WILDEST DREAMS

LOVELOCK BAY
BOOK TWO

ASHLEE ROSE

Ashlee Rose
Copyright © 2024 Ashlee Rose

First Edition

The author has asserted their moral right under the Copyright, Designs and Patents Act, 1988, to be identified as the author of this work.

All rights reserved. No part of this publication may be reproduced, copied, stored in a retrieval system, or transmitted, in any form by or by any means, without the prior written consent of the copyright holder, nor be otherwise circulated in any form of binding or cover other than that in which it is published and without a similar condition being imposed on the subsequent purchaser.

This is a work of fiction. Names, characters, businesses, places, events and incidents are either the products of the authors imagination or used in a fictitious manner.
Any resemblance to actual persons, living or dead, or actual events is purely coincidental.

Cover: Irish Ink Publishing
Editing: Lea Joan
Cover Photographer: Sydnee Rayl Photography

The Dreamcatcher

Some people are like beautiful dreamcatchers,
Absorbing the most terrible things for those they love and leaving
them only the softest, gentlest thoughts behind.

- Nikita Gill

OTHER BOOKS BY ASHLEE ROSE

STANDALONES

Unwanted

Promise Me

Savage Love

Tortured Hero

Something Worth Stealing

Dear Heart, You Screwed Me

Signed, Sealed, Baby

DUET

Way Back When Duet

NOVELLAS

Rekindle Us

Your Dirty Little Secret

A Savage Reunion

RISQUÉ READS

Seeking Hallow

Craving Hex

Seducing Willow

Wanting Knox

Pursuing Hartley

Tempting Klaus

Valentine Belle

ILLICIT LOVE SERIES

The Resentment

The Loathing

The Betrayal

LOVELOCK BAY SERIES

Wildest Love

SINFUL READS

Sinful Brothers

Sinful Affair

All available on Amazon Kindle Unlimited

Only suitable for 18+ due to nature of the books.

PLAYLIST

Scared To Start - Michael Marcagi
Somebody's Problem - Morgan Wallen
A Lot More Free - Max McNown
Growin' Up Raising You - Gabby Barret
Wind Up Missin' You - Tucker Wetmore
What Happens Now? - Dasha
One Number Away - Luke Combs
Lies Lies Lies - Morgan Wallen
Dreamcatcher - Lainey Wilson
Spin You Around - Morgan Wallen
Head Over Boots - Jon Pardi
Worst Way - Riley Green
865 - Morgan Wallen
World on Fire - Nate Smith
Who's Afraid of Little Old Me - Taylor Swift
Pink Skies - Zach Bryan
Here Without You - Acoustic Version - 3 Doors Down
Chasing After You - Ryan Hurd, Maren Morris
Cowboys Cry Too - Kelsea Ballerini, Noah Kahan
Neon Star (Country Boy Lullaby) - Morgan Wallen

Blue Eyed Constellation - Max McNown
Cover Me Up - Morgan Wallen
Fearless (Taylor's Version) _-Taylor Swift
Pick Me Up - Gabby Barret
Watermelon Moonshine - Lainey Wilson
Cowgirls (feat. ERNEST) - Morgan Wall, ERNEST

You can grab the playlist HERE, or through the QR code <3

PROLOGUE
TRIPP

I hadn't said anything, but the word on the street was Austin was going to be arrested.

I'm not buying it. Sheriff Kelcie hasn't mentioned a single thing to me, but then again, maybe he wasn't allowed to.

We all know Austin didn't kill Clay.

Deep down Kelcie knew that too, but they have to have a suspect and it's easier to arrest Austin on suspicion than to not find anyone. My blood runs cold, I always thought I could protect my family, but even wearing a badge doesn't promise that.

The suits had gone quiet, Luke was nowhere to be found and it has me wondering whether he met the same fate as Clay, but fortunately, it wasn't on our ranch.

Kicking off my heavy boots, I settle down in the back room and pour myself a large whiskey. Pondering over the last few weeks, I feel exhausted with it all.

Pacey has shut down; Riggs and Aspen are caught up in their whirlwind and I feel like I am left here picking up the pieces.

Tapping on the side of my glass, I'm not alone with my thoughts long when I hear the sound of tires screeching.

Bolting up, I run for the large window at the front of the house and see a beaten ass car sitting on the side of the road just outside our ranch, smoke funnelling under the hood. Placing my glass down, I move to the front door and grab my hat, placing it on my head and tug my boots on as I run up the driveway to where the car is parked.

"Ma'am!" I call out when I see a woman leaning in the back of the car, the smoke thick and gray and fear prickles at the back of my neck. She ignores me and I hear the sound of a high-pitched cry.

My legs begin to slow as I approach the car, my brows knitting, and my heart is drumming hard against my rib cage.

"Ma'am, is everything okay?" I ask and when the woman stands, wavy brown hair blowing in the wind and eyes as wide as saucers, I feel the air snatch from my lungs.

Standing in front of me, cradling a small bundle in her arms, is the one that got away.

Ten years ago she left town. Ten years ago she left me standing in the dust of her car. Ten years ago she never looked back.

My best kept secret.

The worst heartache of my life.

My wildest dreams.

"Tripp," her voice trembles and all I can do is stare.

Fuck.

CHAPTER ONE
DIXIE

"It's okay baby, nearly there," my voice is soft as I reach behind and try my best to soothe her, twisting my head for just a moment to look at her and that's when I hear a loud horn alarming me. Spinning around quickly, my blue eyes widen when I see my car veering towards the centre of the road, a truck flashing its lights at me in warning.

I go into fight mode, twisting the steering wheel too quickly in an attempt to save myself and my six-month-old daughter, Lainey. Adrenaline spikes, coursing through my veins, my blood hot and pumping so fiercely that I can feel the burn flaming against my skin.

Time moves slow, but whizzes before my eyes and the only thought that consumes me is that your brain lives for seven minutes after you die.

What would my seven minutes look like?

What would I see flash before my eyes just as I plummet into an eternal peace.

My childhood.

Singing.

My guitar.
Sadness.
Grief.
Love.
Tripp.
Lainey.

My tires screech as I slam on the brakes, a loud bang radiating through the car, my ears thumping before a high-pitched noise replaces it as the hood crashes into a wooden pole.

My body jolts forward, panic surges through me but I am helpless. My fingers tighten around the wheel just as my forehead hits into my knuckles.

It takes me a moment or two to come around. Blinking a couple of times, my head feels fuzzy, eyes kind of heavy, a high-pitched ring vibrating in my ears which slowly fades into a piercing cry.

Lainey.

My instinct kicks in.

Twisting and unbuckling myself, I push my door open and stumble onto the grass beneath me. Panic pricks at the base of my neck and my heart rate jumps through my chest. I just needed to get to her.

Tugging the back passenger door open, I unbuckle Lainey from her car seat and hold her close against my thumping heart.

Her little fists are balled, her cries filling the silent roads. My lips are pressed to the top of her head, dusting my kisses over and over, but nothing seems to be calming her down. Lifting my eyes for a moment to look at my surroundings and my heart bottoms out.

Rivera Ranch.

Out of all the places in the town of Lovelock Bay it had to be here.

Shaking it off, I lean back into the car and reach for her pacifier.

"Ma'am," I hear the rasp of his voice and my heart stops beating for just a second.

"Ma'am, is everything okay?"

And that's when I slowly stand, Lainey pulled to my chest and my eyes lock with his.

Tripp Rivera.

I broke his heart ten years ago.

Broke his heart as I booted it out of Lovelock Bay.

But here we were, standing inches from each other.

Heart racing.

Eyes widening.

Old feelings flooring me in an instant.

His hand rubs round the back of his head, his eyes bouncing between me and Lainey.

Dark brown eyes you could lose yourself in and the low sun that's reflecting deep within them make them sparkle in hazel, a shimmer of gold glazing over them. The scar above his eye is still prominent where his brother, Riggs, threw a horseshoe at him when they were kids. Brown stubble hides his strong jaw and his light brown hair still sits as messy as ever.

He never believed in doing his hair when it was hidden under a cowboy hat ninety percent of the day.

Slightly aged, skin a little sun worn and soft wrinkles at the corner of his eyes showing that he has been happy, he has laughed, he has *lived*.

I didn't leave him completely broken.

Shirt tucked into dirty jeans; his thumbs hooked inside his belt loop.

My heart stutters inside my chest as we lose ourselves to the crackling tension between us.

"Are you okay?" his eyes search my face and I watch as his brows softly furrow.

I nod softly.

I'm not.

I am far from okay.

"You're bleeding," concern etches into his face. "Come into the ranch, it's not safe out here for either of you."

My fingers dust softly to my hair line and I can feel the stickiness coating the tip of my fingers.

He steps closer to me, fingers inching closer to my head and I recoil.

"Please, Dixie... if not for you, for your..."

"Daughter," I whisper, shielding her as a truck rolls past at speed and Tripp throws his hand up in the air, cursing into the evening.

"Please?" He begs again.

I reluctantly pull my eyes from him and look at my surroundings again. I have no other choice.

I go to walk to the trunk of my car, but Tripp shakes his head and does it for me, grabbing the diaper bag and small suitcase then stands by my side.

I watch as his hand moves forward, hovering over the small of my back, but he retracts it, giving into his inner thoughts. So instead, he pulls his phone out of his pocket and makes a call arranging for my car to be collected.

I say nothing, just keep quiet and follow him down the driveway of Rivera Ranch.

The same driveway I drove out of ten years ago without looking back.

And I've never felt further from home than I do right now.

CHAPTER TWO
TRIPP

Walking at a steady pace, I force myself not to look behind at the girl I once loved. The one that broke my heart into a million pieces. I have never recovered, and that's the truth. She broke me in ways I didn't even know was possible, but I made peace knowing that I would never see her again. Small town girl turned country singer. She ran so far away from this town. Her mom died young, and her dad couldn't cope with his grief, so while he was physically around he certainly wasn't present. That meant Dixie was left bringing up her younger sister, Lainey, who passed away twelve years ago after being hit by a drunk driver. That day changed the chemicals in her brain. She never was the same brown haired, wide blue-eyed teen I remembered from high school. She soon dropped out then disappeared after a shitty goodbye.

We planned our lives together, but that plan was wrecked as soon as she drove away. The scout came at the perfect time, and he took the only girl I had ever loved.

Climbing the steps to the front door, I hear her

daughter fussing as I twist the knob and step inside my childhood home.

"Ma," I call out, turning and handing the diaper bag to Dixie then dump her suitcase to the ground and watch as it tumbles. Her wide, ocean blue eyes scan the room and memories flood me in an instant, but I shut them down. I don't need to revisit old heartache.

Her daughter begins to cry and I watch as Dixie falls to the ground, rooting through the bag for something and I turn away. Heart scorned, eyes stinging. I made peace that she had gone, and now she's back and making me feel again. I hate it.

My mom walks through the dining room, dark brown hair in a neat, low bun. For a ranch wife, she is always impeccably dressed.

"Tripp?"

Her eyes land on Dixie, mouth a gape before her eyes are on me, silently asking me what the hell is going on.

"Dixie crashed her car at the top of the ranch, hit the sign..." I mumble off, scrubbing my face with my hand. I'm tired. So damn tired. We have so much going on, we really didn't need this right now.

"Oh my goodness," my mom mutters, throwing her hand towel over her shoulder. Dixie is still crouched down and honestly looks like tears are going to shed in her pretty blue eyes.

"I've called Rusty to come and collect her car," I am still rambling, but my mom isn't listening. She is over helping Dixie up off the floor and dragging the diaper bag with her.

"What do you need love?" my mom's voice is soft, as she ushers Dixie forward and leads her to the living room and I stay still, feet anchored, muddy boots all over my mom's floor.

My phone vibrates in my pocket, and I slip it out to see Rusty's name flashing.

"Yeah?"

"Just pulling up, come out and give me a hand." The phone goes silent.

I grab my cowboy hat and place it on my head, turning and walking back out of the door without saying a word. My mom will look after Dixie, and I can go back to my evening and forget this ever happened.

She broke my heart once, I've fixed it, patched it all back up and I'm not about to let the band aids peel away.

I'm not the lovesick teen I was when she left, I am a grown ass man who fixed himself back together again, piece by piece.

Jogging up the dimly lit driveway, I see the bright headlights of Rusty's truck.

Evening is setting in and the sun is getting ready to dip behind the heavy white clouds and all I can think about is my whiskey that I left sitting in the back-room office.

"Tripp," Rusty's deep southern accent fills the open space as he jumps down from the cab of his truck.

"Rusty," I tilt my head as I stop in front of him, hands on hips.

"Was the driver okay?" He asks as he presses the button to lower the bed of his truck, the small crane hook swinging.

"Yeah, she's up at the house," and I see his brows raise.

"Mom is just checking her and her kid over," I mutter, watching as the hook rests on the dusty floor.

"Out of towner?"

I sigh.

"Yeah."

Not about to tell him my whole life story. Rusty was in

our school, but a couple of years older. Always a nice kid. Never caused any trouble.

He kneels down, hooking the back of the car before he stands.

"Push against that sign as I tow the car up, then you can go about fixing it," he winks, and a chuckle leaves me. I do as he asks. I round the front of the car and push against the damaged sign that Dixie ran her car into.

The motor kicks in and slowly, the back end of Dixie's car is pulled up before Rusty secures it.

"All good?"

"All good," he nods, placing the control back in its holder and lifting his hat from his head.

"See you down The Boot tomorrow?" he waits for my answer.

"Maybe, see how things are," I nod slowly, swallowing the lump that's lodged in my throat. So much is going on that the days are rolling into one.

"Of course, well, thanks for the call. I'll let you know when the car is fixed up. Should be a couple of days if I have the parts... longer if I have to order them," he shrugs one shoulder up and turns.

"Sure, thanks."

I stand on the bank of grass and watch as he tows Dixie's car into the sunset, and once again I am left alone with my haunted thoughts.

KICKING MY BOOTS OFF, I place my hat on the coat rack and lift my head listening out for noise.

"Ma?" My voice echoes around the silent house. I have no idea where Pacey is. Dad is with Buck. Riggs and Aspen are up Crooked Valley. And me? I'm here. Like always.

My legs move towards the living room but it's empty. Walking through the large dining room, I enter the kitchen but I'm met with the same emptiness.

"Ma!" I shout at the bottom of the wide staircase, and that's when I see Dixie standing at the top of the stairs.

Hate to admit that she looks like a god damn angel.

Long brown hair cascading over one shoulder, beautiful blue eyes that shimmer in any light like the sun reflecting off the ocean, pouty lips, buttoned nose. Her sun kissed shoulders are on show, a white off the shoulder dress wrapped around her figure. I didn't even get a chance to let my eyes scope over her until now.

"She's just setting up the guest room."

It's the first time she has said more than two words to me.

"Guest room?" My brows raise.

I watch as she slowly steps down the stairs, fingers knotted together.

"Yeah..." she looks over her shoulder, "just for tonight, I mean..."

"Cool," I shut the conversation down in that second and storm towards the back of the house, slamming the door shut and instantly wince when I hear the sound of a baby crying.

Shit.

I fall into my chair, cradling my whisky and rubbing my hand across my mouth.

What the fuck am I going to do.

CHAPTER THREE

I slept awful.

The baby cried most of the night. Stopped myself from going in there far too many times, but my mom was there to help her if needed. But Dixie being Dixie, stood her ground and sent my mom back to bed. Not because she was rude or ungrateful, but because she had been so used to bringing herself up. So used to being the adult in every situation, even when she was just a kid herself.

We grew up together, I always knew of the kid whose mom died when she was eight. She was always scruffy and unkept, skin and bones, but I avoided her. My heart always ached a little when I looked at her. Messy long brown hair that was always tangled, wide fucking heartbreaking blue eyes. So full of wishes and wants, but always looked so damn haunted. She was such a lost little girl. It wasn't just me that avoided her, we all did. She dropped out of high school in her freshman year after her sister died. We didn't see her again for a long while until one night she popped up down The Old Boot, guitar in hand, still the *I am completely broken* look all over her pretty face, but she started playing her guitar, and for just that moment, everything was forgotten. She wasn't the heartbroken, grief-stricken girl she once was. When she sung, she seemed free. No longer haunted by her past.

We started hanging out, but no one knew. She was my secret, and I was hers. We loved fast and fierce until we didn't. She left, drove her car straight out of Lovelock Bay and never looked back until now.

And that's the bit I can't piece together.

Why now?

Padding downstairs, I was a bear with a sore fucking head. The house was warm. Too warm. Wooden shell, wooden floors, every part of this house was a wildfire's dream. Large, open planned rooms that let the natural light pour through. High ceilings, beams and deer antlers on most walls. Family portraits of the Rivera family tree scattered through, and small pieces of history loop around the house, wrapping it in the perfect homely and nostalgic feel. Animal skinned rugs, a whiskey cabinet to die for, and views for miles. Snow tipped mountains on the backdrop of Montana, rolling green fields that never seem to stop. I never tired of living here. I never wanted for much more out of my life than to be happy, healthy and find myself a wife.

But as the years slipped past, I found myself becoming a little bitter. I didn't want any other woman. There was only one that held my heart in her hands, but she dropped it onto the dusty road and drove over it, leaving it bleeding out behind her in a kick up of dust.

But of course, no one knew.

She was just Dixie Walker.

Sad girl turned country singer.

But now she was back, and I couldn't wait for her to leave again.

Rounding the corner and walking towards the kitchen, Pacey and my dad are sitting at the dining table.

"Morning," Pacey beams, backwards cap on his messy blonde hair as he spoons cereal into his mouth. My dad, Jorge, is reading the paper whilst drinking a black coffee like he does every morning.

I grunt. That's all I can manage. A grumpy ass grunt.

My legs keep moving as I reach for the coffee pot and fill my cup up, and when I spin, I see her.

She's sitting at the breakfast bar, all wide eyed and shit. She's wearing a tee, no doubt mine or Pacey's and I can't be in here with her. It's just too much. My lungs feel like they're drowning.

I place my coffee cup on the countertop and turn. I keep my head down and head for my room. It's too much. I need her gone, but until then, I'll be the one to leave.

Grabbing a clean tee and my jeans, I dress then run down the stairs. I can feel Pacey's eyes on me, but I refuse to meet his glare. I am fully aware that they must think I have fucking lost my mind, but that's okay. They can think it.

"Where are you going?" he calls, just as I grab my cowboy hat and place it on my head.

"Out," I rush out, slamming the door behind me and as soon as I am on the porch, I breathe. Inhaling deeply, holding my breath for three then releasing.

Fuck.

Pocketing my keys, I run for my truck. Climbing in, I shut the door and start the engine, and where can I go at seven thirty in the morning on a Saturday? Riggs'.

Driving the car round the turning circle, I kick it down the drive and towards Crooked Creek. The drive isn't far, five minutes if that.

Slowing my truck outside their gates, I cut the engine

and slip the window down. It's peaceful here. The sound of the creek constantly running, the soft breeze dancing in the trees. Giving myself a couple of minutes, I reluctantly get out of the truck and Ace hears me before he sees me, barking but his tail is wagging all happy and shit.

"Ace," I smile, reaching down and stroking behind his ear.

The barks stop, then he trots off happily towards the creek.

Opening the gate, it scratches across the gravel and my heavy boots lead me to their front door.

Knocking, I wait but no answer. I knock again but after the second time of being ignored, I try the handle and I am surprised when it opens.

Honestly, wish I never tried.

I step into the short hallway and just as you reach the end is the kitchen.

And there, sitting on the edge of the countertop, legs wrapped around my brother's head is my sister-in-law, and my brother enjoying his breakfast.

"Oh my god," I bellow loudly and Aspen pushes Riggs away, covering herself up with the shirt she is wearing, and Riggs stands, eyes flicking between the both of us.

"Tripp!" Aspen is flushed red as she jumps off the countertop and hides behind Riggs.

"Aspen," I lift my hat off my head and cover my face and I hear Riggs' deep laugh fill their home.

"It's not funny," she slaps his arm and I try and contain my laughter.

"Maybe lock the door next time," I suggest, letting my hand lower, my hat now resting between my fingers at the side of my body.

"What brings you over..." Riggs looks over his shoulder

at the wall clock, "at seven forty-seven on a Saturday morning?"

Aspen busies herself putting a fresh pot of coffee on.

"Dixie Walker, that's what."

Riggs' brows raise and Aspen spins to face us.

"Dixie?" her brows furrow. Dixie was the grade below us in school.

"Yeah, lived across from Blue Beak."

"Girl whose kid sister died?"

I nod, a sombre mood taking over.

"Poor kid," Riggs grunts, rubbing his hand across his beard.

"Crashed up top of the ranch, damaged the sign. Rusty took her car, and she's at ours with her baby."

"Was that your idea?"

"Absolutely not," I shake my head, stepping into the kitchen and trying to ignore what was going on mere moments ago. "I brought her up to the house to get her off the side of the road, then mom had put her in the guest room with the kid. She didn't stop crying all night."

"Dixie?" Riggs asks as Aspen hands him a cup of coffee and he leans down and presses a kiss to the top of her head just before she hands me a cup and disappears upstairs, all the time Riggs' eyes trailing after her.

"No, the baby."

"Understandable."

"I am wrecked, I have no idea why she came back? Her dad is long gone, she has no other family..." I slump onto the sofa, agitation biting at my nerves. Riggs' takes a slow stroll into the room, leaning against the door frame.

"Maybe she had to come back for work? The kid's dad?" he half shrugs one shoulder up as he takes a mouthful of his coffee.

"Kid's dad won't be here. She hasn't been home in years. The dad will be some bloke back from wherever she is living now."

"Why did you need out?"

"Just got a little bit... I don't know. She keeps looking at me all wide eyed and helpless... I'm not interested in helping her. I done that last night, that's as far as I will go. I have enough people to help, I don't need to add one more to the list."

Riggs chuckles.

"Why don't you crash here tonight, get a full night's sleep then you can reevaluate in the morning after a good night's sleep."

"You and Aspen will keep me awake."

"Not at all, we will be quiet..."

"Bullshit," I laugh, tossing my head from side to side.

"Promise," he wiggles his brows and I roll my eyes.

"Grateful for the offer, but no thanks. I have nothing to reevaluate. I'll get her car from Rusty's then she can be on her way and out of my life."

Riggs says nothing, just sits next to me and we sit in silence, drinking our coffees.

We're not alone long when Aspen comes down the stairs, dressed, fresh eyed and bushy tailed.

"What you two chatting about?"

I'm not sure if she is being sarcastic or thinks she has walked in on a conversation, and we stopped once we knew she was in the room.

"Not a lot, Riggs invited me to come stay whilst Dixie is crashing at ours, but I politely declined," my lips twitch as I fight the smile, Riggs throws his hands up in the air as if to say, *'I tried to help him'*.

"What put you off?" she teases, falling into Riggs' lap.

"Hmm, let me think," I roll my eyes and let my head shake softly as I roll the empty coffee cup over my stained jeans.

"It'll be okay, she will no doubt be on her way home soon."

I shrug my shoulders.

"Hopefully her car is a quick fix and I can get it back to her. At least that way she doesn't have to rely on any of us whilst she is staying here."

I roll my head around to look at my brother and Aspen. They're so blissfully happy and I am desperate for that. One day though.

"Right," I slap my knee then push to my feet, walking across the cosy home and place my cup in the sink.

Riggs is up and leaning against the doorframe.

"Thanks for having me, didn't mean to... ya know," I circle my finger and Aspen's cheeks redden as I stroll towards the front door. "Just maybe lock the door next time?" I half joke, half mean it, brows sitting high in my head.

Riggs just lets out a deep laugh, pulling Aspen into him as he embraces her. Stepping onto the porch, Ace bounds over.

"Is this dog ever inside?" I ask as I crouch down and pet him.

"Nope, he likes running through the fields and down to the creek. He lives his best life. Loves the front of the truck and winding up the cows up," Riggs grunts.

"Atta boy," I smirk as I stand, Ace jumps up and paws my stomach. "Want me to take him back? I can throw him out?"

"Nah, I'll be over soon, just got to finish a job I started..."

"Alright! Bye!" I shout, storming forward and flipping Riggs off as I run down the three steps and march over to my truck.

I do not need any more of a visual than what I got earlier. No thank you.

I shake my head, muttering away to myself as I slam my truck door and push it into reverse.

Turning my music up and pushing my windows down, I drive towards town and head to Rusty's. The quicker her car gets fixed, the quicker I can get her back out of my life.

For good.

CHAPTER FOUR
DIXIE

Slowly stepping out of the room that Orla has so kindly let me and Lainey sleep in, I softly close the door. She slept awful last night, and it didn't help that I had only just got her down when Tripp slammed his office door. I get it though, he is not pleased that I am back home after breaking his heart and leaving it bleeding in the dust as I drove away, but I do still care about him. Whether he chooses to believe it or not. It wasn't my plan to wreck my car outside the ranch, but I did.

It also wasn't my plan to stay here, but alas, here I am.

He is raging. I know it, the whole damn house knows it, but I don't think they know exactly why. They just know me as poor little Dixie Walker who lost her mamma and her sister before she skipped town. But they don't know anything. They know nothing about the childhood I had to endure, the way my daddy treated me and my kid sister. I had one job and that was to protect her, and I failed.

But then there was Tripp.

He was the sunshine on my darkest days.

No one knew about us. I didn't even know what we

were. We just kind of happened I suppose. We agreed to keep it just between us; we were young and I knew I didn't want to stay here. I needed out of Lovelock Bay and as soon as that scout offered me my golden ticket, I snatched it up.

But that soon dwindled. He was a crook and I have tried to get out, but he has his fingers so deeply pressed into my skin that I can't shake him off, even though I desperately want to.

A few nights of fun with a big boy suit ended up with nine months of sickness and leg cramps but look what I got out of it.

My own ray of Sunshine.

I lost Tripp and was plunged back into the crevices of the darkest parts of my soul, but since Lainey, she has lit my world up in a way like never before. I would give everything for her. My last breath if it meant that she could have just a second longer on this earth. I would sacrifice everything for her.

Everything.

Even come back to the town I was so determined to leave in my past forever.

And the reason I am back?

A funeral.

After the day softly clicks shut, I turn and see Orla standing with fresh towels.

"Go and have a nice hot bath, I'll listen out for Lainey," she smiles at me, her eyes kind of watery and my heart swells.

"Are you sure?" I feel like I am taking far too much of her kindness.

"Of course, go and relax. I love having a little bundle in the house and with my three rowdy boys, who knows when

I will get a grandchild of my own," she sighs, but I can see the sadness that blankets her face, her mind elsewhere.

"Thank you, Orla," I reach out, my hand resting on the top of her arm and her hand covers mine for a brief moment.

I drop it and take the warm towels from her as I tuck myself away in the main bathroom. Locking the door behind me, I let out my held breath. What did I do to deserve someone like Orla?

My heart aches in my chest and I find myself rubbing it out.

I miss my mom. I miss the motherly love that she gave me. Maybe I was seeking that out of Orla, wrapping myself up in a blanket of love. But I knew that blanket would be snatched from me soon enough and I would be back, tossed out and brushing myself down again.

Sighing, I hang the towels on the heated towel rail and peel my tee from my sticky skin. I say *my* tee, when it's actually Pacey's.

The Montana sun is warm which heats up the cabin like a furnace.

Looking around the large bathroom, the floors are covered in an off-white tile. To my left is a his and hers vanity sink unit, a large mirror hanging over it. To my right is the toilet and ahead is a beautiful copper tub with a copper free hanging shower and a glass shower door, the floor slightly slopped so the water can run away, and to the left of the tub where your feet would be facing, is a large window overlooking the rolling green and snow kissed mountains.

Folding the tee up, I place it on the sink unit. My eyes lift from the soft material and catch my reflection in the mirror.

Tired blue eyes, puffy bags and pale skin.

I felt every bit broken, every bit tired and worn out.

I wasn't in control and that didn't help. Everything that has happened over the last twenty-four hours have not been conducted by me. This trip here was made because it *needed* to be made. I didn't want to come back here.

Being back in the house that I used to get sneaked into, being back in the close proximity of the only man that ever held my heart so delicately, was not because I wanted to be. I ended up here in some weird, twist of fate.

My eyes fall to my stomach, a little saggy and covered in silver stretch marks from my blessing.

I never wanted kids.

Never wanted to ever put them into a position where they could lose me. No child should lose a parent. No child should grow up without their mother.

I never wanted that for my kids.

So, my solution? Don't have them.

It was that simple.

But Lainey happened. She found me.

And I am so glad she did.

My life has never been the same since.

And I mean that in the best way.

Shaking my thoughts from my head, I tiptoe across the tiled bathroom floor and pop my toe into the copper bath. The warmth splinters over my skin and I feel myself instantly relax. I lower myself down and sink beneath the water. My eyes close for just a moment, my fingers curled round the cool roll top of the tub and my heart slows to a steady beat. When I finally open my eyes, I focus on the view in front of me. It was breathtaking. And just for that second, I was somewhere far, far away from my train wreck of a life.

The way the green hills rolled into the distance, the pretty mountains stood tall and proud, the glisten of the winter snow—which over the next couple of months will gradually melt, but only for a moment before it's back, wrapped around the top of them.

No one can see me, my view is completely unrestricted, and I imagine what it must feel like to live somewhere like this, where this is your view. Every corner of this house has a picturesque view wrapped around it. Every part of it is perfect.

I let my eyes close again, and I lose myself in happy memories.

And only then does my heart feel like it's really beating in my chest.

***

I AM DRESSED in one of the few outfits I shoved into my small suitcase. Bootleg jeans and a white knotted shirt with a gray tank underneath. My chocolate brown hair is in loose waves, tumbling down my back. I walk into the room and see Lainey sitting with Jorge.

My eyes glisten but I blink the unshed tears away before anyone notices.

"Hey," I hold my hand up then lock my fingers in front of me.

Jorge smiles at me, before he focuses his attention back on Lainey.

Orla rounds the corner and pops a fresh pot of coffee on.

"I hope you didn't mind that I offered to bring her downstairs?" she half asks, and I can hear the cautiousness in her voice.

I was drying my hair when Lainey started fussing, Orla kindly offered to help.

"Of course not," I smile, sheepishly walking into the kitchen and dragging a stool out to sit on. The whole house is rustic. Typical ranch home. It's beautiful.

"Are you hungry? I am going to be making brisket shortly for dinner, but I have some fresh bread that has not long finished. I was going to make some sandwiches if you are?" She potters around, and only when I watch her do I realise she has been grocery shopping. There are nappies, formula, baby food, purees and snacks for Lainey. As well as some toys and a highchair that is sitting in the box.

"Did you get her all of this?" and I don't know why, but my voice squeaks.

"I did," Orla turns, "did I overstep?" her face falters for just a moment thinking that she has upset me.

"No, not at all. But please, let me write you a check."

I go to stand and find my purse, but Jorge clears his throat which gains my attention.

"Please, sit back down," the softness in his voice makes me feel warm and I swallow the lump that is lodged in my throat back down. "It's our treat, we have the room, we have space and well, the room is yours and Lainey's if you want it?"

I choke on a sob that I am fighting to hold in and reach for a tissue box that is sat in the middle of the woodwork surface. I grab one and dab my eyes.

"You've been so kind," I sniffle.

"For you Dixie, we would do anything. You deserve a home to feel welcome in, to feel safe in..." Orla's voice is tight as she stands behind Jorge. "I know this is probably a flying visit, but you have a home here, if you want it of course."

I break eye contact and focus on my hands, fiddling with my tear-soaked tissue. I am not used to people being so kind to me, there was only one that had a kind heart, and it was Orla and Jorge's son.

Inhaling a shaky breath, I lift my head to focus on the two people who have opened their home to me and my daughter.

"My plan was not to stay here..." I pause for a moment and look at Lainey. She is reaching up and grabbing Jorge's nose, he is smiling down at her and my heart warms in my chest. "I have some things I need to sort out, but honestly, I have nowhere else to go... I was going to stay at Sylvia's but..."

I see their silently begging eyes on me.

"I would love to stay here, only if you promise you don't mind?"

Orla claps her hands together and rounds the center island, wrapping her arms around me.

"Thank you so much," I sniffle as tears prick in my eyes again, "you'll never know how much this means to me."

"It's the least we can do," Orla chokes, squeezing me a little tighter.

She breaks away and I stand, swooping a fussing Lainey from Jorge and he sets about unboxing her highchair.

"If there is anything I have missed or she needs, please let us know and we can run back to the store..."

"Actually, there are a few things I would like to grab, would you mind taking us?" I ask, popping Lainey's pacifier into her mouth and bouncing her on my hip.

"Of course, let me pack this away and get the brisket on and I will be good to go." Orla says and I take that as my cue to leave.

I get Lainey washed and changed before breastfeeding

her. I didn't want to say in front of Jorge that I breastfeed and didn't need the formula milk, but I'll bring it with me and tell Orla to refund it.

Lainey's chubby little hands reach up and play with my mom's old necklace, a round golden pendant with two crystal stars sitting alongside the moon. The stars connected by a string, tied off with a dainty heart.

She always said we were the stars, she was the moon. Always there, even when we couldn't see her.

Lainey's wide blue eyes are on me, black long lashes framing them. Her hair dark and curly. I am obsessed with everything about her.

The love of my life.

This is all for her.

Everything I do in this life is for her.

This wasn't what I planned when I came back to Lovelock Bay, but I am eternally grateful to Orla and Jorge. I just hope Tripp is okay with what his parents have offered, but honestly, I am not holding my breath.

Orla is patient whilst I scour the shelves trying to work out what I need. I packed enough for a long weekend, but I needed more clothes just in case this trip isn't as quick as I planned. I filled my cart with everything me and Lainey needed. Once paid, we loaded it into the back of Orla's truck then headed back to the grocery store.

We agreed to donate the unwanted formula and I grabbed a couple of must needs. Orla pushed the cart, talking to Lainey and soothing her when needed. We loaded the truck back up and Orla pulled out the carpark.

"Shall we pop into town for lunch? We can dump the bags at home with Jorge?" Orla turns to face me, a wide smile on her face.

"I don't mind unloading? But yes, lunch sounds lovely,"

and it does, but my stomach knots when I think about how much I have just loaded on my already busting credit card.

"No, don't be silly. Jorge can do it, he doesn't do much on a Saturday, so it won't hurt him," she winks and a wide grin presses against my lips as I look out the window at the town I grew up in, but feel like I was robbed of, if that even makes sense.

Looking over my shoulder, Lainey is softly snoring in her car seat and my heart races under my skin, but that racing soon turns to dread when I see Tripp's truck parked back on the drive.

"Don't you worry about Tripp," Orla reads my thoughts and I turn to look at her, brows furrowed. "He comes across grumpy, but he is my sunshine boy. Let me deal with him. You stay in here with Lainey, I won't be a moment," she smiles sweetly at me and slips out the truck. She is so petite and looks ridiculous driving this big truck, but she somehow suits it.

I crinkle my nose as I squint and look over the pastures, the cows free roaming and the silence that I was enjoying is soon clipped short when I hear the sound of a truck approaching. I lower my head slightly and notice the truck slowing beside me, and there he was, Riggs Rivera. A slow smirk tugs at his lips, his eyes hidden behind tinted aviators and of course, his signature cowboy hat.

I see Aspen peek around him and give me a small wave. I don't remember much about her, just knew she was the up and coming show jumper of Lovelock Bay.

I shrink in my chair and just as Riggs rolls to a stop, a thunderous Tripp storms out the house, Orla running after him.

Shit.

My heart jumps into my throat and I feel sick.

Riggs is out the truck, pushing his hands against Tripp's chest, trying to knock him back and Aspen is rounding the front of the hood, trying to squeeze between the two brothers.

My hands are over my mouth and guilt consumes me whole.

"Calm the fuck down," I hear Riggs bellow and Tripp finally seems to calm. Jorge is out on the porch, hands on his hips and Aspen is looking between me and Tripp.

Ground swallow me up, please Lord.

Orla barges past her son, an equally thunderous look painted on her pretty face and Aspen is hot on her heels.

"Aspen, honey, help me with these bags," Orla says, but I don't miss the tremble in her voice.

"Sure thing," Aspen chirps, loading herself with the bags and as she passes, she mouths *hi*.

My cheeks flame.

Riggs walks past and gives a curt nod, a smile on his face the whole time and you just know that he is loving every moment of this.

I look over my shoulder again and look at Lainey. All anxiety hashes out in a moment as I focus on her, but when I turn to face the front, Tripp is standing in front of the truck. His eyes are dark, a scour etched into his face and his fists are balled by his side.

Riggs eventually clasps his shoulder tightly and drags him back into the house, Aspen follows Riggs and presses onto her tiptoes to give him a kiss goodbye before she skips towards the truck.

Orla climbs in the front, Aspen in the back as she quietly closes the door.

"Sorry about that," Orla dusts herself off an imaginary flint.

"No, Orla, I am sorry. Maybe I should just go to Sylvia's." I wince.

"Not a chance. This is *my* home, you're *my* guest. You're staying."

"You don't mess with mama Rivera," Aspen perches herself between the two seat headrests, a wide smile on her face.

"This is Aspen, my Riggs' partner. Aspen…"

"Dixie, yeah I know. You were the topic of conversation over our cup of coffee this morning," and I wince, shrinking.

"I bet," I nibble on my nail bed when Orla pulls my hand away.

"Don't you worry about him. He will come around. He just has a lot going on at the moment." I watch as Aspen sulks back into her chair, Orla's face tightens as she starts the engine.

"Okay," I mutter. The tension continues to grow for the duration of the journey towards the town and I am grateful to get out the car. I unstrap Lainey's car chair and follow Orla towards a small coffee shop called *Sunny's*.

The small bell dings above the door and the smell of fresh coffee entices me in further.

"Mrs Rivera, Aspen," a pretty dark-haired girl says from behind the counter.

"Afternoon Sunny," Orla smiles as she approaches the counter. "How are you?"

"I can't complain," she smiles wide, "I have a date tomorrow night, I am super excited."

"Ooo, who with?" Aspen perches her elbows on the counter, wiggling her brows up and down.

"Just some out of towner," I see the way Aspen's mouth pops open before spreading into a wide grin. "Conrad has asked a couple of times but I am not so sure…" she trails off, eyes moving towards Aspen.

"I can totally see it," she says, straightening up, "you and Conrad… what a couple," Aspen winks and Sunny's cheeks blaze.

Sunny's eyes trail to me and her brows furrow as she waits for my introduction.

"This is Dixie, she is staying here a while up at the Rivera Ranch," Aspen answers for me, then her eyes fall to my daughter. "And this is beautiful little Lainey" she coos and I wave awkwardly.

"Hi Dixie," Sunny smiles before turning her attention back to Aspen.

"How's Austin?" she kind of whispers it, leaning close.

"Hiding," she sighs, her head dropping forward and shaking it from side to side.

"It'll be okay, the whole town is behind him."

"I hope so."

"And Pacey? I miss his cheeky smile every morning."

"He is with Austin. Think he is struggling with it more than he lets on," Orla nods softly. Sunny just nods back.

"And Tripp? He must be struggling after he lost his badge," and my ears prick. *Badge? Was he Sheriff?*

"It's just temporary, conflict of interest and all that," Orla lets out a heavy sigh but stands a little taller.

"It'll blow over, the funeral is this week isn't it?"

I stiffen.

"Yeah Friday, we're all going to go. Want to show how as a town we're all united. The ranches all stay together, and albeit, Clay had an ulterior motive, he was still one of us."

Fuck.

"Yeah, we're closed Friday too, he used to come here

every day for his breakfast roll and coffee," Sunny turns to look at Aspen, "as you well know," a soft giggle leaves her.

Did they used to date?

"It was only once okay, and Tripp told me he came here to order. It was all a set up." Aspen waves her hand in front of her.

Double fuck.

"Anyway, sorry, I have been chewing your ear off. What can I get you?" Sunny smiles, tapping the screen of her till.

"I'll have an oat cappuccino and a cheese and tomato baguette," Orla says, reaching into her purse for her wallet. Sunny turns her attention to Aspen.

"Ooo, I'll have an iced latte with caramel syrup and cold foam," I blink a couple of times, "and I'll have the tuna salad please."

Then all eyes land on me.

My heart jack hammers.

"Can I just have a white coffee and tuna baguette please?" I fist in for my card, but Orla just shakes her head from side to side as she swipes her card through the reader.

"All done, take a seat and I'll bring it over," Sunny smiles as she passes the receipt over to the barista.

"Thank you, Sunny," Orla says softly, popping a ten dollar note into the tip jar. Orla ushers us over to a window table. We all take our seats and Aspen slips her phone out of her jean pocket and checks her emails.

I am grateful Lainey is still sleeping.

"I need to get her stroller out the trunk of my car." I say quietly.

"We can stop at Rusty's before we go home," Orla smiles as she places her sunglasses in her purse.

"Thank you," my voice is quiet as I turn my attention onto the sidewalks of Lovelock Bay town.

"So, what brings you back home?" Aspen asks, pulling my attention.

"Just some personal things I need to finalize," I give a soft nod.

"Ah okay, so you're sticking around for a while?"

What is this? Twenty questions?

"A while yeah, thanks to Orla and Jorge. Just until I sort myself out." I smile at Orla, and she beams.

"Well, I am happy about it. Be nice to have another girl join the gang. It's only me and Harlow and the testosterone is a little much," Aspen says and Orla laughs.

"Try living with it. Always wanted a girl; I used to dress Pacey up in girl clothes when he was a couple of months old, you know, just to get my fix."

And now me and Aspen giggle.

"I do feel for you, them Rivera men..." Aspen puffs her cheeks out.

"Tell me about it," Orla rolls her eyes before laughing.

"What do you do Aspen?" I try and deter the conversation.

"I'm an author," she sits tall, and I can see the pride beaming out of her.

"What happened to the show jumping?" I don't mean to pry, but it makes me a little sad that she didn't get her dream.

"I had to find a new dream," and I don't miss the sad smile that graces her lips.

Sunny appears with our drinks, and we thank her. I reach for my coffee and wrap my hands around the warm cup.

"I had a bad accident, and I just lost all my confidence. I never got back on a horse until a few months ago and I have Riggs to thank for that," her eyes well slightly and I don't miss the glint to her hazel eyes as tears form. Orla reaches across and places her hand on top of Aspen's. "But here we are, things happen. You just have to decide what you're going to do with it. So, I started writing. I wrote mine and Riggs' love story and I go on tour with my publisher in a few months."

"Wow," I mean it. I am in awe. "Congratulations Aspen, that is amazing," and I see the sparkle in her ring lining my next question up nicely. "When are you getting married?" I ask.

"We have so much to sort out so decided the back end of Summer would be better for us. Only keeping it small, getting married on the ranch." She turns to look at Orla and gives her a smile. "We're going for a cookout, haybales, live singers; a proper rustic and country wedding. It'll be perfect. I just want to marry the man I have loved for all my life," and with that, my heart throbs.

"Sounds perfect," I smile, eyes all watery.

"If you're still here, we would love to have you." I roll my lips.

"We will see," I give a shrug of my shoulders, because honestly? Who knows what will happen.

CHAPTER FIVE
TRIPP

I am mad.

Beyond mad.

My parents are too good. Well, my mom more than my dad. He just goes along with it now.

The kitchen is stacked with grocery bags, there is a cute white highchair sitting in the corner and new toys everywhere. I would have liked to have had a say in this, but no, of course I just get it sprung on me.

I'm pacing up and down the hallway and Riggs is watching me, letting out a low chuckle every now and then.

"Glad you think it's funny," I stop for a moment and place my hands on my hips, my foot is tapping. "How would you have liked it if mom and dad moved Aspen in when she first came back?"

That soon shut him up.

His mouth opens then shuts like a damn guppy fish in a bowl.

"Exactly," I cross my arms across my front when I see my dad emerge from the kitchen.

"Stop sulking," he groans, taking some bags up the

stairs and no doubt into Dixie's room. He is back down in moments.

"I don't understand why you asked her to stay," I stammer out.

"You do realise the life that girl had, right?" He stands toe to toe with me, and Riggs stands a little taller, eyes on me the whole time.

Dad has softened in his old age, but we all remember what he was like when we were just kids.

"Fully aware."

"Then let us do something for her, she is back for a reason, but there is something in that girl's eyes that shows just how terrified she is to be back here. So put your fucking differences aside, and for her sake, make her feel welcome. It's the least you could do."

My dad's tone is abrupt but what he is saying is true and I kinda hate it.

"Fine, but don't think I'll be helping out and be a 'step in daddy', I have enough shit on my plate that I need to deal with without having to deal with a broken-hearted girl and her bastard kid as well."

And that's when I hear the front door slam.

I turn to look in that direction and see Aspen, my mom and Dixie.

My vicious words splinter across her face and my heart drops from my chest, plummeting into the darkest depths.

I'm such an asshole.

My dad just gives me a hard pat on the chest as if to say *well done jackass* and I feel like the worst fucking possible human ever.

He walks over to Dixie, taking a fussing Lainey off her and disappears into the kitchen. My mom shakes her head in a disappointed manner and Aspen can't even look at me.

My chest tightens, my heart aches.

"Dix… I…"

She holds her hand up and lifts her nose in the air as she follows my mom and dad into the kitchen, and all that's left is Riggs.

Fighting a smirk, hands fisted into his back pockets, he lets out a low whistle.

"Man," he chuckles, "you fucked up."

"Don't I know it," exasperation coats my tone and then it's just me, standing alone in the lobby.

CLEANING UP FOR DINNER, I am showered and dressed in cargos and a tee. The atmosphere has been tense. Mom and dad haven't spoken a word and Dixie has been hidden in her room.

I'm not an asshole guy, I am a good guy. Was always told that.

It's not you it's me.

You're a really nice guy.

You're too nice for me.

You're too good for me.

I scrub my face. Messing my hair up, I pace into the hallway just as Dixie walks out. Waves of anxiety lap against the ocean blue of her eyes, fingers curled around the baby monitor and I watch as her knuckles slowly turn white from her death grip.

"I… I…" she stammers, and I step forward, holding my hand up.

"You don't need to say a word," I roll my lips and I ignore the ache that is still radiating through my chest hours on. "I was out of line."

She shakes her head, long brown curls masking her face for a moment. "You have every right to be angry with me, I have turned up like an unwanted hurricane, shredding your life to pieces after leaving ten years ago..." she pauses, anchored to the spot outside her room. "I'm only here for a while, then I'll be back on my way," and with that she walks downstairs.

I wanted to say so much more to her, but I didn't.

I admitted I was out of line, but if I kept talking, I would have dug myself a hole. Then I would have buried myself alive, slowly suffocating.

Waiting a beat, I follow her down.

Mom had spent most of the afternoon cooking a brisket for dinner and the whole house smelt amazing. My stomach grumbles and that's when I realized I hadn't eaten a bite today, I have purely survived on coffee.

A clamber has me jumping and I see Pacey stumble through the front door.

"Pace?" my eyes scan over my baby brother and I can't work out if he is drunk or sober.

"Yup," he looks around with a squint, fingers gripped round the doorknob.

"You okay?" I ask and he sneezes loudly.

"Bless you," he blesses himself. "Thank you," he thanked himself.

"You blessed yourself," I blink, head slightly tilted.

"No problem," he okays me with his finger and thumb then stumbles forward towards the kitchen. "Ma!" he calls out and I feel Dixie looking at me. I ignore the urge to face her, to let my eyes sweep over her beautiful face.

Moving forward, Pacey is lifting the pots and pans to see what's cooking. Mom slaps his hand away and tsks.

"Pacey, you're drunk. Go to bed," she scolds, and my

dad rolls his eyes but doesn't move from his spot at the breakfast bar.

"Come Pace, lemme get you up…" I wrap my arms around his shoulders, and he shrugs me off, pushing me in the chest and knocking me off my feet.

"It's all your fault," he slurs standing over me and my brows pinch.

I know he is talking shit. He is angry, I get it, but attacking me isn't going to help.

"Hey!" I hear the bellow of Riggs as he barrels across to where Pacey is stumbling. He grabs Pacey and drags him from the kitchen as I push myself from the floor to my feet.

"You okay?" Aspen asks, rushing to my side and checking me over.

"I'm fine," I grunt, turning myself away from her.

"Jorge, all the kids are home," my mom's tone is uninterested and sarcastic, my dad grunts in response.

"Idiot," I chew the inside of my cheek.

I dust my cargos down and grab the plates from the kitchen cabinet as I start to lay the table when I hear the sound of shouting and banging.

Dixie looks terrified.

We all just continue as normal.

Pacey has had too much to drink, and thinks the whole world is against him.

Austin is his best friend. Sure, there is an age difference, but he and Austin always hit it off. He is protective of him, and what Austin is being dragged through is not ideal. We all know it wasn't Austin, but it's hard to prove an innocent man as not guilty when everyone who cares believes the rumours.

Yes, we were the last people to see Clay alive.

Yes, Austin and Pacey put his beaten body into the back

of the truck. But he was still breathing. He was conscious. Just bruised and bloody.

"Can I do anything to help?" Dixie asks, her sweet voice floating through my heavy thoughts.

"I need to grab some wine, wanna come with?" *I'm* even surprised I have asked her to come with me.

"Sure," she shrugs her shoulders up, placing the baby monitor on the center island and follows behind me.

Walking out the front of the house, I jump the steps of the porch and round the corner of the house when I come to the basement doors. Unbolting them, I tug both open and hold my hand out to help her over the lip and onto the step.

She looks at me, hair blowing softly in the spring breeze, her hand a little cautious to fall into my palm. Her eyes bounce between mine and I watch as the once angry waves are now calm. She makes me feel safe. And I like that.

Her hand slips into mine, if only for a moment as she steps over and I feel the current swarm through me, singeing my nerve endings and as painful as it feels, I don't want to let go of her.

I follow behind her, pulling the light cord as we climb down onto the fourth step and I scoff when I see the fairy lights hung from the oak ceiling beams.

"Fairy lights?" she asks, looking over her shoulder at me.

"Aspen. Scared of the dark. Riggs put them everywhere. He never wanted her to be afraid..." I trail off as we step into the basement, and I look around for a bottle or two of red. "Do you drink red?" I ask, letting my fingertips brush across the dusty bottles sitting in their racks.

"I do," and I don't miss the way a pinch of crimson splashes into her cheeks and my lips pull slightly at the corner into a smirk. But she misses it.

"Merlot?" I slip a bottle out just past it's neck, "or a Rioja?"

"Merlot," she nods.

"Or..." I pause as my fingers dance over to another bottle, "a cabernet?"

"Cabernet," she smiles, giving a confirming nod.

"Two bottles?"

"The whole family is here, so why not," she steps beside me and slides a bottle out.

"Sound perfect," I take my own bottle and hold my hand out for her to take the lead. We walk back towards the steps in silence, and as she climbs the steps, I don't miss my chance to sneak a look at her ass.

Now it's her turn to hold her hand for me, and sure, I don't need her help, but I take it.

Because for just a moment, I feel like she soothes all my worries.

Like my own personal dreamcatcher.

Walking back into the house, I hear the light chatter coming from the kitchen. Anxiety cripples me when I see Riggs' face.

The man can't hide his thoughts even if he wanted to, his expressions always give him away. If he was guilty, his expressions would be the thing to do it.

"What is it?" my chest rattles as I place the bottles on the countertop, Dixie slipping up behind me and placing her bottle next to mine.

Riggs' eyes lift over my shoulder, and I know he is looking to Dixie.

"I'm going to check on Lainey," her voice is quiet, and my eyes follow her over my shoulder as she disappears.

Riggs exhales heavily, head dropping for a moment.

Aspen is nowhere to be seen.

"Shits getting real bad, Tripp," and I can hear the concern that laces his voice.

"What's happened?" my hands rest on the woodblock of the counter, warmth radiating through me.

"Austin is being sent to trial in two weeks," I watch as his throat bobs.

"What?" my eyes widen, and I am already slipping my phone out of my pocket looking for Kelcie's number.

Riggs places his hand over it and pushes it down, shaking his head from side to side.

My brows crinkle, eyes bouncing back and forth between my older brother's.

"Kelcie is the one that pushed for it."

"FUCK!" I shout, slamming my hand on the worktop and instantly regret it, my hand throbs and Lainey screams.

I tip my head back and let my eyes close.

That's why Pacey said it was my fault.

I appointed Kelcie.

He made quick work of getting rid of Pacey as Livestock Commissioner as soon as he was in. I put it down to protecting us, but seems I was wrong.

"What are we going to do?" my voice cracks and honestly, I feel like my chest is going to cave in. I want to cry. Full on sob like a little boy. I want someone to tell me everything is going to be okay, but the truth was, no one could.

I had to deal with this myself.

I just didn't know how to.

CHAPTER SIX
DIXIE

I stand like a spare part as Tripp lays the table, Orla checks on her food and Jorge is sitting at the breakfast bar.

Pacey has just been dragged out of the kitchen like a naughty toddler and sent to bed without supper, Aspen is talking quietly to Orla and Riggs stays away.

Tripp walks back into the kitchen, his eyes skating over me as if he is trying to avoid eye contact and I am desperate for him to look at me properly.

"Can I do anything to help?" my voice sounds hopeful, and Tripp looks up.

"I need to grab some wine, wanna come with?" his brows raise, like he is surprised he has even asked me.

"Sure," I shrug my shoulder up nonchalantly and follow him out the front of the house, down the porch steps and towards the basement doors.

I stand back and watch as he tugs the rusty bolt across and pulls the doors open. The soft spring breeze dances around us, the sweet smell in the air and I look towards the mountains. The stars kissing the tips, the moon full and round, glowing in all its glory. Turning my face, I see Tripp holding his hand out for me. I can easily step over the lip and onto the step, but I take his hand anyway. It fits perfectly with mine and I inwardly gasp when I feel a lightning shock through me, my blood burning as it rushes through my veins. All the feelings from ten years ago consume me whole in an instance.

Snapping back out of it, I step over the threshold and continue walking into the dark basement when I hear a soft click and the whole under build lights up. I look up and see cute, twinkling fairy lights hanging from the beams.

"Fairy lights?" I ask, turning and looking at Tripp over my shoulder, pausing for a moment.

"Aspen. Scared of the dark. Riggs put them everywhere. He never wanted her to be afraid..." He trails off as we reach the bottom, his feet moving towards the racks of wine.

Sweet move Riggs, sweet. "Do you drink red?" He interrupts my thoughts as his fingers brush against the dusty corks of the bottles.

"I do," and for some reason, I feel my cheeks burning. Why am I blushing?

"Merlot?" he continues, slipping out a bottle just past it's neck, "or a Rioja?"

"Merlot," I answer, following him like a needy puppy.

"Or..." He pauses as his fingers dance over to another bottle, "a cabernet?"

"Cabernet." I love a cabernet. White or red. Cabernet is my wine.

"Two bottles?"

"The whole family is here, so why not," I step close to him, my nerves tingling from being in close proximity.

"Sound perfect." He takes his own bottle out of the rack and holds his hand out for me to go ahead of him. We walk back towards the steps in complete silence, and for the first time, I don't feel the tension. I feel at ease.

I turn, smirking as I hold my own hand out for him to take, I don't miss the way his eyes flicker, but soothing as soon as our eyes meet.

He is hesitant, but he takes it, fingers brushing before my hand tucks perfectly inside of his.

Walking back into the house, it all seems calm, but as soon as Tripp notices Riggs, everything changes. I can feel the tension slowly rising and I know I am not going to be wanted here.

"What is it?" Tripp asks, I can hear the nerves cracking in his voice, the way his shoulders are rising and falling a little quicker tells me his heart is racing in his chest. He places his bottle of wine on the countertop, and I mirror him, hidden safely behind him for just a moment.

Riggs eyes lift over Tripp's shoulders and land on me. That's my cue to leave.

"I'm going to check on Lainey," I mutter softly, turning and walking away.

Silence rings loud in my ears as my feet lead me to where Lainey is sleeping peacefully. Opening her door, I sneak in and sit quietly on my bed.

I didn't know what to do. Aspen wasn't here anymore. I didn't even see Orla and Jorge but they might be with Aspen?

Who knows.

I reach for the bedside unit, dragging the drawer open and picking up my phone. My heart sinks a little as guilt weighs heavy on my shoulders. I shouldn't be here. I should be staying at Sylvia's.

I was here for one thing and one thing only.

To say goodbye to my daughter's father and get everything he had.

I check my emails and see a notification from my agent, Lucian. My mood instantly turns sour.

LUCIAN

Dixie, you can't just run away. I will catch up with you, and let's be honest, it's not going to be hard to find you.

Turning my phone off, I throw it back in my drawer when I hear Tripp scream and an almighty bang. My eyes widen and land on Lainey, who screams, and I am up, scooping her against my chest to soothe her back to sleep.

I begin to sing softly, dancing around my room, my hand patting her tooshie until I feel her little body fall heavy. Placing a kiss on the top of her head, I lay her back down and cover her with a light blanket. It's not overly cold, but there is a nip in the air during the evenings.

I go to sit back on my bed when I hear my bedroom door open, and I see Tripp's boot.

"I'm so sorry," he whispers, wincing.

"It's fine, she's back asleep," I smile, standing and walking towards the door, closing it behind me.

He nods, but I can tell he isn't really here with me.

"All okay?" I ask, but not wanting to pry.

"Yeah, fine," he rolls his lips, hands pushed into his back pockets.

"Good," silence creeps over us, my eyes darting around the large space that we're both just lingering in.

"Dinner is being dished up," he almost grunts as he walks towards the stairs, and I follow.

When we reach the kitchen, everyone is back. My brows

furrow, but it's not my place to speak, so, I keep quiet until I am spoken to.

We take our seats; Jorge says grace and Orla tells us to dish up. Brisket, jus, mashed potato and string greens.

I am starving.

"How was your day?" Jorge asks Orla, and I chew on my mouthful.

The brisket is amazing.

"It was nice," she smiles, lifting her eyes to me. "We went shopping for Lainey and Dixie and then we all went for lunch at Sunny's, it was a lovely girls day out," and I can tell that today meant a lot to her.

"It was lovely, I hope you didn't mind me gate crashing," Aspen looks between myself and Orla.

"Of course not," I smile, and Orla gives her daughter-in-law an adoring look.

"How about you dear, how was your day?" Orla asks Jorge and he sighs.

"Same old, popped down to see the cowboys. Seems they all got a little rowdy last night, sore heads this morning. Upped their workloads."

"Dad," Riggs grunts.

"Someone has to tell them. Where were you today?"

"He was busy having a late breakfast," Tripp says through a toothy grin and then groans when I am assuming Riggs kicks him in the shin.

"Took the day off, I only work three Saturdays a month now, you know that," Riggs rolls his eyes as he spoons mash and brisket past his lips.

"Well make sure your guys know what they should be doing, I don't want to have to manage them."

"I didn't ask you to, that's what Conrad is for."

"The town farrier? You have put him in charge for the

Saturday you're not working...?" Jorge seems annoyed as he lets his voice trail off.

"Yup," Riggs whistles and I watch Aspen's lips twist.

"Anyway!" Aspen sings, "Dixie, tell us all about you," her fork and knife get placed down on her plate. "What have you been up to?"

I feel my insides knot.

"Nothing you don't already know," I half laugh, half cough.

Reaching for my water, I take a large mouthful.

"What's it like being a country singer?"

I inhale heavily.

"Not all it's cracked up to be, I have to find a new agent. I love singing, but it's just not enjoyable at the moment and of course, with Lainey... it's not as easy as it once was."

"Is her dad present?"

The question feels like a blow to the gut.

"No, he didn't want anything to do with her."

Lie.

"What an asshole."

"Language," Orla scolds Aspen and she giggles.

"Are you glad to be back in Lovelock? What's the real reason you're back?" she asks, eyes burning into mine.

"I told you earlier..." I smile softly, my throat thickening as panic claws at my throat.

Is it hot in here?

I take another mouthful of water to try and wet my throat, my tongue feels like it's swollen to the roof of my mouth.

"Aspen," Riggs half snaps at her, a smirk on his lips.

"What?" she asks innocently, eyes all wide.

"It wasn't too long ago that you were in Dixie's position and my wonderful Ma here was asking you loads of questions..." he trails off and I see the realisation of what was just happening play across her face.

"Oh my god," she covers her lips with her hands, "I'm so sorry—you're right babe— please, ignore me. It's none of my business why you're back..."

"It's just nice to see you back home again," Riggs chimes in.

My eyes land on Tripp and his jaw is wound tight and, in that moment, I am afraid his walls have been built up again.

"To Dixie," Orla reaches for her wine and holds it up.

"To Dixie," everyone chimes and I feel like a fraud.

The rest of the evening goes off without a hitch, but the tension is still brewing heavily over the Rivera family.

I help Orla clean up after dinner whilst the men all sit in the back office with whiskey and Aspen is drying the plates and putting them back in the cabinet.

The sound of a door opens and closes from upstairs, and I see Orla look up in that direction.

"I'll go," Aspen offers, placing the drying cloth on the sink unit and disappearing round the corner.

"Is Pacey okay?" I pry, emptying the dirty dish water.

"He will be. Just got a little drunk. We have a lot going on and Pacey isn't coping very well."

I was a year younger than Pacey, I knew of him, but I didn't *know* him. The only Rivera boy I really knew was Tripp.

"I'm sorry to hear that."

"He'll be okay, just need to get the next few weeks out the way," she turns to look at me and I can see the pain in her eyes.

"If there is anything I can do, please let me know. You've

been so gracious with letting me stay here, it's the least I could do."

"Thank you, Dixie, that means a lot," she says as she places a hand on my shoulder and gives me a gentle squeeze.

The moment is cut short when Aspen shouts out "Riggs!" and I hear the sound of his feet hitting the floor before we see him.

I give Orla a tight smile as she wanders to where Riggs has disappeared to, and I swipe up the baby monitor and take myself out the front. Closing the front door behind me, I pace towards one of the wooden rockers and settle myself into it. I reach for the blanket box and pull out one of the blankets, covering my legs as I look out to the perfectly clear night. I turn the monitor down so I am not eavesdropping, but the lights stay on so I know if she needs me. And for just a moment, everything feels perfect.

Even though I am fully aware that none of this is.

I had to go and see Lainey's uncle, but I would wait until after the funeral.

Her dad was always in touch, he would have done anything for Lainey, but me and him didn't work. He wasn't a nice man, I instantly regretted my choice when it came to him, but I don't regret having Lainey. She was my world.

I'm not alone with my thoughts long when Tripp walks out onto the porch, completely lost in thought as he steps forward and leans against the wooden railing that runs around the porch.

He hasn't seen me sitting in the corner.

So, I take this as my moment to watch him.

His head is tipped back, hair messy like he has been pulling at the root, eyes glassy as they bounce around the stars.

He looks broken somehow.

The worries laying heavy on his mind.

I shuffle slightly so the chair creaks and his head whips around to see me. Holding my hand up to say *hi*, he strolls across the wooden floor to where I am tucked away.

"I didn't realise you were out here."

"I just thought it would be best to take myself out of that situation…" I pick the skin around my thumb nail bed.

"It's a shit show in there," he huffs, his back against the railings, boot resting on the newel post and hands curled around the rail.

"I'll move into Sylvia's in the morning, you all have so much going on…"

I knew about what Austin was being accused of, everyone did. It's all that has been splashed across the front of the newspapers for the last few weeks. Sure, I haven't been home in years but I still keep up with what's going on.

I even know about the goldmine drama.

Tripp sighs, his defeated brow lifting so he is looking at me.

"You don't have to," he looks tired.

"I know, but I think it may be best," I nod and now it's my turn to bow my head.

Nothing but silence surrounds us, and on that last note, he walks towards me and takes a seat in the rocker next to me.

And that's how we sit until the early hours of the morning.

No words.

No noise.

Just each other's company.

CHAPTER SEVEN
TRIPP

I wake stiff-necked and cold. It takes me a moment to realise where I am.

The sun peeks between the mountains, the low sun ready to greet today and the sound of the eagle's piping notes settle my realization.

Rolling my head to the side, I gaze to where she was sitting last night and I see I'm alone.

Sighing, I push out of the rocker and stretch my arms up then bend my neck, cracking each time and man, it felt good.

Walking into the house, no one is there to greet me. I tiredly trudge into the kitchen, fill the coffee pot and put it on, then my tired legs take me to the bathroom. My eyes are like slits, my head pounds.

Opening the door, a scream wakes me up and that's when I see Dixie wrapped in a towel.

"Shit, sorry—I'm so sorry," I hide my eyes and back out of the room.

I turn, walking to my bedroom and slam my door.

I groan, annoyed that my cock is hardening over the sight of her.

Kicking my boots off, I climb onto my bed and fall face down. My mind fills with images of Dixie. I've seen her body before, many times. But something about it today felt different. It had been years. Her body had changed, in the best way. Curves in places where they never were before, boobs more rounded and fuller.

My cock swells and I am desperate to jerk off, but I restrain.

Rolling onto my back, my eyes pin to the ceiling and I try to think about everything other than her silky wet skin.

I'm not alone with my thoughts long when a glum looking Pacey walks into my room like a stroppy teenager.

"Tripp," he grunts, falling onto the bed next to me.

"Pacey," I roll my head to the side, looking at his side profile. He still looks baby faced. Soft stubble and golden locks.

"I feel like death."

"I'm not surprised," I sigh, my eyes back on the ceiling.

"Did I say anything out of line last night?"

"You blamed me for Austin," and now it's Pacey's turn to look at me.

"You know I didn't mean that man..." he pauses, breath held.

"I know, you were just looking for someone to blame," my lips pull into a soft smile.

"It's just so fucked up," he scrubs his face.

"I know," I sigh. Because it's the truth. It is fucked up.

"He didn't do it man," Pacey rolls on his side, propping his hand under his head.

I hum. "We all know that, but the last person to see

Clay alive was Austin. He was seen dragging him into the back of our truck... then he winds up on our land."

"He can't go to jail; can you talk to Kelcie?" I can hear the desperation in his voice.

My chest rattles.

"There is no point, Kelcie has fucked us every which way possible. I shouldn't have trusted him, and that is on me."

Pacey falls back to the bed, hands over his face.

"I'll fix it Pace, I promise. I won't let them send an innocent man to jail."

The thing is, I had no idea if I could fix it. My confidence was shot.

"I've lost my job, I can't lose my best friend too."

Austin wasn't just Pacey's best friend. He was all of ours. He is Aspen's older brother. We grew up together, days spent down the creek, evenings causing chaos wherever we could. I feel like things are slipping through my fingers and there is nothing I can do to stop them, no matter how much I try and grab a hold.

I needed to protect the land. I needed to make sure they didn't dig down to the goldmine. I needed to protect what was ours.

"You won't lose him, brother." My throat bobs, the lump inside burning through me, "I promise." And I really wish I could keep that promise, but I know that I couldn't.

Because deep down I knew Austin was doomed. Even if we could prove that he was innocent, they would strike him down with something else. They already had their judgement. They already had their man.

Silence crackles between us.

"So, this Dixie chick..." I hear the smile that presents itself on his boyish face.

"What about her?"

"Smoking hot."

I laugh softly.

"I suppose so."

"Oh, fuck off, you know she's hot."

I roll my eyes.

"She's changed a lot from what I remember in school."

"She's all grown up," I remind him.

"She's grown hot. What's the deal, she with someone?"

"No idea, haven't really said much to her. Trying to keep my distance. She won't be around long. Mentioned she is here for a personal issue then will be back to wherever she came from."

"They always say that, then she'll end up staying and you'll both fall madly in love," he scoffs, shaking his head from side to side.

"This isn't some romance movie," I sigh loudly. "She's got a life; she is a singer, no doubt her name in shining lights. She had no life here. There is nothing here for her. Family is all gone, what could she possibly have here to keep her?"

Pacey rubs his hand over his stubble.

"Have you not asked her?"

"No, why would I? We're not friends, I can't just ask her."

He sighs, sitting up before looking at me over his shoulder. "You can, you just won't because you're a pussy."

I scoff.

"I was thinking," he says as he sits up.

"Did it hurt?" I smirk, and he leans over me, slapping me round the head.

I swat his hand away, sitting up and pushing my hand through my tousled hair.

"Anyway, back to what I was saying," he rolls his eyes in an exaggerated manner as he pushes from the bed. "Do you think Riggs would let me help out around here? I need the distraction."

He rocks onto the balls of his feet, hands shoved into the front pockets of his Levi's.

"I can't see why not, there is always something to do around here," I shrug one shoulder up.

"Cool, I'll go over to Crooked Creek," he gives a nod then turns on his heel.

"Oh, make sure you knock," I say a little louder as he gets to the bedroom door and opens it slightly.

"Huh? Why?"

"Trust me on this one..." a soft chuckle escapes out of me, "just knock." Winking, I push up onto my feet and walk out the room behind him, giving him a soft squeeze on his shoulder.

He disappears downstairs and my eyes scan the landing. Stepping towards the bathroom, I lift my hand to knock, but as my knuckles brush against the oak of the door, it opens.

"Dixie?" I call out, not wanting to catch her in a compromising position again.

Nothing.

The room still has warm steam radiating from it, but I take that as my cue to step in. Closing the door and locking it, I peel yesterday's clothes off my body and discard them into the laundry hamper. Turning the shower knob, the hot water spurts from the head and I step under it, the hot water soothing my aching muscles.

Definitely do not recommend sleeping on a wooden rocker.

-10/10.

Once out the shower and re-dressed for the day, I hear the commotion downstairs of my mom and dad bickering and Pacey trying to diffuse the ticking time bomb.

"Hey hey," I call out as I walk in and see my mom and dad toe to toe, chest to chest.

I watch as Pacey's shoulders sag in relief.

"What's going on?" I ask, arms folded across my chest and I feel like I am the parent.

"This whole Austin thing, your dad wants to be the hero and take the wrap for Clay."

"I mean," Pacey runs his hand round the back of his neck, head tilting and I turn to look at him, utter confusion on my face.

Just as I am about to open my mouth, my mom walks over to Pacey and clips him around the back of his head.

"Ow," he half laughs, half grumbles as he rubs out the pain.

"No, Dad, you're not handing yourself in for a crime you didn't commit," I shake my head from side to side and usher my mom to sit down at the dining room table.

My dad's eyes follow, and I know the look that flashes across his eyes. Eyes that widen as I step closer to him, hands on my hips as I lower my voice.

"Tell me you didn't do it."

My dad's head is dropped, eyes firmly fixed on the ground as I hear the sharp intake on his inhale.

"Dad, please, tell me you didn't," and now I whisper, because I am struggling to get the words out.

His dark green eyes finally land on mine.

"I roughed him up a bit, he came onto the ranch late in the evening. Spooked your mother to death. I walked out with my shotgun, and he fronted me out. Telling me that he was coming for my three boys. He was disoriented, like he had lost his head or something. Pupils dilated and his normal impeccable self was scruffy and dirty."

I look over my shoulder at Pacey and nod for him to go and sit with mom. He goes to protest, but with the slight narrow of my eyes, his head is down as he walks towards my mom.

Once I know he is out of earshot, I drag my dad towards the stools and sit him down.

"So, you roughed him around? Then what?"

"I hit him in the face with the stock of my gun," his fingers lock between themselves.

I wait for him to talk. "He went down too easy, nose busted. It took me a moment to realise what had happened. I lowered myself over him, pressed my fingers against his pulse. It was beating, barely."

I am shocked.

Words don't come easy.

"I stepped back, turning on my heel to run into the house for my cell, but when I came back outside... he was gone."

He rolls his lips. Then wets them with his tongue.

"Next thing I know, he was found dead at the bottom of the cows field by the creek."

I suck in a breath, a light whistle filling the room.

"You say nothing, do you understand me?" My tone has bite to it, a fair warning.

He gives a solemn nod and I walk towards the front door, and only then when I turn the corner do I see Dixie standing there, eyes wide and Lainey snuggled into her chest.

Running my hand through my hair, I look over my shoulder then let my eyes connect with hers.

"How much of that did you hear?" I keep my voice low,

her beautiful blue eyes bounce back and forth between mine.

"Enough," she whispers, and my fucking stomach drops.

"Shit," I grit, reaching for her elbow, I pull her to out of the house and onto the front porch.

"Get off me," she tugs away from me, careful not to wake Lainey.

"You don't understand, you shouldn't have been fucking eavesdropping," my temper is slowly slipping.

"Where was I supposed to go?" her brows furrow.

"Anywhere, but not hanging around the corner of the wall listening to something you have no business listening to."

"It is my business if it was *your* dad that killed my daughter's," and my fucking blood runs cold.

"What?!"

Fingers are running through my hair before they're dragging down my face.

She says nothing.

I couldn't believe this. Stepping towards the edge of the porch, my hands are back on my hips as I look out at the picturesque scenery in front of me. Sloped, mountain sides, points that brush fingertips with the angels above us and rolling green hills.

My chest rattles as I exhale.

Letting my head fall forward, I softly shake it before turning to face her. My hand lifting from my hip, fingers rubbing across my mouth.

"So, you were a thing then?" I ask, and I am fully aware my tone has bite to it like I am jealous. I am not jealous. Far from it actually.

The skin on the back of my neck erupts in goosebumps.

"Not that it's any of your business," she begins to bounce a fussing Lainey in her arms, rocking her hips slowly from side to side, "But no, it was a one-time thing."

She averts her gaze from me, looking out at the same picturesque scenery that I was just besotted with.

"Well, maybe a two- or three-times thing but definitely no more than that."

I scoff.

I am judging her.

Felt a dick for doing it, but I couldn't help it.

"Don't scoff at me, you have no right to judge me."

Rolling my eyes, my hands are back on my hips as I begin to pace.

"This why you're back then? Clay's funeral?" My legs stop as my eyes burn into her.

She gives a shallow nod. "Great, so you're staying in my home, under my roof just so you have somewhere to stay before you attend *his* funeral."

I watch as she rolls her lips and I shake my head once more.

"Why didn't you tell me?" rage simmers inside of me as her ocean blue eyes connect with mine.

"I didn't know how," she answers softly, stepping closer to me for just a moment. "But it is also none of your business. Your mom and dad took me and my daughter in. You out of all people should know how hard that was for me, I have nothing here, no family, no home... I packed up and ran. I wanted to make a better life for myself and yet..." she pauses, and I see the glisten of tears in her eyes. Her throat bobs as Lainey's sweet cries begin to fill the tense atmosphere between us.

Her eyes search mine for something, anything, but I

turn away from her and begin to walk down the steps and onto the dusty ground, my boots crunching.

I needed to clear my head, it was full and fuzzy, messy and hectic.

I don't look back behind me as Lainey's cries go from soft whimpers to piercing screams.

I throw my arm up, cowboy hat tilted down, and I walk to the only place that feels like my second home.

The Warren's.

CHAPTER EIGHT
TRIPP

My legs feel heavy from trudging through the fields. The grass is long, wildflowers bloom and my boots are covered in mud. Walking down the fence line and smiling when I see the small nightlights that are lined at every fence post.

I don't knock. Just climb the porch steps and let myself in.

"Blue? Buck?" I call out as I stand in the hallway.

"Tripp?" Blue's eyes widen and she looks so damn tired. I scoop her into my arms, holding her tightly.

Blue was like a second mom to me and my brothers. Always cooked for us, let us stay the night and kept our little secrets from our parents when we were up to no good.

"Is everything okay?" her glassy eyes bounce between mine and I give a heavy nod.

"How are you?" I ask, lifting my hat off and hanging it on the hat rack. I follow her through to the kitchen as she fills an iron kettle and places it on the stove, heating the water.

"I've been better, I am worried Tripp," and I roll my lips.

"I know, but I meant what I said. I will do everything to keep Austin from jail."

My stomach knots.

"I heard my name," I turn on my stool when I see a rugged Austin walk through the doorway. I stand and we embrace.

"Tea?" Blue asks.

"Please."

She doesn't give Austin an option, just makes him one anyway. Austin looks like shit.

Dirty blonde hair, messy. Stubble a little longer than normal, forming a short beard. Eyes hollow, deep set eye bags presenting themselves.

"Have you had an update from your lawyer?" I ask, thanking Blue as I take my tea from her.

"Yeah," he scrubs his face, elbows on the breakfast bar, head hung low.

"And?" I press.

"He is telling me to take the plea."

My blood runs cold.

"Why?"

I knew why.

"Because my chances are looking slim of being proven innocent, I don't see any other way out of it. They've done their investigation and post mortem..."

"And what was the cause of death?"

"Impact to the head, that's what caused him to die," he licks his lips.

I curl my fingers round the mug of my hot tea.

"There was no impact to the head, sure we all roughed him up but he didn't fall back did he? There was nothing for him to have hit his head on was there? He was a little dazed sure, but he ran away didn't he?"

My heart aches. I hate that he is looking to me for reassurance.

"He did," I nod.

"I've told them all of this. I've told them over and over," and I watch as his face falls, his eyes glassy and fuck, my stomach hurts.

"Don't say anything about taking the plea, leave it with me a bit longer yeah?" I clasp my hand over his shoulder, giving him a friendly squeeze.

He nods. And I hear Blue's heavy sigh.

"I don't know what else to suggest..." her eyes find mine, searching for something, anything that will get Austin off the blame train.

"I wish I had the answer Blue, I really do." Lifting the mug to my lips, I take a mouthful.

I know what I could do, I could let my dad turn himself in. But I felt stuck between a rock and a hard place. I didn't know what to do for the best; and then you've got Dixie and Lainey... Clay was her dad. She is growing up without a father because someone killed him.

"Did anyone identify the body?" I ask on a whim, my thoughts cascading over me.

"His brother," Austin turns to face me, "why?"

"Just wondering, just something feels off about the whole thing."

I finish the remainder of my tea; the whole time Dixie's voice plays at the back of my mind.

It is my business if it was your dad that killed my daughter's.

"I've got to shoot off, Austin," I say as I slip off the bar stool, hand back on his shoulder. "Keep your head up, there's enough people that want to see us fall, don't let them see you slip. This will get rectified, I promise."

He mutters something incoherent under his breath and

I give his shoulder one last squeeze. Blue stands and follows me to the front door. Reaching for my hat, I place it on my head before saying my goodbyes to Blue.

She closes the door behind me, and I inhale sharply.

My eyes narrow on my families ranch in the distance as my legs begin to carry me through the fields and back home.

I needed to speak to Dixie. I needed to speak to Riggs. And I needed to speak to Kelcie. Something is going on, I can feel it in my gut and we all know the gut always tells the truth.

Climbing the fence, my boots hit the ground just as Riggs storms out the door, eyes wide and I know he is fuming.

"What the fuck?" he whispers to me, eyes bouncing between mine.

I look over his shoulder and see my dad standing in the door, arms crossed against his chest. For fuck's sake.

I told him to not say anything.

"Elaborate please, it's been a morning, and we have a bigger problem than the one you're *what the fucking.*"

"Doubt that," his nostrils flare as he turns.

"You're on about dad, right?"

I side eye him as we begin to walk towards the bunk house.

"What else would I be on about Tripp?"

"Well..." I pause as Riggs moves across to the bunkhouse and makes sure the coast is clear.

He nods towards the bunk then slams the door behind me as I walk in.

I turn my nose up at the mess.

"You wouldn't last an hour on the ranch anymore," Riggs scoffs, kicking his boot into the floor.

"Funny you mention the ranch, I was thinking of coming back... as well as Pacey... if we can."

Riggs laughs. Loudly. Head tipped back; thumbs hooped through his belt loops.

"Okay pretty boy, both come back on the ranch tomorrow and you can go out with the cowboys. I'll be here too." He steps towards me, "Now, back onto what I called you in for."

"Fine," I nod, "I need to keep busy. I can't be worrying about Austin constantly; I can't just sit and feel helpless. I've lost my badge, Pacey is spiralling."

I shake my head and my big brother closes the small gap between us.

"I've spoken to dad, and mom..." he pauses, and I can see in his green eyes they've made a decision without mine or Pacey's input.

"Don't," I warn, standing toe to toe.

"It's him or Austin, you wouldn't want Austin to go down for something he didn't do, would you? Dad was the last to see him..."

"I've been to see Austin. He has been told to take the plea. He knows how Clay died."

Riggs steps back slightly, a heavy sigh making his broad shoulders rise and fall. "He died of head trauma *apparently*."

Riggs blinks a couple of times.

"He ran after dad roughed him up, he didn't fall to the floor and stay down did he? Same with Austin, he ran. What's to say he didn't have a heart attack then fell and hit his head? They need someone to blame, or more like they want someone to blame and by *'they'*, I mean Clay's family. They won't let this go, and because witnesses came forward to say they saw Austin putting him in the back of the truck, that's their proof. No one official told them that he ran off. We all have. Austin has. But they don't care. Because I can bet you now that Kelcie's pockets are lined."

"Something's off."

"Exactly," I throw my hand in the air, "look, I don't want Austin going down, and I don't want our dad going down either, but I just need a bit of time. We have two weeks until his hearing to be sentenced right? Two weeks is a fucking long time."

Riggs turns away from me, hands moved to his hips as he looks at the artwork on the panelled wall.

"We will not fucking rest until the right person is brought to justice," and he is back looking at me,

"Live by the ranch, die by the ranch," he grunts, and I nod, repeating the words before following him back outside. "Wait," he says as he bolts the bunk house door back.

Fuck.

"What did you want to talk about?"

I squint as I look down towards the creek.

"Dixie," I push my tongue into the inside of my cheek.

"What about her?" Riggs tilts his head to the side.

"She is back for the funeral."

"Right?" his brows furrow.

"Clay was Lainey's dad." I kind of rush out because my chest aches as soon as the words have spilled.

"What?!" he barks, and I look down at my dust and mud covered boots. "Is she a fucking mole? Is she feeding them assholes information?"

I hadn't even thought of that.

"No," I find myself defending her, "they only met up a few times, she hadn't seen him in months then heard the news..."

I had no idea if that was true but for some reason, I was incredibly protective of her which pissed me off a little.

"You better keep your mouth shut going forward, you have no idea what she's up to. Convenient that she happened to..." and he bunny quotes, "crash right outside our ranch?"

I mean, he isn't wrong.

"And she was coming back for that vermin's funeral. I'm sorry Tripp, but I think we have a little snake living with you, ma and dad."

And I can't argue that what he is saying doesn't make sense.

Because it does.

Too much sense actually.

I lift my hat from my head and run my hands through my brown hair, tipping my head back and letting the sun brush over my face for just a moment. The slight warmth feels good on my tired skin.

"This is going to be an outright war with the Attaway's."

"It's going to kick off Friday," I toe the floor.

"Hundred percent, but we will still go and show our respect. Is Austin going?"

I shake my head from side to side.

"Good, I think that's the right move."

"Do you think? Him hiding is just proving to people that maybe he is guilty. Where if he shows up, sure, he will probably be kicked into the dirt, but it shows that he is innocent?"

"I don't know brother..." Riggs pauses for a moment.

"Think about it for a while."

He nods.

"What you doing now?" he asks just as Ace bolts over to us from the house.

"I was going to find Dixie..."

"Come with me, grab yourself a horse and come out with me to find the boys, they're down the bottom field with the cows."

"You sure?" A small smile tugs at my lips.

"Yeah, be good to get you back out with the cowboys, I want to see just how good you are," he winks, and I laugh, slapping him on the back as we walk towards the stables.

The horses are tacked and ready and I place my foot in my stirrups, pulling myself up onto my dark bay horse and kick him on, leaving Riggs to eat my kicked-up dust.

But we both know he will be hot on my tail. Riggs never loses.

Ever.

CHAPTER NINE
DIXIE

My insides knot.

I shouldn't have heard that conversation and I definitely shouldn't have told Tripp. I don't even know why I reacted the way I did. Clay was just a hook up or two. I never felt anything for him. I am sad that he died, I am sad that my daughter will never remember her dad. He was good to her. Every kid deserves to have a dad that loves them unconditionally.

Clay helped with my music, but only when it suited him. He reminded me that he could quickly pull it away from me with a click of his fingers. He was in with some nasty guys from the city, I only met a few of them but they always made me feel uneasy.

My agent is a piece of shit, he will come looking for me but there is no way in hell I am going back to him.

Too many broken promises. He keeps eighty percent of my royalties, and I am broke.

Lainey pulls me from my thoughts when she pushes her bowl of pureed fruit onto the floor, the noise making me jump.

"Oh, Lainey," I sigh, pushing from my chair and grabbing a cloth from the sink. I clean up the mess when I hear Orla.

"Leave it darlin', I'll do it," she ushers me from the floor but I shake my head, not moving.

"No honestly, I've done it now, please," my voice breaks as I look up at her, my eyes are all glassy with unshed tears and I don't even know why.

"Dixie," she whispers as she bends and lifts me from the floor, hands either side of my face. "What's happened?"

I pull my bottom lip between my lips, the words on the tip of my tongue, but Lainey interrupts our moment when she starts a tantrum to get out of her highchair.

Orla turns and takes Lainey from her chair and soothes her, bouncing her gently and walking her out to the front porch to look at the leaves on the trees dancing in the soft summer breeze.

My bottom lip trembles as I walk over to the sink, turning the faucet and rinsing out the dirty cloth. Folding, I hang it over the side of the butler sink then press my hands flat to the surface either side, head hung low as I cry quietly before I am caught.

Is it guilt? All-consuming guilt because I am lying to Orla ad Jorge? They've been so good to me; they've been more of a family to me than my own. I mean, that wasn't hard. My mom died, my kid sister died, and my dad beat me black and blue before I left town.

But even that came with its own problems.

Young girl looking for an escape.

Powerful male promising her a better life.

I'll let you connect the dots.

I hear the sound of heavy boots, my skin prickling, and I

know it's Tripp. Sniffling, I lift my hand and run my finger under both of my eyes to wipe the stray tears away.

"Dixie?" his voice is soft and warm, and I hate that. I spin around, forcing a fake smile upon my lips as I look at him.

"Yeah?" my back is pressed against the sink, fingers curled around the edge of the worksurface.

His eyes roam over me quickly and I let my head drop. The sound of his footsteps become closer and my heart stutters in my chest.

Toe to toe with me, his hand slips from his jean pocket and grips my chin softly, tilting my head back to look at him.

His brown eyes bounce between mine, his pupils dilating slightly, the once harsh frown lines that were dug into his forehead smooth out as worry paints across his handsome face.

"Who upset you?" he asks me, letting his hand fall from my chin.

"No one," and it's the truth. No one did upset me.

"Then why are you crying?" he steps back a little and I miss how close he was to me.

"Hormones."

He hangs on my words a little longer before he gives me a sharp nod.

He is dirty. Hands covered in mud, boots thick with it too. His jeans have hand marks rubbed into the thighs and his face has a golden glow to it from the sun.

"I saw mom out front with Lainey, I just wanted to make sure you were okay."

The breath catches at the back of my throat, and I swallow the burning lump down. Giving him a soft nod, he turns and trudges mud back through the kitchen then kicks his boots off at the door.

"I'll clean this up," I call out, not sure why I offered.

He glances at me as he walks towards the stairs, lips part as if he is about to say something, but he doesn't. He just continues upstairs, and I jump when I hear the bedroom door slam shut.

Moving towards the cupboard, I grab the broom and begin to sweep the dry mud clumps off the floor, then run the damp mop over.

I press the coffee machine on and sit at the table, the house is quiet and for the first time in a long time, I can hear my thoughts.

They're not as heavy or messy as they once were.

I have a lot of shit to unpack, but I am hoping whilst I am here, I can figure out what I need to do next.

And, if I decide to stay, I need a job.

The Rivera's have been far too kind to me the last few days and I can't keep taking from them. I've also got to remember that when they find out my connection with Clay, I'll no doubt be kicked out to the dusty road.

They're not going to want me or Lainey here.

My bottom lip wobbles again but I stiffen it, refusing to let another tear fall through guilt. I didn't deserve to cry.

I also didn't deserve any of the kindness I was being shown.

It wouldn't be long, and everyone would know that Dixie Walker was a fraud.

The sound of a throat being cleared has me turning towards the back of the house as Jorge comes through the boot room.

"Hi Jorge," I squeak, pushing to my feet. "Coffee?"

He shakes his head from side to side and I sit back down, cautiously.

"Why are you sitting here alone?" he asks, now bootless as he drags a chair across the tiles and sits next to me.

"Lainey was fussing, chucked her bowl over her highchair and made a mess. Orla took her out to watch the trees..." I trail off as he just stares at me, opal eyes filled with so much knowledge and wonder.

He grumbles, sitting back, fingers linked together as he rests his hands on his stomach.

"I was thinking about getting a job, I need something to pay my way around here," I say a little too hastily. I haven't even decided if I want to stay or not yet. I know I am not wanted here, especially by Tripp, but I could move into Sylvia's.

My old childhood home still sits at the base of the mountains, the other side of the creek. It's run down and been left to rot. I always said I would go back home one day when I found the courage, but being back here made me realize I don't think the courage will ever come.

"I'm sure we can find you something, people are always looking for help."

I smile at him. His skin worn, his eyes tired. A body that has worked all its life and is still going. The Rivera's have always worked their fingers to the bone. Day and night they're out on their ranches doing what they love.

"I'm sure you could get a couple of gigs singing, Tripp tells me you're causing quite a storm back in the city?"

And my heart falls deep into my chest.

If only you knew.

"I don't know about that," I laugh my nerves off. "I don't have my guitar. I hire one back where I live; my dad broke my one up before I left home." I pause for a moment and I feel a surge of hot tears burning behind my eyes. I haven't thought about my guitar in a long time. My mom bought it for me one birthday, I had been asking for one since I was five. It was the most cherished gift she could have given me. But he took it from me, like everything else and destroyed it along with my happiness. I was just grateful that I still had her pendant. My fingers find it on their own accord and my heart soars back into my chest.

Two stars and a moon. Tied in an infinite bond. Always there, even when I couldn't see her.

My eyes flutter ever so slightly, and a tear rolls down my cheek.

"I'm sorry Dixie, I never meant to make you cry," he grumbles, leaning forward on his chair and resting his elbows on the table.

"It wasn't you, I got upset over a memory," I nod, half laughing, half choking on a sob as I palm the stray tear away.

"But I am sorry, no child should have to go through what you did..." he pauses just as Orla walks back into the room with a sleeping Lainey.

"Oh honey, are you okay?" she says softly when she sees my red rimmed eyes, careful not to wake Lainey.

I nod.

Because the truth is, I am okay. I will heal from this, I will rise, like a Phoenix from the ashes. I will rise, I will soar.

Standing, I say goodbye to Jorge and carefully take Lainey from Orla's arms.

"Thank you," I whisper, as I cuddle my daughter to my chest and walk up the stairs to our bedroom. I huff when I reach the door and it's shut.

The handles are rounded doorknobs and the way I am holding Lainey prevents me from reaching for it.

"Damn it," I say a little louder than intended. Bending my knees slightly, I try and twist the knob with my elbow, but it slips right off causing my arm to jolt and Lainey stirs.

I really don't want to wake her. She fussed all last night, and I could feel the bumps in her gums where two teeth are threatening to break through.

I lean against the bedroom door, head falling back and hitting the wood.

"Do you need help?" I hear Tripp's voice, and my eyes lift to see him standing wrapped in just a towel. Skin all wet and shiny, brown chest hair damp. His muscles ripple under his skin as he walks towards me, arms strong and toned. Dark brown hair flopped against his forehead, water droplets running down his nose. *Hot.*

"Please," my voice is barely audible as I pull my eyes from him. Ten years looks good on him. A little too good if I am being honest.

I step aside and ignore the want to inhale his scent.

He twists the knob and pushes the bedroom door open, revealing my room.

"Thank you," I just about manage as I step into the room and lay Lainey in her cot, settling her down before I walk back out onto the landing, baby monitor in hand as I pull the door two.

Tripp has disappeared into his room and disappointment surges through me.

I make my way downstairs and into the kitchen to pour myself a coffee from the pot I brewed. Glancing up at the time, it's just past two. I have an hour until Lainey wakes and I feel a little lost on what to do.

Everyone goes about their day, their jobs, and then there is me who doesn't quite know what to do with herself.

I'm sitting back at the kitchen table, hot coffee in hand when Pacey walks through the door, a boyish grin on his face.

"Dixie," he greets me as he moves towards the refrigerator and grabs a bottle of water.

"Pacey," I smile back as he plops himself on one of the barstools.

"What's new?" he asks, eyes flitting between mine.

"Not a lot, every day is pretty much the same to me at the moment," I admit, taking a sip of coffee.

"We can find you something to do, there is always jobs to be done on the ranch," he offers, and I place my coffee down on the coaster.

"Thanks." My cheeks blush slightly, "I would take anything at the moment."

A cough fills the room and both me and Pacey turn to look in that direction. Tripp is leaning against the door frame, beautiful arms folded across his chest.

"Am I interrupting something?" He asks, one brow raised.

Asshole.

"Yeah, me trying to find Dixie something to do around here to keep her from losing her mind."

"What about Lainey?" he counters back.

"I'll watch her if Dixie wants to find a little job, I would love to have her, only if that's okay with you?" Orla's voice floats from the boot room, as she places a hand on my shoulder, and I shrink in my chair a little.

"Only if you wouldn't mind? I mean, I still have to find something first but..."

"Like I said, plenty to do on the ranch. I'm back working here since I lost my job, so the more the merrier in my opinion," Pacey gives me a slow wink and I don't miss the low rumble of Tripp from beside me.

"I would love to help out; Tripp, would you mind?"

His eyes are on his brother, and I know Tripp isn't happy about it.

"Whatever, just don't think we will go easy on you."

"We?" Pacey pipes up.

"Yup, I'm back working for the family business too."

And my insides knot.

"Great," Pacey rolls his eyes in a playful manner and I let out a flutter of a laugh.

"Welcome to Rivera Ranch Dix, you're gonna love it," Pacey's smile is wide and my heart beats a little faster in my chest.

"I'm sure I will," I admit, my eyes finding Tripp's. He isn't smiling. His jaw is tight, nostrils flared slightly... he is pissed off. "When do I start?" I beam.

"Is tomorrow too soon?" Pacey asks and his eyes bounce between mine and his mom's.

"Tomorrow is fine with me, Dixie will just need to let me know hers and Lainey's routine..." she pauses for a moment, and I know she is referring to my breast feeding.

"I'll have to run out and grab a couple of bits..." I trail off, anxiety clawing at my throat at the thought of spending more money I don't have.

"Well once Lainey is up, we can drive into town. Get you some clothes and whatever else you both need."

I place my hand over Orla's that is still resting on my shoulder, and she gives me a squeeze of reassurance.

With that, Tripp sulks out of the house, slamming the front door behind him.

"What's eating him?" Pacey looks over his shoulder before his eyes settle on mine.

"I have no idea," I whisper, but the truth was, I did know.

He is upset with me.

Here I am playing house with *his* family when he knows my connection to Clay. Their friend is up for the murder of my daughter's dad. Their dad is willing to take the wrap. Tripp doesn't know my history. No one does when it comes to Clay.

He just helped me when I had nowhere else to turn.

I will tell Tripp the truth, but I'm not ready yet.

I don't want to see Austin or Jorge sentenced for something they didn't do... but who says they didn't do it?

Someone killed Clay, and all arrows point to Austin.

Jorge is a wonderful man and a very proud one, I wish I could understand why he would want to protect someone who isn't even blood. But I suppose I never will. I wasn't even protected by my own blood, by the man who should have kept me safe. But he never did, so yeah, I never will understand.

The hour slips by and we're on our way out. Lainey is fed and happy, gurgling away in her car seat and grabbing the soft toys that dangle in front of her. Orla drives us to the nearest department store, and we pop Lainey in the cart. Her chubby legs kicking happily as she squeals.

"Oh, look at her, she loves riding in the cart," Orla says, pushing it along and I am happy to walk beside her, Lainey's beautiful blue eyes flitting between me and Orla.

"She does," I smile at my beautiful daughter, she's so innocent and blissfully unaware of the cruel world we live in. Walking into the department store, I head straight for the breast pumps. I reach for a manual one but Orla takes it from me and places it back on the shelf.

"Electric pump is better," she says softly and my gut

twists. It's double the price and I can already feel the beads of cold sweat pricking at the base of my neck.

"I don't mind a manual," I offer, a small smile creeping onto my lips.

"Only the best for you, Dixie," and her eyes glisten with kindness and my chest aches.

I pray that my credit card still has enough on it to cover the pump as I place it into the cart.

"Now, shall we look at some more snacks for you, how about some new toys?" Orla sings to Lainey as she pushes her down the aisles, and I can hear her giggling.

She really didn't need any new toys. Orla and Jorge have been more than generous with everything they have already paid out for.

I pause for a moment to watch the glee on Orla's face as she shows my daughter the flashing toy she picked up, Lainey completely mesmerised.

Creeping up behind her, I place my hand on hers and tilt my head.

"Lainey already has so many wonderful things that you and Jorge have treated her to…" I trail off for a moment and ignore the burn in my throat. "But I can only afford the breast pump." I lower my voice and shame blankets me. I have no idea why. I shouldn't be ashamed. I work hard, it's not my fault that my manager takes everything from me and leaves me just enough to put food on the table.

My bottom lip quivers and I look away from her.

"You're under our roof, Dixie. This is not your burden. Let us look after you for a while…" she squeezes my hand before stepping away from the cart and wrapping me inside her arms in a motherly embrace. "You deserve to be cared for, sweet girl," and I choke out a sob.

My tears run through her shirt, but she doesn't push me

away. Just cradles me like I am a little girl who needs their mom. She holds me until I have nothing left to cry.

"Now, wipe your pretty face of those tears, and let's get Lainey some new clothes. Then we will stop at the store for you on our way back into town." Her cool hand cups my face, brushing her thumb across my cheeks. "No more tears," she smiles, and I return it.

Pulling into the parking lot, I slip Lainey from her car chair and feed her in the back of the truck. She was fussing and I didn't know how long Orla was going to keep us in here for. She told me that this is where they've always come for their clothes and the boys still come here now. She told me if I was going to work on the Rivera Ranch, I needed to dress like a Rivera. Just a lot prettier.

Lainey was changed and full and back into another cart. Orla brought her a brown stuffed floppy horse and she hasn't let go of it. Her little fingers grasped tightly round the horses leg as she dangles it over the handle, babbling away to it and my heart melts.

The bell chimes as we walk through the door and the overbearing smell of leather burns through my senses.

"There she is, our favorite Rivera lady," an older man calls from behind the counter.

"Oh, stop it Eddie," Orla waves him off, shaking her head from side to side.

"Riggs need new chaps again?" he rolls his eyes.

"Nope, not here for Riggs today, we're here for Dixie," she turns to look at me, beaming with what feels like pride. But I have no idea why she would be proud of little old me.

"Well, hello there Dixie. I'm Eddie and I own Hats 2 Horses," he runs his fingers around the rim of his hat then tips it down.

"Hi Eddie," I stay close to Orla. "Why the name?"

"Why not? You can literally get hats and horses."

Puzzled I turn to Orla.

"He also sells horses," her lips twist.

"Yeah but she won't ever buy a horse from me, she always uses the Warren lot with the murderer son."

My blood chills.

Orla clears her throat, stepping forward.

"Now, now, Eddie... no one likes a gossip," her brows raise, tone full of warning.

Eddie dips his head for a moment. "She is starting on the ranch, she has nothing so we need to kit her out," his eyes sweep over me, but not in a creepy way. "Can you help us Eddie or do I need to take my business elsewhere?" Orla's tone is clipped, and I know she is reacting to his earlier comment.

I'm wearing a white bardot top, a denim jacket and black high waisted jeans with sneakers.

"Well, you brought her to the right place," he winks at Orla but she is fussing over Lainey. Eddie walks out from behind the counter, and I notice his prosthetic leg. "Wondering what happened?"

My cheeks burn at being caught.

"Used to be a bull rider. Got crushed in the gate one day. They couldn't save my leg." He lets out a soft sigh, but his face is still glowing with a smile. "I'm alive, and I am grateful for that. I live a great life and I am happy. What more could I want or need?" he asks me, and I give a soft shrug of my shoulder.

He gives me another sweeping look before he is off and grabbing all items of clothing, throwing them over the racks.

"Taylor!" Eddie bellows and a young man walks onto the store floor, his eyes searching for Eddie.

"Yeah dad?"

"Reach up and grab the tan cowboy boots for me please son," Eddie nods up at the higher shelf before looking over his shoulder at me. "Size five?"

"Yeah." I give him a puzzled look before looking down at my dirty old sneakers.

Tongue in his cheek, he wanders further down the aisle and grabs some Levi's. Taylor jumps down off the ladder and walks over to me with the shoe box.

"Thanks," my eyes focus on his beautiful hazel eyes. Auburn hair and freckles dusted across his cheeks. Would put him a couple of years older than me. Maybe.

"Not a problem darlin'" he gives a slow wink and I see he has his father's charm. Dressed in plaid green and cream shirt, Levi's, a tanned belt with a huge gold buckle and a tanned cowboy hat to match his boots, he looks the part.

He tilts his hat before disappearing out back.

"Cute," Orla smirks as she begins pushing Lainey towards the clothes that Eddie had tossed. I follow behind her and take over pushing as she fills the cart.

"I wasn't flirting," I find myself protesting, cheeks flaming.

"Of course, not," her lips twitch, "he's a nice kid, maybe he can take you out one night."

A nervous laugh bubbles out of me.

"Not really up for dating at the moment," I mumble as we approach Eddie.

"Okay kid, I think that's everything. Go try some of it on. Orla will let you know if it all fits okay," he beams at Orla and she gives him a soft nod, thanking him.

I follow her to the changing rooms, it's small, with two dressing rooms. Orla perches herself down on a cow skin stool and Lainey is eating puffs. Placing a kiss on the top of her dark hair, I linger for a moment. I have never loved someone as much as I love Lainey.

Grabbing the handful of stuff that Eddie picked, I trudge into the dressing room. Yanking the curtain across, I hang the clothes on the steel clothes rail.

My nose scrunches a little at some of the color choices he has chosen but I trust him.

Stripping off, I reach for the first pair of skinny legged Levi's. Jumping up and down to get them round my waist, I button them and glance at myself in the mirror.

They're high enough that they hide my mom pouch nicely.

Grabbing a plaid shirt, it's dusty pink and beige chequered. Slipping it up my arms, I button it up and tuck it into my jeans.

What do I look like.

I tilt my head in the mirror, letting my eyes roam over my new attire.

"You got an outfit on yet?" Orla calls out.

"Yeah," I inhale deeply and pull the curtain back and her eyes light up.

"Oh I love it, is the shirt comfortable? Jeans fit okay?" she asks, standing with Lainey in her arms, her little mouth sucking hard on her pacifier.

"I think so?" I turn and look at myself in the mirror again before facing Orla. "The shirt isn't pulling around my chest, so I think we're good?" I look to her for confirmation, and she holds her thumb up.

"Put the boots on," she beams and a soft giggle escapes. Bending down, I lift the lid from the box and my eyes widen at the tan cowboy boots. My fingers brush over the cream stitching and my heart gallops in my chest. I had always wanted a pair of my very own cowboy boots, but I never did get them, not until now. I blink away the heavy tears that are forming on my bottom lid and delicately lift them from the box, afraid I am going to break them somehow.

I balance myself as I slip my foot into the boot, and it fits like a glove.

"Well, you look every bit cowgirl," Orla beams and Lainey scrunches her nose at me, arms and legs kicking with excitement.

"Yeah?" happiness radiates through me.

"Yeah," she nods in confirmation.

I try two more pairs of jeans, one straight legged, one bootleg as well as some jodhpurs.

I also try on the tanned chaps to match my boots. I had a handful of shirts and tees to take home with me too. I had been thoroughly spoiled.

Lifting the bags from Eddie, I thank him and for the fiftieth time, thank Orla too.

"Oh, I almost forgot," Eddie smiles, turning and reaching for a large, square box.

My brows raise and I notice the knowing smile on Orla's lips.

He lifts the lid and pulls out a brown cowboy hat with a cream stitching detail.

My eyes widen as he lifts it and places it on my head.

"Now she's a cowgirl," he winks, and I fist my bag for my card but he holds his hand up, shaking his head from side to side. "It's on the house, darlin'."

We say goodbye and make our way back towards the ranch. Orla drives slow as Lainey starts to fuss. She is over tired and over stimulated, but I truly believe she had the best day.

We didn't go out much back home. A lot of our trips were to the recording studio. I became more of a hermit once I had

Lainey. Anxiety used to suffocate me at the thought of going out by myself. What if someone tried to take her from me? What if something was to happen to me whilst we were out, and she was left without a mom? It didn't matter how much I tried; I couldn't stop the intrusive thoughts that crashed over me. I hated it. In constant fear that Lainey was going to be without me one day. I know if I deep delved into it, it would stem from my own trauma of losing my mom at a young age, I never let it bother me until I became a mom myself. I grieved her, of course I did, but I pushed every sad thought that I once had into the deepest crevices inside my chest. They were never coming back out. But having Lainey sparked a new fear. A fear of me dying on her. A fear that she would lose me one day. The thought of leaving her alone was enough to throw me into a panic attack in the back of the truck. Closing my eyes for just a moment, I inhale deeply through my nose.

When I finally open my eyes, I see Orla's bright blue eyes on mine in the rear view and I can see the pain that shines through. Giving her a weak smile, I turn my attention towards Lainey. Gurgling, fingers curled around the toy that is wrapped around the handle of her car seat and her horse teddy is tucked under her arm. My heart warms, glowing even. She was the perfect antidote to all of this, but the creator of all my deepest, darkest fears.

Rolling down the dusty driveway of Rivera Ranch, the small figures in the distance became a little easier to see. There he was. Backwards cap hiding his tufty brown hair and I am sorry but there is something about a man wearing a backward cap that makes me feral, especially Tripp Rivera. Toned, muscly arms wrapped in a damp gray tee and tight dirty denim jeans. He looked every bit cowboy. Lugging barrels of hay from the back of a truck and dumping them into the empty stables. Sweat glistens against his sun-tanned skin, muscles rippling under said skin that I so desperately want to run my fingertips over.

"Close your mouth honey, you're starting to drool," Orla catches me and my cheeks turn pink.

"I wasn't..." I try to counter back but it's no good. She caught me red handed.

Twisting my lips, I drop my eyes from the sights in front of me.

Pushing the car into park, she cuts the engine and Pacey comes bounding over like the golden retriever he is. He greets his mom with a kiss on the cheek as she steps out the high truck. I unbuckle Lainey and lift her from the seat. She is clammy from the car chair. Her dark hair is slightly damp and curling at the bottom. I scoot along the back of the seat and delicately slide out the truck.

Lainey starts to cry, bottom lip trembling before folding down and the tears roll down her cheeks.

"It's okay baby," I soothe her, walking towards the ranch. I feel bad leaving my bags in the trunk, but I need to get Lainey settled.

I look over my shoulder and Pacey gives me a soft nod as he moves towards the back of the truck and I keep walking forward. My skin prickles when I pass Tripp but I refuse to look at him. I must not give into temptation.

Climbing the steps to the house, I push through the door and head straight for upstairs. Turning the corner for my room, I stop outside my bedroom, head tilting slightly when I stare at my bedroom door.

The knob that was once there has now been replaced with a pushdown handle.

My heart stammers in my chest, tripping before

catching itself and resuming its once steady beat. Eyes glass for a moment when I hear footsteps behind me.

Slowly turning, I see Tripp standing there. Chest rising and falling quickly, his skin glistening in sweat, dirty marks rubbed into his cheeks.

His eyes move between me and the door.

Lainey sobs against my chest.

"Did you do that?" I ask, my eyes bouncing between his.

I know the answer. Of course it was him.

His brown eyes soften for just a moment, his hard jaw unclenching. He gives a soft nod before he turns and walks into his bedroom and closes the door.

"Thank you," I murmur to the empty room.

LAINEY IS FED, bathed and down for the night so I take that as my cue to go and soak my body in a hot bath. My muscles ache and I have no idea why. Pushing the door closed, the warm room blankets me. The copper tub fills quickly, and I peel my clothes from my clammy skin. Dipping my toe into the water, my whole body relaxes as I sink under the water. The sun begins to set under the mountains of Lovelock Bay and it's been a wonderful day. Sure, it was made better by Tripp and his sweaty, glistening skin as he worked and suddenly my cheeks flush red.

Me and Tripp happened a long time ago. I left that piece of my heart here in Lovelock Bay and I never wanted to find it again. That Dixie was no more. I'm not the broken little girl I once was, I have patched myself up, fixing all the broken pieces the best I could. All but one.

Tripp made me feel again. He made me realise that I was worthy of so much more than what I had been shown.

But I pushed him away. I had an out to the shitty hand I had been dealt so I took it. Jumped at the chance to leave Lovelock Bay, but in doing so, I hurt the only person who truly loved me for me.

It was brief, a whirlwind romance, each other's secret. No one knew about me and Tripp. We just happened one day... he was there, a comforter that I clung to when I felt bare and stripped of every last fibre of myself. He scooped me up, tucked me safely against his chest and promised to never let me go.

He kept his side of the promise.

I broke the promise into a million pieces.

Shattered him in the process.

Then I ran, far, far away.

I set up a new life in Nashville and vowed I would never step back into my hometown of Lovelock Bay, that was of course, until I got the news from my agent.

Clay was dead.

Murdered and left in the cold.

My daughter had lost her father.

There were no feelings between us. Clay liked to remind me of that every time we were together. I was just his plaything when he came to visit. He had connections in Nashville so whenever he was there for a business meeting, he hit me up. He made me feel cheap and worthless, but I still let him.

I wanted to feel and if that meant feeling with Clay then I was content.

Then came Lainey.

He didn't take the news lightly, but he promised to always be there for her. He didn't know anything about my past, I never went into it with him. I didn't really go into it with anyone but Tripp. Sure, most of the town knew my tragic backstory, but I didn't go out my way to tell them. Most of it was gossip, each time it was spread, another layer of lies coated their tongues. I didn't have it in me to fight my corner, and once I left, I left that part of me behind.

The piece that was tucked deep into the crevices of Tripp's heart.

I never wanted it back.

He hated me.

I wish I hated him. It would make this situation a little easier to cope with.

But I don't.

How could I hate Tripp Rivera. The one who pieced me back together, the one who promised me the world.

Slipping under the water, I hold my breath and let my lungs burn for just a moment before I rise up, a small gasp leaving me as I fill my lungs with oxygen.

I give myself another five minutes in the hot tub before I clamber out, wrapping the warm towel around my slender body and padding across the landing towards my bedroom. Pushing the handle down, I freeze when I see Tripp standing, topless, with a softly snoring Lainey.

My eyes finally move from her to him, his soft brown eyes never lifting from me.

"She was crying," he says quietly, rocking his body side to side. "I didn't want to disturb your bath, so I thought I would try and settle her."

And my heart aches heavily in my chest.

He turns to face me, head tilting to the side, eyes cast down on my brown-haired beauty.

I tighten my towel around my body, now suddenly very aware that I am in nothing but a towel. He steps closer to me, the musky smell of his sweat mixed with his cologne, and I am transported back to the broken teen who looked at

Tripp Rivera like he was my world and everything in between.

But I suppose back then, he was.

I had nothing else to cling onto but him.

He delicately scoops Lainey off his bare chest and holds her out for me to take. My eyes widen, one of my hands holding my towel and I look at him helplessly.

"Shit, of course," he curses quietly, turning his back to me and gently placing Lainey into the crib.

I step back, the wall pressing against my bare shoulders as I try and put some distance between us.

He walks towards the door, eyes finding mine before he gives a soft nod and disappears.

I wait a moment, heart racing beneath my chest before I close my bedroom door and sit on the edge of my bed. My eyes cast over my daughter, and I feel a mix of emotions run through me.

He came in here and soothed her to sleep.

He didn't want to disturb me.

A heavy sigh leaves me as I flop down on the bed and let my whirling thoughts consume me.

CHAPTER TEN
TRIPP

Pulling my tee over my head, I toss it to the floor. It had been a long ass day. I ached in places I never knew existed. Riggs worked me hard. I knew he was going to be a prick about it, but he was so much more of a prick than I expected.

My heart stammers in my chest when I think of Dixie. Was Riggs right to think that she is feeding back information to the Attaway's? I can't see it. I knew Dixie; sure, that was ten years ago but I somehow trusted her and I wasn't sure if that made me an idiot.

The Dixie I knew left.

We had five days to get through until the funeral.

Almost one whole week.

She had been here nearing three days so far and it already felt like a month.

Sitting on the edge of the bed, I push my hand through my hair and a deep sigh passes my lips. Tugging my socks off, I ball them up and launch them across the room towards my tee.

I felt well and truly wrecked.

Pushing to my feet, I'm unbuttoning my dirty jeans when I hear a muffled cry. I ignore it for a moment, pushing them down, but after a minute or two, Lainey's cry gets louder.

Tugging my jeans back up, I rush out of my room and into Dixie's to see it empty and a now thrashing Lainey.

"Shh shh, it's okay," I say softly to Lainey. Holding her against my chest, I bounce gently then reach for her pacifier. Popping it into her mouth, she sucks it in and makes a sweet humming noise as I continue rocking. Her head is against my chest, my heart beating at a steady rate and I feel her getting heavy in my arms.

Everything that was once consuming my mind now fades into silence, and it's just me and Lainey.

A creak in the floorboards has me looking towards the door when I see Dixie walk through, towel wrapped around her wet body. Suds still sitting on her silky skin, beautiful blue eyes wide, dark brown hair pulled into a messy bun. Her eyes skating between me and Lainey.

I lower my eyes back to her daughter, and I feel protective over her in an instant.

This little dot on my chest, soft snores leaving her, pacifier slowly slipping from her mouth.

"She was crying," my voice is quiet, my body still rocking side to side. Her lips part slightly. "I didn't want to disturb your bath, so I thought I would try and settle her."

A soft gasp slips past her lips.

I turn to face her, walking slowly and delicately towards her, careful not to disturb Lainey as she shuffles down my chest.

She tightens the towel around her body and it wraps around her curves like a tailored dress. I force my greedy eyes away.

I shouldn't be looking at her.

I shouldn't be feeling the way I am.

Heart racing, palms sweaty and blood pumping around my body like fire coursing through my veins.

A step between us—maybe half—but I'm close to her. Sweetness fills my senses, daisies and honey swim around the room, and I can't get enough of her, inhaling deeply trying to take as much of her scent in as I can.

I delicately try and scoop Lainey off my bare chest and hold her out for Dixie to take. Her ocean blue eyes widen, one hand still pinched at the top of her towel.

She stands helpless and I internally kick myself.

"Shit, of course," I curse under my breath, turning and laying Lainey down in her crib instead. The urge to brush my fingertips through her soft brown hair is strong but I resist.

Standing tall, I walk towards the door, Dixie pushed against the wall trying to keep me at a distance. Giving her a soft nod, I push the handle down and disappear out of her room and straight into the bathroom.

My skin tingles when her scent is still floating around the bathroom. I shouldn't feel like this. She hurt me.

Broke my heart into a thousand pieces.

Hate her for it.

Stripping my jeans off my tired legs, I drag myself under the shower and wash the day from my skin.

I needed my bed.

Tomorrow was the start of a new week.

The countdown to the funeral.

Five days to get through and then Dixie will be out of my life.

It's just five days.

Five. Long. Tedious. Days.

And from tomorrow, we were going to be working together. I'm going to make sure Riggs puts her far away from me.

Her sad beautiful blue eyes are enough of a temptation to drag me back to her. I promised myself if she ever did return, I wouldn't even spit on her if she was on fire.

Well, she's back.

And I am not going to fall for her again.

I would keep that promise.

My alarm screams at five a.m. Hitting the top of the clock, I groan as I roll onto my back. Sunrise hasn't quite peaked yet and if I can drag my ass out of my warm bed, I can have my coffee on the porch and watch as it greets the day.

Kicking my legs out, I twist and sit on the edge of the bed, scrubbing my face and the sound of my beard scratching against my skin has me realizing I need to shave. I've let my stubble grow a little longer than I normally would, and honestly, I am kind of feeling it. It's been a shitty few weeks and me shaving has been the last thing on my mind.

Scrunching my toes into the rug that lay under my bed, I give myself another minute before I push up, raiding my closet before tiptoeing across the hallway. My wandering eyes drift to her bedroom and I see her door ajar.

Furrowing my brows, I keep moving towards the bathroom and get myself ready for the day.

Moving downstairs, I am the only one awake. Walking into the kitchen, I notice the coffee pot is warm. Crinkling the bridge of my nose, I reach up for my mug and place it under the spout, pushing the button and letting it heat up.

My fingertips drum on the countertop, the soft trickle of coffee the only other noise filling the large house.

Once done, I curl my fingers around the mug and move towards the front of the house and notice the door is already unbolted. My skin pricks and an uneasiness settles in my stomach.

I debate grabbing my dad's shot gun from the cabinet in his office but decide against it and I am glad I did. As I edge out, I see Dixie sitting on the rocker, eyes closed, a soft hum vibrating through her. Lainey is wrapped in blankets as she nurses her.

I try to sneak back inside but bang my head on the doorframe, making it throb instantly.

"Tripp?" she calls softly, and I squeeze my eyes shut, an exasperated sigh leaving me.

"Yup," my voice is full of gravel as I step out onto the deck. I don't look at her, just fist my hand into my back pocket and look at the early morning sky. "I didn't mean to interrupt, er... you know," I dip my head and kick the toe of my boot into the wooden floor.

"You didn't," her voice breezes over me, "you can sit down..." she trails off and begins to hum softly once more.

I debate it.

I did want to watch the sunrise. It had been a while since I had been up and ready for five-thirty in the morning.

"Okay," I sheepishly move towards where she is nursing Lainey, eyes not landing on her once.

Not my place. Kind of weird to watch her nurse her daughter, maybe if she was my own kid, wouldn't be an issue.

I sit in the rocker, hot coffee in hand as my eyes cast down and I see her empty coffee up.

I didn't think breastfeeding moms were supposed to drink coffee?

"I switched the coffee for decaf," she springs on me mid hum as if she reads my mind, taking my mouthful of my coffee and my lips turn down slightly.

Didn't taste any different.

"Why are you awake?" I ask, my eyes pinned forward to the pinky, orange sky.

"Couldn't sleep. Lainey is teething. Thought if I was up this early, I may as well come and watch the sunrise." Her voice is slow, lazy almost.

"You sound tired," I observe, side eyeing as her hand gently rubs her daughter's back.

"I'm okay," her head rolls round to face me, a small smile pinching at the corner of her lips.

Silence coats us for a second.

"Why are you awake?"

I glance down at my coffee cup nestled in my lap.

"First proper day on the job, didn't want to be late. Riggs will be here any minute. He normally gets up about four-thirty, gets to the ranch for five... but since being with Aspen he has become a little lazier." I smirk, scoffing on a small laugh.

"Riggs, lazy? I doubt that," she teases as she moves a snoozing Lainey.

The sun begins to peek over the mountains and the early morning wake up makes it worth it. The creak of the rocker pulls my eyes from the beautiful sunrise and Dixie is standing, Lainey nestled into her.

"See ya later," she gives a soft smirk and I throw two fingers up, flicking my hand back at a half attempt to say *see ya.*

And just like that, I am alone with my heavy thoughts and my warm cup of coffee.

I needed to go over to Kelcie, needed to delve a little more into Dixie's connection with Clay and to find out just how deep it lies.

A sigh rattles from me as I see truck lights approach through the dusk. Riggs.

Pushing from the rocker, one hand folded into my jeans, the other wrapped around my empty mug. Something hits a little different when you drink a hot cup of coffee on the porch whilst watching the sunrise. I'm a simple man. I like the small things in life. The simple things.

Riggs parks the truck and jumps down with Ace in tow. He bolts down the field and Riggs whistles him back. Dog's recall is on point.

"Morning sunshine," his voice gruff as he lifts his cowboy hat from his head and rubs his hand over his curly hair.

"Morning," I nod as he climbs the steps of the porch and walks into the house. I follow him just like Ace does.

He moves towards the coffee pot and pours himself a cup then twists, holding it out towards me and I place my cup under the teat as he pours me another cup full.

"How did you find getting up this morning?" He asks, lower back resting against the countertop as he takes a sip of his drink.

"Yeah fine, felt a little groggy at first but I was alright once I was up," I admit, lifting my own cup to my lips and taking a mouthful.

"Your body clock will soon get used to it," he throws a soft wink as Ace sniffs around the house.

"Sure it will," and my voice rattles around the room.

"All okay?" he asks, head tipped slightly.

"I'm not sure," I rub my hand across my stubble, tongue in cheek.

"Want to talk about it?"

I shrug one shoulder up. "I need to speak to Kelcie," I finally say after a beat of silence or two.

"Nothing is going to change, Tripp," Riggs offers a soft tone, fingers rubbing at his temples.

"I know, but I just want to know what his rationale is behind all of this. He is playing us, and I fucking fell straight into his hands." I tip my head back for a moment and my chest aches.

"You wasn't to know he was playing you, none of us were..."

"I know," I swallow the apple sized lump down, throat bobbing. My eyes settle on my big brother. "I just need to get Austin out of this mess."

"By doing what?"

"Finding out who actually killed Clay."

"You will never find out."

"I beg to differ..."

I hear a throat being cleared behind me and my eyes close for a moment.

"Morning Dixie," Riggs lifts his hat from his head as I turn to look at her. But his tone is not kind. It's harsh. Sarcastic even.

He already thinks she is spying for the Attaways.

"Morning," her voice is low, barely audible. Slowly looking at her over my shoulder, she shrinks as she walks past me and closer to Riggs.

He stands his ground for just a moment, arms folded across his chest.

She doesn't budge.

They are standing toe to toe.

She is tiny compared to Riggs, but she doesn't back down.

"What do you want to say Riggs? It's unlike you to bite your tongue or is it because you're settled down now? Aspen got your leash a little tight?" Dixie goads him, chin lifted, and I chuckle under my breath. Also a little turned on by her.

Riggs narrows his gaze, a rumble vibrating in his throat.

"I don't trust you," his arms drop from his chest. Stepping one step closer to her and he towers over her. I'm not far off the height of Riggs, but for some reason, he has always felt taller.

"And why's that?"

"Because I think you're a snake," his bold tone has her faltering slightly before her back stiffens.

"Why would I be a snake? I'm here to mourn my daughter's dad. There is no ulterior motive..." she pauses a moment and I see the raise of Riggs' brow.

"You are back for something more..." realization slips past my lips as I step closer, "aren't you?"

She looks over her shoulder at me, brows dug into her forehead before she lets that hard-faced mask slip.

"I want to rinse them for every penny they have," her voice is thick, her breath shuddering on its intake.

"Well..." Riggs breathes out, reaching behind him for a coffee then letting out a low whistle. "Seems Dixie is on our side after all."

Her head snaps around as she shoves Riggs in the chest.

"I wouldn't go that far, I'm here to get his money for a better life for me and Lainey. Then I'll be gone. I had no interest staying in Lovelock Bay ten years ago, I certainly do not have any interest now." And for some reason her words sting a little more than I would like to admit. Slicing through me slowly, blood seeps out of the band aids I so delicately placed over my wounds.

"What's your plan then sweetheart?" Riggs asks her and I'm not going to lie, the sound off *sweetheart* rolling off his lips makes my blood boil a little.

I watch as her shoulders rise and fall with a heaving breath.

"You don't have one?" I ask, stepping a little closer to her just as she spins around to face me, eyes bouncing between me and my brother.

"No," she whispers, defeat evident in her timid little voice.

"Then you better start spilling darlin' and we can try and help you," Riggs lifts his eyes from her to me, then up to the soft ticking clock on the kitchen wall, "and we better get to work." I watch as he sweeps his gaze over her. She is dressed in a cotton night dress, frilly hem and pretty frilled straps that sit over her shoulder and all I can think about is dusting my lips across the bare skin on her shoulders.

My lips twitch.

"Shit, yeah... I've just got to go change... and stuff."

And stuff.

Lainey.

She needed to make sure everything was sorted for Lainey.

"Do what you need to do, we will meet you in the bunkhouse about eight..." I trail off and I can feel the way Riggs' eyes are burning into the side of my head.

Until this morning, I didn't know she breastfed. I mean, why would I.

She gives a soft nod then turns on her heel and disappears upstairs.

"This isn't going to work if you're going to make

allowances for her," Riggs grunts as my eyes trail after her, sighing, I face him.

"I'm not making allowances. She has a kid man, she breastfeeds... she can't just... stop." I roll my lips and shake my head softly from side to side.

Riggs' eyes widen slightly before softening.

"I didn't even think..."

"Well maybe use that big brain of yours." I pat him on the shoulder, a chuckle breezing through my lips.

"Fuck off," he grumbles before breaking into a smile.

"There it is," I smirk, "such a pretty boy when you smile Riggs."

Placing my cup into the sink, I turn on my heel and head for the door. "Coming?" I call out.

"Yeah," and with a grunt, he is behind me, and we walk out towards the bunkhouse.

***

SITTING in the saddle of Bucky, a new American quarter horse, I look out at our land. Rivera Ranch. The green rolls for miles and I feel incredibly lucky to call this place my home. Pacey trots up beside me, lifting his cowboy hat and running his fingers through his messy blond hair before his hat lands back on his head.

"It's something right?" he is slightly breathless.

"It is," I nod, loosening the reins for a moment on Bucky.

"You doing okay?" I look over at my kid brother, his skin weathered and tired. The weight of the world lays heavy on his shoulders.

"It's nice being back out doing something other than letting my mind wander with the what ifs..."

My chest aches.

"Yeah," I rumble, watching as the cowboys and Riggs beat down towards us on the back of their horses.

"Wish I could do something," he looks at me, I can see the pain radiating in his eyes.

"I know man, me too, me too." We give each other a silent nod before turning the horses and kicking them on back towards the bottom field.

Time to move the cows out.

"Yeehaw!" Pacey shouts as we gallop towards the herd, Riggs closing in behind us and this right here, in this moment, everything felt okay.

Because I had my brothers at my side.

Riggs to the left. Pacey to the right.

It was a split second if anything, but it was still everything.

CHAPTER ELEVEN
DIXIE

Dressed in bootleg jeans, my new cowboy boots and white frilled shirt, I felt every bit dressed to work. I had pumped and placed my supply into the refrigerator, labelled and ready for when Orla needed it.

"Are you sure you don't mind?" I ask Orla for what feels like the hundredth time.

"Of course not," she smiles, snuggling Lainey, her fists in her gummy mouth.

Teething is hitting my sweet girl hard and I can't wait till her teeth fully break. Not sure why I am wishing that on myself, because once the bottom ones break, the tops follow soon after.

Well, that's what my mom forums say anyway.

"Okay, so I think I have covered everything when it comes to her routine, I mean, you probably know most of it anyway," and I am fully aware that I am rambling, but I am nervous. I have never left her before, and sure, I know I am only going to the ranch to work, but it still feels a little too far.

"Any problems, I will come find you," she gives me a reassuring nod, and my heart races under my skin. Lainey is babbling, eyes all glassy and wide. She's so precious. Chubby little arms and legs. Brown curly hair, long dark lashes. She is perfection.

I glance up at the time, it's seven-fifty.

"Okay, it's time for me to get to work then," and I half laugh, half choke on my intake of breath. I had never worked on a ranch. Didn't even know how to ride a horse so this was going to be a bundle of fun.

"You will do great sweetie, dinner will be served at five. Chicken pot pie with creamed mashed potato and greens, sound good?" she asks, bouncing a fussing Lainey.

"Sounds perfect," I nod, stepping towards Orla with Lainey and placing a soft kiss to the top of her head. "Mommy loves you honey," I whisper, because speaking out loud feels too much. I feel silly for getting teary eyed, I am literally just outside.

It doesn't matter what I keep telling myself, a tear rolls down my cheek.

Swiping it away, Lainey reaches out for me and I grasp her little hand in mine, kissing it tenderly.

"Mommy will be back soon okay? Orla..." I feel strange calling her that, "Orla will be looking after you." Not sure why I am having a conversation with my six-month-old, but I felt like I should tell her, so she knew I wasn't leaving her for good.

My eyes lift to Orla, she gives a warm smile. She would be such a good nanna.

"Okay, I'm going to go," I smile, leaning up and ignoring the way my heart aches heavy inside my chest.

"I normally do lunch around noon, sometimes the boys

eat in the bunkhouse, sometimes they don't eat at all. No pressure to come back to the house, but it'll be made up if you do want it.”

I give a shallow nod and have to walk out the door before I change my mind on this whole working thing.

The sweet breeze dances across my skin, my head tips back slightly and I inhale.

When I let my eyes open, I see Riggs walking towards me. Cockiness painted all over his face.

“At least you're early,” he tips his hat and I roll my eyes.

“Where do you want me?” I ask, placing my own hat on my head and walking down the steps of the porch to stand in front of my boss, hands on my hips.

“The stables need to be cleaned, the vet and farrier are coming at noon. You'll need to help them. I'll come and check on you around two. We're just about to go down and fix the fence line and then the sign that some out of towner crashed into...” his lips twitch and I can't fight the smile that spreads across my lips.

“Yea, sorry about that,” I shrug, fisting my hands into the back pockets of my jeans. “What happened to the fence?” I find myself asking, eyes on Riggs.

“Not sure, seems tampered with but can't work out for what reason,” he shrugs back at me, turning and leading me towards the stables. “You ride?” he asks as I try to keep up with his long strides.

“No,” I admit, feeling a little shameful really. A pink blush crept onto my cheeks.

He stops in his tracks, turning to face me. Dressed in a long sleeved black crew neck, dirty Levi's and heavy black boots.

“You fuckin' kidding me?” he smirks, but his eyes are dark and thunderous.

"No," I say again but this time it comes out in a squeak.

"Fuck," he scrubs his face, exasperation leaving him as the seconds tick by. On a groan, he turns on his heel and continues walking down the dusty trail towards the stables.

Stepping over the metal threshold, my eyes glance at the large stables in front of me.

"How many horses do you have?"

"At the moment," his voice is low, as he picks up a broom and continues walking down the concrete path between stalls, "fifteen."

"You want more?"

"We have a couple of mares that we want to put for foaling this year, so hoping to get a few more," he smiles, twisting and handing me the broom.

"Start here in Travis' stall," he hooks the stall door back, "then work your way down on the left side. That should keep you going until Harlow and Conrad arrive."

I knew of Harlow.

But I never met her.

She's the same age as Aspen. Always seemed nice enough in school.

"Right," I nod, wrapping my fingers a little tighter around the broom handle.

"Obviously, if you need to erm…" he pauses for a moment, cheeks a little crimson as he wraps his hand around the back of his neck. He feels awkward and I am relishing in this.

"What?" I goad.

"You know, if you need to attend to…"

"Lainey," I smile. I could easily drop the conversation.

"Lainey, then you can just go. You don't need to ask my permission and shit."

"Noted," I give a firm nod but inside happiness blooms in my chest. Makes me wonder if Tripp said something to him.

"Okay, any problems then come find one of us. We'll be down the bottom field. Takes a while on a horse... will take even longer walking," he tilts his hat towards me then disappears towards the exit of the stables.

The stables are large, shaped like an L. The stalls are all pretty big and the hay store is next door, but the stables have a built-in archway so you can slip in there from here.

I watch as Riggs disappears and once he is gone, I get to work. I have four hours to clean out ten stalls on this side, then I can carry on with the right side once Harlow and Conrad get here.

Hitting the broom head onto the concrete, I get to work.

SLOWLY STANDING UP, I wipe the sweat from my brow. I've managed eight stalls, which honestly, I don't think is bad going. My boobs are solid and beginning to ache. I need to pump. Placing my hand over them, I wince.

I turn around and focus on the large clock that hangs at the back of the stables, it's just before twelve.

Placing the pitchfork next to the broom, I step out of the stall to see Tripp walking in with a horse. He notices me straight away.

Slowing his steps, his lips tug at one corner, but his eyes are like stones as he stares at me. I am aware I look a mess.

My braids are messy, strands loose. Brow sweaty and three shirt buttons undone.

The closer he gets, the more I struggle to catch my breath.

Something about him being all dirty and sweaty does things to me that it shouldn't.

But there is nothing there between me and Tripp anymore.

"You okay?" He calls out, brows furrowed as he loops the leading rein through the hoop on the stall wall.

"Yup, just need to pop up to the house, but don't want to go until Conrad and Harlow are here," I say, brushing a loose strand of my dark hair off my face.

His eyes drift down, eyes widening slightly when they land on my chest.

Slowly slipping my arm across my body, he turns away from me.

Fuck.

The sound of tires fill the stables, overriding any tension that was once brewing between me and Tripp.

Two doors slam and that's when I see them.

Harlow and Conrad.

Harlow is pretty. Light brown hair, long, brushed off her face in a high ponytail. Slender body, dressed in a tee and jeans. Cream cap on her head.

Conrad places his hand in Tripp's, giving it a firm shake. Messy brown hair, floppy kind of. Thick denim covered thighs nestled in dirty chaps. Deep brown eyes that would consume you in one. Whole. Killer jaw, perfect smile and that's when he catches me staring.

Glistening eyes, lips parting a little wider as his gaze roams up and down my body.

"Who's the new girl?" he smirks, eyes not lifting from me as he asks Tripp and I watch as Harlow rolls her eyes.

"I'm Dixie," I step forward, holding my hand out for him to take, which he does, gladly.

"Dixie," my name rolls off his tongue a little too easily and I feel myself blush.

Damn. I needed to pull myself together.

"I'm Harlow," she says, pushing past Conrad and giving me a wide grin.

"Hi Harlow," I hold my hand up.

She turns and strolls towards the pretty chestnut.

"Hey, Amber."

Ah, a mare.

Harlow runs her hand down her neck as her and Tripp fall into conversation.

"Are you here for Amber too?" I find myself asking Conrad and he shakes his head from side to side.

"Nah, I'm here for Raff. Riggs should be bringing her down any minute." I give a shallow nod as if I know who Raff is. "So, how long you been working here?" he asks, leaning against the stall.

"Today's my first day. Just helping me out until I am back on the road again. I crashed my car at the top of the ranch, the Rivera's took me in and said I could stay until I was ready."

"Flying visit then?"

"Something like that," I smile and that's when I hear Tripp talking to Harlow about Austin.

"I'm really worried about him Tripp, I don't know what else I can do. He is pulling away from me..."

Harlow and Austin, dating. Noted.

I take that as my cue to leave.

"I'll be back shortly," I say to the stables, not that anyone really listens but I felt it was the right thing to do. Lowering my head as I walk past Conrad, I don't miss the sultry look he gives me. I have a feeling Conrad is a bit of a player and I am not into that.

But I would be lying if I said I didn't like the small bit of attention I received from him.

It had been a while since anyone had looked at me the way he did. It felt nice.

Ignoring the eyes that were burning into the back of my skull, I keep my legs moving towards the house. Climbing the steps, I push through the door and peak inside the kitchen. It's empty. Moving to the living room, I see Orla and Lainey sitting on the rug on the floor, stacking blocks.

Her eyes lift from my daughter to me, and she gives me a smile.

"All okay?" I mouth, and she gives me a thumbs up. I am mindful not to let Lainey see me. I have no idea how she has been since I have been out, but I didn't want to rock the boat now. "I'm just going to pump," I whisper and she gives me a soft wink. Kicking my boots off, I move upstairs and into my room.

Fumbling with my buttons, relief swarms me when the material is not suffocating me. My boobs are spilling from my bra, hard and swollen and I cannot wait to pump. Standing, I search my room for the pump and that's when I realize I left it downstairs on the sink drainer.

"Fuck," I whisper to myself.

My head tips back and I ignore the irritation that is currently coursing through my veins.

Sighing heavily, I walk towards my bedroom door, fingers grabbing the fold of my shirt to cover myself when Tripp walks into the room, us bumping into each other and knocking me back. He falls on top of me, hands pressed on the floor either side of my head.

"Oh fuck," he calls out, our bodies pressed together, and my eyes widen as they bounce between his. He pushes up, lazily dragging his gaze over my heaving chest.

I scramble up, pulling my shirt across my body once more to cover myself.

"What were you doing bursting in here like a mad man?" My brows are pinched as I push myself up, hands behind me, elbows bent.

"I just..." he licks his lips, all panty and his eyes are flitting.

"Just what?"

"You and Conrad, I didn't like it."

"There was nothing not to like, he introduced himself, I introduced myself," I throw my hand in the air, that irritation that I once felt was slowly building back up.

"He looked at you like he wanted you," he snaps, and I can't help but laugh at how stupid he sounded.

"And!?" I shriek, waiting for him to answer but before he can I snap, "He looked like a player," I shake my own head and push to my knees.

Tripp's eyes soften slightly, mouth opening and then closing.

"He used to date Aspen," he tells me.

"Okay?" No idea why he is telling me this.

Nothing.

I am confused. Fully. I have no idea what he thought he saw but it really was nothing.

"Are we done here?" I go to walk away, and he meets me, toe to toe.

His green eyes draw me in every damn time, but still he keeps quiet.

"Okay, cool, because I really need to go pump," I nudge my shoulder into him as I begin to walk downstairs. He is hot on my heels.

Ignoring him, I move towards the kitchen, and I am

grateful that Orla has taken Lainey away from the living room as she definitely would have heard me. Grabbing my pump from the drainer, I turn to look at him, eyes ablaze with some kind of fury masked with irritation.

He is following me like a lost puppy and the more he follows, the more he annoys me. Climbing the stairs, I hear the sound of his boots when I turn around on the step and face him. He is two down, but our eyes are level.

"Go away Tripp, why are you still here?"

I watch him. Watch as his expression changes. Hard to soft. Wound up to relaxed.

He says nothing. *Again.*

So I turn and head to my room, slamming the door behind me.

WALKING BACK into the stables and feeling a lot more comfortable and definitely not as irritable as I was half an hour ago, I see Conrad shoeing a dark brown horse.

I scan the room, Harlow and Tripp are nowhere to be seen.

Not entirely sure why, but the thought of Tripp not being here disappoints me.

I try to walk past Conrad unnoticed, but I fail.

"You're back."

"I am," my voice a little higher, a small smile playing on my lips, but I continue walking to where I left my barrow, broom and fork.

"Did you fancy getting a drink with me one night?" He calls out, his voice echoing down the stalls, and I stop in my tracks as I turn to face him.

"I'm not into dating at the moment..." my voice trails off.

"Who said anything about a date?" his head cocks to the side, a stupid ass grin on his face.

"I... erm," shit, I feel like a fool. My cheeks flame, burning as I stare at him.

"Just a drink," he counters, stepping closer to me.

"I don't think that's such a good idea..." I shrink back against the wall. I'm not good in situations like this. His face softens and it's like he feels sorry for me almost. Am I that readable?

"Okay okay," he stops in his tracks, and I swear it's because he saw a flash of fear strike through my eyes, he holds his hands up. "I didn't mean to scare you."

"You didn't," I laugh it off.

"Well, your face says different," he smirks, his eyes raking over my body.

"I'm just not very good at things like..." I pause, moving my finger between the both of us, "this."

He says nothing, just stands as if he is waiting for me to explain. But I don't.

"Not a problem, the offer will always be there..." he reaches for my hand and scoops it into his as he brushes his lips across the back.

"Thank you," I give a courteous nod before he turns away and I sigh, a deep painful sigh as I watch him walk away. "What an idiot," I mutter to myself, turning on my heel and losing myself in horse manure and fresh bedding.

Walking through the door at four p.m., I am wrecked. Boobs are full again and I'm miserable. I trudge my achy legs up the stairs and I hear Lainey giggling from the bathroom. Pushing the door two, I see Orla on her knees bathing my daughter. Bubbles fill the tub, and she watches in awe at the way they move and float through the air as Orla blows them from her palm.

My heart throbs in my chest.

This is what Lainey deserves. A Nanna that loves her like Orla does.

I step back, not wanting to intrude on their moment and sink into my bedroom. I flop down on the bed; I just needed a couple of minutes. I feel suddenly overwhelmed. I'm tired. I know that. It's been a busy day and sure, I've spent the day cleaning stalls out but I'm not used to being on my feet all day. Not used to lugging heavy barrows of manure and hay up the manure hill.

I didn't see anyone apart from Tripp, Conrad and Harlow and they were flying visits.

My mind whirls and my chest caves in. Memories of my childhood flash before my eyes and I don't want to go back there. Not today.

A soft knock on the door has me resting onto my elbows to look at the door and I see Tripp standing there, dirty and grubby, and I ignore the way my stomach knots at the sight of him. The way my heart beats a little quicker in my chest.

"Hey," he says quietly, boot in the door as if testing to see whether I will invite him in or not.

"Hey," I breathe, sitting up a little more.

"You okay?" I can hear the concern in his voice, did Conrad tell him I freaked a little. How embarrassing.

"Tired," I smirk, one corner of my lips lifting a little higher.

"I bet," he smiles back and I don't miss the way his green eyes glisten.

"Everything alright?" I ask, not quite sure what his reason for being here is, not that I mind him being here... it just feels a little weird.

"We're heading down to the Dusty Old Boot tonight... didn't know if you fancied coming? We normally go on Fridays but..." he trails off.

"The funeral," I nod, licking my lips.

"Yeah..." one hand is still on the handle of my door, the other curls around the back of his neck.

"I mean, it would be nice but I also need to check with your mom... she's had Lainey all day... and I need to feed her because..." I look down at my chest and sigh.

"We won't be heading out till about eight, would that work or...?"

"Like I said, I need to check with your mom," and he looks away from me, also a little disappointed maybe.

"Do you need to pump?" he asks, and his question has my lips parting. "It's on the drainer... I don't mind getting it for you."

I would try and hold out for Lainey's bedtime, but that's four hours and I don't think I have another four hours in me.

So I just give him a nod.

"I'll go grab it," he thumbs behind him and disappears downstairs.

I fall back into my bed and I feel wetness dampen my cheek.

I'm not alone long when I hear footsteps and giggling.

"Shall we go and find mommy," Orla says in a baby voice, Lainey squeals.

I wipe my eyes and sit up, plastering a huge smile on my face just as Lainey's head pops around the door.

"There she is!" Orla says with excitement lacing her

voice and Lainey's blue eyes light up, her legs kicking in excitement.

"Sweet girl," I murmur, standing as I scoop a freshly bathed Lainey into my arms, pressing my lips to the top of her head as I inhale her scent. Honey and oats.

"How are you sweetheart, how was your day?" Orla asks as she loiters in the doorway.

"Good," I smile, I'm not lying completely but... "How was Lai—"

"Here we go," Tripp barrels through the door interrupting us, Orla snaps her head around to look at her son who is holding part of my breast pump.

"Thanks," my cheeks redden, and I watch as Orla's lips twist into a smile.

"Not a problem," he rushes out before disappearing.

"Oh, Tripp!" I call out, and he is back in the doorway, leaning against the doorframe.

"Yeah?" His brows raise.

"Any news on my car?" and I watch as his shoulders sag.

"I spoke to Rusty earlier, needs a few more days."

I give a little nod and with that, he turns and walks away.

Lainey snuggles into me and my God I have missed her.

"How did you get on?" I ask the question that I wanted to before Tripp walked in.

"We got on perfectly. I can't wait for tomorrow," she beams, and Lainey begins fussing, hands grabbing at my top.

"I'm going to feed her I think, give her a bottle before bed," I say my thoughts aloud. Not sure why.

"She has a diaper on, I put her fresh sleepsuits away," she smiles before turning on her heel and walking out the room. "Oh, and supper will be dished up shortly," and with that she disappears downstairs.

Holding a now fussing Lainey, I use one hand to unbutton my shirt just enough to be able to slip my nursing bra down and she latches on; the relief I feel in an instant makes my head fall back.

Heavy footsteps pull my attention and Tripp is back in the door, head down as if he isn't allowed to look at me.

"You don't have to duck your head," I say and try not to laugh.

"I didn't want to stare," his voice is quiet.

I scoff.

Lowering my eyes to my daughter, I brush my free hand over her soft hair and my heart thumps in my chest with so much love.

"I spoke to my mom..."

Snapping my head around to look at him, my eyes narrow on him.

"Tripp," his name comes out more as a whine.

"She said she'll watch Lainey," his head is dipped once more. He knows he fucked up.

"It's not your place to ask. She is *my* child Tripp. What if I didn't want to leave her? What if your mom felt obliged because *you* asked her?"

I let my questions linger in the air for a moment more.

"It wasn't your place to ask. I said I would... now it makes me look cowardly and that I have sent you down to do it for me."

Anger rattles inside of me.

"Not at all, it wasn't like that," he tries to defend himself, his voice a little louder.

I turn away from him and ignore the sting of angry tears.

"Come?" he asks so delicately, it pulls on my heart strings.

"I'm not sure..."

He gives a heavy nod and then walks back out of the room without another word to pass his lips.

"Oh, baby girl, what am I going to do," I sigh.

CHAPTER TWELVE
DIXIE

Lainey sits in the highchair, smashing her hands down on the tray, food going everywhere, but it doesn't matter how much I try to stop her, she won't.

"Orla, I am so sorry."

"Please," she closes her eyes, lips pursed, "I have raised three boys, please don't apologise about Lainey throwing food to the floor."

I give her a soft nod, letting my eyes flutter shut for just a moment.

Riggs and Aspen are in light chatter with Pacey. Jorge and Tripp are talking about the cattle and I feel like a spare part as my daughter trashes the floor with what little food is left on her plate.

"How was your first day of work?" Jorge surprises me with his question, I blink a couple of times and turn my face to look at him at the head of the table and that's when all the soft voices simmer to a deafening silence.

"Erm," a soft cough tickles at the back of my throat before I let my eyes fall into my lap. "It was good, my muscles ache and I'm dog tired so that's a good sign..." my eyes lift to steady on Jorge, "right?"

"Sounds like a damn good day to me," he chimes, and the table falls back into their chatter.

Once dinner is ate and Lainey is down for the night, I help Orla clear the table and do the dishes. Orla washes, I dry, and Aspen puts away whilst the Rivera boys are talking to Jorge in the back office.

"How's Pacey been?" Aspen asks and I roll my lips.

"Up and down. It's been hard on him. But his feelings feel minuscule to him in comparison to what Austin is going through."

I step back and place the dish on the countertop. Aspen still has one in hand.

"We just don't know how to get out of this mess we've fallen into," she admits, head tilting to the side ever so slightly. "He is pushing everyone away, he hasn't seen Harlow in weeks."

"She was down at the stables today," I pipe up then internally kick myself.

"I think she is trying to keep busy, act normal as such," her eyes find mine as she gives a soft smile.

I nod. Not wanting to involve myself any more than I have in this conversation.

"He won't let her near though, he is fully in his head that he will accept the plea," and her voice cracks.

"Oh Aspen," Orla pulls her washing gloves off and encases Aspen into a motherly embrace. I clear my throat, feeling like I shouldn't be here. Placing the dish towel down softly, I take two steps forward just as Orla breaks away from Aspen and her eyes are on me.

"It felt like a private moment..." I admit, fingers locked in front of me.

"Everyone knows what's going on in the Warrens' household, it's not a secret." Aspen palms a stray tear away from her reddening cheek.

We hear the sound of heavy boots coming towards us and Aspen spins quickly, grabbing the plate from the countertop that I'd placed down and then pops it in the cupboard.

"Ready?" Riggs asks, his eyes searching Aspen's and with three long strides, he is in front of her. Hands cupping her face, eyes volleying back and forth between hers. "What's happened?"

"We were speaking about Austin," Orla says softly and Riggs' eyes slice over to me before they're back on Aspen.

"Everything will be okay Wildflower, I promised, didn't I?" he speaks softly and quietly and my heart melts a little in my chest. Eyes burn into me, and I know it's Tripp but I refuse to look over towards him.

Riggs' fingers lace through hers as he leads her towards the front door, Pacey bounding out behind them and Orla disappears to find Jorge.

It's just me and him left in the room.

"Did you want to come?" he asks, hands fisted into his jeans.

"Maybe another night, I'm wrecked."

He gives a shallow nod, then turns to walk out the door, following his brothers. I jump when the door slams a little harder than expected, the sound echoing around the large kitchen.

I stand for a moment, kind of annoyed with myself. Shaking my head, I move back to the wet dishes and continue to dry.

"Oh," I hear Orla's voice and I don't miss the slight

surprise in her tone. "I thought you were going with the boys?" her brows furrow.

"I'm tired, it's been a long day and I know Tripp asked you to watch Lainey but, well..." I pause for a moment, not wanting to stammer over my words, "you had her all day today and—"

"And nothing, you deserve a night out. You have done this for far too long with no support system. Well, now you have it. She's no trouble anyway. She's asleep so why would you choose to miss out? I mean, you're welcome to sit with me and Jorge, but he will be asleep in..." she pauses and twists her wrist towards her, "twenty minutes tops, and then I'll sit with a warm cup of tea and crochet."

A sigh vibrates in my chest as I fold the dish towel over my hands.

"Go, I can run you down there and then you jump back in with the boys to come home."

"They might not want me there, I think Tripp only asked out of kindness."

"Tripp doesn't ask out of kindness, darling. If they didn't want you there, they wouldn't have asked at all," her brows raise, a knowing smile pressing onto her lips as she strides towards me, taking the dish towel from me. "Go get ready, I'll meet you in the truck at eight-thirty," and with that, she turns her back on me and finishes the rest of the dishes.

I'm dressed in a white off the shoulder knee length dress. Pretty sage flowers with pink petals are dotted over the thin material. A light wash denim jacket sits over my shoulders, and I slip my cowboy boots on to finish my look. My hair is in loose waves, tumbled down my back. Pushing a set of medium, gold hoops through my ears, I stack my wrists with bracelets and look at myself in the reflection as I fiddle with the delicate pendant on my chain.

I contemplated getting changed but the longer I took, the more I would disturb Lainey and if she wakes, then I wouldn't go. Inhaling, I puff out my cheeks on my exhale.

Grabbing my perfume, I walk out of the door, softly closing it as I spray myself. I give it a minute to seep into my skin before delicately pushing the door and placing it on the floor just inside of my bedroom. With one last look over at Lainey, my heart thumps a little harder in my chest. Leaving her was the worst, but I know she's safe here with Jorge and Orla.

Closing the door behind me, I make my way downstairs. I peek a look at Jorge, who like Orla said, is sitting in his chair, eyes closed, mouth open and soft snores fill the room.

Grabbing my purse from the hook, I place it over my body and walk towards the truck.

"Well, don't you look pretty," Orla smiles and pushes the truck into reverse.

"Thank you," I mutter, looking down at my hands.

Why did I feel so nervous?

CHAPTER THIRTEEN
TRIPP

Sitting in The Boot, the usual crowds are here. Conrad is with us, and I am surprised to see him here alone. He normally would have some pretty little thing on his arm, but he has chosen to fly solo tonight. There is one regular missing and that's Austin. As much as he knows that everyone in The Boot believes his side of the story, he refuses to come. Harlow sits between me and Pacey and I'm glad she is out, but knowing Austin, he probably sent her away.

Riggs walks over with our bottles of beer and places them in the middle of the table, Riggs settling down next to Aspen with his whiskey. Not a big drinker that one, but if he does have a drink, he'll normally have one glass of whiskey.

"I have started finalising bits for the wedding," Aspen pipes up as she takes a swig from her bottle. "Guys, I need you to go to the tailor and get your suits fitted."

Pacey rolls his eyes.

"Can't I just come dressed like this?" he looks down at himself then back at Aspen, shrugging his shoulders up.

"Absolutely not," she shakes her head from side to side.

"Fine," he huffs, and I chuckle softly as I take a sip of my drink.

"Just let us know when, we will be there," I give her a curt tip of my hat and Riggs leans over, knocking it off the top of my head so it lands on the dusty floor of The Boot.

"Take your damn hat off; manners," he tuts, and I ignore the rage that simmers within.

"Where is Dixie?" Aspen asks, looking over my shoulder and I shake my head.

"Not coming; sort of glad really," I half admit. It's not a lie, she's pulling me in again and I don't need my heart broken again.

"Yeah?" Aspen pokes and Riggs grumbles beside her. God, I love her but she is nosey.

"Yeah, it's bad enough she is living under the same roof as me, I dunno... just a little too close?" I look up at Aspen and I can see she gets it, almost like she hears what I'm not saying.

"Do we know why she is back yet?" Harlow asks and this is my chance to scope and see if Aspen knows.

"Nah, just personal issues," I breathe out, fingers picking the damp beer bottle sticker.

"You know," Pacey pipes up and I know what is about to come from his mouth before he even says it. "They say that's a sign of being sexually frustrated," his hand is curled around his bottle as he points to where I am picking.

"Yeah?" I smirk, tilting my head back and looking behind Harlow towards my kid brother and Pacey chuckles to himself, letting his head drop. "Look, I don't have time for any of that. What with everything that happened, losing my job... that is the last thing on my mind."

"Yeah, it's been a bit of a ride hasn't it," Conrad pipes up from beside Aspen and we all nod.

Silence swarms our table for a moment before I hear the sharp intake of Riggs breathing in.

"Need you boys up early in the morning, we need to get the herd across the creek and into the top field, we've got cowboys moving up there tonight to settle for a couple of weeks whilst the cows birth the calves. Then once they're strong enough, we will bring them back down to the ranch."

I nod.

"It's quiet up in the top pasture, the cowboys will be there if any trouble comes their way and they're out the way of coyotes."

"Just let me know when you need me," Harlow says and her eyes linger on Riggs just a little longer than they should have. We know Harlow loves Austin, but we also know she holds a soft flickering candle for Riggs. First love and all that bullshit.

"Will do," Riggs doesn't even meet her gaze, he is too focused on Aspen.

"How is the writing going?" I ask Aspen, softly rolling the base of my empty beer bottle on the table.

"Ugh," she huffs, chest rising and falling, "hit a bit of a block. Not sure where I want the story to go," she admits, nodding to herself. "I need to get a move on though as my tour is coming up and people are wanting the second instalment..."

"You can't force a turd," Pacey shrugs up.

"Pretty sure the saying is, you can't force a fart..." Aspen nibbles on her bottom lip, "but thanks for the advice." Soft laughter rolls across the table when I notice Riggs looking behind me.

"Oh my," Aspen whispers. Whoever it is, is gaining the

attention of the table. Twisting and looking over my shoulder, I see her.

Pretty white dress, her new cowboy boots and her long brown hair sitting in waves down her back. Wide blue eyes seek me out and she holds her hand up awkwardly. She looks so damn pretty.

"Fuck," I hear Conrad mutter under his breath, and I snap my head around to look at him, eyes narrowing. "What?" he smirks, and I shake my head.

Riggs stands up, walking over to the table behind us and grabbing a spare chair, carrying it across the floor before placing it at the top of the table. I know he doesn't particularly like Dixie, but he isn't an asshole.

Well... mostly.

She walks over cautiously, her eyes bouncing around the table before they settle on mine, and I see the twitch of her lips.

Pretty as sin.

Inhaling sharply, I go to stand and she looks up at me.

"Drink?"

She eyes the table and sees that we're all drinking beer.

"I'll have whatever you guys are having," her voice is soft and I give her a gentle nod.

"Beers all round then?" I ask the table and they all chime a yes. Walking across the floor, my boots feel heavy as I rest against the wrap around bar.

"Same again?" Tabitha asks.

"Same again," I smile, "just add one more on," and I look over at the table, everyone talking and laughing like our lives haven't been completely turned upside down in the last few weeks. And then I see her.

The girl that broke my heart ten years ago, and

somehow, it feels like she belongs here. Like she has always been here.

"There we go darlin'," Tabitha says as she passes me the tray.

"Thanks, just pop it on the tab," I give her a wink.

"Riggs'?"

"You know it," I snort a laugh as I walk back to the table and place the tray down.

Everyone reaches for one, and Dixie looks like a deer in head lights.

"You okay?" I say softly as I sit down, my head dipped slightly.

"I think so," and I watch, the dimples digging into her cheeks.

"What made you change your mind?" I fall into easy chatter with her whilst the rest of the table slip into their own conversations.

"Your mom," she tilts her head, eyes volleying between mine.

"So, my mom could get you to come out with us, but I couldn't," I place my hand over my heart and act wounded which causes her to shove me away playfully in the arm.

"It's nothing personal," she licks her full lips, and my eyes drop as I watch.

"Kind of feels that way," I whisper.

"Hey, Tripp," Conrad shouts across the table. Annoyance grates inside me as I turn to face him.

"Yup?"

"Stop hogging her," he smirks, and I want to throat punch him.

Harlow whistles and Pacey chuckles low.

"How are you feeling after today?" Riggs asks, arm firmly wrapped around Aspen's shoulders.

"It was good, I'm tired but that's good, or so I have been told…"

"It is for me, sleep hasn't been great and being back on my horse, back in the saddle… well, I'm going to sleep like a damn baby tonight," Pacey says before swallowing a mouthful of his beer down.

"You done good, kid," Riggs tips his head towards me. Conrad is staring at Dixie, and I watch as her cheeks blush under his gaze.

"Stop staring at her man," I grab a cardboard coaster from the table and flick it in his direction.

"I can't," he lifts one shoulder, he does not give a fuck. Ballsy bastard.

"Do you want him to stop staring?" I can't hide the smile as I ask her, there are no hard feelings between me and Conrad, but still.

"Doesn't bother me," she smiles as she purses the rim of the bottle to her lips and takes a mouthful. "But I am curious Conrad," she says, placing her drink down, "do you ask everyone you just met out on dates?" and Riggs bellows a laugh, Harlow shakes her head shamelessly and Pacey's mouth drops open, and I hate it. Hate that he asked her.

"Seems to be a bit of a pattern when any new girl rocks up into town," Aspen side eyes Conrad.

"Dirty dog," Riggs chuckles to himself, hand stroking his beard.

"So is it still a no?" Conrad rests his elbow on the table, head on his hand as he looks down the table at her.

"It's still a no," she smirks, lifting her bottle to her lips.

"Damn," he laughs, sinking back into his seat. "Worth a shot though, right… you don't ask, you don't get."

I manage to simmer my thoughts for just a moment when I see Riggs lift his brows at me and I give him a nod.

"Conrad," my voice is a little louder as he looks towards me, smirk on his face as he shares a joke with Harlow.

"Yeah?"

"Walk with me a minute," I scoot from the cherry red seat and my boots hit the dusty ground.

Riggs and Aspen move out of his way so Conrad can reach me.

I begin to walk and he is behind me, I tug the door of The Boot and step outside into the cool spring evening, Conrad's boots beating down behind me.

Turning, I tilt my head to the side and his hands fold into his jean pockets.

"Just letting it be known..." I run my finger across my bottom lip, head resting down as I close the gap between us. "She's off limits."

"Is she?" he fucking scoffs a laugh, eyes glistening as they dance around the fire deep within mine.

"Yeah, she's *mine*." And even I'm a little shocked at my own admission. Dixie broke my heart and trampled over it, but the thought of her being with someone else floors me in an instant.

Conrad lets out a deep laugh, shaking his head from side to side.

"So, what, you Rivera boys get to put claim on any fresh meat that comes across that town line?" his eyes lift to look behind me at the dusk evening sky.

"Not at all, but the two girls you have tried to make a move on have been connected to me and Riggs, maybe you need to look a little closer at the girls already in the town before you come for ours."

Conrad steps towards me, our boots toe to toe.

"Okay princess, I'll leave her alone but if she makes a move on me..." his lips twitch into a smirk. "I won't be pushing her away," and with that he turns on his heel and walks back into The Boot, soft laughter following him as he does.

"Fuck it," I groan, lifting my hat and rubbing my hand over my messy hair before placing my hat back on my head, and making my way back to our table to sit with the girl that I have claimed to be mine, yet can't even hold a decent conversation with.

CHAPTER FOURTEEN
DIXIE

Conrad walks in, boyish grin on his face as he settles next to Riggs. They shuffled up when Tripp took Conrad outside and couldn't be bothered to keep moving every time one of them needed out.

"Hey," he smirks, resting his hands on the table just as Tripp walks in, eyes pinned to me.

"Hey," I whisper, my mind ticking over with what may or may not have happened outside.

Tripp says nothing as he sits down next to me, his eyes move from Pacey to Riggs before landing on Conrad.

"Was thinking," Riggs breaks through the visible tension that seems to be blanketing our table. "I might call some cowboys down from across city instead of using our boys, we need to get the cows settled and I am a little worried if I take a group of mine out to cow watch, so, I think we should call a favor in."

Tripp scrubs his face with his hands.

"I don't mind sitting up there?" he offers, and Riggs laughs at him. "What?" Tripp answers, back clearly up.

"Trust me, you do not want to have to sit up in that field

for two to three weeks whilst they birth and look after their calves," Riggs smirks, "plus we need you down on the ranch."

"I'll put a call into Marty on Monday, see if he can help," Tripp responds, taking a swig of his beer.

"Ew, why are we talking business?" Harlow rolls her eyes and Pacey sighs.

"Because we have to," he snipes at her and Riggs raises a brow, Aspen shaking her head towards Harlow.

They fall into chatter, and I feel his gaze cast over to me. I am lost, I have no idea what they're even talking about, so I just sit, lost amongst the chatter of cows and calves.

"You doing okay?" Tripp asks, sinking the last of his beer and placing the bottle on the table. He turns his body to face me, so his back is to Harlow and Pacey.

"Yeah," I say softly.

"You're bored aren't you," he smirks, eyes not leaving mine.

"No," I lie, and my cheeks betray me as I laugh.

"You are allowed to admit it," he leans closer to me.

"Okay, I'm a little bored."

"Well, what can I do to cure that?"

I sit for a moment, eyes gliding around the table at the group before they're back on his.

"Tequila," I wiggle my brows and deep down I knew this was a terrible idea.

"Tequila it is," he slams his hand down on the table before he stands and walks towards the bar and I follow. I order two trays of tequila shots knowing full well I will regret this in the morning, but right here, right now... I'm living in the moment.

And that moment was Tripp and Tequila.

The trays are placed down, and everyone reaches in for one except Riggs.

Placing the salt on my hand, the salt shaker is passed around the table as Pacey shouts out, "Lick, shoot, suck!"

My eyes land on Tripp as I lick the salt, knock back the shot and ignore the burn as it slips down my throat before I suck on the lime.

"Woooo!" Pacey shouts out as he slams his glass down, "Again!"

Three trays of shots down and everything is hazy. In a good way. It feels good to just sort of let go of all the tension that has been brewing deep inside of me. Clay. Coming back home. Tripp. All of it has built up to something so big that I feel like I am ready to snap.

But tonight, being able to let go just that little bit has me feeling slightly better.

Aspen drags Riggs up and leads him towards the jukebox as he slips a quarter in and she selects the song, and within a few seconds *Head Over Boots - Jon Pardi* begins to play.

Conrad is up, holding his hand out for me, but I shake my head from side to side as I watch Riggs spinning Aspen around before his hand skims around her lower back, pulling her body close to him. Her head tips back slightly, they're muttering quietly between themselves, lips pressing into smiles just before they kiss.

Conrad drags one of the bar girls out and spins her around and I smile at them. I hear shuffling beside me and when I turn to look at Tripp, he is standing in front of me, hand held out, cowboy hat tipped down slightly.

"Ma'am," he smirks as I place my hand in his and my heart stutters in my chest, "may I have this dance?" and my cheeks pinch crimson.

I nod, and for a slither of a second I feel bad for turning Conrad down.

But this is Tripp.

The only man who has ever had my heart and soul.

He pulls me up softly, arm snaking around my back, holding me close to his body as he begins to dance with me, his lips moving slightly to the song that plays through the bar.

And in this moment, the way his eyes are glistening, burning into my soul, takes me back to when we were just kids.

Truck pulled up, lights the only thing lighting up the evening as he would turn his truck radio up as loud as it would go and he would spin me around in the parking lot, lips meeting then once we were hot and bothered, we would skinny dip in the creek.

And how amazing would it be to be teleported back to those summer nights, just before it all turned tragic.

He must see the way my brow crinkles, the way my lips part and my eyes dull for just a moment because he slows us down, and then it's just us, the only thing around us is Jon Pardi's voice. His hand cups my chin, tilting my head back to look at him.

"What's wrong?" he breathes, our eyes still dancing.

"Just thinking back to when we were younger," and I give him a lopsided smile which has his thumb brushing across my bottom lip.

"Yeah?"

"Yeah," I nod as his hand cups my cheek and I find myself leaning into him just as he turns me around, swaying me from side to side as *Spin you round - Morgan Wallen* begins to play.

"I'm always up for a reenactment," he teases, and my heart skips a beat in my chest.

"Maybe someday," I mutter as he holds me close against him.

"Don't say maybe; it'll never happen," he rasps, his lips brushing against mine, but I pull away slightly.

"Tripp," I breathe, head dizzy, breathing laboured.

"Dixie," he whispers and everything around us goes silent and all I can focus on is our breathing.

"I vowed to never fall for you again, I'm sure you vowed that too..." I just about manage to squeeze out.

"I never stopped falling, little Dreamcatcher."

And my heart stops beating for just a second.

"Ever."

For just that split moment all of our messy past was forgotten.

TRIPP

Riggs broke the party up and with a few groans, we all made our way to the waiting trucks. The tension that filled Riggs' truck was heavy. A few *accidental* finger brushes, shy giggles and burning crimson cheeks looped as we pulled into the driveway.

Pacey stumbled from the truck, not looking back as he climbed the steps and wandered into the house, closing the door a little loudly and I watch as Dixie winces. Her eyes draw back to me and I lose myself in them.

The soft summer breeze wraps around us and for just a moment, it's me and her, lips edging closer to hers, but a whistle pulls me away. Eyes casting over my shoulder,

Riggs gives me a curt nod of his head, his lips pulling into a smirk as he waves me off. Aspen lifts her hand and wriggles her fingers, nose scrunching as she says goodbye. I watch as their truck turns and drives down the dusty drive, their rear lights blurring before they disappear.

A soft sigh has my shoulders lifting as I turn to face her.

Her.

Her, the one who showed me what it was like to love. Her. The one who has held my heart over the last ten years. Her. The one I adore.

Her.

It's always been her.

My trembling fingers inch towards the loose hair that blows, cascading around her face and tuck it behind her ear, her eyes not leaving mine as they dance and glisten under the clear night sky, the stars twinkling in her beautiful blues.

"I'm glad I came tonight..." she trails off.

"I'm glad you came as well," and I reluctantly drop my fingers from her hair, my intake of breath catching at the back of my throat.

"I don't want the night to be over," she whispers into the quiet evening.

"It doesn't have to be," a small smile plays on my lips. She drags her eyes from mine as she looks over her shoulder towards the house. "But I understand..." my voice is quiet. I want to be selfish, but it's not about me. Her eyes soften as she meets my gaze.

"Stay here..." she pushes onto her toes and kisses me softly on the cheek and my skin warms under her lips.

She kissed me.

"I don't plan on going anywhere darlin'..." I rasp, my head tilting to the side and her cheeks turn pink as she spins on her heel and moves towards the house, slipping inside the door and I am alone, under the stars waiting for my dream girl.

My eyes cast down, kicking the toe of my cowboy boot into the dusty ground, a boyish grin spreading across my lips as I watch the stones loose, gliding across the floor.

"Tripp..." her angelic voice floats through the air, the breeze picking it up and wrapping it around me like a blanket.

Lifting my head, I twist around to look at her. Eyes alight with want, eyes alight with desire, eyes alight with adoration. I never thought she would return—maybe in my wildest dreams—but never did I think she would be walking towards me, the soft moonlight illuminating her, making her look like a god damn angel. Everything about her was perfect.

"All okay?" I ask, not sure if she is coming to wish me goodnight, or whether she can spend an hour more with me.

"All is fine. Lainey is fast asleep. Had to take my..." she pauses for a moment and that blush that paints across her cheeks is back and I have to admit, I love it a little more each time I see it.

I nod, no words were needed.

Silence echoes around us and suddenly, I feel like a giddy love struck teen all over again. Reaching my hand out, my fingers slightly spread, I watch as her beautiful eyes cast down.

"Walk with me?" I ask softly, and my heart rate spikes as she slips her hand into mine.

We didn't speak, just let our hearts lead us to the place that only we knew about. Tucked away over the other side of the creek. Kicking our shoes off, a giggle bubbles from her and I cast my eyes over my shoulder as I look at her, all starry eyed and giddy.

My fingers lace with hers once more as I lead her across the stepping stones of the calm creek. My heart gallops in my chest like wild horses, nerves growing stronger the closer we get to our spot. My feet land on the soft grass and I turn to face her, eyes searching her beautiful face.

"I never thought I would be back here, let alone with you..." she trails off and her head drops. My brows furrow and my chest aches a little. Dropping my shoes to the floor, my hand reaches forward as I place my finger and thumb on her chin and tilt her face back, her glistening blue eyes on mine.

"Hey, hey," I whisper, eyes bouncing between hers. "No sadness, I'm sure neither of us expected to be here again..." and now it's my turn to trail off. "But things happen for a reason, in some twisted game of fate you ended up here. You came back." I ignore the lump in my throat that has lodged itself there, when I know in fact she didn't return for me, but admitting that out loud will only crush my heart again.

She gives a soft nod as she drops her boots to the ground and my lips twitch into a slither of a smile.

Walking her towards the large blossom tree, my eyes fall to the trunk and that's when I see it. Our initials carved into it; TR <3s DW.

"We really did love with our hearts on our sleeves didn't we?" she hums, leaning into me and I lower my face to kiss her on the top of her head.

"And what a way to love," I smile into her hair just as she breaks away and I instantly miss her. Her fingers fall from mine and my brows furrow as I watch her intently. She glides towards the tree, fingers brushing against the wild flowers that stand just under her knee and my heart throbs in my chest. She looks so beautiful.

She stops in front of the tree, her fingers delicately tracing around our initials.

"We always said we would get married under this tree," she laughs softly, slowly spinning to face me.

"And we still will," I surprise myself by saying it, but it's true. I know deep down that she is the one for me, the one I will marry.

But she shakes her head from side to side.

"Don't say the words," I whisper as I step closer to her, closing the gap in three long strides, a hand sweeping her face up to look at me. "Please baby... just promise me tonight," my voice cracks as I edge closer to her, lips hovering over hers.

"Tonight," she whispers back, nodding as a tear rolls down her cheek, I swipe it away with my thumb.

"Let me get you out of your head," I murmur and she nods again, another glistening tear escaping just as my lips press against hers, ever so softly, ever so slightly. The feel of her trembling fingers dust up my clammy tee, clutching it in her small grasp when her kiss becomes desperate, needy almost. Her other hand curls around the back of my neck, fingers pinching the hair that sits at the nape and tugging. Her tongue sweeps past my lips like a hunger burns deep inside of her. Her head tilts just as my hand cups her cheek, my heart explodes deep inside my chest, obliterating into a million tiny pieces before our souls intwine and piece both of our broken hearts back together piece by piece.

"Take me back Tripp, take me back to when we were teens and everything was perfect," she whispers, unshed tears evident in her crystal blue eyes, "just for tonight."

And I am nodding, panting, begging her, desperate for

her as my tongue glides across hers in a soft but tantalizing stroke.

My fingertips graze down her cheek, her jaw, skimming them down her collarbone as I slip the shoulder of her dress away and allow my lips to dust the trail I marked with my fingers. Her head rolls back, her eyes dusting shut as I continue my kisses over her sensitive skin.

"Tripp," she breathes a whisper of a moan, blending with the sound of the trickling water.

"Yes Dreamcatcher," my breath strokes against her skin.

"Swim with me," she dips her head, hands cusping my head in her delicate hands as she drags me up, eyes bouncing between mine. "Then take me home," her last request comes out as a plea and I smirk.

"Always, darlin'," I rasp, kissing her once more before dropping my hands from her skin and watching her as she undresses.

My hungry eyes roam over her body, the body I have seen so many times ten years ago, but I feel like I am watching her for the first time with brand new eyes.

Heart drumming in my chest, blood pumping loudly around my body and every feeling I had supressed for Dixie Walker was slowly and torturously bubbling closer to the surface, pricking at my skin as I watch her slowly peel her pretty dress from her body, the hairs on the back of my neck standing one by one.

A shrill ringtone pulls me from my love drunk haze, and I shake my head, eyes widening as Dixie bends down and rummages in her purse for her phone.

"Orla, is everything okay?" she asks softly, but I can see the worry slowly etching itself onto her face as the seconds pass and my heart is in my throat as I step closer to her, my eyes volleying between hers.

"I'll be right there."

She cuts the phone of and is bent over collecting her purse and boots.

"What's happened? Is everything okay?" the panic is evident in my voice.

"Lainey is unsettled, your mom has tried everything but she won't stop screaming," her words come out rushed as she twists her head to look over the creek towards the ranch.

"Let's get you home," I lower my head, waiting for our eyes to connect.

"I'm so..." she whispers but I press my finger against her lips and shake my head from side to side.

"Don't you dare," my voice is low, "come." I lace my fingers through hers, taking the boots into my hands, I lead her through the fields and towards the house.

It just wasn't our night.

I'm not upset or disappointed; Lainey will always come first.

And I know that.

CHAPTER FIFTEEN
TRIPP

Dixie has plagued my mind in the few days since that night. Small *accidental* finger brushes, a few longing stares but we've never had a moment alone since. I could have easily followed her up to her room, before dragging her back into mine, but I didn't. I stayed away. I took myself back out onto the porch with a glass of whiskey to keep me warm as I sat in the rocker and watched the stars.

"Right," Riggs claps his hands together, wincing at the loud sound and Pacey moans, letting his head fall as it hits the breakfast bar with a thud. "Ow."

"It's far too early for this, my head is pounding," I groan as I nurse a cup of coffee. We decided to hit The Boot last night to try and hash out the last few details before the funeral.

"And this is why we don't drink on school nights, children," Riggs smirks, but scolding us at the same time.

"Idiot," I shake my head, my hand pressed to my forehead. My head is pounding.

"We need to be switched on, we're not going to be welcome at Clay's funeral, but we need to go. We need to show the town that we're not going to cower away. Yes, Clay died on our land, but we did *not* kill him."

Pacey sighs, his eyes darting to the door once he sees Dixie standing there holding Lainey.

"Carry on," I grit, eyes moving from Pacey and nodding for Dixie to come in. She walks in but keeps her head down, cautious almost.

"Is there any word on Austin showing his face?" Riggs turns his attention to Pacey and he just sits tall, eyes cast down as he puffs his cheeks out.

"He hasn't said."

"I think he should go," Dixie turns around after placing Lainey in her highchair, my mom waltzing through and taking over whilst ushering Dixie to sit down next to us.

"And why's that darlin'?" Riggs raises a brow, dragging his own stool out to take a seat, boyish grin tugging at his lips.

"Because if you say he isn't guilty of killing Clay, then by him going surely it would work in his favour?" her blue eyes bounce around the room and my heart drops.

"But then it's like leading a sheep to a pack of wolves," Pacey eyes her, and she sits a little taller.

"But are you shepherds going to leave him alone with the wolves?" she counters back, and I hear my mom snigger softly.

"No," he tightens his lips as he shuffles in his seat.

"So, I think he should go."

Silence fizzles around the table, eyes bouncing between all of us when we hear my dad, "I agree with Dixie. We all go. We're united and we won't let one of our own take the blame for something he didn't do."

Riggs smirk grows wider, whistling through his teeth.

"Someone better go and get Austin then," he chuckles.

"Leave that to me," my dad says as he reaches for his cowboy hat and walks out the door before even giving us a chance to argue with him.

"Where is the wake?" I ask, bringing my cup to my lips and taking a mouthful just as my mom places a fresh coffee down in front of Dixie.

"Across town, some bar called Mules," Pacey chirps up.

"Never heard of it."

"Probably run by them or something," he shrugs a shoulder up.

"Mules is my dad's bar," Dixie slips out as if it's not a big deal and all eyes are on hers. "Or was, still is? I don't know," she lets out a shallow breath.

"Your dad? He left town years ago didn't he?" I ask, a little confused by her admission.

"He did... unless he is back?" and I see the fear in her eyes.

"But then if he abandoned it, maybe the Attaways took it over?" Riggs suggests and now it's his turn to have all eyes on him.

"Maybe..." I throw out into the conversation because I am to focused on Dixie again. Her eyes drop from Riggs' as she plays with the delicate gold chain around her neck.

"Looks like we're going to the wake as well," Riggs rubs his hands together before standing. "I'll be back at noon, we will ride down to the church," and with that he walks out the back door.

Pacey and I nod as we push ourselves from the table and place our cups in the sink.

"Mom, will you ride down with us or take a truck?" Pacey asks and I hover close to Dixie.

"I was going to offer to stay home with Lainey, a funeral is no place for a baby," her eyes slice from Pacey's to Dixie and she gives my mom a soft nod. "Your dad will ride down with you," she smiles at Pacey, cupping his cheek as she rubs her thumb across it. "Take your guns, you never quite know what will happen once you're in that church."

I swallow the lump that forms in my throat.

I have no idea who is going to be inside that church. Sure, we have Clay's brothers, uncles, cousins... but he was also in with the big boys from the city.

"I don't think I can go," Dixie whispers beside me and I turn to look at her, crouching down so I am level with her.

"Why not?" I whisper, eyes focused on her ocean blues.

Her lips part to speak but she rolls them instead, shaking her head from side to side as I watch her eyes well. She pushes from the table and disappears upstairs.

I stand, eyes roaming between Pacey and my mom, waiting for one of them to tell me to follow her.

My mom rolls her eyes and I take that as my cue. Turning, I climb the stairs two at a time and stop outside her bedroom. Lifting my hand, I curl my index finger and hover it over the wooden door. Inhaling heavily, I knock softly.

She doesn't answer.

I knock again then push down the handle of the door, popping my head around the doorframe. And that's when I see her. Sitting at the edge of her bed. Tears soaking her cheeks, hands buried into the lap of her pretty white nightdress.

"Talk to me," I usher softly, not stepping into her room until she asks me.

Her glistening eyes meet mine, and I watch as she sucks in a breath, bottom lip trembling.

I have no idea what the hell is going on, but what I do know is I don't like seeing her upset.

"Can I..." I pause for a moment as I push the door a little wider and she gives me a nod. Slowly stepping into her room, it's cosy. It's always just been a spare room with a single bed. Sage green walls, cream carpet, cream-stained oak furniture and a little lamp.

Sitting next to her, I place my own hands in my lap and we sit in silence.

She sniffles beside me and my heart aches.

"What's going on Dix..." I trail off as her watery blue eyes meet mine.

"I can't do it."

"The funeral?" I ask stupidly, but I want her to say the words out loud, I want to hear it come from her lips.

She nods.

"Why? What's changed... wasn't that what you were coming back for?" and I hear the way her breath trembles on her intake, fresh tears streaming down her face, and she nods, eyes cast down into her lap as she picks the skin around her nailbed.

"There is so much you don't know..." she whispers.

"Then tell me," I reach my hand across, grabbing her chin softly and turning her head to face me. "I have nowhere else to go."

That was a lie.

I had the funeral to go to.

But in this moment, she was more important than the funeral.

"That's a lie," she half laughs, half chokes out a sob.

"Okay, fine, but still, I'm not going anywhere," my thumb pad brushes against her cheek, catching a tear that rolls from her beautiful eyes.

"When I left town, I was signed by a guy called Lucian."

I nod. I have no idea who Lucian is but still, I find myself nodding as if I do.

"He promised me the world; the tours, the fame, the fortune—" she stutters.

"Yeah?"

"Yeah," she whispers, "but after a few months, things started to change. I was chained to him at every moment, I only done the shows he wanted me to, only toured where he said... and then Clay turned up." She sniffles.

I stay mute for just a moment. I want her to keep speaking. I don't want her to stop.

"He seemed so kind, he and Lucian were friends and that's when I was thrown into a whole new world. I was taken to the city, to be wined and dined and shared amongst friends," she swallows, and I see the way her throat bobs up and down, eyes glistening.

"Until one day he didn't want to share anymore. Lucian had got all he wanted from me and my singing career begun dying a slow and painful death. That's when Clay swooped me up, cocooning me into this false pretence of safety. He was bored within a few weeks, the visits from wherever he was coming from were getting less and less and then I found out I was pregnant with Lainey. I knew she was his. I hadn't been with anyone apart from Clay at that point. He was pissed, I told him I didn't want him in mine or the baby's life, but thought he had a right to know so if he decided down the line he wanted to meet her, he knew about her."

She shudders as she intakes a deep breath.

"After a couple of months, he turned up telling me he wanted to know his daughter. Wanted to be just her dad though and anything romantic between me and him was long gone. He said he would be back a little more as he had business to attend to with the big suits and that's the night I overheard him talking about his plans for the land, the ranches, the empty gold mines…"

I roll my lips.

"I had no idea what they were going on about, but then it clicked. They were talking about the old mines at the top of the creek… the ones that filter into your land… the same mines that run directly under your ranch…" her face tips up to mine and I can see the concern etched into her face. "Lucian was involved in all of this, Clay promised him a cut of whatever they made when they explored the gold mines, then Lucian heard of his death and well, the suits have pushed him out. He used me for ransom, but they didn't care. I was nothing to them, didn't mean anything. I was just Clay's baby momma," she sighs. "Lucian told me I was never going to leave Wyoming, he had originally had plans to take us to Los Angeles, make me the star… but we both knew that was never going to happen, not now that I had Lainey. I love singing, I wanted to pursue that as a career and don't get me wrong, I was noticed, people knew who I was in Wyoming, but not here, not in LA. I would have been plankton in a sea of fishes. Single mom, down and out, broke. Lucian took everything from me, so I had to run. The only place I knew I could come back to was here… then with Clay's funeral, it seemed like the perfect time." I don't miss the tear that rolls down her cheek and runs off her chin, dissolving into her dress. She slowly looks at me, eyes bouncing between mine, "I came back hoping for some money; hoping to collect what Clay promised for Lainey. I didn't even think…" she pauses for a moment shaking her head from side to side. "Lucian is going to be there, and once he sees me, he will drag me back to Wyoming kicking and screaming," and that's when she looks away from me.

My blood is boiling, and I am so fucking mad at this whole situation. The situation with Clay, the situation with her shitty manager. Old feelings chip away at the surface and the need to protect her blazes through my veins.

I push from the bed and step towards her, her eyes still cast down as if she is ashamed of what she has just told me. Gripping her chin softly, I tilt her head back to look at me and her glassy blues break my fucking heart.

"Nobody is going to get to you, nobody is going to touch you... anyone and I mean *anyone* lays a finger on you, I'll chop their fucking hands off and shove them up their asses."

She blinks, her lips parting and that's when she stands in front of me, trembling hands resting on my chest, my erratic heart beating under her fingertips as I let my fingers lazily sweep her hair away from her face.

"You promise?" she whispers.

"I promise," I breathe, just as I lower my lips to hers, softly, delicately before my tongue pushes through and everything inside of me burns like wildfire. Her hands are in my hair, mine cupped around her pretty face as our kiss deepens, as if she's all the oxygen I am allowed, kissing her is like breathing, like living... existing. Ten years of pent-up misery and heartache rolled in with protectiveness and a blazing love all mixed up and poured into this kiss.

The one kiss that ripped my heart from my chest and delicately landed in her small hands, for her to keep and protect.

And I was just praying she done just that.

Dressed in an all-black suit, white shirt and black cowboy hat and boots, I was ready to go. We knew this was going to be reckless, like playing with fire, but we all agreed that we were going.

Not only to pay our respects to a man that had died, but to also clear our name of this bullshit once and for all.

Walking across the hallway downstairs, I saw Riggs and Aspen waiting for us in the small lounge area, Riggs cradling a crystal glass of whiskey, Aspen eyeing him occasionally as Pacey joins them.

"Well, don't we look handsome," Pacey jokes, smirking as I walk into the room and reach for my own glass of amber. I needed something to calm the nerves that were shocking me with every heartbeat that thumped in my chest.

I rolled my eyes, slipping the sleeve of my blazer up as I checked the time.

"Is Marty meeting us here?" Riggs asks, arms protectively wrapped around Aspen's back. She wears a knee length black dress, hair pulled into a neat bun with a few loose strands framing her pretty face.

"Nah, he is going to meet us up at the church, we don't need to give the Attaways anymore reason to think he is on our side. But then what does it matter? Kelcie is in their pockets..." I take a mouthful of my drink and wince at the burn, "I am so fucking mad I stepped down so easily, thought I was doing the right thing," I shake my head from side to side as disappointment surges through me.

"Look, what's done is done, all we can do is show up, show everyone that we're still the same group of brothers. We have our enemies; we don't need to make any more. So, with that," Riggs turns and places his glass on the oak mantel above the fire. "We go in there," he pauses, stepping forward as his eyes dance between me and our kid brother, Pacey, "we take our guns, but we do not be the first to pull, do you understand me? We're taking them for protection, not to start a full-blown fucking war," his voice is stern, and me and Pacey give him a firm nod. "No one fucking draws their guns until I tell you to, no fucking fighting unless they provoke it."

And my mom walks into the room holding Lainey at that very second.

"We don't need any more drama brought on our name, please boys..." and she doesn't just look at me and Pacey, she focuses on Riggs too. "No fighting. Be the bigger men, heads held high and walk away."

Riggs nods.

He would never start a fight for fun, but we do need to protect ourselves. We have no idea who will be here today and just who Wallen, Clay's brother, has on his side. His brother was killed, his dad long gone... he only had himself. The suits would be there, Wallen will want to keep this going, he will fight for the land just for his brother's legacy. And for Lucian? Well, that cunt can rot in hell. Dixie didn't need to tell me anymore; I had already made my own mind up just how that fucker treated her over the last ten years and I am done letting it happen. She stays with me, with us.

No more running for her.

"So, we all understand?" My mom says as she stands next to Riggs and we all nod.

"Yes ma," me and Pacey say in unison and Riggs leans down and places a kiss on her head, Lainey's wide blue eyes staring at Riggs.

He softens slightly, tilting his head to the side as he reaches out for her, and she grasps his fingers. A low rumble of a laugh courses through him and his eyes go all sparkly.

Aspen steps up beside him, hand tucked under his arm as she watches the grumpy ass cowboy turn to putty in front of Lainey. I get it. I think we've all got a soft spot for her.

I hear the sound of heels clicking across the wooden floor and I turn to look over my shoulder to see Dixie. Mid length black dress, laced cuffed sleeves and heeled pumps. Long brown hair wavy and cascading over her shoulders.

She looks beautiful.

She dips her head as she slips past me and the urge to reach out and grab her just so I can hold her close is overwhelming. But I don't. I watch as she walks over to Lainey and scoops her out of my mom's arms. Lainey reaches up and places her chubby little hands over Dixie's lips just as Dixie kisses her.

"Ah man, I want one," Riggs groans and Aspen leans into him.

"Soon big fella, soon," she turns her face up to look at him just as he leans down and places the softest of kisses on her lips.

My eyes scope over to Dixie, and she is staring at me, all starry eyed and shit and I am desperate to take her out on a date; dancing in the parking lot under the stars and a late-night swim in the creek. Just like old times. Just like before.

The front door closes, and we all turn to see Austin, Harlow and my dad.

"Austin," my mom breathes, walking over to him a little quicker before wrapping him in her embrace, Harlow still firmly holding onto his hand, fear burning through her eyes that if she lets him go, he will bolt like a wild mustang.

"Hey Orla," he smiles, eyes closing for just a moment.

His dirty blonde hair is cut, tidy. He wears a matching black suit, same as me and my brothers but he doesn't have a cowboy hat.

When his eyes open, they scan over the three of us and we see the way his shoulders relax a little.

Mom steps back and only then do me and my brothers, one by one, pull him into an embrace. Just a little reminder that we will always have his back, that we will always be here for him, we will *always* choose him.

God didn't make him our blood relation, but he did make us family.

"Right, are we ready?" my dad asks, eyes moving between us all.

"Ready as we will ever be," I chime as I go to open the front door, the girls walking out first, Harlow still gripping onto Austin.

"I'll take the girls and Austin in the truck, you three ride the horses down." We nod.

My mom follows us onto the porch, leaning in and giving each one of us a kiss on the cheek.

"Be safe, I love you," she tells each of us as we pass her and walk down to where the horses are tied up.

Steps faltering, I turn to look back towards the house and I can see the worry etched onto my mom's face and I hate that she feels like that.

Dixie kisses Lainey on the top of the head, lingering for just a moment more before passing her to my mom. I watch as she lets out a deep exhale, taking the steps slowly as she walks across the dusty floor. I wait for her and give her a look.

"You feeling okay?" I ask softly as I walk her to the truck.

She nods. But I am not convinced.

"We won't leave your side, you've got all of us. This is how we work," I smile at her just as my dad places his hand on the small of her back. "I'll see you at the church," and she gives me a ghost of a smile before getting into the truck.

"I'll keep them safe," my dad says before opening his own door.

"I know," I tip my hat towards him, "I'll see you soon."

My heart jack hammers in my chest as I walk towards my brothers already on their horses. Footing the stirrup, I pull myself up onto Bucky's back, Riggs on Travis and Pacey on Chase.

"Ready?" Riggs asks, Travis stepping forward, tail high.

"Ready as I'll ever be," I swallow down the nerves.

"Then lets fucking go," he kicks his horse on and me and Pacey follow across the fields and towards the church.

And for some reason, I feel like we're heading to our own funeral.

CHAPTER SIXTEEN
TRIPP

We sit just a little bit up from the church as we watch the funeral car pull into the parking lot. I turn to look at Riggs, his eyes are firmly settled on the car and we're waiting for him to make the move for us to go.

Dad is already there with the truck, just pulled around the corner so still out of sight.

I have no idea how this is going to go down. I am praying that it'll be smooth, that we can all be adults about this.

The sound of horse hooves has me and Pacey looking over our shoulder to see Marty, he was our town's Livestock Commissioner. He has always been on our side.

"Afternoon," he stops his horse between me and Riggs. "How's the land lying?" he asks, his eyes gazing across the same view as Riggs.

"All looks okay, just want to wait until the coffin is out of the car, don't want to stand around any longer than I have to."

He gives a steady nod.

"Thanks for coming with us," I murmur, tightening the rein on Bucky as he stamps his back hoof down.

"Sure thing, couldn't have you walking into war on your own," he sort of smirks which gets a growl from Riggs.

"We're not walking into war, and we're not alone," Riggs snaps at him a little too easily. He is nervous, I get it. I am too. Marty just laughs, shaking his head.

"Riggs buddy, you're walking into an all-out war. I don't see no white flags about to be waved, do you?" he questions, but Riggs says nothing as the coffin is pulled from the car and up onto the pallbearers shoulders, one of them being Wallen.

"It's time," Riggs clicks his tongue into the roof of his mouth as he kicks Travis on, and we follow close behind.

Walking across the lot, heads turn to look at us just as dad climbs out the truck with the three girls and Austin. Harlow leads Austin towards us, and we bury him in-between the horses as we walk past the crowds and over to the horse rings to tie our boys up.

We can hear the hushed voices, but we hold our heads high as my dad follows behind the us.

Riggs halts, jumping down from the horse and once Travis is secured, me, Pacey and Marty dismount. The sound of hooves in the distance makes me lift my head to see a crowd of cowboys riding towards us and I look over at Marty.

"Couldn't have you go in there without your army," he tilts his head, fingers holding the rim of his cowboy hat and I have never felt more thankful than I have now.

Most of these cowboys are from neighboring ranches, a few out of towners, but we all know each other, and of course, leading them is Hudson up front and center, our own cowboys tucked behind him and then my eyes settle on Conrad and I give him a firm nod, him returning it with a smile on his face.

Pacey whistles as he ties Chase up and one by one, we walk towards the door, Austin still safely nestled between us.

There is no way in hell he is going in without us. Harlow slips in beside him, fingers lacing just as Dixie stands next to me, Aspen next to Riggs and Marty stands shoulder to shoulder with Pacey.

Inhaling deeply, I feel Dixie's fingers brush against mine just as I flex my fingers out. She turns to look at me, fear gallops through her eyes like wild horses, but they soon settle just as my fingers link with hers, palm to palm.

"I've got you," I whisper as we slip into the stream of people walking behind the coffin as Clay makes his final journey and that's when we hear *Go Rest High On That Mountain - Vince Gill* begin to play as we enter the church.

We tuck ourselves out the back, the whispers still so loud and echoing around the small church, heads turn, eyes narrow and the main focus is on Austin.

Watching in silence as the coffin slips onto the catafalque, Wallen hanging back for just a moment, hand placed on the top of his brother's coffin, head bowed, and his shoulders visibly shake.

I swallow down the lump.

I'm not sad for Clay. I'm sad with the situation. Sadness drowns me at the thought of being in Wallen's position as he lays his brother to rest, as he spends his final journey with the only family he has left.

The priest stands up front, clearing his throat as Wallen steps back, his head lifting and that's when his eyes settle on mine, then Riggs, then Pacey and lastly on Austin.

We all watch as his fists ball at his side, and that's when

Riggs stretches his arm out, his hand pressed out as he hovers it in front of me and Pacey, a warning but also a protection to let Wallen know that no one is getting near his kid brothers.

Wallen finally slices his eyes away and tucks himself into a pew, whispering in an older man's ear who then in turn looks over his shoulder, but he isn't looking at me or my brothers. He is looking at Dixie.

Lucian.

She whimpers next to me, hiding her face behind my arm, head down so her long brown hair hides her pretty face.

"I've got you," I say quietly, tightening my grip on her hand.

Surprisingly, the service goes off without a hitch. Fanning out of the church, we decide to avoid the burial, but we are going to head straight to the wake.

The cowboys greet us, all sitting tall, shotguns in hand as they form a wall of horses.

Riggs gives them a tilt of his cowboy hat and Hudson kicks his horse on, breaking the formation and moving forward towards my dad's truck. We wait until the girls and Austin are safely inside before we mount our own horses. Half the cowboys break off and lead the truck towards Mules and the other half sit back and wait for us, Conrad stuck to our side too.

"Wasn't as bad as I predicted," Marty half laughs, his horse circling.

"We still have the wake to get through," Riggs grunts as he kicks his horse on.

"Well let's all pray that it goes off without a hitch too then."

We all let out a soft laugh, because we know if anything is going to kick off, it'll be at the wake.

The ride takes us about thirty minutes, which works well as we get there just before Wallen and the rest of the funeral attendees.

My eyes lift as I look up at the bar that sits in the middle of nowhere. Worn out panelled exterior that is desperate for a lick of paint, roof tiles slipped and sitting in some of the gutter. What the hell were they thinking holding it here?

Opening up Bucky's rein, I turn him around and look at our surroundings. There is nothing here. We're sitting on a dusty parking lot.

Harlow, Aspen and Austin join us; Harlow still very much holding onto Austin's hand.

My brows furrow when I look over at the truck and see that Dixie is still sitting in there. Kicking Bucky on, I trot across the large, empty lot and jump down from the back of my horse, holding onto his reins as I duck my head down to look in the back of the truck.

"Hey, you okay?" I ask, her eyes pinned forward, fingers curled into the soft leather of the seats. I glance over at my dad, and he gives me a sombre look.

"No," she whispers, and I don't miss the way her voice trembles.

"Baby..." it falls from my tongue, but I don't regret it. "Look at me."

And she does. Red rimmed watery eyes land on mine.

"I promised you, didn't I? I swear it Dixie, Lucian isn't going to get near you,"

and she nods, and I hate that she is crying. "Come. Come stand with me," I hold my hand out for her to take, and as she reaches her fingers out to me, I hear the sound of a gunshot echo around the parking lot.

Panic rings in my ears, screaming, drowning out my thoughts as I step back and slam the truck door. Footing the stirrup, I'm on Bucky's back within seconds as I turn him around and that's when everything moves in slow motion.

A rusty truck pulls into the parking lot, Wallen falls from the passenger side, pistol in hand as he aims it towards my brothers and Austin.

"Shit," I am already pulling my gun out as I kick Bucky towards where Wallen is stomping across the lot, gun pointed at Austin.

I shoot in the air, trying to deter him when he points the gun at me, shooting twice towards me and I feel the reins go slack and Bucky goes down, taking me with him.

And that's when an all-out war kicks off, but in that moment, all I can hear is Dixie screaming.

Don't get out the truck, don't get out the truck.

I look towards the truck and my dad is clambering down and the fear is crippling me, the pain that radiates through me is nothing compared to the fear that I feel.

I scream out, Riggs looking over at me as I watch the next few moments pan out. Lucian is running for Wallen, just as he pulls the trigger once more and I am sure it hits Austin, but it's not until I see Aspen move to the floor, that I realise Austin is still standing.

Another guy who is with them is still shooting bullets, and I feel a hand in my gun belt. Eyes widening when I see Dixie.

"No, no, go get back in the truck," I pant, the feel of Bucky's weighted body crushing me a little more.

Her eyes are fuelled by gasoline, and I know I won't stop her from walking into the god damn fire. She gives me a small smile before she is up and walking into the crowd, my gun loose in her hand as it hangs by her side and I watch as she lifts her arm slowly, aiming it towards where Wallen is standing. But just as she pulls the trigger, he steps back and she hits the guy who is reloading his gun, the bullet hitting through his temple as he falls to the ground like a sack of shit and I watch as she drops the gun as if it's just burned her.

"Fuck," I mutter, slightly in awe, slightly terrified.

Lucian whistles and drags Wallen into the waiting truck as it speeds off and that's when I see Harlow on the floor. Austin falling to his knees as he screams.

Marty and the cowboys are following the truck across the dead grassed fields, the sound of guns still echoing in the distance and I want to run to them, but I can't.

Bucky is dead.

Falling and crushing my leg underneath him as he died.

Tears wet my cheeks and it doesn't matter how much I scream and try to move him off me, I can't. A searing pain burns through my shoulder and it's not until I glance down, I see that I am bleeding. He shot me.

The upper half of my body falls back into the dusty ground beneath me, and I am frozen. I can't do anything.

All I can hear is Austin crying, Riggs shouting and Aspen trying to console her brother and that's when I feel hands on my head.

"It's okay son, you're going to be okay," my dad is on his knees, lifting my head and resting it into his lap and I can't stop the tears that are flowing.

Rolling my head to the side, I see Riggs on the floor dcing CPR on Harlow, Austin is sitting on the ground, knees tucked into his chest and Aspen is now the one screaming.

Conrad is on the phone, no doubt to emergency services

and it's not until Conrad steps aside, I see Pacey on the ground, sobs pulling from his lungs as pain blankets him.

"Dad," I croak, tapping his hands that are cupping my face. "Go be with Pacey, I'm fine," I reassure him, and I can see how torn he feels. "He needs you more than me, dad."

"Here, I'll stay," Dixie says softly, tears streaming down her pretty face as she helps my dad up then takes his place, my head on her lap, her fingers brushing my hair from my face.

I watch as dad jogs over to where Pacey is laying, him unbuttoning his shirt before he falls to the ground and pushes it against Pacey's stomach as he screams.

And just as I roll my head around to look up at Dixie, my little dreamcatcher, the world around me goes black.

CHAPTER SEVENTEEN
DIXIE

I'll never forget what I saw when I was tucked inside the back of the truck.

I'll never forget the way I watched the bullet hit Harlow.

I'll never forget the way I watched Pacey hit the floor, a cloud of dust rising around him like his soul leaving his body as a bullet tore through his skin.

I'll never forget watching the man I love go down in slow motion as his horse was killed at the hands of Wallen.

I'll never forget the way Tripp cried out as his leg was crushed and a bullet burned beneath his skin.

I'll never forget the way Jorge ran over, ripping his shirt from his body to stop the bleeding in his son's stomach.

I'll never forget the way Austin cried over Harlow's lifeless body.

I'll never forget the way I snatched a man's life away by my own hand.

I'll never forget the way Pacey screamed in pain, choked sobs ringing through my ears.

I'll never forget the way I held Tripp's face in my hands as he passed out.

I'll never forget the way Orla screamed when we told her two of her sons were on their way to hospital.

I'll never forget the way Orla sobbed when we told her Harlow was dead.

I'll never forget the way Harlow's parents fell to their knees when Jorge told them that their daughter wasn't coming home.

I'll never forget the way the Rivera family were ripped limb from limb.

I'll never forget.

CHAPTER EIGHTEEN
DIXIE

I sit next to the crackling fire. I didn't want to leave the hospital, but Jorge basically dragged me away from Tripp's bedside as he was taken down to surgery. Not even sure why the fire is on, it's not particularly cold outside yet I can't stop shivering. A blanket is thrown around my shoulders and my fingers are wrapped around a hot cup of tea.

I think it's the shock.

The shock of what happened earlier in the day. And even though everything happened only a few hours ago, it feels like a lifetime has passed.

Orla is beside herself, muttering the Lord's prayer under her breath repeatedly.

I watch her pacing. Up and down, back and forth. Jorge is standing at the window, as if waiting for something to happen. He is on guard. Constantly.

Riggs told us he would keep us updated, but I couldn't just sit here. I needed to know that he was okay. I wanted to be there when he woke.

"Jorge," I say softly, placing my cup on the side table

next to me. He turns to look at me, eyes hollow, soul tired and face lifeless. "I want to be there when Tripp wakes up..." I stand slowly, shrugging the blanket off my shoulders.

"Dixie..." he tilts his head, and I don't miss the worry that wraps around his hoarse voice.

"Jorge," Orla steps towards her husband and places a hand on his chest where his heart sits. "Let her go, let her be by his side."

"I'll take Lainey..." I glance over at my beautiful daughter who is sitting on her play mat stacking blocks.

"No, leave her here with me," Orla smiles, "I could use the company."

"Why don't you come with me?" I step towards her, but she shakes her head, tears rolling down her cheeks.

"I can't, no, I'll stay home," she whispers as she picks up her pacing again.

I sigh, turning my attention to Lainey, blissfully unaware at what this cruel world has taken from us all today.

"Come," Jorge says softly and I walk over to my daughter, placing a kiss on the top of her head before scooping up my bag and following Jorge out to the truck, but now without our entourage of cowboys that ride in front and behind as we make our way down towards the hospital.

Jorge has his shotgun down the side of his door, eyes focused on the road ahead and I would be lying if I said I wasn't nervous.

What if they come back?

I shut the thoughts down instantly, I couldn't think like that.

They got what they wanted.

An eye for an eye.

Austin supposedly took Clay's life, so they took Harlow's.

Bile rises up my throat and the flashbacks replay over and over in my head. The way Tripp went down, the way Pacey fell to the floor and the way Harlow's lifeless eyes were on Austin, a tear running down her cheek as she took her last breath.

Choking out a sob, I drop my head into my hands.

I hear Jorge sigh before I feel a soft pat on my knee as I let the tears flow.

I cried for the duration of the journey.

My heart weeping, soul aching.

Today should have never happened.

And now we were all in mourning.

CHAPTER NINETEEN
TRIPP

ingers laced through Dixie's, we run towards the creek. We're laughing, carefree and down here, we didn't have to sneak around. No one knew where we were.

We met at school, we knew each other but hardly said two words to each other until her mom died. She became more secluded, withdrawn and I worried about her. One afternoon after school, I waited for her at the bottom of the steps and asked her out to the diner. Just for milkshake and burgers. I was waiting to be shot down into a ball of flames, but she said yes.

The conversation flowed, it was easy with her, like breathing. I didn't have to think about it, just knew what to do.

She didn't open up about her past, but we spent a long time speaking about her future.

So, from that day on, every Thursday I was studying in the library if you asked my family, but to me, I was courting Dixie.

I have no idea why we kept it a secret, but we both enjoyed it being something between just us. No one could ruin it, no one could take it from either of us.

It worked.

"You sure about this?" I ask, kicking off my cowboy boots

and unbuttoning my pants and she giggles, nodding her head as she unbuttons her pretty cream sundress and pushes it off her shoulders. The way her sun kissed skin basked in the glow of the low afternoon sun. Her dark hair wavy and blowing in the soft breeze, shimmering hints of copper that catch my eye every so often.

"So sure," she whispers just as her dress falls from her body and I groan in appreciation. She is picturesque. Beautiful. So, so, beautiful.

Lifting my tee above my head, I toss it into the pile of my clothes. I don't even care that I am standing in my boxers. Don't care that I am out in the open with just Dixie.

Because she is all I cared about.

We passed each other our hearts, both promised to keep them safe and never let them break.

I had fallen in love with her.

And it terrified me.

We stand for just a moment, eyes dancing together in a slow waltz. The summer breeze wraps us in her embrace, and I knew I needed to have her lips on mine. I didn't want to wait anymore.

Two steps forward and I was in front of her. My fingers fumble as I softly brush a strand of her hair away from her stunning blue eyes that glisten as she looks up at me. My hand cups her cheek, thumb brushing across her bottom lip and my heart skips a beat or two deep within my chest. Edging forward, my lips are on hers, slow and sensual without tongues and my body flames against hers, every nerve ending shot, my blood pumping hard in my ears and I am lost in her.

Her tongue creeps past my lips as our kiss deepens and I feel her body mould against mine.

Her fingers walk down my body before they're linked between mine, her lips breaking into a smile as she pulls away from me.

She drags me towards the creek and stops on the bed, her eyes playful and glistening as she slips her fingers from my hands.

My brows crinkle before she reaches up behind her, unhooking her bra and letting the straps fall down her arms and away from her perfect body. Next is her panties, she shimmies out of them and there, the love of my life, my wildest dream is standing there in front of me, baring all herself to me.

She steps into the calm water before plunging her body beneath the surface, a smirk still pressed against her lips.

"You coming to join me? Or you just going to stand there, chicken?" she teases, splashing water at me.

"I'm no chicken darlin'," I smirk, pushing my boxers down and off my feet as I step into the cool water and swim towards her, wrapping my arms around her and I groan when her legs circle my waist.

"I love you, Tripp Rivera, thank you for reminding me what it's like to feel alive again."

My heart throbs deep inside my chest.

"I love you, Dixie. Never did I think I could love someone as much as I love you. I want to be with you every waking minute, and in my dreams I am waiting for you to find me." I rub my nose against hers, "During the good, the bad, the ugly... you Dixie Walker, are the one that takes all the darkness from my life, the one who keeps me safe... the one who has my whole heart. You're my own little Dreamcatcher, Dixie. My wildest dream and it's one I never want to wake from."

Her lips crash into mine and that's how we spend our afternoon, limbs tangled on the bank of the creek, away from everything and anyone as we finally become one.

Mind. Body. Soul. Heart and Dreams.

She never did leave my dreams after that day.

And even now, as I lay here as my favorite day flashes

before my eyes, she is with me. Standing on the bank of the creek, wearing her pretty cream summer dress as she holds her hand out for me to take.

But I can't reach her.

I never can.

"Tripp," her voice is soft and in the distance.

I try to move, but I am grounded.

"Tripp, Tripp..." she continues calling my name, but it doesn't matter how hard I try, I just can't get to her and I watch as she fades away and that's when I am plunged back into darkness.

CHAPTER TWENTY
DIXIE

He looked so still.

"Tripp," I say softly, my hand resting on his chest. I am desperate for him to wake up. Desperate to see his beautiful brown eyes. "Tripp," I try again, my voice cracking. "Tripp..." I trail off and my heart shatters in my chest.

I hear footsteps by the door, and I lift my red rimmed eyes to Riggs. He is leaning against the door frame, arms crossed against his chest.

I palm my tears away and step back from the bed.

"You okay?" he asks, and I nod heavily, sniffling as I play with the hem of my dress. "You sure? Because you sure as hell don't like fine from where I am standing," he scoffs a soft laugh as he walks a little further into the hospital room.

I look up at him, his kind eyes pinned to mine and I break down when I feel his arms wrap around me, and I sob into his dirty and bloodied white shirt.

I don't even care.

Every one of us lost something today. Every one of our souls altered slightly after today.

"How's Pacey?" I ask, refusing to step out of his brotherly embrace.

"In the ICU, he lost a lot of blood, they think part of his spleen was damaged, but they just wanted to get the bullet removed, get the bleeding stopped and they will keep an eye on him." His low voice rumbles through his chest where my head rests, my eyes pinned to Tripp. "But the next forty-eight hours are critical."

I feel myself shiver.

"And Tripp?" I can barely manage to squeeze his name past my lips without a tear cascading down my cheek.

"It's going to be a long road to recovery. Ligament and muscle damage around his hip and pelvis, broken femur and fractured tibia. They've pinned and caged it..." he trails off and I know that, I can see the cage around his leg, can see the way the pins have penetrated through his skin, the dried blood stained. "The bullet went straight through the flesh in his shoulder. They said it was clean. No remnants of the bullet. Also, a few stitches in the back of his head from the fall."

I nod, not sure why.

"Have you had any news from Marty and Hudson?"

And I realise that I am still standing happily wrapped in Riggs' warm embrace and I know I can step away, but I don't want to. His hard exterior has been left at the door, and I am enjoying the softer side of Riggs. It won't be long before his walls are back up and his armour is on.

"Nothing as of yet, but they probably don't want to bother us."

"Ahem," I hear Aspen clearing her throat, but there is not an ounce of jealousy swarming in her voice.

"Hey Wildflower," he looks over his shoulder and smiles at his fiancée.

"Hey," she smiles, pushing onto her toes and placing a kiss on his lips.

I push away, eyes red and watery.

Aspen's eyes meet mine, and she throws herself at me, holding me close to her.

"It'll be okay," she whispers and my heart sinks.

"How are you doing?" I find myself asking, Harlow was her best friend, her sister from another mister. "And Austin?"

"Austin is..." she pauses, her eyes glassing.

My heart.

Her lips part but then they close again, her bottom lip trembles.

"I am so sorry," I whisper and now it's my turn to comfort her.

We hold onto each other, when we hear a croak of a voice.

We all turn to face Tripp as his eyes flutter open. He blinks a few times, eyes moving slowly between us all.

"Tripp," I whisper, heart stuttering in my chest and he gives me a small smile, lips pulling at the corners.

"Hey Dixie," and my feet are moving towards him.

"I'll go get the doc," Riggs says quietly, leading Aspen from the room.

Sitting on the edge of the bed, I'm mindful to be gentle and not to cause him any discomfort.

Reaching forward, I brush his hair from his face as my eyes settle on his.

"I dreamt of you," he rasps.

"Did you?" I choke on a sob, tears threatening to fall.

He nods, closing his own eyes as he swallows.

"It was the afternoon we went down to the creek... you in that pretty cream sundress," he smirks a boyish grin and my heart jack hammers in my chest. "The way the water glistened over our bodies," he continues, and my breath catches in the back of my throat.

"Always dream of that moment, the best of the best," he sighs, moving slightly and he winces, head thrown back into his pillow as he grits his teeth.

I stand up, slightly panicked.

"Was it me? Did I hurt you?"

"No, baby, no," his glistening brown eyes seek mine out. *Baby.*

I go to sit back down but Riggs walks through the door with the doctor.

"Tripp," he smiles over at him, and I take that as my cue to step away.

Moving for the door, Tripp calls out, "Dixie?"

"I'm just going to the restroom," I give a small smile and he meets me with his own before I walk out the door and leave the man that I once loved; but the truth was, I have never fallen out of love with him.

So, what do I do?

I run.

CHAPTER TWENTY-ONE
TRIPP

Panic swarms me when I see Dixie moving for the door in which my brother and the doctor just came through.

"Dixie?" I call out.

"I'm just going to the restroom," she gives me a small smile, eyes glistening with something but I have no idea what. My own smile slips onto my lips just as she disappears, and I instantly miss her.

What is happening to me?

"Tripp," the young male doctor smiles at me as Riggs falls into the chair beside me with a low growl.

"Hey doc," I wink at him, as he reaches for my chart just a nurse walks in behind him to check my monitor.

"How are you feeling?" his head tilts to the side as his eyes bounce between mine.

"Better than I look," I smirk, and I hear the nurse giggle softly.

"That's good," he nods, flipping over the paper on my chart, "we cleaned your bullet wound up and made sure there was no remnants of any kind. A bit of physio on your shoulder and you'll be good as new," he chimes, and I watch as his face drops slightly but I don't miss it.

"But?" I ask and I hear Riggs clear his throat.

"Your leg..." he looks up from his chart. "It was bad Tripp; you were in surgery a long time. Your pelvis wasn't broken and honestly, I am shocked. Muscle and ligament damage around your pelvis and hip, your femur is broken, and your tibia is fractured... along with a few broken toes. Not to mention you had concussion when you came in. We did carry out the relevant scans to make sure there were no bleeds on the brain, and you were all clear."

"So, you fixed me back together again," my eyes cast down to my caged leg.

"We did, few pins here and there... couple of bolts," he gives a boyish grin, and I nod. "But it's going to be a long recovery. You're going to have to have rehabilitation for your walking; physio and so on..."

"How long before I am on the back of a horse again?"

My heart feels heavy at the mention of riding again, my mind flashes to Bucky. The way that coward shot at my horse, killing him instantly. He took my horse's life. The horse I always loved a little more than the others... he destroyed him in under a minute.

"All in all... with the breaks you have, around two to three months."

My eyes widen.

"But, it will depend on when you're up and about and well... we won't know for sure."

"Get me up now," I throw the covers back and try and move myself, hissing as I do with pain shocking through my body.

"Brother," Riggs is beside me, hand resting on my good shoulder as he shakes his head from side to side.

"You need to rest, Tripp. You can leave hospital in a few days, but not until we know you have a set up at home."

"We're going to move you into dad's office," Riggs says softly.

I throw my head back on the pillow and nod, swallowing down the large burning lump that has lodged itself there.

"I'll be back to check on you soon, nurse Sarah will administer another dose of pain killers," and just like that, he is gone.

"Pacey?" I turn to look at my older brother.

"Stable, but critical. Lost a lot of blood. They had a lot to repair, they think his spleen is damaged, but they were more focused on getting the bullet out and stopping the bleeding." And I watch the way Riggs' face changes. He looks haunted.

"I want to kill every single one of them," hot tears burn my cheeks as they cascade down, my jaw tight as I grind my back teeth.

"Don't you worry brother, they'll get what they deserve."

"You promise?"

"I never break a promise," he grunts. I raise my brows. "Fuck you," he shakes his head.

"Can you grab Dixie for me?" He sighs and walks out the room and I am alone whilst I wait for Dixie to return.

My dreamcatcher.

Riggs steps back in, popping his head around the doorframe.

"She's gone."

"What do you mean she's gone?"

"She's not here. Restrooms are empty, she ain't in the waiting room... it's like she's disappeared."

I try to sit up and wince.

"I'll go find her." He nods, whistling as he walks out the room and I see a handful of his cowboys following him down the hallway.

Don't leave me now.

CHAPTER TWENTY-TWO
DIXIE

I have no idea why I ran to here, but I did.

Looking at the derelict house that sits on a large field, tucked alongside the creek, it was very picturesque when I was a child. Now, not so much. Nothing but harboured bad memories here.

I deserved so much more than the hand I was dealt. But I was never the 'woe is me' type.

My legs begin to move towards the wrap around porch, which has seen better days. Wood weathered, some beams broken, some missing completely, which cements the fact that my dad just up and left. I have no idea if he is still running Mules. But I would be shocked if he was.

Stepping cautiously onto the porch, I inhale deeply as I step back and look out at the view. The mountains stand tall and proud, the dusk settling in just over the snow tipped tops. Always loved this view. The sound of the creek trickling by, it was the same creek that ran through Rivera Ranch and The Oaks, but this is where the mouth of the creek was.

Our house felt like it was at the base of the mountains,

even though it wasn't, you would think that if you saw how it sat.

It was such a beautiful plot.

Not so much anymore.

Moving forward, my hand reaches out as I push gently on the front door and my brows crinkle when it doesn't open. Not sure why I am shocked.

I turn and find myself sitting on the top step of the porch. I should go back home. And by home, I don't mean Rivera Ranch. I mean to Wyoming. I don't belong here. My past will eventually catch up with me, Lucian is no doubt still here, hopefully with a bullet through his skull, but if he is still alive and kicking, he will sniff me out. He won't leave without me in his grasps.

My chest aches.

Hate that I ran out on Tripp.

I just needed some fresh air.

Realising that I was still utterly in love with him suffocated me. Seeing him lying in that bed, pinned and caged... I couldn't breathe. I needed out, and truthfully, I don't think I can break my heart or his again. The thought of losing him is too much to even think about.

Dropping my head into my hands, I sigh. It had been such a long day.

"Well, well, well..." I hear his voice before I see him and my skin prickles with goosebumps. Slowly lifting my head, my eyes meet his.

Lucian.

"Pretty good aim for a useless little girl."

I crinkle my nose, arms wrapped around my knees that are bent up.

I wish I could ignore him.

"Not that useless when I shot one of your guys dead

with a bullet to the temple," I shake my head from side to side.

He laughs.

I drop my head again, not wanting to give into the fear that is currently crippling me as the seconds pass.

His boots scuffle across the dirt that sits just in front of me, and my eyes are pinned to them, dirty and scuffed.

"We're leaving in four weeks, I suggest you get yourself packed up."

Snapping my head up to look at him, my eyes widen.

"Who said I am leaving?"

He rolls his eyes. "We have a show…"

"There is no *we*. I am not leaving. I don't want to leave with you."

He lowers himself in front of me, black eyes on me.

"Who said you had a choice?" he reaches out and grabs the top of my arm, squeezing tightly as he drags me to my feet. "Remember why you came back here, Dixie? This was always the plan." His finger runs across my bottom lip, "We already eradicated one problem; the focus is the gold mines. We said we would split it three ways… Unlike some *greedy* assholes."

"I didn't want to be part of the plan, I left you, I gave you all I had and told you it was over," I try and pull my arm from his grip, but he just tightens it. "I came back here for Clay, and to get what is rightfully mine—his money—I need it for Lainey. I don't care about anything else; I have no interest in being your mole."

The sound of the back of Lucian's hand marking my cheek fills the emptiness, my head spinning from the force and tears sting behind my eyes. "If you do not do as I say, I will take the Rivera Family out one by fucking one and make you watch as I sink a bullet between their eyes." His tone is cold, heartless, "Then I'll kill Lainey."

Swallowing the bile that coats my throat, my eyes fill with unshed tears.

"And I mean it Dixie, I want to know everything those bastard boys are up to in regard to the gold mines, that's my golden ticket, and if you play along, it'll be yours too,"

he shoves me back and I fall onto the steps of my childhood home with a crash, pain radiating up my back.

"Do you understand me?" he asks, his eyes steady on mine and all I do is nod.

"Good," he stands tall, brushing his hands off of invisible dust. "Wallen is meeting up with the big suits that Clay was in dealings with next week, so hopefully he gets a move on with taking over the land too. We're sitting on a damn goldmine... *literally.*"

I stay mute.

"I'll see you in four weeks," Lucian says and I bury my head back in my hands, and when I finally look up, he is gone.

CHAPTER TWENTY-THREE
RIGGS

Galloping along the creek, I am starting to panic when I can't find her. She wasn't back home at the ranch, mom said she hadn't seen her since dad run her back to the hospital.

I'm not one to panic normally. But after what happened today, I am on high alert.

I approach the edge of the town, just at the foot of the mountains, when I see a little beaten up house and I realise it's Dixie's childhood home. Kicking Travis on, I gallop across the dirt track that leads me to where I see Dixie sitting, head tucked onto her knees, arms wrapped around them. She looks so small sitting there.

"Dixie?" I say softly, and her head lifts, eyes red rimmed from her tears. "Shit," I grunt, jumping down off Travis and jogging towards her as I kneel down. "Who hurt you? Are you okay?" and she sort of nods but then shakes her head from side to side, tears rolling down her cheeks. "Come," I say, offering her my hand and after a moment or two, she takes it and I pull her to her feet.

We stand in silence for a moment, her face turned away

from me as she looks across the empty plane in front of us. I tilt my head as I look at her, it's as if she has the world on her shoulders.

"Wanna talk about it?"

She shakes her head before finally meeting my worried gaze.

"Let's get you home." She steps towards the horse, eyes widening. "Shit," I hiss, "I forgot you don't know how to ride."

Her cheeks pinch crimson.

"It's fine," I sigh, nudging her towards Travis. "Grab the reins," and as she does, I foot her into his saddle and once her feet are into the stirrups, I take her reins into my hands, and I walk us back towards the ranch in complete silence.

Tying Travis up, I help her off and she mutters the word 'thanks' before disappearing into the house. I want to follow, want to ask if something happened, but it's not my place. Mom will get it out of her no doubt.

"Riggs," I hear the sound of Hudson's deep gravel of a voice.

"Yeah?"

"A word?" he nods his head towards the bunkhouse, and I grunt. I am exhausted. I just want to go home and curl up next to Aspen and sleep this shitty day off.

Following behind him, he opens the door and I walk in after him.

"What's wrong?" I cross my arms across my chest.

"We followed those two guys, no one got hurt."

"What a shame," I let out a soft chuckle, "their names are Lucian and Wallen," I nod.

"We think there is some connection between Tripp's girl and the Attaways."

I raise my brows. Of course, I know this is true, but I am intrigued to where this conversation is going.

"I sent the rest of the guys away, then I tucked myself away. As they got out the car that Lucian guy was talking about getting Dixie back to Wyoming, but Wallen told him to hold off a few weeks because he is meeting the suits that Clay was dealing with... then they were going on about that place Mules and how everything will come full circle..." he pauses for a moment, "I heard them say about killing Lainey if the plan doesn't work."

And my blood boils.

No fucking way am I going to let those two cunts anywhere near Lainey or Dixie for that matter. I may not like the girl much, but I can tell who she is to Tripp and because of that I care enough for her to protect her at all costs.

"They won't get a chance to get near her."

Hudson nods, and I can see concern etched into his face.

"Is there something else?" I ask as I begin to walk towards the door of the bunkhouse, his skittishness has me on edge.

"They're coming for Austin."

I swallow.

"They can fucking try," I grunt, as I march towards the house, slamming the door behind me as I scan the room for my brothers. The two I would call for a family meeting, the two that would be stood by my side... and then it hits me.

Neither of them are here.

I'm all alone in this war that the Attaway's have brought onto my family.

Realization sinks and settles deep into the crevices of my chest.

Dixie and Lainey are my family.

CHAPTER TWENTY-FOUR
TRIPP

I'm not alone for very long when Aspen walks through the door.

"Hey," she smiles, sadness still evident in her pretty hazel eyes.

"Hey," I sigh as she sits in the chair next to me. "How are you?" I ask first, having to remember that she watched her best friend get murdered.

She drops her head, her fingers twisting her engagement ring around her finger. I wish I could take all her pain away.

Wish I could make all of this disappear.

Wish I could go back in time and stop all of this from happening.

"I'm so sorry Aspen," and she finally looks at me, tears dampening her cheeks and she gives a little nod.

"I just..." she tries to speak but stops herself, shaking her head from side to side.

"I know," I reason with her, I have no idea if it'll even make her feel better, but she shuffles forward and scoops my hand into hers, her thumb brushing back and forth across the back of it.

"You doing okay?" she asks me now and my heart thumps inside my chest.

"I've been better," I smirk, head resting into the pillow.

"I bet, you've been through it."

I nod.

"This is nothing in comparison to what Pacey has endured... and..." I went to mention Harlow but stopped myself.

"Don't invalidate your own trauma and injuries," she scolds, wrinkles forming on her forehead as she furrows her brows.

"Sorry," I roll my lips and I sigh.

"Where's Dixie?" she suddenly asks, looking around the room.

"No idea, haven't seen her in a couple of hours... Riggs went looking for her."

"Oh," she sounds surprised, but I am not sure if she is surprised about Riggs or Dixie running.

"Mm," I hum just as my phone buzzes. "Can you grab that for me?" I ask Aspen and she stands and reaches for my phone that is sitting on the bed table at the foot of the bed. She passes it to me, and I see Rusty's message.

> **RUSTY**
>
> Heard about the funeral, fuck man, my thoughts and prayers are with you all. Send my love to Austin.

I swallow the lump down of the reminder that is burned into my retinas.

ME

Thanks man, I appreciate it.

RUSTY

Btw, cars done. No rush. Took a little longer
than expected as had to wait for parts but
all good to go.

ME

Thanks, might need you to hold onto it a bit
longer. I'll be out of action for a while.

RUSTY

No problem. Rest up. Look after you.

Letting my phone rest on my lap, I look up at Aspen.

"What a complete shit show."

She scoffs a laugh, and her bottom lip trembles before she breaks down again.

"Aspen," I sigh, she's breaking my heart.

I lift my arm up as she rests her head on my chest, and I comfort her whilst she cries.

Aspen is so much more than just my brother's fiancée, she is family, she is my sister. We grew up together and when all the shit went down between Pacey, Riggs and Aspen, I was the only one she would talk to, until Riggs told me to back the fuck down, and annoyingly I did. Then she up and left. Broke all of our hearts in the process, just not as much as she broke Riggs'.

Riggs appears at the door, he looks pissed off. Permanent scowl on his face, heavy footsteps on his way towards the room and hands balled by his side, but as soon as he sees Aspen, everything disappears. He scoops her up, holding her to his chest as she sobs silently into his shirt.

"I am going to run her home; I'll be back soon..." and the look he gives me is not a good one. Something has happened. "Dixie is safe," he mutters just as he walks out of my room and relief swarms me in an instant.

Time slips by and my eyes feel heavy. Letting them close for a moment, I can feel myself drifting in and out of sleep when there is a knock on my door.

"Yeah," I say muffled, refusing to open my eyes.

The sound of the boots hitting the floor and the clink of the spur spinning has my eyes bolting open. I knew who it was before I even looked.

Sheriff Kelcie.

"Well, hello Tripp," a lopsided smirk pulls at his lips, thumbs tucked into his belt loops and a dark brown cowboy hat covering his balding hair.

"What do I owe the pleasure?" I sigh, closing my eyes again, hands resting on my lap, fingers interlocked.

"Just thought I would pop in and check in on my *favorite* Rivera brother."

"Cut the bullshit," I scoff.

"Fine," he sighs, "I need to know what the fuck went down at Clay Attaway's funeral," he pauses for a moment as he drags the chair that sits in the corner of the room along the lino floor tiles and sits right next to my bed.

His breath is rancid.

I turn my face away from him for a moment.

"You know what went down," I roll my eyes.

"I do, but what I can't seem to understand is that whenever you and your brothers are anywhere near the Attaway's there is violence."

I go to open my mouth but slam it shut, before starting again.

"Sounds like you're picking sides, Kelcie."

He scoffs, shaking his head from side to side.

"I only pick the innocent side Tripp, the side that matches the badge that sits on my belt."

"*My* badge."

"Technically, it's *my* badge. You gave it to me."

"Leant it to you," I raise my brows, "don't get it twisted Kelcie."

He laughs, tipping his head back and I have never wanted to punch someone in the throat as much as I do this dickhead.

"We will see what happens when you're back on your feet, aye Rivera," he leans in and snarls, his hand on my shoulder as he pushes his thumb into my bullet hole wound, and I scream out.

"Get the fuck off him," my brother's voice bellows around the room and Kelcie shrinks back into his seat, but Riggs is fuming. His temper is short, and I can see in his eyes he has lost it. Grabbing Kelcie by the scruff of his shirt, he drags him out of the room and tosses him down the hallway of the hospital.

"I'll have you charged for that Rivera!"

"Try it, where are your witnesses?" and Kelcie stands from the floor, and I watch as he looks up and down the hallway. "Exactly, now fuck off Kelcie, don't come anywhere near my family again," and Kelcie knows better than to not listen to Riggs.

He steps back inside the room and grunts when he sees blood trickling down my chest. Reaching for the call button, he presses it over and over until someone comes in, but I have no idea what happens after because I black out.

CHAPTER TWENTY-FIVE
DIXIE

Tucked into an armchair, I have Aspen's latest book on my lap but I'm not reading. My mind is with Tripp. My mind is on the stupid threat Lucian has now hung around my neck like a noose, and as the hours go on, I can feel it getting tighter.

Orla walks into the room and hands me a cup of cocoa, and I feel like a fraud. Both of her sons are in hospital and she is the one waiting on me. Make that make sense.

"Orla," I sigh, taking the cup from her, "please, sit down, let me fix you some food," I offer, a small smile pulling on my lips.

"Don't be silly," she waves me away, shaking her head from side to side.

I lift my eyes to watch her as she potters around an already pristine living room. She hasn't slept for more than a couple of hours a night, and once she is up, she is constantly busying herself. The ranch, the house, Lainey... we've tried to step in but she shoos us away. It's her coping mechanism, I guess.

"Can I do anything?" I offer like always, but she just

spins to look at me, tilting her head and giving me a lopsided smile.

"No darlin', you just enjoy your book," she gives me a wink and then disappears out the room.

Sighing, I close the book on my lap and let my head rest onto the back of the armchair.

A moment or two passes and I roll my head around to see a tired Jorge walking through the door, kicking his boots off and reaching for the door frame as he holds himself up. He looks dishevelled and exhausted.

I push up from the sofa, stepping towards where he is standing and wrapping my fingers softly around the top of his arm, rubbing gently.

"You okay Jorge?" I ask, concern lacing my voice.

"Yes sweet girl," he stands a little taller and gives me a smile.

"Sure?" my lip twitches at the corner.

"Sure," he nods his head as he lifts his cowboy hat and walks across the hall to hang it up.

"I'll go down the hospital and do the night shift," I speak a little louder, heart thrumming in my chest.

"You don't need to do that," he sighs.

"I know I don't need to, but I want to."

"Riggs can go with you."

"Riggs was on last night, he is exhausted. Conrad?"

Jorge rubs his chin like he is thinking.

"Take Hudson down with you. Don't want to get Conrad mixed up in this anymore than he already is."

I give him a shallow nod and walk into the living room to collect my belongings before climbing the stairs and grabbing a crochet blanket from the foot of my bed and a few other little things I may need. Lainey stirs behind me in her crib, and I feel an ache present itself deep inside my chest.

Leaning over her, I stroke her brown hair, soft whimpers leave her, and I just want to scoop her into my arms and run far, far away. But I couldn't.

I am too grounded here. Anchored even. Even thinking about leaving hits me right between the shoulder blades with force, winding me in an instant.

Lifting my hand from Lainey's head, I step back, clutching my bag and tossing it over my shoulder. Walking out the room, I pull it until a small gap is all there is stopping the door from hitting the doorframe.

Walking downstairs, Jorge and Orla are nowhere to be seen, but standing in the large lobby is Hudson.

"Ma'am," he lifts his hat from his head, uncovering curly blond hair. His eyes are piercing green and his skin has a glorious sun-kissed glow to it.

"Hudson," I smile before walking into the living room and seeing Jorge and Orla cuddled up asleep on the sofa, Lainey's baby monitor wrapped in Orla's clutch. My heart skips a beat or two as I look at them both. Bending, I grab a blanket from the blanket box and cover the both of them up.

Walking towards the armchair I was tucked into, I grab my book and begin walking back towards Hudson.

"Ready?" he asks as he opens the front door for me to take and I give him a soft nod.

The drive is silent as I watch the pretty pink sky settle over the mountains of our hometown. Hudson keeps looking over at me, checking on me to make sure I am okay. But honestly, I have no idea how I should feel.

I feel guilty for taking a man's life, but that same man

took the life of Harlow. My daughter's uncle shot Pacey Rivera and Tripp, the only man I have ever loved.

If I could have, I would have taken them all down.

But I couldn't.

Tilting my head, I look down at my hands. They're clean with no marks, yet all I see is them tainted with blood.

"Get out your head, kid," Hudson mutters as we pull into the hospital car park, and I snort a laugh. "Think about the future, not what's going on right here, right now. The Rivera boys will be alright, they're made different. A little bullet isn't going to keep them down for long. Kids are wild at heart, like mustangs, you can't keep them pent up for too long."

I turn my face to look at him, my eyes feeling heavy with unshed tears.

"Come," he says as he puts the truck into park and jumps down, then opens my door and helps me down.

We walk in silence towards the reception, Hudson giving the reception ladies a little nod as he walks past and their cheeks blush a pretty pink. He is very easy on the eye, but he is no Tripp Rivera.

The ward is quiet, the sound of machines beeping softly in the background as we walk down the long corridor to where Pacey is. Walking into the room, my heart stutters in my chest as I see the boy who is like a ray of sunshine laying lifeless with a tube in his mouth and hooked up to a machine.

"Hey Pace," I whisper as I walk into the room and take a seat next to him. I am unsure what to even say to him and I am sure I am the last person he would want to see here, but I don't want him to be alone.

I turn to look at Hudson and he gives me a nod.

"I'll go sit with Tripp, come down when you're ready

and we will switch it out," I smile at him just as he walks out the room and disappears.

"Everyone is real worried about you," I say softly, hand reaching for his. "Austin misses you, he really needs you." I sigh for a moment, "He is lost; not only has he lost Harlow, but he has kind of lost you too in a way. You're the person he would turn to if you were at home," I rub my thumb across the back of his hand, my eyes pinned to his handsome face. "Wake up now Pace, show everyone just what you're made of," I whisper through a tear that rolls down my cheek. "Please," my voice trembles and I think everything has hit me.

Tripp.

Pacey.

Orla.

Jorge.

Lucian.

Even Harlow.

I begin to hum softly, my eyes closing as I begin to sing a song I wrote years ago when my mom gave me my first guitar.

I repeat the bridge as I fade my voice out and back to a hum.

My eyes stay pinned to Pacey's face. No one deserves this. Especially not Pacey. He is the kindest kid I have ever known. Will always show up for you, will always have your back.

Sighing, I let go of his hand for just a moment and sit back, losing myself in the silence.

Soft shakes make me sit bolt upright, and I see Hudson with a sappy smile on his face.

"Wakey wakey, it's time to switch," he whispers, and I rub the sleep out of my eyes.

"Any change?" He asks, standing tall and looking over his shoulder, but I shake my head from side to side. "Damn," he lifts his hat from his head and places it on the foot of Pacey's bed.

"He will wake up, won't he?" I ask as I push from the chair.

I watch as Hudson's brows crinkle for just a moment, a line forming on the bridge of his nose.

"I hope so, ma'am. I really do hope so."

The walk is short down to where Tripp is, and nerves rattle inside of me. I ran from him yesterday and never gave him an explanation. I panicked. Things were getting a little too... I suck in a breath as I stand outside his door. Giving myself a second, I step into the room and am surprised to see him awake.

His eyes light up, the smooth lines at the crease of his eyes disappearing as he smiles at me.

"You came back."

I nod, fingers locked together as I walk cautiously over to the seat next to his bed, but he reaches out for me, fingers wrapping around my wrist as he tugs me towards him.

My eyes widen but a boyish grin pulls at his lips.

The same boyish grin he would flash me when we were both up to no good.

"Tripp," I whisper as he pulls me into his arms.

"You're never running from me again Dixie Walker," he breathes as he wraps his arms around me, holding me close to him. He hisses in as I try to move but he doesn't let me.

"I..." I pause for a moment, bodies flush, and I push up, mindful not to hurt him by putting my full weight on him. Riggs must have told him. My blue eyes bounce between his deep brown pools and my heart hammers in my chest.

One of his hands brushes up and tucks a strand of my hair away from my face and behind my ear.

"I never stopped loving you Dixie, not for even one day," he whispers, and I swallow the large lump that has formed in my throat. "Tell me you never stopped loving me," he asks on a beg, the sound of his voice cracking.

"Not for even one day," I whisper back, eyes filling with tears.

"Then promise not to leave me, promise not to run away from me again. My heart couldn't stand it."

I lower my face as a tear rolls down my cheek and drops onto his bare chest.

"I can't promise you that," I choke on my words.

They way he pulls in a breath has me feeling guilty, like my words were too painful for him to hear, his chest aching as if it was too hard for him to breathe.

"Then promise me tonight," his eyes are back on mine, burning into the depths of my soul.

"I promise," I nod as his hand cups my cheek, his thumb brushing away a rogue tear that trickles down as our lips edge closer.

His breath catches at the back of his throat the moment our lips touch and I melt into him. Tongues dancing, his hands are in my hair as I cup his face with mine.

"I can't wait to get home," he whispers against my lips, his eyes lowered watching my mouth.

"And why is that?" I whisper back.

"Because I need you Dixie, I want to trace my fingers over every single freckle, mole, scar and blemish on your skin, I want to remember what it feels like to have you, to remember the way your skin melted against my fingertips, the way you taste on my tongue... I want to remember it all Dreamcatcher."

My heart is weeping deep inside my chest. Because I want all of that too, but Lucian's threat is too loud in my mind.

"Why Dreamcatcher?" I ask, my voice a whisper as I try and change the subject.

"Because you take all the bad away, keep me safe in the storms Dix... you make me feel peace." His hands are still cupping my face and I lean into him, "I don't feel haunted when you're here," and his lips are back on mine and that's how we spend our evening until I fall asleep on his chest, comforted by the noise of a hundred soft galloping horses replacing his heartbeat.

***

THE MORNING SUN shines through the metal slated blinds and it takes me a moment to realise where I am. Slowly pushing myself up, Tripp is still softly snoring. Creeping from the bed, his hand darts out and wraps around my wrist.

"You promised," his voice is gruff, eyes still closed.

"I'm just moving off you," I whisper through a smile.

"Okay, I'll let you off," his fingers uncurl and rest on his stomach.

"You feeling okay?"

He rolls his head to face me.

"Apart from feeling like a horny teenager, I feel great," and I giggle.

"Well, I don't think you'll be up for any loving anytime soon," I scrunch my nose.

"Oh don't you worry about that baby, I'm sure we can make it work... I remember the way those hips moved when you were on to—"

"Woah!" Riggs bellows into the room and my cheeks burn red.

"Don't you dare *woah* me," Tripp shakes his head, a soft laugh filling the room and it's up there with one of my favorite sounds, parked right next to Lainey's laugh. "I walked in and actually caught you eating—"

"Enough boys," Aspen walks in rolling her eyes. Hands full of coffees from Sunny's and two brown bags. "Who's hungry?"

"Famished," Riggs groans as Aspen hands me a coffee cup and I lift the lid and smile, then shoves a brown bag in my face.

"You remembered my order?"

"I did," she winks, "I mean if it was one of those fancy mojo dojo coffees then you would have had no hope in me remembering," she laughs as she walks towards Tripp and kisses him on the forehead before dragging his bed table over him and placing a coffee and a breakfast bap down for him.

"This smells so good, so much better than the shit they serve here," he smirks as he peeps inside the bag.

"Only the best for you Tripp Rivera," she beams at him and Riggs coughs. "Yours is coming darlin, don't be getting jealous now big man," she winks, patting Riggs on the chest before handing him a coffee and his own breakfast bap.

He grunts in response and Tripp's eyes are on me as I grab my bag.

"Where you going?" the panic is evident in his voice.

"Nowhere," I reassure him as I sit down and reach for my book.

"Oh," he nods, then whistles to get Aspen's attention, brows raising towards me and what I am reading.

"Oh my god," she jumps up and down as she watches

me opening my book. "You're reading *my* book!?" she screeches, and Riggs closes one eye, tilting his head as her screech pierces all of our eardrums.

"I am," I smile at her, eyes glassy at how happy she is.

"And... are you enjoying it?!"

"Devouring it," I nod, taking a mouthful of my coffee and licking my lips. "Must admit though... the cowboy is a bit of a grumpy ass isn't he," I raise my brows as I look at Riggs through my lashes.

Aspen sighs, tucking herself under her fiancé's arm and pats him on the chest.

"Yeah, he is, but trust me, he redeems himself."

"Not long till your signing, you getting excited?" Tripp asks and we watch as Aspen's face falls and she turns her face up to look at Riggs.

"I've cancelled," and I see the way her shoulders sag forward. "I couldn't leave, not after everything that has happened."

I nod silently.

"So sorry Aspen," Tripp mutters as he lifts his coffee cup to his lips.

"Don't be sorry," she smiles at him and my heart swells.

"There is always next year," Riggs wraps his arm around her small frame and pulls her into him, placing a kiss on the top of her head.

Silence crackles around the room before Hudson runs through the door.

"Pacey is awake," he rushes his words out.

"Let's go," Riggs places his coffee and food down on the table and follows after Hudson.

Me, Aspen and Tripp sit and wait.

The last thing he will want is everyone crowding his room.

"Can you call my mom and let—"

"Already on it," Aspen smiles as she lifts the phone to her ear.

Tripp throws her a wink before his sole attention is on me, his boyish grin painted onto his face and my heart skips a beat.

And just like that, we're teens again.

CHAPTER TWENTY-SIX
TRIPP

Never did I think that I would be dressed in another black suit so soon.

Difference was, this time, it was someone on our side.

I would be lying if I said it's been all rainbows and sunshine since I have been home from hospital; it's been hell.

But I won't give up.

"Ready?" Dixie's soft voice pulls me from my thoughts, her hand resting on my shoulder. Looking up at her, I smile. She is so beautiful. Wrapping my fingers around her delicate wrist, I lower my lips and kiss softly over her pulse point.

Mom and dad are waiting outside for me, Pacey is up and about, slowly, but he is up. I cast my eyes to my crutches, but I know it's going to be a long day, I don't know if I have it in me to be on my feet all day.

Sighing, I push the brake off my wheelchair and Dixie

begins pushing me until we're at the edge of the porch. Riggs and Hudson lift me down and I hate it.

I try to hide my shame, but I can't.

She catches me.

She always does.

She gives me a sad smile and I hate it. Hate seeing her sad. Especially over me.

Mom hands Lainey to Dixie, and she holds her close as Conrad begins to push me towards the truck.

"You doing okay?" He asks me softly, and I shrug my shoulder up.

"Been better," I huff as Riggs pulls me from my chair and I stand and hobble myself to the truck, but before I can even try and get myself in, Riggs is lifting me in.

"There we go," he half smiles and I hide my face from him. My throat burns as I try and swallow down the thickness, try and blink the tears away before anyone sees them.

Dixie slides in next to me before putting Lainey into her car chair and buckling her in.

Her hand rests on my thigh, and I turn away from her, looking out the window as Riggs puts my chair into the bed of the truck.

Dad and Mom ride with us. Pacey rides with Riggs, Aspen and Austin. Blue and Buck follow in their own trucks and I am already dreading the next few hours.

None of us were ready for this day.

How could we be?

We were burying one of our own.

I am overcome with emotion, and it doesn't matter how much I try and stop it from seeping from me, I can't.

Dixie peeks at me under the rim of my cowboy hat,

before her hand is buried inside of mine. And as we begin to drive, I choke on silent sobs.

Suddenly, everything has got a little heavier.

THE SKIES ARE GRAY, clouds thick and full of the tears of God. We all wait outside, all dressed in black as we wait for the horse and carriage to arrive with Harlow's casket.

Austin stands at the front of the church along with Joy and James, and Harlow's kid brother Harrison.

His head is bowed, his shoulders shaking softly as he cries and fuck, he breaks my damn heart.

The sound of hooves has us all looking to the left as two beautiful Friesians trot softly across the gravel of the church parking lot, Harlow's wicker casket tied to the back. Aspen's sobs echo as Riggs holds her tightly, letting her tears soak his shirt. A lot of her pain will be masked with guilt. They lost so much time together.

Austin begins walking down with Harrison and James, Riggs pushes Aspen into Pacey's arms as Conrad and my dad step forward ready to carry Harlow into her final journey.

Tears stream down Austin's face and all I want to do is wrap him in my arms and hold him tightly.

Joy drops her head, shaking it from side to side as if in utter disbelief that this day is here. The day that she is burying her little girl.

Harlow was well loved throughout our small town and to see the crowds standing here waiting to say their goodbyes is something to feel proud of.

Sunny stands next to Aspen, her head ducking every now and again to make sure she is okay.

The carriage drivers slide her casket off slowly and into the hands of the pallbearers.

They all listen as the undertakers tell them what to do, and on the count of three, she is lifted onto their shoulders.

And that's when Joy loses it, falling down to her knees and my mom rushes over to her, trying with all of her might to pull her to her feet. Dixie slips her hand from mine as she moves quickly over to Joy's side and helps my mom lift her.

"We've got you," Dixie says softly as they begin leading her into the church. Joy's screams will haunt me for the rest of my life.

The undertaker begins walking in front of the casket as the boys carry her into the church, and we all follow. I wheel myself, not wanting to take the attention away from the people that need to be comforted. Wheeling myself up the ramp of the church, I puff as I move into where the ceremony will be taking place, mindful not to take anyone out with the leg rest of my chair.

As the casket enters the church, *pink skies - Zach Bryan* begins to play.

I watch as they place Harlow's casket onto the catafalque and they all step back, apart from James and Austin. Their hands stay resting on the lid, Austin sobs and James wraps his arms around his shoulders.

I swallow down the lump that is swelling as the seconds pass.

Listening to the song, my heart breaks a little more and this song is so fitting for all of us. The way we all grew up together. The best of friends until the very end.

The church is filled with sniffles, quiet sobs and some loud. The pastor clears his throat as he begins the ceremony where we all say goodbye to our friend.

We say goodbye to our Harlow.

Here without you - 3 Doors Down plays as we exit the church, Harlow back on the shoulders of the pallbearers as they lead us to her final resting place. Tucked under a cherry blossom tree just before the creek. We used to hang out around the church as kids, this cherry tree was one of our many climbing adventures.

A smile pulls at my lips as I remember the fond memories, but the fond is soon forgotten as I watch them lower her into the ground and my chest aches.

"Ashes to ashes, dust to dust..." the pastor says as he throws dirt onto her casket and the rest of us throw soft yellow roses into where she lays.

My eyes move to Austin who has his hands fisted into his pockets, eyes red rimmed and swollen as tears freely flow down his cheeks.

He is the last to throw his rose, and once he does, he shakes his head from side to side before turning on his heel and walking away.

Me, Riggs and Pacey all exchange looks but Riggs shakes his head softly, and we know not to follow. He needs his space. He needs some time. He has just put the love of his life to rest, where she'll find peace whilst he lives in eternal hell until the day they meet again.

We're the last to leave, and when we do, the drive is silent and slow.

No one is quite ready to say goodbye, but we had to.

She'll live on through the wind in the trees, the sound of the birds chirping, the wildflowers blooming in the fields... she will live on among us, reminding us when needed that she is with us.

Always.

———

THE WAKE IS at our ranch. Joy offered but mom thought it was only right that we hosted. I sit in the corner, just watching as the range of emotions take over every single person. Sadness, happiness, joy, anger, laughter and grief. Pain stricken grief. Dixie appears with the baby monitor clasped in her hand as she seeks me out.

"Hey you," she smiles, leaning down and kissing me on the cheek, her scent surrounding me.

"Hey," I smile back at her, her hand is on my shoulder and I cover it with mine.

"Has Austin returned yet?" she asks, her blue eyes scanning the room.

"Nope," I sigh, and I didn't want to admit it out loud, but I was beginning to worry.

And just as I sent my prayer up to let him return safe, Hudson bursts through the front door. Riggs storms over to him, a thunderous scowl on his face.

"Sorry to barge in Riggs." He glares around the room before his attention is back on Riggs. I wheel myself over, Pacey hobbling to stand behind Riggs too. "Austin has turned himself in."

"What?!" Riggs' gruff voice booms around the room. Buck is up and raging like a bull as he storms across the floor towards where Hudson stands.

My dad is close behind, grabbing Buck and holding him back. Not that he looks as if he is going to fight anyone, but we can see the emotion that is building behind his eyes. The anger and grief all mixing into one. It's a dangerous combination.

"Said he has nothing left to fight for."

"Fuck," Riggs covers his mouth with his hand as he rubs his chin.

"Now what?" I ask, looking up at my older brother.

"We're fucked."

The evening hit a further downward spiral after the news that Austin had turned himself in. The sombre mood just grew and one by one, people left.

Sighing as Riggs fills my glass with whiskey, I give a shallow nod as thanks.

"Fuck," he sighs, his deep voice vibrating around the room as he falls into the chair in the corner. Aspen is at home with Blue and Buck trying to get in touch with Austin's lawyer, but with him handing himself in, I'm not sure if there is much more they can do.

My dad has been quiet since finding out. I think a lot of that is because of guilt. He wanted to turn himself in, but selfishly I told him not to. Not because I wanted Austin to go down, but because I wanted to find out what actually happened that night.

I know in my heart of hearts that Austin didn't kill Clay. I also know my dad didn't either. He was dazed and roughed around, all it had to take was one slip for him to hit his head. The way Austin and my dad dealt with him wouldn't have caused his death.

Rubbing my finger along my bottom lip, I try and wrack my brain for something to give, for something to click on what may or may not have happened to him.

Pacey lets out some form of grunt, and my eyes slice across to where he is sitting. His face a constant scowl. A rumbling, dark cloud hanging over his usual sunshine and rainbow self.

"You okay?" I ask the stupid question and he returns a raise of his eyebrows. The last time I saw Pacey in this kind of mood was when everything went down with Riggs, Harlow and Aspen.

Harlow.

A pain sears through my beating heart at the loss of her. I know she wasn't always the nicest, but people liked her. Sure, she had a few enemies and some probably wanted to see her downfall but that didn't mean that any of those would have wanted to see her dead.

She didn't deserve that.

No one did.

Not even Clay.

But I would keep that to myself.

"All sunshine and rainbows brother, how about you?" he snarls, lip turning like a rabid dog, and I shake my head from side to side.

This hasn't just changed him; it's changed all of us.

Altering our brain chemistry somehow, throwing it out of balance.

It was weird. Couldn't really explain it.

"Don't be a dick man," I scoff, shaking my head as I sip on my whiskey and welcome the warmth that the amber liquid gives me.

"Not being a dick at all, just a little sour," he hisses at me, rolling his eyes.

"Pacey!" Riggs snaps, a little more assertive than he was probably wanting to be.

We hear the huff that passes Pacey's lips and we all sigh.

Silence creeps around us, Conrad sits in the corner, eyes moving between me and my brothers slowly as if trying to read the room.

"We need to go down to the mines," Riggs finally says, breaking the crackling tension that was growing as the seconds passed.

"What?" and I have no idea why I am questioning him, I know it as much as him that we need to see what's down there before Wallen and the fuck head suits get there.

"How are we going to get down there? Your ranch sits over it..." Conrad says softly, nursing his own whiskey, sipping it.

"Don't you worry about the how son, I grew up here, I've been down that mine a few times," my dad says loud and proud as he walks into the living room and pours his own whiskey.

"Is there anything down there?" and now I ask because I need to know. I need to know if this an outright suicide mission or whether there is something down there that is worth more than life itself to these suits. If it meant they took the mines and left our ranch and land alone, I would gladly pass it up, but I am terrified that wouldn't be enough for the greedy sons of a bitches.

"There was... once upon a time," he says with a gruffness to his tone, perching himself on the arm of a chair, both fingers wrapped around the crystal etched glass.

All eyes are on my dad.

"Years and years ago, I'm talking about when I was a youngster, a fourteen carat diamond was found down that mine by my grandpa, Dusty," my dad shuffles, readjusting himself before taking a sip. "He hid it for years, never told anyone about it. I had no idea just what it was, just knew it was my grandpa's special stone."

We all stay silent as he continues.

"One day some men came, telling my grandpa it was theirs and that he needed to hand it over. He swore blind that he had no idea what they were on about and he was arrested there on the spot. Times were different back then, you didn't get away with half the shit you youngsters do now..." and he fucking eyeballs all of us. Including Conrad.

"Anyway," he clears his throat, "he never came home, my dad—your grandpa—refused to talk about it, and still till this day, we have no idea where he hid the stone. Rumour has it that the Montana Pearl still sits down in those mines, but team after team have been down there, until it was shut off and deemed redundant."

"What are your thoughts?" Riggs asks, sitting on the edge of his chair, his whiskey swirling in his glass as he softly moves it.

My dad sucks in a breath before puffing his cheeks out.

"There have been many that have looked, many that have failed and lost their lives. My grandpa was very secretive, if it's down there, he would have made sure it stayed hidden unless he *wanted* you to find it. The land itself would be worthless to the suits if they found the Montana Pearl, but alas, I can promise they'll never find it."

"How can you be so sure?"

And my dad chuckles, letting his head tip back softly.

"Why do you think my grandpa built this ranch in this location, why do you think Rivera Ranch sits bang in the middle of the X on the sky view map? He wants them to think it's buried here. I can bet you a hundred bucks that he hid it somewhere with no relevance to that mine. Or, I could be completely wrong, and it is just buried deep within the mine somewhere," my dad shrugs a shoulder up, "but it doesn't matter, because no one is getting down there."

I raise my brows.

"We're down half an army dad, we can't fight them off."

"You're right, *we* can't. But I have plenty of allies that owe me a favor or two that would be happy to step in and help if needed. Trust me son, don't you worry your pretty little head over it," he stands slowly, hand resting on the small of his back as he straightens himself out. "But don't you four concern yourselves, there is no need. No one is getting to the mines. No one is getting our land. You just focus on the here and now, and that means you and Pacey need to get better."

I drop my head for a moment.

"Raise your glasses," my dad orders and I lift my head to look at him before stretching my arm out, holding my glass in the air. "To Harlow," he chokes, and my chest tightens, "may you always rest in peace our sweet girl."

"To Harlow," we all chime, knocking back our whiskeys as my dad slams his glass down on the table with force and walks out the room.

"One more?" Riggs asks as he walks slowly towards the decanter and we all nod one by one, still dressed in our black suits. It didn't seem right getting changed when we were still mourning Harlow.

Looking over my shoulder, I will for Dixie to walk into the room, but I know Lainey was unsettled, no doubt picking up on the mood of the household, and I know that Lainey will always come first.

Before me.

Before anything.

Just how it should be.

"So, I have a date with Sunny," Conrad interrupts my thoughts and Riggs wolf whistles. "Stop that," Conrad laughs, rubbing his palm down his thigh.

"Finally managed to get one of the girls from town," I wiggle my brows, "hopefully that means you stop going after mine," I wink at him, a smirk tugging at my lips and he flips me off causing me to let out a rumble of a laugh. Riggs smiling from ear to ear before he breaks into his own laughter.

"Well you fuckers took every single girl that came into town, had to get my hands on Sunny before Pacey claimed her," and Conrad smirks, side eyeing Pacey and he just returns a kind of growling noise.

"Where has my little sunshine Pacey gone?" Conrad leans across and nudges Pacey softly which causes him to push up with force and hiss as pain sears through him. Riggs is up, grabbing our kid brother and letting him use him as a support.

"You okay?" I ask, and there is a sense of worry coating my tone.

Pacey's eyes are squeezed shut as he clings onto Riggs like he is his life raft. Knuckles white, fingers digging into Riggs' arms and my chest aches, breath shallow and I wish I could take his pain away. But it's not just a physical pain, it's a mental pain too.

Hate it.

Hate it for all of us.

"It's okay, I've got you," Riggs reassures Pacey, holding him for as long as he needs.

I wish I could help. But I am useless. Trying to get up without help is impossible, so now I'm stuck, watching like an outsider as my younger brother sobs in the arms of my other brother.

My heart is breaking.

Conrad shuffles in his seat, guilt written across his face at making Pacey react and rush up, but it was only banter. It wasn't meant in a malicious way. Pacey would have once just flipped him off, laughed and then shrugged him off. But not now.

It's like the light side of Pacey has been completely eclipsed by a darker side, a side that he has been buried away and only now it's raising its ugly head to claim any ounce of light that was left in Pacey's soul.

Squeezing my own eyes shut as I try and block out the sounds of Pacey's pained sobs, I hear the sound of footsteps hitting down the hallway and my dad is in the room, slipping his arms under Pacey and pulling him off of Riggs softly. Riggs tilts his head, as if he is trying to get his own emotions in check and that's when we see the blood on Riggs' white shirt. Our eyes skate across to Pacey whose shirt is saturated.

"Get him to the truck," Riggs barks and Conrad is up and off the sofa before lifting Pacey like a little child, carrying him out the room when my dad and Riggs follow, and I hate that I can't go and follow. Hate that I am now left here alone with my thoughts, and like most nights, flashbacks roll of the day of Clay's funeral and how everything went down, but it all happens in slow motion. The sound of Harlow's screams, Pacey crying and the constant echoes of shooting guns.

I feel a hand on my shoulder and jump before looking behind me and seeing her dressed in her pretty white night dress.

"Sorry, I didn't mean to startle you."

"It's okay," I whisper, letting my eyes shut for just a moment as I try and calm my racing heart. My hand reaches over hers, clasping tightly and I realise that I never want to let her go.

Not just tonight.

Forever.

"Where's everyone gone? I heard the front door slam," she slips her hand from under mine and I miss her instantly. She walks slowly towards the decanter filled with whiskey and I let out a heavy sigh.

"Pacey stood too quickly, think he may have busted his stitches. He was bleeding, they've taken him to get checked out," my lips roll and my brows pinch.

"Oh no," worry wraps around her whispers as her beautiful blues are on me.

"Hate all of this," I admit and let my head drop for a second.

"I know," she hums, and I hear the sound of whiskey pouring, making me lift my head as I study her. Long wavy brown hair falling forward, button nose, full lips, crystal blue eyes that penetrate into my soul with each gaze that meets mine.

"Fuck," I rasp, swallowing down my words. I feel like a nervous teen again, as if I am seeing her for the first time.

"What?" and I don't miss the panic that laces her voice as she stands, her small hand moving as her delicate fingers tuck a strand of loose hair behind her ear.

"You're so fucking beautiful."

And I am winded when her cheeks turn a pretty pink, eyes casting down and lashes fanning out as if she is embarrassed by what I said.

"Don't ever shy away from me," my hand lifts, fingers brushing along the inside of her arm.

Placing the decanter back on the table, she stands in front of me, glass resting on her bottom lip as she takes a sip of the burning amber teasingly slow.

And I am jealous.

Jealous of a glass. Jealous of whiskey. Jealous of anything that gets to be on her lips, her tongue, down her throat.

Fuck.

I feel my cock stir in my pants, my stomach knotting

with want and a need to have her. She was a craving that I so desperately needed.

An addiction.

Her hazy eyes cross with mine, her chest rising and falling a little faster than before as she drains the rest of her glass. She turns her back to me, and my eyes roam down her back and land on the hem of her cotton nightie, sitting mid-thigh against her sun-kissed skin and I am desperate to run my fingertips under it, to feel her skin beneath them, to claim every inch of her as mine, tarnishing her with that word. *Mine.*

I watch her like I am a predator stalking his prey. Watching her every move until I can pounce. She leans slowly, reaching for the decanter giving me a tiny view as to what sits underneath. My finger runs across my bottom lip as I fantasise. Swallowing, my mouth suddenly dry as she fills her glass to the rim before she spins, hungry eyes pinned to me.

"Thirsty?" I ask as she lifts the glass to her lips and takes a large mouthful, swallowing it down and I am jealous of the silky liquid slipping down her throat, my eyes watching as her throat bobs.

She nods, pulling the glass away and licking her upper lip.

My lips twitch as I take my own mouthful and I watch as her eyes skate down to my chest, my stomach, my groin and her cheeks burn flaming red.

"What's the matter Dreamcatcher? Seen something you like?"

And I know I am teasing her, but my cock is evidently hard in my pants.

Her eyes are back on mine as she takes another mouthful of her drink.

"Do you know how desperate I am to stand in front of you, to wrap my arm around your back and pull you close?" I whisper.

She says nothing, just listens to me.

"How desperate I am to dust my lips up the column of your throat, to drag them across your collarbone and scatter butterfly kisses against your perfect skin?"

I swallow.

My throat suddenly dry.

"Do you know just how fucking *desperate* I am Dixie?" my voice is tight.

She shakes her head from side to side, her silky brown hair moving as she does.

Curling my finger, I call her over waiting for her to refuse, but she doesn't, she walks herself over to me, decanter of whisky loose in one hand, fingers pinched around the rim of the glass with the other. Her steps towards me are slow, lazy maybe but she looks hot as sin. My head tips back as I look up at her, and I lose myself in her eyes, her smile, her dimples... everything about her I lose myself in.

She leans forward, placing the decanter on the round side table next to me, her fingertips brushing against my chest as she slowly stands up, teasing me.

My eyes don't leave hers as we start a game of stare off.

Lifting my glass, I drain the remainder of my drink and let my glass hang off my knee. I watch as the minx smirks at me, tilting her head to the side as she brings her knee up, resting it between my legs, but she's mindful not to touch my cast. I feel like a King about to be worshipped as I sit in the armchair, my leg resting on the footstool on top of a pillow.

"Head back, mouth open," she whispers, breathing a

little heavier and the smell of whisky surrounds me, consuming me as it mixes with her heavenly scent.

I do as she says, tilting my head back and all the time not lifting my hands to touch her. Even though I am desperate too.

But I want to see who breaks first in this little game of teasing we have going on. Hands still either side of me, glass still empty.

Opening my mouth, my eyes are burning into hers as she lifts the decanter and hovers it over my mouth, slowly pouring it past my lips and onto my tongue, my tastebuds exploding and before I can even swallow, her hand is on my cheek, tilting my head forward just as she locks her lips with mine, swirling the amber liquid between us as our kiss deepens, our tongues swirling, mixing our want and whiskey together. *The perfect whiskey kiss.*

She pulls away just as I swallow it down and a guttural groan vibrates through me.

Heart pounding.

Blood pumping.

Her whiskey laced eyes burning deep into my soul. Wild. So fucking wild.

"Kiss me again," I rasp, the burn of the whiskey still coats my throat. Placing her glass and decanter on the table next to me, her lips pull into a smirk as her sole focus is back on me.

Her smile widens, and this time she leans down and straddles me, legs either side of my lap.

"Darlin," my voice is low and raspy, her eyes locked with mine, her hands are on my face. "What are you doing to me?" I whisper.

"Loving you Tripp," she leans into me, her kiss soft as

my hands curl around her hips, fingers digging into the soft cotton material that clings to her body.

She breaks away for just a moment and my eyes volley back and forth, waiting for her to falter, but she doesn't. Her lips curling into a smile before they're back on mine as she kisses me like it's the last kiss she'll ever give.

And this time, we don't hold back. We don't tease. We don't play.

We're all in.

CHAPTER TWENTY-SEVEN
DIXIE

"Darlin'," he rasps, his voice tight and constricted, our eyes locked and loaded with each other's, my hands cupping his handsome face. "What are you doing to me?" he whispers, the smell of whiskey on his warm breath surrounds me.

"Loving you Tripp," I lean into him, a soft kiss dusting across his lips and I feel his hands on me, *finally* on me. Hands curling around the curve of my hip, fingers pressing a little harder into my dress and I know I'll have marks on my burning skin.

His eyes bounce between mine for just a moment, vulnerability hazes them along with a desiring want and need and I can't remember the last time I saw that, and then it dawns on me, it's always been that way with Tripp. He has always looked at me like this. *Always.*

My lips break into a smile before I press them back on his, our kiss hot and messy as our tongues dance with each other in a tantalising routine.

Rolling my hips gently over his lap, mindful not to hurt him as I feel his evident bulge in his pants.

"Fuck," he groans, hands skimming down my body to my bare thighs, his finger and thumb squeezing into my sensitive skin before gliding under the hem of my dress. My breath catches at the back of my throat, breaking away from him. The tips of his fingers brush delicately across the front of my panties, rubbing my clit gently through the soft and thin material.

And my god, it feels so good to be touched by him again. Two of his fingers curl around my panties, my skin erupting into goosebumps from the small touch of his fingers on my bare skin, on the most sensitive part of my body. Slipping further, his fingers press against my clit, gasping when the shot of pleasure cascades down over me, my head rolling back as he works my body up, plays me like a guitar with a song that only he knows because he was the one to write it.

I feel like we're teens again, hands on each other at any moment we get.

But we're not teens.

We don't have to hide this anymore.

I have loved this man with everything I have for ten years, I'm not about to waste a second more hiding it from him or anyone else.

Hips roll over his hand just as his fingers tease at my soaked opening.

"Tell me you want this," he rasps, teasing me with the tip of his fingers, slipping in and out of me. The burning ache that was once a spark is now a raging ember intensifying in my stomach.

"Yes," I nod, hands splayed against his chest and my mouth hangs as he slips two of his fingers deep inside of me, fucking me with them slowly.

His head tips back as he watches me, watches how the

pleasure that he is causing possesses me, taking over my body bit by bit.

I clench and a knowing smirk tugs at the corner of his lips.

"You getting close baby?" his voice quiet just as he teases a third finger and my hips roll forward, silently begging him to do it.

I nod, chest rising and falling as I try my hardest to not come, I don't want it to be over yet. Letting my hand slip down his shirt covered chest, my fingers wrap around his wrist as I shake my head from side to side. Confusion paints over his handsome face, and he slips his fingers from me, and I whimper at the loss.

"Did I hurt you?" he asks, eyes bouncing between mine and I shake my head.

"I'm just being selfish... not ready for all of this to be over," I admit, cheeks turning crimson.

"Baby, it's far from over," he smirks, his fingers back rubbing my clit, but I stop him again.

Shuffling back slightly, my fingers skim up and down the silhouette of his cock as I begin teasing him.

"How is this fair?" he cocks his head to the side, and I smirk, "It isn't."

Pulling my bottom lip behind my teeth, I sink them into my bottom lip as I readjust myself over him. Legs widening so I am sitting deeper into his lap, my fingers dancing up my bare thighs as I lift my dress up around my waist.

Tripp sucks in a breath as his eyes fall between us, watching as my hips begin to rock over his cock.

"Little Dreamcatcher," he rasps my nickname and my eyes lock with his as the breath catches at the back of his throat, my hips circling getting the friction I so desperately need. "You're going to make me come in my pants like a horny teen," his hands rest on my thighs, and I bite the inside of my bottom lip.

"Good," I whisper, lowering my lips to his as we kiss, his hands move to my bare hips as my pantie covered pussy rubs against his pant covered cock.

My stomach tightens, pussy clenching as I rub myself off over him, kisses getting lazy, and he pins me to his lap as he presses his cock against my clit.

A moan slips past my lips as I roll myself over him.

"Fuck," he whispers against my lips.

His hand slips up to my throat, squeezing gently before it curls around the back of my head, his fingers wrapping around the hair at the nape of my neck. Tugging my head back softly, his lips dust up the column of my throat as I shamelessly move my hips, getting all I need from him.

"You going to come baby? You going to make a mess all over my lap?" he nips at the sensitive skin of my throat.

"Yes," I whisper as he groans. "Are you?" I turn the question on him, and his mouth hangs open a little, eyes all hazy, my hips rocking up and down his cock.

"It seems I don't have a choice, you're just too good," he smirks but his breaths are laboured, harsh, intoxicating. I let my head roll forward, looking down between us and continue to rub myself off on him, but I manage to catch just as his eyes roll into the back of his head. His grip on my hips tightens, pushing his hips up and against me again causing his cock to press just where I need it to. Rocking my hips back and forth, I ride him. Head falling forward, my breaths become laboured and my movements lazy, but I don't stop. Rocking myself slowly against him, my clit rubbing over the tip of his cock and I feel him stiffen beneath me, head tipping back as he comes and he sends me spiralling. My back arches, head back and just as my orgasm rips through me, two fingers are fucking me as his thumb presses against my clit and the rough waves that crashed over me moments before calm down to soft laps against the shore.

Our eyes are hazy, lips parted as we both pant, lips pressing into wide smiles.

"Fuck," he laughs, cupping my cheek and I lean into his hand. "I'm going to need some…" he pauses as I wiggle myself over him, "help cleaning up."

"I've got you big boy, come," I say softly climbing off of him, my dress falling down back to my thighs as I smirk at him. Lifting his casted leg off the footstool, he hisses as I place it on the floor gently. "You okay?" I ask, panic lacing my voice and he nods.

I loop my hand under his arm and on the count of three, I pull him up. I help him hobble over to his wheelchair and sit him back down.

"I cannot wait to be out of this cast," he groans, as I begin pushing him towards the back of the house where his temporary bedroom is.

"I bet," I say quietly.

"You not going to ask me why?" I can hear the playfulness in his tone.

"I think it's pretty obvious; so you can walk."

And he laughs a boyish laugh.

"Not even close," he says as I push him into the bedroom and walk around to face him.

"No?" I tilt my head to the side.

"No," his eyes are burning with desire.

"Why is it then?"

"I cannot wait to be out of this cast so I can fuck you. Hard. Dixie. To pin you against a wall and fuck you until you come undone, coming all over my cock, my tongue, my fingers. God," he sucks in a breath, "I am desperate to fuck you Dixie, desperate to taste you."

My skin burns, cheeks flaming, and my stomach tightens as I fidget on the spot, clenching my thighs together to try and ease the building pressure that grows between my legs, my clit pulsing with need.

"Would me fucking you be enough?" I ask, letting my fingers brush the strap from my night dress off my shoulder and letting it fall down my arm.

His eyes burn, throat bobbing.

"It'll never be enough when it comes to anything to do with you Dixie... nothing will ever be enough."

***

TRIPP

I sit and watch her undress.

"Would me fucking you be enough?" she asks me and fuck if it's not the hottest thing I have heard. Hungrily watching the straps of her pretty nightie slip down her arms and my cock is already hard.

I came like a schoolboy in my pants as she dry humped the fuck out of me, getting herself off too.

"It'll never be enough when it comes to anything to do with you Dixie... nothing will ever be enough," I rasp, my voice low and husky. Desperate to stand, desperate to walk over to her and run my fingertips across her skin. My eyes trail down her body as she lets her dress fall from her curvy frame and it pools at her feet. Standing in nothing but her cotton panties that are tarnished with her arousal from just moments ago and she looks every bit stunning. Her confidence vanishes as quickly as it came on as she tries to cover her stomach in front of me, her head dropping as she hides.

My heart aches, chest tight and my throat burns.

Pushing from my chair, I balance myself then hobble slowly to where she is standing, shielding herself from me.

"Hey," I say softly, fingers gripping her chin and tilting her face up so she has to look at me. My eyes volley back and forth between hers and my heart gallops in my chest.

"Don't ever hide yourself from me, you are the most beautiful woman in the world Dixie Walker."

She shakes her head from side to side.

"I'm not the same girl from all those years ago Tripp," and damn she breaks my heart as her voice cracks.

"No Dreamcatcher, you're not," I whisper, not letting her drop her eyes from mine for even a second, "but look what you did... you grew a beautiful little girl who adores you. Sure, you've changed in your eyes baby... but not in mine, not even a little. You're still the girl who held my heart all those years ago, you'll always be her Dixie."

My other hand skims down the side of her body, tracing the curve of her hip before I gently push her hand away. Gently brushing my fingertips over the silver stretch marks that she thinks taint her beautiful skin, but they don't. I follow them like a trail, gliding them across her lower stomach before I skim them over her hips, and slowly, I let them glide delicately up the side of her body towards her chin, her eyes burning into mine.

"Don't ever hide from me, I have dreamed of this moment for the last ten years... you're it for me Dixie. My wildest *dreams*, my wildest *love*, my wildest *forever*."

She chokes out, hands resting on my racing heart as her lips press into mine. She's needy and wanting and I want to give it all to her. Everything I have is hers, my heart, my soul, my love, my desire. *Everything.*

She slowly and gently turns me around so I am standing where she was and ever so gently she pushes me back so I am on the bed, sitting on the edge. She stands between my legs, hands on my face as her eyes bounce between mine.

"I love you Tripp. I never stopped," she whispers as she kisses me softly. My fingers kneading her hips as I lay back, taking her down with me so her chest is pressed against my shirt. She smirks, and my hand trails up her spine before my fingers are tucking a strand of hair behind her ear.

Her fingers fumble with the buttons of my shirt as she slowly begins to undo them. Gently pushing them over my shoulders as I rest up onto my elbows and I see her eyes fall to my bullet hole scar, trembling fingers tracing over the bumpy surface of skin before they descend over my tattoo that sits over my heart *'live by the ranch, die by the ranch'*.

She's in her head, her eyes tearing.

My large hand cups her face, thumb brushing over her cheek.

"Eyes on me baby," I whisper to her, and she does, her beautiful blue ocean eyes find mine. Dragging her fingers across my toned stomach, they stop at the button of my pants, and I nod softly. Hopping from me, her feet are firmly on the hardwood floor as she pulls my pants down my legs. Once she has got the shorter side off my cast, she holds them up and giggles. They look ridiculous. We had to cut one leg to accommodate my shitty cast.

Tossing them to the floor, her attention is back on me.

"Can you move onto the bed anymore?" she asks all coy, but I know deep inside of her, the minx that is Dixie Walker is still buried within.

I push myself back up, and grunt as I move towards the

headboard, so my back is resting against the hard surface, both legs fully on the bed.

She reaches for a scatter cushion and pops it under the foot of my cast, and I smirk.

Bending my good leg up and widening my thighs I watch as she crawls up the bed before she straddles her legs either side of my lap, her pantie covered pussy rubbing against my cock.

"You sure about this?" I ask just as her lips dust over mine.

"Always," she whispers back as my tongue pushes into her mouth, a soft whimper escaping as I hold onto her hips, desperate to be inside of her.

Her fingers walk down my stomach and into the waistband of my boxers and I groan as her thumb brushes against the sensitive head of my cock. My eyes flutter open as I watch her, letting my fingers dust up her side from her hips before they're on her tits, kneading and rolling her nipples between my fingers. Her head rolls back as she lifts her hips from me and her arousal has soaked through the thin material of my boxers.

Her greedy hands are in the waistband as she tugs them down, my cock bobbing with pre cum sitting on the tip as it rests against my stomach.

"Fuck," she whispers and I watch as her cheeks turn pink. This is not the first time we have been together, but somehow, it feels like it.

"Let me see your pretty pussy," I rasp, eyes grazing down her perfect body. She is still on her knees hovering over me when she thumbs her panties and slowly slips them down until she has to stand to kick them off her feet.

A moan vibrates out of me, bottom lip dragged into my mouth by my teeth. My hand slips between her thighs, rubbing her clit and my cock pulses, desperate to be buried deep inside of her.

Her small fingers wrap around the thick girth of my cock as they slowly and teasingly stroke up and down.

"You still want to fuck me?" I ask, eyes burning into hers, breaths slow and I am trying so damn hard to control myself.

She nods, her breath shuddering as I slip a finger into her soaked cunt.

"Good," I lean forward, nipping at the skin on her neck and her back arches as her hips roll forward, her clit rubbing over the palm of my hand as my fingers fuck her.

"I need you," she whispers, eyes all hazy and wild. Her hips tilt and I slip my fingers from her, bringing them to my lips before pushing them into my mouth and sucking them clean. Eyes roll in the back of my head as her hand strokes me still. Pushing to her knees, she rubs the head of my cock over her clit before gliding me between her pussy lips and teasing at her opening.

"Not as much as I need you darlin'," hips rolling up and my cock slips just inside of her and fuck it's euphoric.

Her head falls forward as I fill her slowly, her body trembling and her breathy moans like music to my ears.

"Oh my god," her head rolls back, hands pressed against my chest as she takes a moment.

"You feel so damn good," my hand cups her face and she leans into it just as her hips begin to circle over me. A low moan passes my lips as she takes control, legs widening as she sits lower, sucking my cock deep inside of her. "Fuck," I rasp, my teeth grazing against her jaw as she rocks back and forth, her pants growing louder.

The front door goes and we both freeze, and just as I am about to lift her from me, she lifts herself slightly and my eyes fall between our bodies, my cock glistening and coated in her arousal, it pulses inside of her. She rests her feet onto the soft mattress, fingers curling around the top edge of the headboard as she slides herself up and down my throbbing cock.

I moan every time she lowers herself down, rolls her hips forward then lifts herself up again before sliding down my cock. The sound of whiskey filling glasses and clattering makes my breath hitch, but on my exhale my moans echo around the room.

"Tripp?" I hear the sound of my brother calling my name, my eyes roll into the back of my head, whimpering as her cunt tightens around my cock, sucking me deep inside of her.

"I'll go check on him shortly, let me get this drink in me first," Riggs grunts.

"You need to be quiet, baby, can you do that for me?" she whispers, knowing exactly what she is doing. The bedroom door is open and knowing that they could walk in at any minute sends a thrill through me and has me whimpering a little louder as she rides me like a damn fucking pro bull rider.

"You like me fucking you like this Tripp?" she asks, smirking as her sweet cunt slides up and down my cock with ease, arousal dripping from her pretty pussy.

My eyes roll in the back of my head as she moves a little faster.

"You like watching the way your huge cock fills me to the hilt?"

"Fuck Dixie," I rasp, fingers digging into her hips as my spare hand skims down her shimmering stomach.

My moans grow louder as her tight little cunt clenches around me.

"I'm so close," she pants just as my fingers rub her clit.

"Your pussy looks so fucking good with my cock fucking it," I rasp, moaning as my eyes lift to hers, watching as she slowly begins to unwind, coming undone thrust by thrust.

"Quiet," she whispers, "they're going to hear you."

But I don't care, I can't stop my moans. With each roll of her hips, with each thrust of my cock inside her pussy is one stroke closer to exploding and filling her tight cunt with my cum. She's everything I dreamed she would be.

She covers my mouth just as she lifts herself to the tip of my cock, teasing me as she lets the swollen head of my cock sit inside her wet, hot pussy, hovering ever so slightly as she slips me just inside her cunt, in small, teasing, pulses.

"There's a good boy. You're going to come for me now, I want you to fill my pussy full of you," she moans as my fingers dance across her clit, and with one last roll down onto my cock, I whimper behind her hand as I pulse deep inside of her. That's when I feel her body sag, finally giving in, as she rides me deep and hard into the mattress as her own orgasm crashes over her. My eyes are full of lust, watching mesmerised as her back arches on top of me and I drag her hand away from my mouth, leaning forward, arms around her back as my hot and needy mouth finds her full tits, tongue wrapping around her nipples as I suck. They leak onto my tongue, my eyes widen, but I continue as her whimpers fill the room, her body trembling as she comes all over my cock. Her legs shake and her breaths shallow as our heads press together. We don't relish in our hot as fuck sex, because she is rolling off me and then I see her eyes widen.

"We didn't..." she pauses, reaching for her nightie and panties as she pulls them on with quickness.

"I've not been with anyone since..."

She blinks a couple of times, head tilting.

"Only you Dixie," I breathe, chest rising and falling, feeling laid open and vulnerable in front of her, my heart beating openly in my chest, waiting for her to wreck me again. "It's only ever been you," I rasp as I pull my sheet over me, covering myself up.

"Tripp," her eyes glass, head dropping for just a moment. "I'm sorry," she chokes, and I want to be there, holding her, wiping the tear that is no doubt rolling down her cheek away with my thumb.

"Why are you sorry?" I find myself sitting forward, hanging on every word that falls past her lips.

"For leaving you, for running..."

"It's okay Dix, I promise it's okay."

She shakes her head from side to side and finally, after what feels like a lifetime, she looks at me. Blue eyes full of her unshed tears, and like I predicted, a glistening streak of wetness drawing a glittering line down her pink cheeks.

"I broke your heart."

"And I broke yours too, I am sure," I whisper.

"You were never with anyone else..." she sniffles, wrapping her arms around her body.

"I never wanted to be with anyone else because in the deepest crevices of my heart baby, I knew you would come back. There could never be anyone else when I had you, Dixie."

Her shoulders roll forward as she chokes out a sob, and my heart aches heavily in my chest.

"Please don't cry," I beg, my own voice cracking.

"I don't deserve you," she whispers, palming her tears away.

"You deserve everything Dixie, don't ever think you don't baby. Because you do. You deserve it all." I pause for a beat. *"I love you."*

She walks over to me slowly, fingers brushing my hair away from my forehead, her eyes volleying between mine, brows crinkled slightly.

"I will never deserve you Tripp Rivera," she whispers against my lips and my heart flatlines in my chest as I wait for her to tell me she loves me back, but as the seconds tick by, the more I worry that it's never coming and she is ready to walk away from me again.

Say it Dixie, baby...

Our lips are inches from each other, our heavy breaths mixing, hearts beating as one.

Three words, my little dreamcatcher... say them.

"But I love you," she breathes out, her voice trembling and I edge forward ever so slightly as I kiss her, heart enveloping together as our souls knot with an invisible string, connecting us forever into the infinite world of love.

She pulls away and I groan at the loss of her lips on mine.

"I love you Dixie Walker."

"I'll be back soon," she whispers, lips pulled into a small grin, eyes glistening, cheeks pink.

I give her a nod, fingers laced with hers and I try with all I have to hold onto her as she walks away, but eventually her fingers slip from mine and she is gone.

Sighing, I watch as she walks down the hallway and within seconds, she has disappeared, but I'm not alone for long when I see Riggs walking towards me, a boyish grin on his face.

"Alone now?" Riggs smirks, leaning against the doorframe. His eyes scan the room. "Smells of sex in here," he grunts, "good on you man," he chuckles as he sips his whiskey.

"Fuck you," I laugh, running my hand through my

messy brown hair. "How's Pace?" I ask, desperate to move, but kind of stuck in my bed. Naked.

"Back in surgery," Riggs rolls his lips together and I go to move but he shakes his head from side to side. "Dad and Conrad are there."

And I close my eyes for just a moment. I am so fucking angry. He's my baby brother, I should have protected him. And I hear the rattle of Riggs' heavy breathing.

"They will get their karma, don't you worry," as if he can hear my thoughts.

"I feel useless." I let my head drop for just a moment, shaking it heavily.

"Well don't. You're not useless. It's just a shit situation. They knew what they were doing, it wasn't a random attack... it was premeditated. Carefully planned out."

I sigh.

"We need to use Dixie, get her in with Wallen. Use Lainey..."

"No fucking way," I move forward, shuffling myself to the end of the bed.

"Tripp."

"Riggs," I hiss as my leg hits the ground and I cry out.

My brother is there, next to me as his arm wraps around my shoulder, holding me close to him.

"We need to end this war Tripp."

"And we will, just don't use her as bait..." I whisper as tears burn behind my eyes.

"Okay," he whispers, holding me close and suddenly I burst into tears. The heaviness of the last two weeks laying heavy on my soul, and I have tried to be strong, tried to be the perfect big brother, but something had to break eventually. And that something was me.

"I've got you," Riggs whispers, and he stays sitting with

me until every emotion has left my body, and suddenly, I am exhausted.

DIXIE

The house is silent, and I managed to sneak away to check in on Lainey and swipe the monitor before I made my way back downstairs to Tripp.

Back inside his arms, I listen to the way his heart beats beneath his warm skin and I feel like I am finally home.

"Why did you choose the name Lainey?" He asks as I lay my head on his chest, his fingertips brushing delicately up and down my spine.

"Because I loved the name, also because my kid sister was called Lainey," I whisper to the quiet room, and I feel the burn in my throat at thinking of her.

"It's a pretty name," he brushes a kiss into the top of my head.

"I think so too," I look up at him, sleepy brown eyes pinned to me, but his mind is elsewhere.

"You okay?" I ask.

"My soul is tired," he admits with a low voice.

I feel that.

I give a small smile, eyes creasing as I do.

Reaching forward, I place a soft kiss on his lips.

"Sleep baby," I whisper as I rest my head back on his chest, and within seconds, soft snores fill the room. Content, heart full and eyes falling heavy, I slip into a peaceful slumber with him, praying that we find each other in our dreams, because the thought of sleeping for hours without him suddenly feels too much.

CHAPTER TWENTY-EIGHT
DIXIE

I was awake before Tripp and as much as I wanted to stay in his bed for the duration of the day, I had to mom and work. Sneaking from his bed like a one night stand that was filled with hot and dirty sex, I wince. My boobs are rock solid, and I need Lainey to feed. Tip toeing past his door, I close it behind me. Walking quietly down the hallway, I reach for the newel post and step onto the first step when I hear a soft chuckle coming from the kitchen and my eyes cast over to where it's coming from.

Riggs.

My cheeks burn and I shake my head.

"Sneaking out his room," he continues to laugh as he spoons a mouthful of cereal into his mouth.

"Screw you," I smirk, flipping him off as I run up the stairs and into my room without being caught by Orla. Pressing my back against my closed door, I let my eyes flutter shut for just a moment, a soft smile pulling at my mouth as I sink my teeth into my bottom lip. I replay the memories of last night and how good it felt to be with Tripp again.

I am brought back down to earth as Lainey stirs, crying on cue.

"Shh shh," I hush her, scooping her up and holding her close to me as she rubs the sleep out of her eyes, my lips pressing soft kisses on the top of her head. "Morning baby," I coo, bouncing her as she begins to fuss.

Sitting on the edge of my bed, I slip my nightie down and let her latch on. My eyes flutter closed again as I sit in perfect silence thinking of what my life could be like if I didn't have to leave, if I didn't have to walk away in order to save Tripp and his family.

My breath stutters at the back of my throat at the thought and I ignore the burn that lodges itself there, making it hard to breath suddenly.

Lowering my face, my hand strokes over her brown hair, her long lashes fanned out as her hand rests on my chest.

"God, mama loves you," I whisper, suddenly feeling overwhelmed with emotions.

Her little hums as she suckles make my heart skip a beat and I push everything from my mind as I focus on her, my world, my daughter.

Once she is fed and changed, I walk her downstairs, still wearing my nightie. I hadn't had a second to get changed because every time I laid her down, she sobbed.

Orla is standing at the sink, coffee in hand as she distantly looks over the ranch, no doubt her mind with Pacey.

Riggs sits at the table, a stupid smirk on his face and it makes sense, he actually *knows* what me and his brother have been up to. He didn't just catch me sneaking out of his room after maybe accidentally falling asleep in his room.

Shit.

"Morning," I say softly, and Orla snaps out of her trance, turning to face me.

"Morning my beautiful girls," she smiles widely, stepping towards me and Lainey as she places her mug on the worksurface before she kisses me on the cheek and takes Lainey from me who goes willingly, arms out for Orla as she babbles away.

"I see how it is," I smirk, walking towards the coffee pot and pouring myself a hot cup.

"She's granny's favorite girl," Orla dances around the large kitchen area and I just stand and watch, heart slowly disintegrating inside my chest. My fingers pinch at the delicate pendant of my gold chain. I wish my mom was here, wish she could have met her granddaughter. But I am grateful that in some weird twist of fate, my baby has Orla. *Her Granny.*

She sings to her, *I Will Always Love You - Dolly Parton* and a lump bobs in my throat as tears threaten. I can feel Riggs staring at me, and my cheeks flush. Turning my face slowly to look at him, my lips turn up slightly into a small smile and he gives me a shallow, knowing nod, lips rolled into a thin line.

Bringing my mug to my lips I take a sip just as Tripp wheels himself into the kitchen.

"We need to get you on your crutches man," Riggs sighs, shaking his head.

"Yeah, yeah," he waves his brother off.

"The physio is due today, I'm sure she'll work me out and get me on my feet," and my ears prick, eyes slicing across to him and Riggs laughs into his cup, not just a gentle laugh, no, a full on belly laugh that gains the attention of everyone in the room.

"What's funny?" Orla asks, Lainey's face flush with her cheek as Orla keeps swaying.

"Nothing," I snap my lips shut and I see the glint of playfulness in Tripp's eyes.

"Little Dixie here getting jealous over the physio," Riggs says through bouts of laughter and I step towards him, swatting the top of his arm with my hand.

"No I'm not," my cheeks turn red, blazing fucking hot and my ears feel like they're on fire.

"You are darlin'," Riggs says softly, shrugging his shoulder up. "It's okay to admit it, we won't judge."

"Don't you have cows to sort out?" I snap back in a lame ass attempt of a comeback.

"Waiting on you sweet cheeks, I'm two men down... I need all the help I can get ahead of the branding in a few weeks."

"Oh shit, I forgot about that," Tripp grunts, wheeling closer to me smirking.

"Morning," I whisper as I turn quickly and reach for a mug and place it under the coffee machine.

"Morning little dreamcatcher," he winks then looks over at my mom. "Morning ma."

"Morning my angel boy," she smiles sweetly at her son as she places Lainey into the highchair.

Riggs coughs, "Do I not get a morning?"

"Morning sweetie," Tripp teases and Orla rolls her eyes.

"I said *morning* to you this morning mama's little cherub," she walks over to Riggs, pinching his cheek and he laughs before she grabs a yogurt out for Lainey and some mushed-up blueberries.

"Thanks ma," Riggs beams, draining the rest of his coffee and sliding from the stool before placing his empty cup into the sink. "Dixie, go and get ready, we've got a full day," he huffs, reaching for his hat off the coat stand. "I'll meet you in the bunkhouse," he gives me a nod and my heart thumps a little louder.

"Riggs," Orla calls out, her voice timid.

"Yeah?"

"I need to go and see Pacey..." she trails off, eyes bouncing between me, Lainey and Riggs.

"Oh shit," Riggs rubs his beard and sighs as he steps back towards the kitchen, heavy boots echoing around the large space.

"It's fine, Riggs, can you find som—"

"I'll watch her," Tripp says, and all eyes are on him.

"Tripp," Orla says softly, head tilting to the side.

"I'm more than capable," and his tone is sharp.

"Of course you are..." she looks at me, eyes widening slightly.

"It's just a lot for you, plus you have physio..." I try, my voice soft.

"I can manage," he softens his tone as he looks at me.

"I won't be long," Orla says placing Lainey's breakfast in front of her, her little lips pursing into a pout as her little fingers grab a handful of smashed blueberries, lifting them to her mouth and I smile as she tries to fit them all in one go.

"And I'll be just on the ranch," peeling my eyes from my daughter and back to Tripp.

"I know," he nods then averts his gaze to his mom, "and I'll be fine."

"You better let that physio work you hard man, gonna need you on them crutches sooner rather than later..." and Riggs' eyes are on me the whole time.

The bastard knows what he is doing.

"Riggs," Orla shakes her head as she steps outside the

kitchen for a moment and Riggs follows her before his eyes are bouncing between me and Tripp.

"Surely you want to be able to... you know... without being in a cast. Can't be ideal," he says a little louder from across the kitchen, rubbing his hands together and Tripp glares at him.

I cover my face, shame painting my cheeks.

"Fuck off Riggs," Tripp reaches for a dish towel from the side and launches it towards his brother who just laughs.

"Fine, I am leaving," he rolls his eyes. "Dixie, go get dressed. We've got a lot of work to do," he tips his cowboy hat and begins to walk away. "Oh and Dix," he calls back.

"Yeah?" I answer him all whilst Tripp's fingertips are brushing against mine.

"You're gonna learn to ride today, become a proper cowgirl," and then the door slams.

"You know how to ride," Tripp wiggles his brows in a playful manner and I smirk down at him.

"Horses baby... I don't know how to ride horses," and the smile falls from his lips.

"I want to teach you," he sucks in a breath, and I clasp his hand in mine, bending down so I am kneeling.

"I know... but I need to help out, so I need to learn now."

"How about..." he leans in close to me, "later on, you climb on top of me and show me what you learned," and he winks at me, causing me to laugh. "Most beautiful sound," he hums.

"You, Tripp Rivera, are a very dirty man."

"You love it," he presses a kiss to the back of my hand, and I sigh.

"I do," I whisper, "I really do."

Walking downstairs, I grab my cowboy boots from the boot cupboard and slip them on. I am wearing my Levi's, white tee and my cowboy hat that matches my boots.

I hear a wolf whistle and I turn around, Tripp staring at me all hungry eyed.

"Hey you."

"God, I wish I could be with you today," he wheels himself over, "I would sneak you away in the stables," his voice is low, "and fuck you against the wall, making you see the stars as you come all over my cock." My breath hitches, chest rising and falling.

"That's not fair."

"No?" he pushes his tongue into his cheek.

"No," I whisper.

"I promise to let you come later on tonight when you ride me, cowgirl," and my cheeks burn as Orla steps into the room, and I move backwards.

"You sure you're going to be okay?" I ask, nerves engulfing me.

"I'll be fine, and if there are any problems, I'll come find you," and I raise a brow. "Fine, I'll call or shout and someone will come and get you," he smiles, "I promise, we will be okay," he nods at me and I find myself nodding along with him.

"I've brought Lainey's cot down and put it back up in your room Tripp," Orla says as she grabs her purse from the hook.

"Okay."

"She will have a bottle around two, I have already made it up. It's in the refrigerator so just get it out around twenty minutes before she's due it and she'll drink it at room temperature."

"Milk, refrigerator, room temp... got it," he nods as if making a mental note in his head.

"Then she will eat lunch around noon, again, all prepped in the..."

"Refrigerator," he smirks and I nod.

"If it's too much getting her in the highchair, I have a little seat and tray that I have left in the lounge on the sofa... obviously—" he cuts me off.

"I won't leave her alone. I'll have eyes on her the whole time."

"She will be due a nap around ten, then again at three. But don't let her sleep any longer than an hour."

"Morning or afternoon nap?" he asks, looking over at Lainey who is sitting playing blocks.

"Afternoon."

"Okay, cool. Well, that works well because my physio is due at eleven... should be gone for twelve."

And jealously swarms in my stomach.

"Don't be getting jealous little Dreamcatcher," he smirks and Orla hovers behind me.

"I should be home before she goes down for her afternoon nap anyway," she smiles at her son and walks towards him, placing a kiss on the top of his head.

"Okay ma."

"Any problems..." she goes to speak but Tripp smiles.

"I'll call," he nods at her and she steps towards the door, blowing us both a kiss before she disappears.

"I promise I'll be okay," he reassures me, nerves still building as the seconds pass.

"I know," I look over at her, guilt shaming me.

"She will have the best time, we will have lots of fun,"

his voice pulls me back around to look at him and I stare at him with adoring eyes.

"I know," I beam at him, "I just feel guilty."

"Well don't. Get used to this Dixie, get used to me being here, used to me showing up for both of my girls, because this is how it's going to be," and his fingers lace through mine, pulling me closer to him as our lips hover over each other's. "I love you Dixie Walker, this is your life now. Our life. Now go, before my brother drags your ass out of this house," he kisses me quickly and my blood pumps loudly in my ears as I smile against his mouth.

"I'm going," I whisper, lips still locked.

"Good, go," he smiles back.

"If your physio gets too handsy..."

That has him pulling away, laughing loudly.

"Baby, I'm pretty sure I told you last night that it's only ever been you..." And I nod. "But, if she does..."

I swat him and pout, sticking my bottom lip out as I sulk.

"I'm joking baby, if she gets too handsy, I'll let her know that I belong to my beautiful Dixie Walker."

I smirk, leaning in for one more kiss before I reluctantly pull myself away from him and walk over to kiss Lainey on the head. Turning, I move towards the front door when he grabs my attention.

"Dixie?"

"Yeah," I breathe, a permanent smile on my lips.

"Wear the cowboy hat when you ride me tonight."

"Tripp!" my body flames in heat, my stomach knotting at the thought, but I have to calm myself down and I rush out of the front door and run until I am at the bunk house.

Tripp Rivera.

Hot as fucking sin, and he is all mine.

CHAPTER TWENTY-NINE
DIXIE

Knocking on the door of the bunkhouse, I wait for a second or two before opening it. Stepping inside with caution, nerves ripple through me. All eyes are on me, and I hate it.

Riggs whistles which gains the attention of his cowboys. Some I have seen before loitering, some I haven't.

"This is Dixie." He calls out, looking at me with soft eyes and I appreciate him. "She is going to be joining us for the foreseeable until both of my brothers are back on their feet."

I hear some light chatter at the back, a pair of eyes roaming up and down my body.

"She's Tripp's girl, we all know we don't cross the line on the Rivera girls don't we now boys?" Riggs' voice claps around the room and Hudson smirks. He is the only one I actually know and have properly met.

Tripp's girl.

Be still my beating heart.

Voices of agreement fill the room.

"Now, we're starting a little later today as Pacey was in

surgery during the night, so we have a lot that we need to do. The new vet, Opal, is coming to the ranch today, and I need to get down to the calves." Riggs' eyes are back on me, "I'll be taking Dixie with me."

They all nod.

"Hudson will lead half of you down to the bulls. James, can you go across to Maple Farm and grab a couple of the mares that are due for breeding? Opal will check them over to make sure we're good to go. Paul," Riggs calls out and a young boy stands up, he must be around sixteen if that, "you stay back with Billy. The yard needs to be cleaned, horses need to be mucked out and if anyone asks you to do something, you do it, do you understand?" They both nod.

"Right then, let's go," Riggs is authoritative, but they listen. "You," he points at me, "you're coming with me." I nod, dipping my head and following him outside. My eyes cast to the house and the urge to run over there and make sure everything is okay simmers in my stomach as Riggs catches my attention. "He'll be okay, I promise you."

"I know he will, I'm not worried about his capability..." I trail off as we walk towards the stables

"Then what you worried about, Kid?" he asks, looking over his shoulder as he grabs a saddle and nods for me to do the same, my heart jack hammering in my chest.

"Worried about him. Worried about if he gets hurt whilst looking after her, worried that he will try and do too much then be stuck somewhere because he didn't want to let me down."

"Dixie," he stops in his tracks, turning to face me as we stand between the stalls. "He is a tough kid, but he knows his limits. He wouldn't do anything to put Lainey or himself in danger. Trust me."

And I nod.

"He wouldn't have offered if he didn't think he was capable," he smirks, turning and walking towards the back of the stable. "So," his voice echoes around the stalls, "have you ever ridden before?"

My mind flashes back to last night and the way I rode Tripp and I have to clench my pussy at the thought.

"No," I whisper, worried my voice will give away my dirty thoughts.

"This is going to be one hell of a ride," he chuckles as he throws his saddle on to the back of his horse. "Let me guess," he rasps, his eyes on me, "you've never tacked a horse before?"

I shake my head from side to side.

"Come," he nods me over and I walk towards him, the leather saddle still tucked over my arms. "Watch me, then we will saddle your horse."

I watch as he tosses the saddle blanket on the back of his horse before the saddle is placed on top. He readjusts it so it's sitting perfectly in the dipped part of the horse's back. He reaches down and grabs a long leather strap that sits under the horse's stomach, just behind it's front legs and he buckles it tight against the horse.

"That's called the girth," he looks over his shoulder at me, "it needs to be tight, but you still want to be able to get two fingers underneath, so it's not too tight against the horse's skin," he shows me as he slips two fingers under the girth and I nod, knowing full well I will spiral into a panic soon.

He stands up, grabbing the bridal.

"Right, always do the bit first," he smiles as he rests the metal bar in his hands, with two circles either side.

"How do I get that into his mouth?" I ask, eyes

widening as the panic I was talking about starts circling in my lower stomach.

"Like this," he smirks at me before holding his palm flat, bit sitting in it with the loops sitting either side of his hand. Lifting his hand to the horse's mouth, he moves his hand in a soft side to side motion as if rubbing the horses teeth with the cool metal and he slips it into the horse's mouth, pushing it towards the back.

"Can you see?" He asks and I step a little closer. "The bit needs to be under the horse's tongue, and pushed back, this is how you're going to control him. If the bit is over the top of the tongue, you're going to struggle, plus, it's not great for the horse either."

"Okay."

"If the horse doesn't open his mouth, a thumb in the corner of his mouth with a soft press into his tongue should get him opening for you," and I just stay silent. "Now, pull the bridal up and move the horse's ears forward over the headpiece."

I am shitting myself.

"Now, do the first strap under his head, the second under his nose," and Riggs makes it look so easy. "Your turn," he beams at me, his horse now tied back up outside his stall.

He walks across the concrete floor and opens the stables to a dark chocolate horse with a beige nose.

"This is Betsy," he smiles, "one of our new mares from Maple Farm," his eyes on Betsy as he rubs her neck.

"Hi Betsy," I murmur as I step towards her, and I watch as her ears go back.

"She can sense you're nervous."

"That's because I am," I admit, and he scoffs a laugh.

"She'll make your job real hard if you don't get brave

quick," and the sound of Betsy stamping her hoof against her straw covered floor makes me jump. "Snap out of it," his tone cool as he runs his hand up and down her neck.

"Okay okay," I rush forward, pulling the saddle blanket from underneath the heavy saddle, my arms feel weighted. I toss it over her back and Riggs smooths it out for me before I lift the saddle up, moaning as I do and the relief I feel when it's out of my arms is amazing.

"Straighten it up, make sure it's sitting on her back properly otherwise you'll hurt her," he says softly, his eyes watching my every move, and he makes me more anxious.

"Stop watching me," I snap, getting flustered.

"I have to watch you Dixie, because if you fuck up, the horse gets hurt or you do. Ideally," he smirks as his eyes lift over the top of the horse's neck, "I don't want the horse hurt," and I snort a laugh, shaking my head from side to side.

Faffing with the saddle, I step back and look at him. "There? Is that okay?"

"That's perfect," he praises, and I beam. "Now, the girth. Remember what I said?"

"Not too tight, two fingers under."

"You got it."

I drop the girth down off the top of the saddle gently, trying not to hit Betsy. Leaning down slowly, I bend and reach for the girth as I buckle it in and tighten it, worried I am going to pinch her skin.

"Is this tight enough?" I ask.

"I dunno Dixie, is it?"

And I can feel myself getting flustered.

Slipping two fingers under the girth, I can wiggle them. "Seems okay."

"That's not good enough, what will happen if when

we're riding, the saddle comes loose because you haven't done the girth tight enough? You'll slide off along with the saddle and end up on the floor hurt," his tone is a little harsh and my cheeks burn.

"Don't be an ass Riggs."

I stand up, hands on my hips and I throw a dagger glare at him.

"Sorry," he grumbles then walks around my side, slipping his fingers under the girth and pulling it out. "It's fine," he nods as he hands me the bridal off the stable door. "Bit first," he reminds me, and Betsy's ears are flat to her head.

"What if she bites me?"

"It'll hurt," he chuckles softly and fear pricks at the nape of my neck.

"Thanks," I sigh as I lay the cool metal into the palm of my hand as I raise it closer to her mouth, the horse's lip curls and her mouth opens ever so slightly and that's when I slip it under her tongue and into the corners of her mouth. Betsy rolls her tongue around and I look at Riggs.

"It's normal, imagine having a metal bit put in your mouth and under your tongue," he smirks

"I would gag."

"Shit, I better tell Tripp not to tack you up then," and he elbows me before bursting into laughter.

"Idiot," I sigh as I pull her ears forward and behind the headrest then pull her fringe out, so she looks all pretty.

"There," he smiles, "now do the bridal up."

"Okay bossy," I sigh as I fiddle with the delicate buckles and tighten them.

"Well done you," he chimes, and I stand back, admiring my work. "Now," he passes me the reins, "fix your stirrups."

"What?" I snap my head to look at him.

"You need to lengthen your stirrups."

"Back up bud, you missed a step," as I look back at the lengths of leathers that hang down against her belly.

"I am going to show you now, so, fun fact," he nudges me out the way as he lifts the saddle flap up and loosens another buckle. "You can measure your stirrup length from your armpit to your fingers, then double it to get the right length, there or there abouts," he nods, "you want your knee slightly bent, heels dug down."

He is talking a different language.

"I was never a horsey girl, I was a singer Riggs. I learned to play the guitar, not how to ride a horse,"

"Well Dixie Walker, it's never too late to learn a new hobby."

"Okay, I'll make a deal with you right here, right now Riggs Rivera."

"Go on."

"I learn to ride."

"Well from what I heard..."

"A horse Riggs, I learn to ride a horse, *not* a cowboy," I roll my eyes and he chuckles beside me, "then you learn to play the guitar." He inhales heavily, turning to face me and I watch as the smirk pulls at the corner of his lips.

"Deal," he holds his hand out for me to shake and I do, gladly. "Now, fix your stirrups and get onto your horse."

Shaking my head, I measure out my stirrups like he said and they look too long but I trust him. Footing the stirrup, I hold onto the horn as he gives me a leg up, swinging my spare leg over Betsy's back and sit in the saddle.

"How does that feel?" he asks as I wiggle my boot in the stirrup and push my heel down.

"Feels pretty good."

"Stand in the stirrups," he asks and I blink a few times. "It's exactly as it sounds, stand in the stirrup, heels down."

I do as he says, holding onto the saddle as I do.

"Perfect," he smiles as he passes me the reins. "Now stay there whilst I get onto Travis." As soon as he walks away, Betsy starts moving.

"Er, Riggs," I call out and Riggs rolls his eyes, pushing Betsy back into the stall.

"You know the metal bit you put in her mouth?" I nod. "It's connected to the reins. Hold onto her, pull back slightly, but not too much or she'll start walking backwards," he shakes his head from side to side and I tighten my grip around the reins and hold her still.

I watch as Riggs mounts Travis with such ease and I am a little jealous. He clicks the tongue at the roof of his mouth as he kicks Travis on and only then do I release the reins and Betsy just follows.

"Riggs."

"Yes," and I can tell he is so over my shit already.

"Do I need to kick Betsy on like you just did?"

"Only when you want her to trot or move on."

"Right."

"But I'll tell you when to kick on, and try with all you have to keep your ass in the saddle."

"How far have we got to go?"

"A little up the highlands."

"That's quite a ride," I say softly as I take in the sights in front of me, and even though I have seen the same view, the same rolling green fields and the same trees that dance in the wind, it all looks a little more beautiful on the back of a horse.

"Then you better get ready to ride Dixie."

Riggs kicks Travis into a faster pace and I do the same,

kicking Betsy on as her legs move beneath us, carrying me behind Riggs and I bounce in the saddle.

"Ass in the saddle Dixie, heels dug deep," he shouts out and I focus on doing as he said, ass in saddle, heels dug deep, and alright, I am no horse rider, but I managed not to fall off.

That's something right?

CHAPTER THIRTY
DIXIE

I smile ear to ear as I watch the once heifer's nursing their calves, some are jumping around in the full wildflower fields, others are curled up not too far from their moms as they snooze in the mid-afternoon sun.

"It's something right?"

"Yeah," I breathe as two younger cowboys sit in the distance, watching. My eyes scan to them before Riggs notices.

"They watch the cows, make sure they don't get into any trouble... they even sing to them of a night," and a smirk pulls at my lips, thinking that he is pulling my leg but when he doesn't falter, when his lips don't turn up into that boyish grin we all know, I realise that he is being serious.

"What do they sing?" I find myself asking as my eyes pull away from the two cowboys and watch as a young calf leaps through the flowers.

"A little bit of Dean Martin, some Kenny Rogers, bit of Dolly Parton..." and I side eye him and he bursts into laughter. "I have no idea what they sing, Dixie, why don't you trot yourself over there and ask them?" he smirks, eyes glistening in the high noon sun, and I shake my head from side to side.

"Not overly interested... just thought I would ask the question seeing as you were the one that mentioned they sing."

He scoffs a laugh, sitting relaxed on the back of his horse, shoulders rolled back as he slouches slightly, reins loose in his glove covered hands.

"I can see why you like doing this," I say quietly as I lift my eyes from him and back out to the stunning views in front of me.

"Yeah, it's peaceful, kind of takes you away from the bullshit of everyday life..." he sighs heavily, "don't get me wrong, it isn't all rainbows and butterflies. This job is hard going too. It has its perks... but it also comes with its downfalls."

"I can imagine, but isn't that the same with every job?"

"I suppose so," I hear his deep intake of breath as Travis moves forward slightly, hooves hitting the ground softly. "But I wouldn't want any other job than this," he smiles at me.

"Not even when Aspen left?"

And he looks at me, head tilting slightly.

"I had my own dreams, but once she left I kind of just fell into this. My dad made it pretty clear I wasn't to leave... made it clear that he wanted me to run this place so my dreams kind of fell on the back burner as such. Everything sort of fell into place and life just continued as normal, whether she was in my life or not."

Sadness swarms my chest.

"Look at you now though," I breathe out, trying to change the subject slightly. "You got the girl and the dream job."

He laughs softly, letting his head fall forward, shaking it from side to side, his worn cowboy hat firmly on his head.

"I am certainly living my dream, but not sure if it's the dream job. But I definitely got the dream girl and that's all I care about," he smiles a wide toothy grin at me. He averts his gaze behind him when he hears the cries of one of the heifers and I watch as his brows furrow into a scowl, jaw a little tighter than normal. He nods his head for me to follow, kicking his horse on with a click of the tongue. I nudge Betsy on and trot behind Riggs as we continue down the fields and towards the two cowboys that are sitting watch over the new moms and their babies.

"Boys," Riggs grunts as he slows Travis down and I slow just as I approach.

"Boss," the young boys nod at Riggs then move their attention towards me.

"Eyes on me."

I know they're probably only looking at me because they're wondering who I am and what the fuck I am doing here. I question myself daily.

"Everything been okay?" He asks, Travis circling around before Riggs pulls him to a halt again. Betsy just stands and I loosen the reins slightly.

"Yeah, we lost two calves this morning," the older one of the two says quietly and I hear Riggs tut before whispering *fuck* under his breath. But by the way he acted when he heard the heifer, he already knew this.

"We tried everything, the vet took too long to get here," his lips roll into a thin line as he stares down Riggs.

"Where are the heifers now?" Riggs averts his gaze, looking over the field for the crying heifers. It doesn't take him long to notice them in the field again. "Why didn't you call?" he snaps, opening his rein and turning Travis towards the back of the field. He shakes his head in a disapproving manner as he kicks Travis into a canter and I stay put, my eyes volleying between the boys who I am still trying to work out if they made an honest mistake or were just too stupid and reckless to care.

The younger one looks guilt ridden, the eldest can't hold my gaze for more than three seconds max before looking away.

"Did you fuck up?" I ask as Betsy starts to get antsy beneath me, my eyes searching for Riggs and the younger one shuffles uncomfortably in the saddle of his horse. "Shit," I groan as I kick Betsy on and she finds her gallop as my hands move up her neck, my body leaning down, and my heart is thrashing in my chest.

I finally catch up with Riggs and he is seething.

"What can I do to help?" I ask, feeling like a spare part as Betsy circles around.

"Just try and keep the herd away from these two," he nods his head and anxiety swarms my stomach. How the hell am I meant to do that. I turn Betsy around and trot towards the cows, and they move down towards the two cowboys. I wave my hand in the air, whistling and they gallop up.

"Keep the herd away, can you do that?" I ask a little more condescending than I wanted too, but I heard the urgency in Riggs voice and for some reason, I didn't want to disappoint him.

Pulling on Betsy's rein, I open it up and move towards Riggs who is reaching for his rope.

"Stay close," he says softly as he loops the rope and begins to swing it above his head, "we're going to rope the heifers and lead them back to the ranch."

I nod, swallowing the nerves down and the cows must

sense what is coming because they begin to move, calling out for their lost calves and my heart aches heavily in my chest. Riggs moves along the side of them, throwing his rope and catching one of them just as he slows his horse down and pulls the cow towards him.

I watch in awe, somewhat mesmerised with what I am witnessing. Glancing over my shoulder, I see the two young cowboys herding the cows further down the field and relief swarms me.

"Hold onto her," Riggs orders as he trots over to me, pulling the cow behind him.

"What?"

"You heard me, hold onto her... don't let her escape," he passes me the rope that is wrapped around the cow's neck, and I look up at Riggs. "Can you do that for me Dixie?" he asks, clearly out of breath, hand resting on his thigh as he waits for my answer.

I nod, fingers tightening around the rope like my life depended on it.

Riggs returns my nod and kicks on his horse down the field as he goes to hunt down the other heifer.

The cow pulls against me, and I panic. Moving Betsy forward, I begin to lead her down the fence line as I wait for Riggs to catch up with me, and I feel relieved when I see him trotting over the hill with the missing heifer as he slows and begins to walk beside me.

"Ready to get these girls home?" He asks, tilting his cowboy hat towards me.

"Sure thing, boss." I beam as we make our way back towards the ranch in a comfortable silence.

Once we're back, Hudson greets us as he walks out of the bunkhouse.

"All okay?" Riggs asks, but Hudson's eyes move to the

two heifers behind us. Riggs follows his gaze, hands resting on the horn of the saddle before he is back turned towards his cowboy.

"Lost their calves," he answers the unspoken question.

Hudson gives a solemn nod, then takes another step towards Riggs.

"Bulls are good, all health checked and hopefully we will get another good breed from them."

"Good," Riggs grunts.

"What do you want me to do with the girls?" he rubs Travis' neck, giving him a soft pat as he waits for Riggs to answer.

"Call around, see if we have any calves that need moms, if not... well..."

"Not a problem," Hudson bobs his head in a knowing nod as Riggs begins to move forward, leading his cow into the pasture, I follow his lead as Hudson steps aside and watches us.

"Where will they go if they don't get a calf?" I ask.

"Slaughterhouse maybe, might keep them for another breeding cycle... but I'm not sure."

"Why?"

He laughs softly, "Why the slaughterhouse or why the breeding?"

"Why aren't you sure?" Riggs jumps down from his horse, tying him to the metal railing then leads his cow into the pasture and through the metal gate.

I follow suit.

"They've both lost a calf before this, just not sure if it's worth the heartache and the money to keep breeding if their calves don't survive."

I roll my lips. I mean, it makes sense.

I say nothing. Because honestly, my heart hurts a little

more today than usual. Sucking in my bottom lip, I try and ignore the tremble and the way my eyes are stinging and clouding.

I know it's because I want to cry. I just don't want to.

And yes, the reason I want to cry is because of the cows.

I. Am. Wrecked.

Every muscle in my body aches.

Riggs hits the trim of my hat as my heavy legs carry me across the dusty trail. "You done good today, kid," he smiles as he unlocks his truck. "See you tomorrow."

"Yeah?" I smile feeling all proud of myself.

"Yeah, Dixie... you're a cowgirl now," he winks at me just as he climbs into his truck and shuts the door, and just for that moment, I feel like I am doing what I should have all along.

Walking through the front door, it's just past four p.m.

The house is quiet, but the smell that surrounds me has my stomach rumbling. I hadn't eaten today. We had been so busy down the fields; lunch was the last thing to enter my mind.

"Hey," I call out as I sit on the small bench by the front door in the lobby and take my boots off, sighing in relief at how amazing it felt.

"In here darling," Orla calls out and I float across to where she is cooking over the stove. Looking over her shoulder, her cheeks are rosy, eyes glistening. "Did you have a good day?"

I can barely nod. "So tired though," I half laugh as I look at the empty highchair then back to Orla.

"She's with Tripp, they've been inseparable," and my heart swarms deep inside my chest.

"How's Pacey?"

"He is doing okay," I watch as her face falters for just a moment, "but he is a strong boy. He'll be up and about in no time causing havoc around the ranch like he does," and my lips curl at the corners.

"That's good to hear."

She hums, "Jorge is still down there, won't leave his side. I'm going to take dinner up to both of them."

"They'll appreciate that," I let my eyes drift for just a moment.

"Dinner will be done in about an hour. Chicken in a white wine sauce, potatoes and all the veg," and my stomach rumbles loud in appreciation, my boobs aching. "Has my son not fed you today?" she spins, crossing her arms across her chest.

"Honestly, we have been so busy, even if we did sort lunch, we wouldn't have had a chance to eat it," I half laugh. Last thing I want is for her to call Riggs out and snap the already thin line between us. He has only just started warming up to me, I don't want him to pull away now.

"Okay," she gives a knowing nod before she turns around and continues cooking.

Forcing my weighted legs to move I walk out of the kitchen and turn left as I walk out of the double archway and down towards Tripp's room. I have missed Lainey immensely. I have missed Tripp an immeasurable amount. My two favorite people.

My steps falter when I can hear a soft lullaby coming from his room. Standing still, it takes me a moment to realise he is singing *Neon Star - Morgan Wallen*. Walking quietly, careful not to draw attention to myself, I peek my head around the door frame and listen. He is resting in the armchair that sits in the corner of his makeshift bedroom. His head is drooped, eyes cast down on my daughter. Her wide blue eyes are glued to him, corners of her mouth lifting into a smile as she babbles at him.

I'm not watching them long when I am caught. Tripp's eyes light up, his lips pursing into a wide toothy grin as he continues to sing.

"And look who is home Lainey," he sings in a similar tune as he delicately lifts her up, turning her so she can see me. Her little feet resting on his thighs, one on each and I worry about his cast. His hands tuck under her arms softly and when her big, beautiful eyes land on me, she squeals, her smile growing as she begins to jump up and down with excitement on Tripp's lap.

"Hey baby," I coo, walking in and scooping her from Tripp's arms as I hold her close, my cheek on hers before I kiss her for what feels like a million times. "God I missed you," I whisper into the top of her head as I hold her close to me, eyes fluttered shut for just a moment before they find Tripp's. "Missed you too," I croak and his eyes glisten with a shimmer of blue.

"Not as much as I missed you," he sighs, as if the words lay heavy on his chest.

Stepping closer to him, I lean down slowly and place a soft kiss on his lips. Whilst holding Lainey against my chest, her grabby hands trying to get inside my shirt.

"The day went so slow, but somehow the hours slipped away."

"Welcome to parenthood," I smirk as I stand and bounce Lainey in my arms but she fights to get towards my boobs.

"She's an angel," he breaks his gaze from mine before he

is watching Lainey, small creases in his forehead appear as his brows crinkle whilst he studies her. "Honestly, she has been a dream."

Smiling, I drop my head as I look at my daughter and a wave of unconditional love blankets me.

"She ate well, drunk her bottle and napped for a few hours. Mom was back before she was due her next one, so she took over," his eyes move to me. "Kind of hated that she did to be honest," and I laugh softly.

"Well, I have to work tomorrow so," I nibble the inside of my cheek and his face lights up.

"I'll watch her," he shuffles forward, and I let my gaze linger on his handsome face a little longer. Small wrinkles either side of his eyes, probably from squinting at the sun a little too much. They're a beautiful dark brown, flecks of honey drizzled through and in some lights, they look almost black. Golden skin that has a constant glow. Soft dark stubble brushes across his chin, jaw and upper lip. Full pink lips that I am always so desperate to kiss. His hair caramel brown, messy and long on top, short around the sides. My eyes fixate on the small scar above his eye from when Riggs hit him with a horseshoe, and suddenly, I am desperate to trace my fingers over the small indent in his imperfect skin.

A shallow hiss has me pulling from my dreamy gaze, his eyes are slammed shut, teeth gritted as he tries to move.

Popping Lainey in her crib, she starts to cry because I put her down. I move quickly to where he is, crouching down on my knees.

"What do you need?" I ask him, eyes volleying back and forth.

"Just..." he grits, "help..." *sigh,* "me move." His voice comes out more as a beg and I nod. Unsure what he wants me to do. Pushing to my feet, he reaches out for me, and I grip under his arm as I pull him closer to the edge of the seat.

"Do you want to get up or...?" I ask what seems like a stupid question.

He chokes out a cry as I try and pull him to his feet.

"Slowly," I whisper, trying my best to hold his weight against my frame as he hobbles forward, my legs moving back.

"I am struggling," he whispers, vulnerability written all over his face.

"You're doing so well handsome," I smirk, trying to lighten the mood but I can see the pain behind his eyes. We keep slowly moving until he is next to his chair, his trembling hand moving to grab the arm rest. His grip around my hand tightens and he slowly moves to lower himself into his seat. I don't let him go, and even though my body is screaming with the way my muscles are being stretched, I help him until I know he is safe.

His head falls back softly, and if I wasn't looking at him, I would have missed it. A glisten streaks his cheek and my heart aches.

Lainey's soft cries soon turn into full on wails.

"Thank you," he can't even look at me, his eyes are still closed.

"No need to thank me," I whisper as I turn on my heel, but his fingers curling around my wrist has me looking over my shoulder at him.

"Honestly Dixie..."

I smile at him, and I feel myself getting choked up as I look at the man before me, soul broken and wounded.

"It's no problem," I nod, slowly pulling away from him and walking towards Lainey's crib. Bending slowly, I pick her up and cradle her as I unbutton my shirt with one hand and let her latch on. Turning to walk from the room, my steps falter and I realise I haven't asked him about physio. *What a bitch,* my inner thoughts lash against my skin, burning me with their marks.

"How did you get on today?" and I hate myself for not asking sooner.

"Good, hard work… but good," a twitch of his lips causes one side to lift into a lopsided smile.

"That's good, baby steps right?"

"Yeah, she thinks I'll be on crutches in the next week or so, then cast comes off in four."

"You'll do it, I have every faith," I mutter and begin to walk as Lainey's whines turn into sobs. His fingers brush across my forearm as I pass him, causing my breath to catch in the back of my throat.

"Stay with me tonight," his voice comes out more of a beg than a question.

"I have to be up early," I whisper, my eyes dusting over Lainey as she suckles.

"So, please, stay with me," his eyes burn through to my soul showing me just how vulnerable he is. "The nightmares don't plague me when you're next to me," he rasps, voice thick and cracking, "you're my dreamcatcher, Dixie. Please."

His fingertips brush slowly up and down my already sensitive skin, causing it to erupt into goosebumps.

"Always," I just about manage to croak out and he curls his fingers around my delicate wrist, bringing it to his lips as he places soft, wet kisses along the inside.

"I love you Dixie."

"I love you," I choke before slipping my arm from his soft grasp and walking out of his room to settle Lainey.

Guilt buries itself inside my heaving chest as Lucian's words ring around my ears.

"We're leaving in four weeks, I suggest you get yourself packed up."

"Who said I am leaving?"

"We have a show..."

"There is no we. I am not leaving. I don't want to leave with you."

"Who said you had a choice?" he reaches out and grabs the top of my arm, squeezing tightly as he drags me to my feet.

"I left you, I gave you all I had and told you it was over," I try and pull my arm from his grip but he just tightens it.

"If you do not do as I say, I will take the Rivera Family out one by fucking one and make you watch as I sink a bullet between their eyes. And I mean it Dixie, I want to know everything those bastard boys are up to in regards to the gold mines, that's my golden ticket, and if you play along, it'll be yours too."

Two weeks had already passed in the blink of an eye, and Lucian is not a patient man. He knows where I am, no doubt he has his beady eyes on me at all times, but I am not ready to fight him yet.

He wants information out of me, wants me to run right back to him and Wallen and feed him everything I have heard, but there is nothing. Two out of the three Rivera brothers were down, Austin turned himself in for a crime he didn't commit.

Worst of all, I knew everything.

I was part of this sick plan, but I didn't want to be.

But once they threatened Lainey, I was their prisoner. Bound to them so fucking tightly that even though I wanted to, I would never escape.

Death would be the only way out of this.

But I couldn't leave Lainey.

Shaking my head from side to side, I ignore my thoughts.

I was going to fix this, I needed o.

I loved Tripp.

Always have. Always will.

I will not let Wallen or Lucian get to them. I would sacrifice myself ten times over for them. For *him.*

The sound of my bedroom door opening has me jumping and trying to cover myself as I still nurse Lainey.

"Only me sweet," Orla's soft voice fills the room and I smile, relieved that it wasn't Jorge or Riggs.

She walks into the small room, unfolding the travel crib that was downstairs in Tripp's room.

"Thought you would need this up here," she smiles softly as she places it on the hardwood floor before putting it up.

"Thank you," I whisper as my eyes lock on Lainey who is milk drunk and dozing.

"Don't thank me sweet girl," she sighs as if my words are wasted on her.

"I do need to thank you," and I feel the familiar burn crawling up my throat as tears threaten to fall. "You took me and Lainey in for a few nights and we're still here nearly a month on," I sniffle as I stroke Lainey's soft brown hair, her fingers curled around my pendant.

"You're family Dixie, you and little Lainey make all of our days so much brighter," she tilts her head to the side.

I choke out a sob and hate that I have let the tears fall.

"You're helping around the ranch, you and Tripp are well... whatever you are," she smirks, "and I know how hard it must be for you to be back here again, back where your memories are not happy ones." She steps towards me, slowly sitting next to me on my bed.

I nod.

"But we're all glad you're back," she wraps her arms around my shoulders and pulls me into her for a cuddle.

"I'm glad to be back," and I kind of wish it was a lie, but it's not. I was terrified of coming back here, but now I am... I can't imagine being anywhere else.

"Good, our sweet girl," she whispers into my hair as she kisses me like my mom used to and my heart breaks, slowly shattering into a million tiny pieces inside my hollow chest. "Now, go get cleaned up. You stink and dinner will be done in twenty," she whispers, and I can see the smirk pulling at her painted red lips.

I sniffle, laughing softly as I stand with a snoozing Lainey, kissing her forehead and lingering for just a moment before I lay her down with her comforter.

"Night baby," I whisper, my fingers dusting through her hair.

"I'll take the monitor down, see you shortly," Orla says as she picks the monitor up and walks out of the door, not looking back.

The smile quickly slips from my lips and the anxiety rips through me, but I push it down and head for the shower.

Not tonight Dixie... not tonight.

CHAPTER THIRTY-ONE
TRIPP

Dixie was quiet during dinner, but to be honest, mom was too.

The house felt too quiet. Too empty. Haunted almost. Dad, Riggs and Pacey were missing from our table. My mom kept looking at the head of the table where Dad would normally sit and sighing before her eyes dragged across to where Pacey would normally be sitting.

"Won't be long, ma," I smile, stabbing my fork into a potato. "Table will be full again," I try and force a smile out and she nods, silent tears building behind her eyes.

"I know," her voice is a whisper, "hate a quiet house," she admits before her eyes are cast down to her plate.

"Dinner is delicious Orla," Dixie's voice floats across the table, the sincerity loud in her tone.

"Thank you, sweet girl."

Slowly sinking my hand under the table, I rest it on Dixie's bare thigh and I don't miss the way her breath catches at the back of her throat at the feel of my fingers on her skin.

"I'll be at the hospital late tonight, might even stay

there." My mom says a little louder as my fingertips trace circles on her thighs.

"Okay," I answer as I reach for my glass and swallow down a mouthful of water.

"Will you be okay?" she asks and I can see the worry that etches into her face.

"Of course, I have Dixie," I turn my face to look at her and she gives my mum a wide grin. My gut knots, her eyes look empty, her mind elsewhere maybe.

Shit, did I do something wrong?

Slipping my hand from her thigh, I bring it back on top of the table and pick up my knife and fork as I cut into my chicken, coating it in the thick white wine sauce.

"I'll look after him," she reassures my mom as she takes a mouthful of her own drink as if she is trying to wet her dry mouth.

"I have no doubt about that," my mom responds, placing her napkin over her half full plate before she pushes it away. Her voice is cold, her eyes glazed over with tears.

"Mom, you need to eat," I say softly, reaching across to try to place my hand over hers.

"I'm just not very hungry," she admits, giving me a sad smile and standing from the table. "If you'll excuse me, I'm going to clean up before I leave for the hospital."

We both nod as my mom lifts her plate and glass then walks away into the kitchen, just leaving me and Dixie alone. My heart aches and I wish I could do so much more.

"Is everything okay?" I find myself asking as I look at her, studying every little marking on her face.

She doesn't look at me, just keeps her eyes on her plate of food as she pushes it around and after what feels like a lifetime, she gives me a nod.

"Have I done something to upset you?" and that's

when she turns her face up to look at me, eyes brimming with tears as she shakes her head from side to side. "Dix, fuck," I rasp, turning my body to face her as I cup her cheek in my hand, brushing my thumb across her soft skin as I wipe her tears away and hold her still so she has no other option but to look at me, eyes burning into my soul.

"Honestly, I am fine. I'm tired," she chokes, half laughing as a sob breaks in her voice.

"Then how about we get to bed, hm?" I say softly as I lean into her and place a delicate kiss on her forehead.

She nods, sniffling.

"Okay, well eat up then we will settle down."

I know she is lying, when you've known someone as long as I've known Dixie, you come to notice their little traits and quirks. Dixie can't lie for shit. Her bottom lip quivers ever so slightly, and if you weren't looking for it you would never notice it. Her eyes fixate on yours, slightly widening. It's like her whole body freezes.

But I won't push.

There is a reason she isn't talking, and I will find out eventually, but tonight I just want to wrap her in my arms and have her head on my chest as she falls asleep to the sound of my steady heartbeat.

We finish dinner in comfortable silence and once we're done, she stands and clears the table. I protest but let's be honest, she is quicker than me at the moment. Dishes cleaned, and kitchen tidy, she is leant across the countertop, eyes fixated on the view in front of her.

The sun is beginning to set, the skies a mix between pink and lilac as a blanket of navy begins to creep in.

My eyes roam up and down her body. Cute satin pyjama shorts that cut off just above the crease of her ass cheeks, the frill of her satin matching vest sits on her lower back, most of it hidden by her long brown hair.

I wheel closer to her, my fingertips delicately brushing up the back of her legs and her breath stutters at the feel of my soft touch on her skin. She averts her gaze from the evening and looks at me over her shoulder.

"Hey," her voice is soft, a small smile picking at the corners of her mouth.

"You would tell me if something was wrong, wouldn't you baby?" my voice is low as my fingers curl around the inside of her thigh, my lips pressing softly where my fingertips were just dusting.

"Yes," she breathes, my fingers digging into her skin a little harder, my kisses still soft.

"Good," I murmur between my lips touching her thighs.

"It's just been a long few weeks," she admits just as I lift my mouth. She spins around, fingers curling around the edge of the worktop, hair falling gently and framing her pretty face. Her head tilts as she looks down at me.

"I know," nibbling on my bottom lip, "but it'll get better. It won't be like this forever."

She nods, pulling her eyes from me for a moment.

"Do you know..." my voice is hushed, a boyish smirk tugging at my lips as I curl my finger inside the waistband of her shorts. "How desperate I am to taste you on my tongue Dixie?"

Her cheeks flame red, mouth popping open for just a second before her teeth are sinking into her bottom lip.

Her grip tightens as I drag my fingers down the front of her shorts, brushing them across the front of her pussy before they slip between her legs and rub her through the thin, satin material.

Her breath hitches as I let them slip inside her shorts,

grinning when I feel her bare and soaked. Fingers glide through her pussy lips, teasing the tips in her arousal.

"Take them off," I order as I drag my hands out of her shorts.

She nods, uncurling her fingers and hooking them inside the waistband as she slides them down her gorgeous legs. They pool at her bare feet and she goes all shy on me, and it's hard to see her like this when she took control the night before when she rode my cock like a god damn pro bull rider.

"Don't be getting all shy on me now, baby," I rasp, my eyes falling to her perfect pink pussy, and I can't wait to bury my tongue inside of her. "Up on the counter," and she does, she lifts herself up, a hitch in her breath as the cool surface meets her hot skin.

She is the perfect height, and sure, I would rather eat her sweet cunt on my knees instead of my chair, but beggars can't be choosers. I needed to taste her, needed her cum on my tongue as she moans around the room.

Her fingers curl around the edge of the counter, ass right on the edge as I tease my fingers up her inner thighs, slipping one, then two fingers deep inside her hot, tight, cunt.

She shudders as my lips dust up the inside of her thighs.

"You make me feel like a queen," she whispers and my brows knot as I lift my heavy brown eyes to hers.

"Always baby, I would never treat you as anything less," I rasp.

"I wish it had only been you," and I slip my fingers from her and I see sadness bloom across her beautiful face. I go to speak but she stops me. "I haven't been with many... just two after you."

I have no idea why she is telling me this now, but I

listen. If this is what has been bothering her, I don't want to shut her down now.

"But after Lainey, he…" and her eyes glisten as they find mine and I nod knowing full well who she is talking about. "He said I was ruined… damaged…" and my fucking blood boils. I didn't need any more ammunition to hate Clay more than I did, but hearing those words leave her pretty mouth has me reeling.

She sucks in a heavy breath.

"He told me no one would ever want me because I birthed our daughter," and it's taking everything in me to keep calm. I know what she is insinuating. But there is no fucking chance in hell the man knew what the fuck he was talking about. Inhaling deeply through my nose and exhaling a shaky, but angry breath through my mouth, I tilt my head to the side. Her eyes are bouncing between mine, chest rising and falling as she lays herself bare in front of me.

"Baby," I whisper, my own anger slowly simmering down into nothing as my fingers tease up her inner thigh, dusting across her perfect cunt. "I can promise you…" I kiss where my fingers have left a trail that only I can see, "you're not ruined," *kiss,* "or damaged," *kiss.* My fingers are teasing at her pussy, her lips parting as I slowly slip one, then two, fingers back into her, stretching her. "Your pussy was made me for me and only me, and…" I smirk as I let my lips brush on the top of her thigh as my other hand spreads her leg a little wider for me, my fingers slipping in deeper. "Your cunt feels just as good as when I took your virginity ten years ago," my thumb brushes against her clit, and her head falls forward as she watches me fuck her sweet cunt with my fingers.

"Look how perfect you are, Dixie," I moan, a third finger

teasing, and her mouth drops open, "you're not ruined baby," I choke just as I lean closer and swipe my tongue across her clit.

"Tripp," she whispers.

"Feet on the counter," I lift my lips from her, smirking as a string of her arousal connects to my lips. She does as I ask, her feet on the counter and her thighs wide, her pussy begging to be eaten as my fingers fuck her slow. Flattening my tongue, I swipe through her cunt as my thumb pulls her pussy lip, burying my tongue deeper. Pussy full of my fingers, tongue working her clit and I am desperate to have my cock in her too.

I moan against her clit as she clenches around my fingers, a drip of arousal coating my tongue and I tease another finger inside. Hips rolling forward, her moans vibrate through her. She watches, eyes all wide as she focuses on the way my mouth moves over her clit, stroke by stroke, my tongue closer to pulling her orgasm from her.

"I'm so close," her fingers lock around my hair as she tightens her grip, my head tilting to the side, rubbing her clit with my tongue. Pussy tightening around my fingers as I fully push the third into her now and I groan as wetness trickles down my hand.

"Fuck," she sobs, and not once has she lifted her eyes from her pussy.

Letting my tongue glide and tease at her opening, I am desperate to have her coming on my tongue. She grinds her greedy cunt onto my fingers, taking all three deeper with each roll of her hips.

"You getting all needy Dixie?" I tease, lifting my mouth from her and her blue eyes are masked by pleasure, her body trembling as I push her closer with each curl of my finger towards her orgasm, waiting to watch her free-fall in front of me.

"I need to come," she chokes, and I moan, leaning back for just a moment as I look at how hot she looks. Needy and sweaty, cunt full of my fingers. Rubbing my thumb over her clit, I pull her pussy apart as I lower my lips back over her swollen clit, sucking it into my mouth as she cries.

"I'm going..." and she can't even finish her sentence. My fingers fall from her soaked cunt and wrap around her hips as I lift her to my mouth, her fingers holding her upper weight as I eat her deep and fast and she comes on my tongue, her body convulsing under my mouth and I smirk as I lick her fucking clean.

"Shit," I groan as she pulls back. She looks so fucking pretty. Eyes wild and full of her shattered orgasm, skin all dewy that I am desperate to feel under my fingers, lips parted and full that I so badly want to kiss.

She slips off the counter, legs trembling as she reaches down to pick up her discarded shorts.

My hand presses against her lower stomach, stopping her from moving away from me.

"You okay?" and she nods, the sadness still threatening to take over in her pretty blue eyes. I go to speak again but she shakes her head from side to side and presses her finger over my lips.

"No more talking," she nods at me, "I need you Tripp."

My cock hardens, throbbing in my cotton shorts.

She slowly stands and saunters her way to my bedroom, grabbing a bottle of whiskey from the side unit as she does and I give myself just a second, because I am scared if I go in there right now, I'll cum in three seconds.

CHAPTER THIRTY-TWO
DIXIE

I swig from the whiskey bottle and ignore the burn. I shouldn't really be drinking, but I'll pump and dump before bed like I did the other night when me and Tripp drunk whiskey. The warmth settles my anxiety and guilt, and I need to come clean. I will. Just not tonight. Tonight I want Tripp to make me forget everything.

My cheeks flame at my vulnerability back in the kitchen, telling him just some of the stuff that Clay said to me, and I have no idea why I told him. Maybe it was my own insecurities shining through and mixed with the guilt I already felt, something had to give.

I take another mouthful and wince at the bitter taste. My eyes lift to the door when I see Tripp there.

"Fuck," he rasps, "I can't wait to be out of this damn cast," he rolls towards me, and I smirk.

"And why is that Mr Rivera?" I tease.

"Because I *need* to fuck you."

"Is my fucking you not good enough?" I pout, crossing my legs in front of me as I stand, one hand on hip.

"Oh baby, you're fucking is top tier..." he smirks, "but

the way I *want* to fuck you... well," he winks and my insides alight with desire, my pussy practically dripping and needy for him.

"You forgot your hat..." he tuts and my stomach flips.

"Oops," I roll my lips as a smile spreads across my face.

"Go get it baby," his throat bobs and I place the bottle on the bedside unit and do as I am told, scarpering away and grabbing my cowboy hat from the stand in the hallway. Walking back into the room, the trim of the cowboy hat between my fingertips.

My eyes devour Tripp laying on his bed, ripped body on show, cotton shorts hanging around his waist.

"How did you get there?" I sigh, a little annoyed that he moved himself.

"Magic," he winks and I laugh softly.

"Idiot," I kneel on the bed, reaching for the whiskey before swinging my leg over his body and sitting over his lap. "Thirsty?" I ask as I hold the whiskey bottle up, he shakes his head as I take a mouthful.

"The only whiskey I want to be tasting is off your lips, your tongue..." he trails off just as I lean down and cover his lips with mine, our tongues dancing and the taste of whiskey still evident on my tastebuds. He moans into my mouth, his hand clasping my face and his cock rubs over my clit.

Rolling my hips over him, I smirk as our teeth clash.

"Don't be a tease Dixie," he whispers, rocking my satin covered pussy over his thick cock.

"I don't tease Tripp," my tongue dips back into his mouth and his fingers knead my hips.

"I beg to differ baby," he whispers as I slowly sit up, wriggling my needy pussy over him.

He wraps his fingers around the bottle neck of the

whiskey, but I snatch it back, tilting it and his eyes widen as I let it drip onto his stomach, filling his belly button.

"Dixie," his shrill laugh fills the room as I lean down and run my tongue over his body, lapping up every ounce of spilt whiskey before I dip my tongue and clean him.

Pushing up, I can feel wetness pooling in my satin shorts.

"I am so wet for you Tripp," I breathe, becoming a little brazen as the whiskey makes my cheeks flame red.

And this time, I let him take the bottle from me.

My eyes flicker to the baby monitor that sits on the side, just wanting to make sure she was okay.

Lifting my hips, I move back slightly and wrap my fingers into the waist band of his shorts and tug them down his thick, toned legs, careful not to catch his cast.

Pulling my bottom lip into my mouth, I lower myself down between his legs.

"Baby, what are you doing?" he asks, but his words soon escape as a soft moan catches at the back of his throat when my tongue runs up from his balls to the tip of his cock and I smile as his dick bobs against his stomach.

Kissing down his thick length, my tongue flicks across his balls and he moans, neck craned, eyes on me as he watches as my tongue strokes him.

Dragging back to the swollen head of his cock, I curl my fingers around his length, pursing him on my bottom lip as I look at him through my lashes.

"Fuck, Dixie," he rasps, head rolling back for just a moment. I am leant over him, ass in the air. "I am desperate to fuck you like that, your ass high as I pound your sweet cunt," and his hips roll as I take him to the back of my throat. His fingers grip onto the bedsheet beneath his hot body, his muscles tense as I tease the head of his cock on the tip of my tongue.

His eyes are back on me as he watches me suck his dick, my cheeks hollow as I wriggle, trying to relieve the pressure that is building deep inside of me. One of my hands skates underneath my body as I circle my clit. Rubbing the head of his cock on the inside of my cheek, I slip him from my mouth for just a moment as my eyes connect with his. I'm on my knees, rubbing my clit as I moan, my other hand still tightly wrapped around his cock.

His mouth is loose, hanging slightly, eyes hooded as he fights against his pleasure.

Slipping my hand from my clit, I roll my hardened nipple through my vest and lower my lips slightly so they're hovering just above his swollen head. I spit on his cock, rubbing my thumb over his sensitive tip before swallowing him down, fingers tight around the base of his dick as my mouth moves up and down his slippery cock.

"Shit," his hand is in my hair, gripping at the root as he pulls me off him. Whimpering at the loss, he nods his head back for me to move closer to him. I crawl over his body, brushing the head of his dick against my clit as I do and his fingers dig into my cheeks as his tongue swipes past my lips.

"I am fucking feral for you," he groans, his spare hand palming my ass cheek, lazily skating his fingers under my shorts as he pushes two fingers into my soaked cunt.

"Oh," I moan, back arching as my hips begin to move. My eyes fall between my legs, I'm on all fours over his body and I am desperate to be fucked hard in this position. "How long till you can fuck me like this?" I moan as my pussy tightens around his fingers.

"Soon baby," he hushes me, grabbing my chin, lifting

my face to his and locking his lips with mine. Whimpering at the loss when his fingers finally slip from my dripping pussy he brings them to his mouth and pushes them between his cushioned lips as he licks them clean.

"So fucking good," he groans.

"Let me taste you," I whisper, trying to lower myself but his hand is on my face, cupping my cheek as he shakes his head from side to side.

"I need my cock inside of you, I am begging you," he pants as my hips roll over his cock.

"You all needy baby?" I taunt and he growls.

"I am," his voice is all shaky as my pussy rubs up and down his length.

He says nothing, his eyes watching as I bring him closer to his orgasm.

"What do you want Tripp?" I tease, not letting up.

"Let me fuck you, let me fill your pretty cunt with my cock. I need you Dixie..." he moans and I feel wetness coat my satin shorts and I know it's from him.

"Let me fuck you..."

"*Please*," the beg in his voice has me hot and bothered.

"Such a good boy," I praise him, lips on his as my hips still slip back and forth over his hard cock.

His greedy hands are on my hips, his fingers digging into my hot skin and I am desperate for him. Pulling away, his eyes burn into mine as I reach for the hem of my tank, lifting it over my head and his hands are on my skin, skating up my sternum and grabbing my full breasts, groping and kneading and I am grateful I pumped before I came down.

Reluctantly, I move, lifting from him and his hands reach for my hips, pulling me back down.

"You want me to ride you cowboy?" I let my tongue run

across my top lip and he nods eagerly. "Then let me get my hat," I wink, and he finally lifts his hands from me as I climb from the bed and grab my hat from the far end of the side unit. Slipping my fingers into my shorts, I slip them down, the whole time his hungry eyes on me. Kicking them off my feet, I climb back onto the bed and before I even get the chance to sit on his lap, his hands are on my ass, pushing me forward as he buries his tongue deep inside my pussy, tongue fucking me as his nose rubs against my needy clit.

"Tripp," I pant, eyes rolling in the back of my head. With every thrust of his tongue and stroke against my clit, my orgasm is getting closer and I want to make a mess on his cock, not on his tongue. "I want to cum all over your big, thick, cock," I moan as my hips roll.

"And you will," he groans as his tongue slips from my wet cunt, "I just needed one last taste," he smirks as he lets me move back, legs either side of him.

Placing the hat on my head, I tilt my head to the side and my cheeks pinch a rosy pink.

"Fuck, you're so hot," he sings, voice smothering me in goosebumps.

Kneeling up, I wrap my fingers around his cock, rubbing his swollen head over my clit then slipping him through my pussy lips.

"Your cunt is just…" he loses his trail of thought as I line him up at my soaked cunt, and slowly, teasingly I sink down onto his cock, inch by fucking torturous inch as he fills me.

My mouth hangs as pleasure splinters through me. I will never get used to his size. His cock is thick and long and just the most perfect I have ever seen.

My hands splay against his chest as I lift myself slightly, rocking my hips over him as I fuck him slowly, but this position is never enough for me, I need him deep. I need more of him. Spreading my legs a little more, I bury him deeper inside of me.

Lazy strokes from his fingers make their way to my hips as he curls his hand around them and lifts me, using my pussy how he needs it.

"Use me Tripp," I beg, eyes fluttering shut, back arched slightly as his cock rubs against my g-spot.

"Reverse cowgirl," he rasps, voice all tight. "I want to watch my thick cock stretch your perfect cunt out."

Arousal drips from me as I move and his finger buries deep inside of me, his thumb brushing over my clit as he fucks me.

"I can never get enough of you," he moans, and I watch as his fingers work me up, his cock covered in my wetness.

Wrapping my fingers around his wrist, I tug on his wrist and he lets his fingers slip out of me and he lifts his hand, pushing his fingers between my lips as I suck my arousal from them.

"Fuck," he hisses.

Moving before he buries them back inside of me, I climb over him, my back to his chest and he lines himself up at my pussy, teasing me but I can tease him right back. My hips rock back and forth as I slip the head of his cock just inside my pussy and just as I try again, his fingers are curled around my hip, the other lost in my hair as he grabs a handful and pulls my head back so I am arched whilst riding his cock.

"Shit, you're so hot Dixie," he moans, the soft whimpers leaving him every time my pussy sucks his cock deep inside of me. "My cock looks so good buried in your cunt," and his dirty mouth has my skin smothered in goosebumps.

Slipping himself to the tip and clenching my pussy around his swollen head has my orgasm teetering.

"Do that again," he rasps, the hand that was curled around my hip dragging down to my ass cheeks, spreading them.

Doing as he asked, I lift myself up his cock, leaving just the tip inside myself and I clench. Primal growls fill the room, his fingers digging into my ass and using it to slam me back down on his cock.

"You're such a nasty girl Dixie," he pants, making my pussy clench. "Ride me baby, make me cum so I can fill your sweet little cunt up."

Leaning my upper body forward slightly, I wrap my hands around his thighs, mindful not to hurt him as my hips roll over his cock, burying him inside of me.

"I need more," he begs, and I still, looking at him over my shoulder.

"Okay," I whisper.

"Don't move," he smirks as he drags us back towards his headboard. My back to his chest, his good leg bending up, his bad one hanging off the bed and I'm worried he is going to hurt himself.

"Hold your legs," and I do, I hook my hands under my thighs, pulling them wide and holding them in the air.

"Good girl," he whispers in my ear, his fingers finding my clit, working me up once more. "You might be the dominant one now Dixie, but once I have been given the green light, I am going to ruin you for any other man, ruin you for your own hand, your toys... everything. I will pound into your cunt hard, just like you want me to. Make the most of being the one in charge, because it's not going to last," he rasps just as his hips begin to move, his cock fucking me deep and slipping in and out of me with ease.

The sounds of wetness and skin meeting all mixing with our moans as we chase our orgasms.

"That's it, keep holding your legs baby," he whispers, nipping at the shell of my ear as his hands skate under me, spreading my ass cheeks just as a finger teases there and my pussy tightens.

Fingers rubbing my clit pull me from the feel of a finger slipping into my ass, and I explode as his cock fucks me deep and hard.

"Tripp, shit," I sob, head throwing back against his chest.

"Yes baby, come all over my cock," his voice is tight as I ride through my orgasm and just when I am spent, body trembling, I let go of my legs, pushing his knee down and I take control, riding his cock until his breath labours and his cock pulses inside of me.

"I'm going to fill your tight little cunt full of me," he moans loudly as his own orgasm shatters through him, and he throbs deep in me, filling me with his cum.

THE LAST FEW days whizzed by quickly and we somehow fell into a new routine. Tripp helped with Lainey whilst I was on the ranch with Riggs doing what I could to help lighten the load. He looked tired, working long hours then up most of the night dealing with Austin's lawyers along with Buck and Blue.

Pacey was due home tomorrow so Orla was trying to get everything sorted for him, whilst Jorge stayed at the hospital until he was ready to leave. As the hours ticked by, I was getting more cautious about Lucian turning up. He said four weeks. We were rolling into the third week, and he had gone silent, and I wish I could say that was a good thing, but it wasn't. He was planning, plotting, no doubt with Wallen.

Uneasiness settles in my chest, and I have to take myself away from the table, a crushing weight falling onto my shoulders.

Tripp calls after me, and in this moment, I am glad he can't follow me. Shutting myself away in my room, I slide down the door and try my hardest to suck as much air into my lungs as possible, but it didn't matter how hard I tried, nothing seemed to help. The weight on my shoulders rolled down into my chest and the uneasiness was replaced by a tight elastic band sitting just under my breasts. I was being crushed. This is how I was going to die.

Closing my eyes, my fingers curling into a ball and flexing straight. I continued this rhythm as I focused on my breathing, willing that it would soon be over.

A knock on my bedroom door has me jumping when I hear Riggs' voice.

"You okay, kid? Tripp sent me up."

"I'm fine," I choke out, the air snatched from my lungs as the tightness presents itself again.

"Let me in," he tries to push against me, but I push back.

"No," my voice cracks.

"Dixie, let me in," his voice is urgent now, the familiar Riggs gruffness filling the small space.

I ignore him, tears streaming down my face.

"If you don't let me in, I'll break the fucking door down," and I know he means it. He would rip the door from its hinges if he needed to.

I sniff, nodding to an empty room and only then do I

twist onto my knees and open the bedroom door. His eyes find mine, and I feel like a child.

"Shit," he grunts, lowering himself down and pulling me in for a cuddle. He holds me like this for what feels like forever. I would never have dreamt that me and Riggs would grow closer. We never crossed paths until the day I turned up all those weeks ago, but now, I have never been more grateful for him. He was the big brother I never had but somehow always needed.

"Thank you," I mutter, hands on his chest as I push away gently.

"Do you suffer with them a lot?" he asks, placing his hand on his bent knee as he stands up, a grunt leaving him as he does.

"With what?" I ask, dumbfounded.

"Panic attacks," and suddenly it all makes sense. I shake my head from side to side.

"What set you off?" he asks, and my mask is torn off with his question, my vulnerability bleeding at his feet.

I keep quiet for a moment, but my eyes deceive me, tears filling my ocean blue eyes and I ignore the burn that radiates behind them as I refuse to blink, because as soon as I do, fresh tears will roll down my cheeks.

"You can talk to me Dix..." his voice is soft, eyes full of worry.

I whimper as I hold it all in.

"Are you going to break my brother's heart?" he asks, and I shake my head violently from side to side. But when the question actually settles in my brain, I realise I have just lied. Because either way, one of us going to end up heartbroken, or perhaps both of us. Lucian never breaks his word.

"You over worked?" and I see the guilt flash in his light

green eyes as I shake my head again. "Then what? Is it Lainey?"

"No," I whisper, I am still sitting on the floor, throat hoarse from crying.

"Is it that fucking cunt who followed you to your house?" and my eyes widen.

"Lucian," I whisper the name, worried in case saying it out loud makes him appear.

"How did you..." I pause and furrow my brows.

"Give me some credit," he scoffs a laugh, but there wasn't any harshness to his voice.

"Of course I looked into you, especially when I found out your history with Clay."

Shit.

"He won't get near you Dixie, not whilst you're under our roof," and I swallow the bile that is slowly creeping up my throat.

"He has threatened me," and I clasp my hand over my mouth, eyes bugging as I shrink that I so freely blurted that out.

"What?" Riggs hisses, his tone sharp but he keeps his voice down so Tripp doesn't hear.

I nod, tears streaming down my cheeks.

Riggs steps further into the room, closing the door softly behind him and I am grateful Lainey is downstairs with Orla.

"Tell me everything," he stands over me, hands on his hips, his eyes burning down into mine and I can feel the fire radiating behind my eyes.

"They want the goldmines; they want the land." I choke out.

"I know that bit, what is he threatening you with?"

"They wanted me to be their mole."

And I watch as his nostrils flare, and suddenly he can't look at me. Pure fucking disgust painted over his face.

"Is that why you were back?" and when he finally turns his face to me, I can't even lie my way out of this. "I fucking knew it," he growls, running his hand over his head, fingers knotting in his curly hair.

"But I haven't spoken to them," I choke out through sobs, pain splintering through my heart. "Lucian found me after everything went down at the funeral," tears stream down my face. "I haven't said anything, my lips have been sealed. I have one week until he takes me home to Wyoming."

I watch the shift in Riggs' expression, it softens ever so slightly before angry Riggs is back with vengeance.

"Have you told them anything?" I shake my head from side to side.

"There was nothing to tell, and as the days passed, I wanted nothing more to do with Lucian." My breath shudders on my intake of breath, "He told me that if I don't do as he said, he would put a bullet between each of your eyes," my voice cracks, "and then kill Lainey." The words burn my tongue as they roll off it and I feel physically sick at the thought.

"Listen," Riggs lowers himself, wrapping his fingers around the top of my arm as he pulls me to my feet, "no one is getting near you or that little girl." He steps back, reaching to open the door and as he goes to walk out, he spins to face me. "Oh, but Dixie..."

"Yeah?" I answer, palming my cheeks.

"If I find out you're lying, I'll put a bullet between your eyes."

He walks out the door leaving me in a cold sweat.

CHAPTER THIRTY-THREE
TRIPP

Dixie didn't come back down from her room; Riggs told us all she had a migraine. I was desperate to go up to her, to make sure she was okay, but I couldn't. Mom settled Lainey to sleep and took her up to bed and for the first time in nearly a week, I was sleeping alone.

I knew sleep wouldn't come easy tonight. Since the accident, my sleep is haunted by that day. The day where time stood still and claimed the life of one of our own. But when Dixie is next to me, my sleep is peaceful. She takes all the bad away.

And now I am terrified of falling asleep without her.

So instead of waiting for sleep to come, I drink enough whiskey to settle my mind and eventually, I drift off into a darkness that I can't seem to claw myself out of.

———

MORNING COMES and Dixie was nowhere to be seen. Riggs told me last night that they would be up early to go down to where the calves were, but when she didn't kiss me goodbye, I knew something was wrong.

I didn't have long to dwell on it when the physio knocked at the door, and I wheel myself to let her in. Mom had gone to meet dad at the hospital to collect Pacey, so I was here on my own with Lainey, and I was grateful that she went down for her nap a little earlier than usual.

"Morning Tripp, how you doing?" she asks before walking through to the living room.

"Not too bad, in pain today."

"Yeah? Where abouts?" her eyes on me as she kneels down and starts unloading her backpack.

My heart.

"My upper thigh, constant ache." I sigh, wishing to rub the pain out.

"We worked hard yesterday, it's hardly surprising that you're hurting." She gives me a little raise of her eyebrows before she stands. "And you're pushing yourself more than you should be, I know you're desperate to be out that cast and on your feet Tripp, but rushing the healing process won't help at all. If anything, it'll make you worse and put you back a few more weeks."

I sigh heavily. "I know, I am just fed up."

"And I get that Tripp, I do. But we have a plan... four more weeks and you should be out of cast and back to walking mostly unaided."

I scowl, slicing my eyes to where Lainey sleeps.

"My family needs me; the ranch needs me..." my voice is thick with emotion and I try to push the lump that is trapped in my throat.

"But you're no help if you're not healed, Tripp."

Sighing, I fold my arms across my chest and she raises one brow at me as she tucks her arms across her own chest.

"You ready?" she asks and I shake my head. "That's already the wrong attitude. Positive mind…"

"Yeah, yeah; positive mind set," I roll my eyes.

"Tripp," she steps towards me, head tilting to the side as her eyes burn into mine. "What's going on? You're normally so positive… smiling ear to ear and ready to smash our sessions."

I look away from her, because I don't want her to see the sadness that hangs over me.

"Just having a shit day, one of those… pent up and trapped in this house, everyone is going about their lives and here I am, sitting here festering with nothing but my thoughts." Clenching my jaw hard, my teeth grind. "I haven't even been to the prison where my innocent friend handed himself in… I am stuck. And then…" I trail off, finally looking at her.

I can see the worry etched into her face, but it doesn't matter. I am feeling lousy and sorry for myself.

"And then?" she says softly.

"Nothing, honestly, I'm fine," and I plastered the fakest smile on my face. "Let's do this."

But truthfully, on the inside, I am wilting.

I REFUSED to let anyone wheel me into the sheriff's office where Austin was being detained. I dragged myself through the door on my crutches, shoving the door open with my shoulder. Grinding my molars down, agitation nips at my skin when I see Kelcie sitting at *my* desk, dirty as fuck boots resting on the desk as his eyes bore into mine. No offer to help me, just fucking sits there like the useless sack of shit that he is.

I'm panting by the time I am through the door, dragging my casted leg behind me before I move forward using my crutch, keeping my foot off the ground.

"Well, look who it is," Kelcie spits into the metal trash can and I screw my nose up.

"Where is he?" my tone is flat, I am in no mood today. Dixie has pulled away from me, it's been four days since she was last in my bed, and I am beginning to take it personally.

"Have you booked in?"

I roll my eyes, turning my head to the side and softly shaking my head.

"Let me in to see him," I grunt, slowly facing him again.

"Can't do that unless you book in," and this cunt is beginning to grate on my already short temper.

"Let. Him. In." I hear the sound of Riggs' voice behind me, and I have never been more grateful for him to have followed me.

"What you gonna do big man?" Kelcie kicks his boots off the desk and pushes to his feet, thumbs tucked into his belt, *my* badge sitting on there.

"Don't push me, I am in no mood."

"You throw your weight around this town thinking you own it... newsflash, you don't. There are bigger and more powerful men in this small town that will rip you and your families legacy to shreds." Kelcie stands toe to toe with Riggs, but he has nothing on my brother's height.

Riggs' lips twitch and he shakes his head. "Don't get too comfortable with that badge, *Sheriff.* It'll soon be back on Tripp's belt and Pacey will be back as a Livestock Agent. The Mayor is on our side, Marty is on our side. You really want to pick your battles today?" Riggs' brows raise and Kelcie just eyeballs him.

"They can try big man, I was sworn in."

"Don't mean shit," Riggs chuckles softly and I watch as Kelcie shoves Riggs in the chest, but he doesn't fucking falter. A low rumble of a growl vibrates through Riggs' chest as he shoots his hand forward, wrapping it around Kelcie's throat as he walks him towards the wall behind him and pins him there. "Don't. Fucking. Touch. Me." Riggs spits, jaw wound so fucking tight.

"Sorry, sorry," Kelcie squirms, his voice tight and constricted by Riggs' large hands. I watch as Riggs squeezes a little tighter, his face going red, and I know he is too far gone.

"Riggs," I say softly, and I watch as Kelcie's eyes scan to mine and I see the pure fear closing in on them as Riggs strangles the life out of him slowly.

Would I love to see the downfall of Kelcie? Of course.

Do I want another death associated with us? Absolutely not.

"Riggs!" I bark, my voice filling the room and Riggs drops his hand from Kelcie's throat in an instant. We both watch as he falls to the floor, hands around his own neck as he gasps for breath.

"Do we have an understanding, *Sheriff?*" Riggs stands over him, heavy boot resting on his back as he presses him to the floor.

"Yes," he whispers, and I smirk.

"Good," he spits on him, and I roll my eyes. He always has to take it one step too far.

He keeps Kelcie pinned to the floor under his boot as he nods for me to walk through the cells and find Austin.

I probably shouldn't leave Riggs and Kelcie alone, but Austin is more important.

I discard the crutches and hobble through, hissing

when I look at my palms and see the blisters forming and my heart drops when I see him. Sitting curled up in the corner of the cell.

"Aust?" my voice is soft, and I wait with bated breath as he slowly lifts his head to look at me, eyes hollow, soul empty, heart completely obliterated.

"Tripp," he chokes as he pushes to his feet, fingers wrapped around the bars.

"I'm so sorry it's taken me so long."

"Don't be, you've had a lot going on." A hint of a smile ghosts his face, but it soon disappears.

"How's it going?" and I wince as soon as I ask it knowing full well he is living through hell.

"Not much to report, dad and mom are working with the lawyer, he thinks he can get me out on bail," he puffs his cheeks out as his eyes cast down.

"That's good news bud," I try and keep my voice upbeat but he just shakes his head, defeat blanketing him in an instant.

"What's the point?" and when his eyes find mine, they're full of tears. "Harlow is dead, the woman I was planning to spend the rest of my life with..." he sniffles for a moment. "Had a ring for her and everything," he just about manages through the tremble in his voice. "Put it in her casket, and when I meet her on the other side, she'll have it with her and we will be together for eternity. Nothing will tear us apart."

The edges of my heart crumble.

"Everything good has left man, what do I honestly have to lose? They think I killed Clay. I can't keep wasting my breath on trying to make them believe me. I am tired Tripp, so fucking tired."

My best friend bows his head in defeat, and I know

there is nothing I can say or do to make him feel better about any of this.

"You let us worry about getting you out, just keep your head down and do as they say, okay? Your hearing is in two days, a lot can happen in two days."

He doesn't look at me, he doesn't even acknowledge what I said.

"Hold on a little longer bud, we will make this right."

A soft chuckle fills the small cell room.

"You've been trying to make it right since the night it happened... and look where I am," and I don't miss the venom that drips from his tone, but I don't take it personally. I take the hit like a bullet, ignoring the pain that sears through my skin.

"I'm sorry." The words leaving my mouth wind me, sucking the air from my burning lungs as I choke on my exhale. Tears prick behind my eyes like a thousand needles and guilt consumes me whole. My chest tightens as I feel it cave in on itself making it impossible for me to catch my breath.

"I needed you," the crack in his voice echoes around the room like a gun shot.

"And I needed you," I shout, everything becoming too heavy to carry and I am ready to give in, let my legs give out and crash to the floor. "I've been through hell myself. I have tried Austin. Tried to be the best friend, tried to keep you safe. I. Have. Tried." I am angry and sad and broken. A tear rolls down my cheek and I don't even wipe it away. I will not be ashamed to cry. "I need you to fight with me man, I need you to want to get out of here, because if you don't..." I pause, licking the saltiness from my lips, "what is the point."

Dropping my head, I suck in a breath and ignore the shudder as I do.

"Exactly," Austin's voice is low, "what is the point."

I give a heavy nod, refusing to look at the boy I grew up with, the boy who was so much more than a best friend, he was my brother, my family. He broke my damn heart just like I have broken his. Closing my eyes, I turn my body and hobble out of the room and back into Kelcie's office.

Riggs sees my face and all I can manage is a slow shake of my head. He goes to step forward and I hold my hand up against his chest.

"Leave him," I whisper, ignoring the way Kelcie is glaring at me.

Riggs gives a heavy nod, turning on his heel and getting the door for me.

"We will see you soon Kelcie," he smirks, lifting his hat from his head as I walk past and once I am outside, I crumble.

CHAPTER THIRTY-FOUR
DIXIE

The atmosphere that was surrounding the house was heavy. It was the day of the trial, Tripp and Riggs had been up most of the night trying to see if they'd missed anything in regards to Clay's death.

I wracked my brain whilst my eyes stayed on the ceiling of my bedroom to try and pick out something that had been said that could pin point me in a direction of where I could be any help.

Lainey clings to me as I pace the hallway. Tripp knows something is up, he knows I am avoiding him. After my chat with Riggs, I didn't want to get Tripp caught up in this shit with Lucian. He was a nasty man; he knew powerful men who would line us up in a firing line and take us out one by one.

Orla waltzed down the stairs dressed in all black as if she was in mourning. She didn't stop to wish any of us good morning, just opened the front door and walked down the driveway. I looked over at Pacey who was leaning against the door frame and gave me a shrug.

"She's going to the Warrens'."

I nod, then turned and walked into the lounge to place Lainey on her playmat. I decided to stay home, it didn't feel right going to the hearing, it didn't feel right to sit and listen to people argue over if Austin did in fact kill Lainey's dad. I didn't think he did, but then again, I don't really know. I didn't know Austin well at all.

Sighing, I lean down and give Lainey a kiss on the top of her head as I push to my feet, and I hear a whistle coming from the front door.

"Well, isn't this nice," and my blood runs cold at the sound of his voice, followed by another set of footsteps.

Riggs rushes out, standing in front of Pacey and I feel Tripp's hand curl around my hip and pull me back towards where Lainey is.

"Don't panic," he whispers softly in my ear and my eyes are wide and locked on Lucian and Wallen.

"Get the fuck out of our home."

Lucian scoffs, tugging on the cuff of his white shirt before looking over his shoulder at Wallen, a stupid smirk on his face.

"Now, now, boys," he holds his hands up in some kind of peace offering. "We're merely here to get what belongs to us," Lucian smirks a wicked grin as I mould into Tripp's body.

"Then we're heading to the courthouse to see Austin get sent down for murdering Clay."

"You're not getting anywhere near her," Riggs' voice is low, and fear sprinkles deep inside of me. Tripp's grip tightens on me as my eyes shift to Lainey, but before I even get a chance to get there, Pacey swoops her up into his arms and tucks himself beside me.

"Oh," Lucian grins, "look how precious you all are protecting her." His black eyes settle on me, "Don't make me follow through with my threat Dixie," and my eyes widen as he opens his suit jacket revealing his handgun.

Blood thrashes in my ears and suddenly, that's all I can focus on.

"I'm not afraid of you," Riggs steps towards Lucian and bile rises in my throat.

"You should be," he slips his hand onto the handle of his gun.

"Probably," Riggs shrugs a shoulder up, "but I'm not."

Relief swarms me when I see Conrad, Marty and Hudson quietly walking into the house and before Lucian can even swipe his gun, Marty has the barrel of his own pressed to Lucian's temple, Hudson's pressed into Wallen's.

"If you do not get off my property, I will tell these two to put a bullet in both of your skulls."

Lucian laughs softly and I can see the panic in Wallen's eyes. He is a coward. Just like his brother was.

"Okay, fine," his hands are back up in front of him as if surrendering, and after a heartbeat, Marty and Hudson drop their guns, but don't put them away. "Dixie," the way my name falls from his tongue makes my blood run cold, "don't forget what I said." And with that, he turns on his heel along with Wallen and walks out of the house and once he is gone, I finally exhale.

Marty and Hudson exchange looks before all eyes are on me.

"Dixie..." Tripp turns me around to face him, "what is going on?"

"I promise I will tell you all, but not now," I shake my head from side to side, tears filling my eyes, *"please."*

His eyes are burning into mine and after what feels like hours, he drops my gaze.

"Okay," he whispers but I can see the disappointment etched onto his face. Riggs passes him his spare crutch just as Pacey passes me Lainey.

They all walk out of the house in an united bond and I instantly miss Tripp and I hate that I have disappointed him.

Hate it.

TRIPP

We walk into the courthouse united. I didn't go and see Austin again after our last visit, I couldn't do it to him or to myself. Blue and Buck are sitting in the front pew along with Riggs and Aspen. Me and my family all sit the row behind.

Marty, Hudson and Conrad sit next to me and Kelcie sits in the other front pew, his eyes bouncing between me and Riggs.

My heart aches when I see Austin being led in and seated behind the desk with his lawyer, and there sitting across from him is their lawyer who looks like he is worth five hundred dollars an hour, and beside him is Lucian and Wallen.

Nerves cripple me and my hands lock in front of me.

Austin turns to look at us all, and I am waiting for him to look at me, but he doesn't.

Letting my head fall for a moment, I lift my eyes and that's when his gaze locks with mine. A slight, gentle nod towards me makes my nerves ripple out into nothing but calmness.

Everyone stands apart from me as the judge walks in, and once she takes her seat, they all take theirs again.

Blue is clinging onto Buck like he is her lifeline, Aspen's arm is locked through her mom's and Riggs places his hand on Aspen's thigh as she bounces it up and down.

The proceedings start, and the whole time my heart is in my mouth. They argue the toss back and forth, both lawyers going for each other, sniping a little deeper with each fact or lie that spills from them.

My eyes glue to the back of Austin's head, zoning out as the noise all fades into nothing.

They have no evidence on Austin. Nothing at all.

But still, the way this conversation is unfolding, he is going down.

Commotion stirs in the courtroom and my eyes widen when I see my dad stand up.

"If you're going to charge Austin with the murder of Clay Attaway, then you need to charge me too," and my fucking heart drops inside my chest. Riggs' head spins around, brows furrowed and lips rolled into a tight line.

Shit.

"Excuse me?" the judge says a little louder.

"I saw Clay the night of his death. He threatened me on my ranch. Fists were thrown and I roughed him up a bit. He spooked my wife, scared her half to death. He kept rambling that he was coming for my sons. But something didn't seem right with him. He was disoriented, his pupils were dilated. He looked scruffy and dirty, eyes rolling... he came for me. In self-defence I hit him in the face with the stock of my gun," he pauses for a moment and looks down at my mom, tears streaming down her face. "He went down easy, I had busted his nose, dazed him no doubt. I lowered myself down, felt for his pulse and it was there... barely though. I ran back into the house to reach my cell to call 911, but when I came back outside, Clay was gone."

I swallow. I can't believe he just outed himself.

The judge sighs, her mouth opening to speak when Conrad stands up.

"If you're going to charge either of them, then you need to charge me too..."

"And me," Marty stands and so does Hudson.

"And me," Riggs stands, his fingers laced with Aspen's still. "I put a bullet in his dead body once the sheriff was called," and I see the pain flash across his eyes.

The judge bangs her gavel against the sound block.

"Order, order," she says loudly, trying to silence the courtroom.

Slowly, they all take their seats.

"Can I see the autopsy results for Mr Attaway again?" she asks, eyes bouncing between Austin's lawyer and the Attaway's lawyer.

"They should have been given to you prior to the hearing."

Austin's lawyer stands up, hands in his pockets.

"I would like to see them again," her eyes narrow on him before they move towards Wallen and Lucian.

Reluctantly, the Attaway's lawyer bends and slips out a manila envelope and I see how both of their eyes widen. He steps forward with the sealed envelope, Lucian and Wallen rush to their feet and you can see the panic that is slowly suffocating them.

He passes it to the judge, and I realize that this is evidence that hasn't been put forward.

They fucking gave a fraudulent report.

Her brow raises and I see the lawyers shoulders sag forward.

She pulls the envelope open and pulls the paperwork out, a loud sigh filling the deafly silent courtroom.

"It says here that Mr Attaway's cause of death was a heart attack. Yes, he had head trauma, but none of which killed him," her eyes slice to Lucian and Wallen. "Sheriff," she calls up Kelcie and he stands tall. "Detain both of these men until I have had a chance to actually sit and read through this case file again... it seems I have been lied to," she shakes her head from side to side before her green eyes land on Austin.

"Mr Austin Warren..." she trails off for just a moment and I know that we're all holding our breath. "You're free to go."

The courtroom erupts in cheers as the judge hits her gavel again.

Silence trickles over the room as she turns her attention towards the Attaway's lawyer.

"I would also like to know if Mr Clay Attaway had any legitimate children. If so, another hearing will be arranged to go through his estate."

And my heart thrums in my chest.

"Court dismissed," the loud sound of the gavel hitting the sound board echoes as we all stand ready to embrace Austin, but there isn't even a hint of a smile on his face. The court guard walks across and unlocks Austin's handcuffs before leading him out back to collect his belongings. Blue is wrapped in Buck's arms, and our mom is crying happy tears whilst my dad is comforting her.

I shuffle, reaching for my crutches as Pacey helps me to my feet.

"Where you going?" his brow crinkles.

"Just need some air," I nod.

"I think we need to go to The Boot. This calls for a celebration." I smirk, but sadness consumes me.

"I don't think Austin is going to want to celebrate, he told me he has nothing to live for anymore... we need to just keep an eye on him."

Pacey sighs, then gives a heavy nod.

"You're right."

"Always am," I smirk as I hop myself outside the courtroom and keep going until I am out in the fresh air.

Sitting alone with my thoughts, the sun is beating down on my tired soul. The town is busy and I feel like I haven't been out in so long, trapped inside a house, and it's not even like I have hated it. I haven't. I hate it more now because Dixie has pulled away from me, I am lonelier than ever, and I have no idea what I have done to upset her. Worry settles deep inside my chest that she is about to shatter my heart for the last time.

I close my eyes, the world is quiet for a moment as my mind takes me back to when we were teens.

SNEAKING out of the house well past curfew, I climb into my truck and start the engine. Looking in the mirrors as I creep down the driveway, relief swarms me just as I get to the ranch sign. Picking up speed, I drive just outside of town and park my truck in a dusty lay by and reach for my phone.

ME

Outside baby xx

I wait for a couple of minutes and begin panicking that her dad has found out, what if he has stopped her from getting to me?

My phone beeps in my lap.

DIXIE

walking out now xx

Looking to my left, I smile when I see her running across the field, her house small in the distance. Unlocking the truck, she climbs up and her beautiful smile grows as she leans across the middle of the truck and kisses me softly on my lips.

"You sure about this?" I whisper against her lips.

"So sure," she nods, slipping back into her seat and buckling herself in, slipping her hand onto my thigh.

"Ready?"

"Ready."

Pushing the truck into gear, I move back onto the road and head back towards town. Dixie has always wanted to dance in a parking lot, night sky above us, nothing but the truck headlights shining on us as I spin her around the parking lot.

But I want tonight to be so much more than just this.

I want her in every sense of the word.

We've had a few kisses and slid into third base, but we haven't gone any further, until tonight that is.

Pulling into an empty parking lot, I give her a soft wink before stepping out of the truck and walking around to her side. Opening the door, her eyes glisten like the stars in the dark navy sky. Her hand slips into mine as she climbs down and out of the truck, my heart thrashing in my chest. Walking her to the back of the truck, I reluctantly let her go and climb onto the bed of my truck. Lifting the picnic blanket, I drag the boom box to the edge and press play.

Spin You Around - Morgan Wallen *begins to play and my heart stutters in my chest. Her beautiful blue eyes light up,* cheeks pinching that beautiful pink and her lips pressing into the most stunning smile I have ever seen.

Nothing would beat this moment.

This would stay locked away deep inside my heart for eternity.

"May I have this dance?" I whisper against the back of her hand that I scoop towards my lips and dust them across her soft skin.

"You may," she giggles as I stand a little taller and spin her around, her pretty dress lifting as she turns.

Pulling her close to me, my arm snakes around her back as we begin to sway, her hand in mine and I have never felt more content than I do in this moment.

Her beautiful eyes stay on mine whilst we dance around the empty parking lot. My lips wear a constant smile, our heads bowed.

"Be mine Dixie," I whisper as I edge closer to her lips. "Forever."

Her eyes glisten with unshed tears.

"I'll always look after you, we have room on the ranch. You don't have to be scared anymore Dix, it's just me and you against the world."

She smiles, her beautiful blues bounce between mine.

"We can move out of Lovelock Bay, wherever you want to go my little dreamcatcher, we can go," I kiss her softly just as the song dies down and Worst Way - Riley Green plays.

"You promise?" her voice cracks as she asks me.

"I promise," I nod, arm unwrapping from her back and let my fingers travel up her side before I am cupping her face. A stray tear rolls down her cheek as she leans into my hand.

"I love you Tripp."

"Not as much as I love you," I brush my nose across hers, "be mine?"

She nods, soft laughter escaping her and damn it's the most beautiful sound I have ever heard.

Letting her out of my grasp for just a moment, I lift my brown cowboy hat from my head and slowly lower it onto hers.

"Mine," my voice is low, a cocky smirk pulling at my lips.

"Yours," she whispers, both of her small hands clasping my face.

"You know the rule baby, you wear the hat..." Her cheeks turn crimson. "You become mine forever my Dreamcatcher."

Her smile only widens before she kisses me, her tongue pushing past my lips as her body melts into mine.

"Make me yours in every way, Tripp," she begs against my lips, my heart jack hammering in my chest.

"Fuck," I groan, hands on her hips, fingers digging into her skin through her dress.

Breaking away reluctantly, I step back and look at her.

Pretty white dress, freckles scattered across her nose from the summer sun, long brown hair in loose waves and brown cowboy boots. My heart bangs in my chest. Finally my eyes land on my hat that sits on her head.

She's mine.

Scoffing a soft laugh, I climb onto the bed of the truck, pushing the boombox towards the back and laying down the picnic blanket.

"Come sit with me for a moment," I smile, reaching my hand out for her to take. She takes a moment to clasp her hand in mine, but when she does, my heart jack hammers in my chest, my skin tingling from my fingers up to the base of my neck before my skin erupts in goosebumps.

We lay on the bed of the truck, pointing out the constellations above us. Turning my head to face her, I am in awe. She's talking softly about her favorite stars and constellations but all I can do is stare at her, the stars have nothing on her. Sure, I am a fool in love, but damn, she is pretty.

I didn't need to look at the night sky for beauty and wonder when I had her next to me.

Her head rolls around to face me, her words trailing off when she realises I have probably not listened to a single word she has said.

"You okay?" she whispers and I nod, a stupid ass grin spreading across my lips.

"I am perfect Dixie," I whisper as my hand cups her cheek, pulling her lips to mine, the night slipping away beneath us on the bed of my truck in an empty parking lot with the love of my life.

THE TRUCK ROLLS to a stop outside the house and Riggs and Hudson are there to help me out. I have over done it. My body aches. I am dog tired and the only thing keeping me going is seeing Dixie's beautiful smile. I shouldn't have been on my crutches all day, but I am desperate to get some normality back into my life. I was a stubborn fucker at times.

Sighing when Riggs drops me into the armchair, I wince as he lifts my cast up and rests it on the foot stool.

"I'm shooting back to the station, want to see what is going on with Lucian and Wallen..." he trails off, rubbing his beard before trudging over to the whiskey bottle and pouring a small glass, knocking it back in one with a wince. "Also, want to know what the fuck is going to happen to Kelcie because let's be honest, we all know that his pockets have been heavily lined. That son of a bitch is getting away without any repercussions," he shakes his head from side to side before he walks out the room, a high whistle echoing as he calls for Hudson and I hear the sound of Ace's collar as he barks at Riggs.

Minutes pass, and the silence is deafening.

"Dixie?" I call out, head resting on the cushion of the armchair. Nothing. "Dix?" my voice is a little louder now and slowly I sit up, heart thrashing in my chest like a feral great white. Pushing up from my seat, I groan as an ache radiates through my leg and slowly travels up my body.

"Baby?" the voice slips out not quite sounding like my own and my chest tightens.

Worry begins to prick at the back of my neck, my stomach knotting as I move slowly.

The kitchen is empty, pristine and clean and Lainey's stuff is exactly where it should be. My eyes move upstairs, and I debate trying to climb them, but I know if I fall I will fuck myself completely.

"Dixie?" my voice grows louder and so does my worry. What if something has happened to her and Lainey? What if Lucian or Wallen's men came for her?

My heartbeat bangs in my ears, blood rushing through my veins.

Hobbling down the narrow hallway to my makeshift bedroom, I stand in the door way, wrapping my fingers around the frame as I steady myself and ignore the burn that is consuming my leg.

Moving slowly into my bedroom, the glint of gold catches my eye from the afternoon sunlight. I step closer and my brows furrow, confusion masking my face and my heart bottoms out.

Three bullets sit on my bedspread along with a note and my throat burns, a lump lodging itself there and it doesn't matter how much I try and swallow, I can't rid it. My stomach knots and twists as anxiety cripples me. Scooping

the bullets into the palm of my hand, I look at them before
—lump growing—my eyes slice across to the handwritten
note that lays on my bedspread.

> *Tripp,*
> *I promised a night, not forever.*
> *The three bullets are the ones that would have*
> *killed you and your brothers if I didn't keep up my*
> *end of the bargain.*
> *The fourth I have with me was meant for*
> *Lainey.*
> *I thought it would be best to leave when you*
> *were gone, but just know we will be safe.*
> *I will never stop loving you, and no doubt you*
> *will hate me now.*
> *But I do Tripp. I love you.*
> *Me staying would only bring more hurt and*
> *upset to your family, and I couldn't be the reason*
> *for that any longer.*
> *I've not run, just stepped away.*
> *Yours always,*
> *Dixie xxx*

She fucking left me.

Reaching for the note, I read it again. And again. And
again.

Tears well in my eyes as I screw the note up, crushing it
into a small ball and tossing it behind me. My head drops,
my eyes locked on the three bullets.

She saved our lives whilst destroying mine. My heart is

screaming at me to find her, hunt through the town until I find both of them, but my heart is telling me to stop. She left me. She broke me, again. My heart can't take much more and neither can I.

A choked sob vibrates through my chest. Clasping my hand shut around the bullets, my nails dig into the palm causing a small sting. I should stop, but I don't. I keep squeezing until the pain consumes me.

My whole body begins to tremble and all I can do is scream, shattering my heart into a million pieces all over again when she was finally piecing it back together.

I hobble towards the door, tugging it hard I nearly pull it from the hinges. I ignore the way my body screams at me, the way the pain becomes too much but I keep moving forward.

Pacey is just walking up the steps when he sees me, Mom and Dad behind him.

"Tripp?" his eyes bounce between mine, trying to find a hint of what has me raging like a damn bull.

"These fucking bullets were meant for us," my voice is hoarse from my screaming.

Pacey's eyes fall down to look at my bleeding palm before they're back on me. "Dixie left these with a note. Lucian was planning to put a bullet between our eyes if she didn't leave."

I hear my mom gasp and my dad's is furious. He pulls my mom close as she hides in his chest.

"Where is she now?"

"I don't know," my voice trembles and I am so fucking angry.

Just as Pacey steps towards me on the porch, mom and dad still standing on the dusty pavement, Riggs pulls up on the driveway.

"Boot?" he asks, standing on the sidestep of the truck and my chest feels like it's about to cave in.

Pacey gives him a nod whilst mom walks past me to get my chair, all the while sniffling.

"I don't want to go, you guys go," I sulk, turning my back on my brothers as my dad wraps his arm around my back and for the first time in a long time, I lean on him, just like I was a little boy again.

CHAPTER THIRTY-FIVE
TRIPP

I have no idea how long I have been laying on my bed, eyes pinned to the ceiling as I toss the bullets into the air and catch them.

My heart obliterated into a thousand shards inside my chest, and I feel like beat by beat it is slowing, until finally, it will stop beating all together.

I have no idea where she has gone, it can't be far. As far as I am aware, her car is still at Rusty's garage.

The silent house is filled with emptiness. Dad joined my brothers to celebrate Austin's trial, mom stayed at home with me and honestly, I think she is grieving for the grandchild that she had also lost.

Sighing heavily, I sit up with difficulty, my eyes trailing towards the closet in the corner of my bedroom, eyes sting, throat burns.

My dad and me rode over to Dixie's childhood home a week ago. I wanted to see if her guitar was still there, and with Marty's help, we got into the boarded-up house and sure as shit, her broken guitar was hidden in her dad's closet. Dad took it into his workshop, and whilst Dixie worked, we got started on fixing it up and I finished it off with a small dreamcatcher that I painted in a light pink on the lower bout.

I was going to give it to her this weekend.

I wanted her to know that she could still chase her dreams, and that she could do it with the guitar that meant so much. Sure, we had to replace certain parts, but most of it was patched up from what was left.

My heart rattles in my empty chest on my inhale of breath.

I was so close to having it all, only for it to be taken away in a blink of an eye.

My phone beeps and I wait a minute or two before I cast my eyes on the screen. *Sunny.*

I roll my eyes. I like Sunny, but we're not on friend basis.

SUNNY

Wanted to let you know Dixie is crashing here. She is safe, so is Lainey. Just give her space. xo.

Pointless text. Tossing the phone into the bedspread, I reach out for the handrail that sits on the wall beside my bed and pull myself to my feet.

I'm done moping.

But before I can sleep this day that went from happy to shit real fucking quick, I need mom's help.

"Ma." I call out as I slip my hand into my crutch and wrap my finger around the handle, hobbling down towards the living room where she sits. Her eyes pinned to the window, fingers knotted together, and she looks so sad.

"Mom?" my voice is soft as I approach. Turning her head to look at me, I see the sadness that is painted over her face and my heart hurts.

"You okay?" and I don't miss the way a heavy sigh wraps around her question.

"Can you help me with something?" I ignore her question as her brows pinch, eyes searching my face.

"Sure," she nods, pushing up from her seat and following me into the bedroom.

I SHOULDN'T BE DRIVING, but it's fine. My casted leg is not even on the gas. I needed to get to Dixie. Hudson had text me and told me that she was on her way to The Boot. My phone screams in the cup holder of my truck. I want to ignore it, but curiosity gets the better of me. The sky is dark, the odd street lamp dim. My phone continues dancing in the middle of the truck and I finally sweep it into my hand and see Riggs' name.

"Yeah," I groan, rubbing the sleep from my eyes.

"It's Dixie."

The way his voice rasps, breathless and urgent causes my heart to flatline in my chest. I ignore everything else, pushing the gas to the floor and driving as fast as I can, my eyes widening when I see why Riggs is calling me.

Panic claws at my throat, and I am desperate to get to her.

Desperate to know if she is okay all whilst silently praying that she is.

Nothing can happen to her.

Not my Dixie.

CHAPTER THIRTY-SIX
DIXIE

I am curled on Sunny's sofa feeling sorry for myself. Guilt lashes against my skin like a whip, never letting up, my skin bleeding.

Sunny hands me a warm cup of tea as I sit up, blankets wrapped around my shoulders.

"You doing okay?" she asks, rubbing the top of my arm, head tilted to the side. Her short brown hair is glossy, bright blue eyes that pop against her pale skin. She seems to have her shit together, she is slightly younger than me and I feel kind of envious of her. I shouldn't. She has worked hard and life hasn't been great to her but she never gave up.

"Not really," I roll my lips, bringing the hot tea to my lips and softly blowing. "I am mentally exhausted, my heart aches so heavily in my chest. I hate that I left them all, but I was so terrified. The four-week mark had hit, and at least if they got there and saw that I am not there anymore then they'll come for me, and not the boys. I would have never forgiven myself if anything had happened to the Rivera boys," I shudder at the thought. I sigh before taking a mouthful of the sweet tea and hum in appreciation. My eyes lift from my lap as I look around at Sunny's apartment. It's above her coffee shop, it's cosy. Warm creams, sage curtains, oatmeal carpets. The layout is mainly open planned apart from the two bedrooms and bathroom. Her kitchen and lounge flow, it works. She has bookshelves lining the back wall and a small television that sits on a corner unit. Large sash windows make the small room feel that much bigger as she overlooks the quaint little town of Lovelock Bay.

"Babe," her voice is soft, pulling me from my thoughts as she perches herself on the edge of the oak coffee table.

I blink at her a few times.

"You do realize that Lucian and Wallen have been detained?"

My eyes widen, heart jackhammering in my chest.

"What?" I barely whisper.

"They gave a fraudulent autopsy report as evidence..."

A high-pitched ring pierces through my ears, the blood rushing through my veins before it pumps loudly in my ears, slowly drowning out the ringing.

"No," my chest rises and falls quickly.

"The judge is arranging a hearing to go through Clay's estate... and because you have Lainey..." she trails off as she slowly slips the mug from my hands and places it next to her on the coffee table before she clasps her hands over mine.

"You've won, Dixie," she whispers, smiling from ear to ear.

"I didn't know... I..." my voice stammers and the breath catches at the back of my throat as tears prick behind my eyes.

A knock at the door has me jumping and Sunny's brows

furrow as she looks at the door. Dropping my hands, she stands and I palm the tear that runs down my cheek.

Looking over my shoulder, Sunny peeks through the spy hole then pulls the chain across.

"I have a parcel for Dixie Walker," the sound of a low voice makes my skin prick.

"Sure," Sunny says as she takes the large gift box from him. Who delivers this late in the evening?

"Can you sign here please?" and I zone out for a moment, eyes glued to the light pink gift box. That always was my favorite colour. A light dusty pink.

The sound of the front door closing snaps me back into reality.

"You have a parcel," Sunny's voice is tight as she picks up the box that looks huge against her petite frame.

Pushing from the sofa, I grab it from her and she gives me a thankful smile.

"Late isn't it?"

She half shrugs.

"I've had later," she takes her seat back on the coffee table as I place the gift box on the sofa.

Pinching the note that is attached to the box, I turn it over and my heart stutters in my chest.

– Never stop dreaming, ever x

My brows furrow, as I untie the white ribbon and lift the lid slowly and I freeze.

"What is it?" Sunny asks, standing behind me, eyes looking over my shoulder.

There, laying on soft satin as my old guitar, a light dusty pink bow wrapped around the neck. Cracks are evident but they're smudged, giving it a marble effect in the wood, the odd veins crossing. Tears stream down my face when I notice the little pink dreamcatcher that is painted on the lower bout, then underneath, as if etched into a tree 'TR <3 DW'.

Memories flood me of the old blossom tree down where we used to swim in the creek, and drink moonshine, marked with our initials and we vowed that we would get married under that tree one day, but here we are, ten years later, and I have never felt further away from that memory than I do now.

"Is this yours?" Sunny asks and I nod silently, slowly reaching down and wrapping my trembling fingers around the neck of the guitar and lift it gently.

"My mom got me this guitar for my birthday; my dad destroyed it years ago and I feared I had lost it but..." I am lost for words as I turn to look at Sunny. "Tripp must've fixed it up," my head falls forward as tears fall onto my guitar, my thumb brushing across the delicate string. "He pieced it back together again, just like he did my heart. Bit by bit..." I choke and Sunny wraps her arm around my shoulder, pulling me into her.

"It's not too late to make this right Dixie, they're all at The Boot. I'll stay with Lainey."

Stepping away, my eyes bounce between hers.

"Go," she ushers softly as she takes my guitar from my loose hold. My eyes sting from the tears that fill them, my heart thrashing in my chest. "Go get your man," she smiles, and I nod, wiping away my tears and stepping towards the door.

I turn to face her, a little hesitant.

"You deserve a happy ever after Dix," she tilts her head to the side, and I smile at her.

Looking in the mirror, I swipe my ring finger under my

eyes and rid my face of any smudged mascara. My long brown hair is in a loose messy braid, hanging over one shoulder, baggy oversized tee and mom jeans that are a little too ripped at the knees and banged out sneakers, but I don't care. Tripp loves me and I love him. In every single form.

Opening the door, I rush onto the street and grab my phone from my pocket, scrolling till I see Hudson's name.

He answers on the first ring.

"Yeah?"

"Can you take me to The Boot?" I am breathless as I stand on the sidewalk of the quiet town, the warm summer breeze dancing across my skin.

"I'll be there in five," and he hangs up.

I wanted to surprise Tripp.

I needed to apologise.

It was time to finally get my dream, and that dream was Tripp Rivera.

CHAPTER THIRTY-SEVEN
RIGGS

The atmosphere in The Boot was buzzing. Austin was a little sour, but after we managed to get a beer or two into him, he loosened up ever so slightly. He was grieving, he had a lot going on and I get that. But he needed an escape, even if just for a night.

This is the first time we have been in The Boot since Harlow died, and to say it was bittersweet is an understatement. We all know she is missing, but we all feel her here and I hope that means she is with us, sitting beside each of us in her eternal peace.

Hate that Tripp isn't here.

But I get it.

He is wounded.

Dixie will come back, I have every faith.

I needed to debrief my brothers on my findings, but all work talk stops tonight. We were here to celebrate, and I didn't want to be the one to bring the evening down with work shit.

World On Fire - Nate Smith begins to play, a few of our

group up dancing, Austin sits nursing his beer, eyes just watching what's going on. Conrad sits next to him, Aspen the other side, closest to the floor.

My smirk pulls and I stroll across to her.

"Wildflower," I rasp, leaning down and placing a kiss on her lips.

She smiles, cheeks pinching pink underneath her freckles.

"Dance with me?"

"How can I say no to *the* Riggs Rivera," she playfully winks, standing as I wrap my arm around her back and pull her close to me.

"You can't," my lips brush against her ear as I sway with her across the dusty sawdust floor.

"God, I love you," she smiles against my mouth as I kiss her, and I've missed her. Our life has been a hundred miles an hour since Dixie crashed into town. Mixed with Austin and Harlow, our lives have somehow frozen in time, but we've been existing in these strange few weeks. We would have just started the first leg of Aspen's book tour, but she couldn't leave, neither of us could. The only thing I refused to push back was our wedding.

I've waited over ten years to marry this woman, there is no damn way in hell I am waiting any longer.

"Not as much as I love you Wildflower," her arms loosen around my neck, mine around her waist.

"Not possible," she whispers between our kisses.

My eyes lift from my beautiful fiancée when I see Dixie push through the door, flustered, eyes wide as she scans the room. She seeks me out, nearly tripping over her own feet as she approaches me and Aspen.

"Where is Tripp?" she asks, breathless, sadness creeping onto her face.

"He didn't come," I roll my lips and softly push Aspen to my side, arms hung around her back, thumb looped into the pocket of her jeans.

"What?" her voice cracks, her lips pull into a smile, but her eyes tell me everything.

"Is everything okay hon?" Aspen asks, her eyes moving from me to Aspen.

"Why did no one tell me? Why did no one say anything about Lucian and Wallen?"

"I thought you knew," my voice is gruff as the music lowers.

"How would I know? I left him. Left a note, broke my own heart and his in doing so. I was protecting you," she chokes on a sob.

"That's the first mistake, you could never protect us kid. If someone wanted bullets between our eyes, they would do it," and Aspen shivers beside me. Harsh but true.

"I need to go to him," she turns to walk away, and I grab the top of her arm pulling her back.

"We'll take you," I give a soft nod, "I need to round these guys up anyway. Work doesn't stop for cowboys." I wink and Aspen's hand rests on my steady heart.

"Okay," she nods, looking at the floor.

I turn my face, pressing a kiss into Aspen's hair.

"Go sort Austin out, I'll get the cowboys sorted."

"I'll meet you outside," Dixie says softly, before disappearing into the restroom.

Within ten minutes, I have them outside and one by one, load them into the back of our trucks like I am herding cattle.

Aspen helps Austin in and gives him a soft smile.

"You doing okay?" she asks as I place my hand on the

top of the passenger door, eyes bouncing between her and The Boot.

"Yeah... I think," he looks up at us through his long lashes and dirty blonde mop of hair. He needs a haircut. "Thanks for dragging my sorry ass out," and I know he is aiming that at me.

"Not a problem," I wink when the smell of smoke has me turning towards The Boot.

Black smoke comes thick and fast bellowing out the back of the bar, fire spreading through the timber framed building and my heart drops. People come scuttering out, mouths covered with hats. Tabitha collapses as she reaches the parking lot. Pacey is already on the phone to 911.

Running towards the building, Aspen is screaming out my name.

I stop, turning and looking as I try and count up the heads I can see.

"Dixie!" I scream, Aspen begins rushing to open the truck doors shouting, 'No' as she does. "Fuck!" I can't get in. The fire is too wild.

Slipping my phone from my pocket as I stand back from the ablaze building, I dial Tripp's number.

"Yeah," his voice is low, quiet but I can hear the low hum of the truck. Is he driving?

"It's Dixie," and just as my words slip from my mouth, I hear the sound of his tyres crunching down the driveway and across the parking lot.

Cutting it off, he falls out of the truck and I am running to him, trying to lift him to his feet.

"I need to get in there," he shouts, fear etched into his face.

"No," I shake my head.

Before I can even volunteer, I hear Aspen scream out to my dad.

"The fuck," I drag Tripp over to Austin, perching him against the seat. "Don't move."

Running after my dad, I try to stop him, but it's no use, I can't. He disappears into the building that is slowly crumbling in front of me, The Boot sign falling from the front of the bar and screams echo around the empty parking lot. I feel the grip of a hand on my shoulder and when I look, it's Tripp. He has hobbled himself over towards me and I feel helpless.

There is nothing I can do.

***

TRIPP

Dark black smoke bellowing, fire ablaze and getting wilder as the seconds pass. The sound of sirens in the distance wailing feel like a million miles away. Each heavy beat of my heart, is one beat closer to me losing the only one I have ever loved.

Another hand clasps my shoulder and I know it's Pacey.

"I need to get in there," I whimper but we all know if I go in, I'm not coming back out. Dropping my head against Riggs' shoulder blade, I sob into his white shirt, already grieving for my dad and Dixie.

"Tripp," Riggs' voice vibrates through his body and when my red rimmed eyes lift, I see my dad stumbling out with Dixie in his arms just as the fire truck pulls into the parking lot. They file out in a group as two rush towards my dad and Dixie, the rest of the group rush into the burning building whilst the other group stands guard and waits for orders with their hoses.

Riggs begins moving, trying to drag me with him, Pacey hooks himself under my arm when suddenly I feel another arm wrap around us. Looking over my shoulder I see Austin. My three best friends lifting me across to where my dad lays Dixie down before he himself collapses in a heap on the floor next to her, his fingers brushing over hers before he goes still.

"Dad!" Riggs screams as they place me next to Dixie and lay me down as softly as they can a dead weight of a man.

"We need help!" Pacey shouts, his voice cracking as the emergency services arrive, paramedics running across and rolling my dad onto his back as they press for a pulse.

"Dixie," I whisper, brushing my trembling fingers across her smoke covered cheek.

Laying my head on her chest, I try and listen for her heartbeat.

"Don't leave me baby, please…" I beg as I hear the paramedics calling for oxygen.

"We need you to move away," they call, their voices floating over from where they're trying to get to my dad.

"I'm not moving," I hear Riggs' voice, it's broken and gravelly. My eyes lift as I look at my dad on the floor, Riggs palming his cheeks and I realize he is crying.

"You need to, I have to start chest compressions," and the pain that sears through my heart is unbearable.

Closing my eyes as the tears roll down my cheeks, I press my ear back onto her cheat and try to listen, try to hear a slither of her heart beating when I am gently lifted from her body.

"No, no, no, no," I beg as another group of paramedics

try and move me but I cling onto her lifeless body. I don't want to let go.

"We can't save her if you don't move," but I am frozen. I don't want to leave her. I can't.

I feel arms wrap around my upper body and lift me as I start screaming.

"No, I can't leave her, please, no," I am full on sobbing through screams, tears burning my cheeks and when I look, it's Conrad.

"I've got you; she is going to be okay," and I watch as they begin pumping on her chest, trying to kick start her heart and all I can do is watch as two of the most important people in my life lay on the dusty floor whilst paramedics try and bring them back to life.

Everything after that slows down, the greedy flames consuming The Boot, the way the smoke tarnishes the clear night sky, the way we all stand helpless as we watch. Riggs, Pacey and Austin standing over my dad as we watch as they work on him before my eyes finally drag across to Dixie. She's all alone.

Press.

Breathe.

Press.

Please Dixie.

Press.

Don't leave me.

Press.

Come on. If not for me, for Lainey.

Press.

I love you.

"We've got a pulse, get her in the ambulance," the medic screams as they help slide her onto the bed and lift her into the ambulance and my eyes follow as she gets taken away. Slowly, ever so painfully slowly my eyes skate across to my dad.

I watch as they still work on him, and with each press, comes a new stroke of fear.

And I know when they lift their heads and give *the* look, that we've lost him.

CHAPTER THIRTY-EIGHT
DIXIE

Walking into the restroom, nerves prickle at the base of my neck.

I'm nervous to see Tripp.

But I know I need to make this right.

Need to fix what I have broken. Again.

Washing my hands, I look at myself in the mirror and give a haunted smile back to myself.

I miss him.

I needed him.

I didn't know how to breathe without him.

And now I know the threat is gone, I can be with him wholeheartedly.

They would never let anyone hurt me.

Like Riggs said, I couldn't protect them. But this is the problem with being left the way I was. My mom died. I did everything to protect my sister Lainey, but I failed. I did everything to protect myself and only ended up being hurt.

Splashing my face with cool water, I was hoping it would make me feel a little fresher. I had been slowly dying inside, I was miserable, and it was because I was away from the ones who have loved me like a family should have. Because I was away from the only man I have ever loved, the only man who has showed me what *love* should feel like.

Grabbing a paper towel, I pat it against my skin before discarding it.

"Time to be a big girl, Dixie," I whisper to my reflection before giving myself a smile.

It was time to take back control on my life.

Walking towards the door, my fingers wrap around the handle as I tug it open and as I do, I bump into a body.

Head tilting back, my brows pinch when I see Sheriff Kelcie standing there.

"Kelcie?" worry pricks at my skin, and I find myself stepping back.

"Hello Dixie," a smirk pulls at the corner of his mouth. He steps towards me, cornering me. "Lucian wanted me to give you this, a final goodbye I think he called it," he scoffs a laugh as he hands me a piece of paper.

With trembling fingers, I take it from his grasp and unfold it.

I'M PUTTING AN END TO YOUR RUNNING, DIXIE. IT'S OVER. I'LL SEE YOU IN HELL.
    - LUCIAN

Swallowing the thickness, I feel bile swirl in my stomach, and I shake my head from side to side as I try and decipher the cryptic message.

"What does this mean?" I ask and Kelcie just shrugs his shoulders.

"I hope you kissed your beautiful daughter goodbye," and with that, he turns and walks out of the restroom.

I give myself a moment, chest rising and falling as I reread the note. *See you in hell?*

Slipping it into the back of my jeans, I tug on the handle of the restroom, but it won't open.

"Kelcie!" I shout, banging on the door.

"It's over Dixie," he calls back just as I see soft smoke drifting under the door.

"No, No, No!" I bang harder, "Please don't do this, please let me out," I scream, banging again but I hear nothing back.

Looking around the room, there is no other way for me to escape.

Shit.

Banging again, the smoke is getting heavier.

"Please, someone help me!"

Bang.

Bang.

Bang.

Tears stream down my cheeks as I cry, knowing this is it for me.

I am never escaping.

It doesn't take long for the smoke to eventually take over the small restroom so I lay myself down and close my eyes, and before I am plunged into darkness, memories flood me of Tripp and Lainey and what our life could have been.

They say your brain lives for seven minutes after you die.

What would my seven minutes look like?

Lainey.

Tripp.

Orla.

Jorge.

Riggs.

Aspen.

Pacey.

Tripp.

Lainey.

At least I know she'll be loved.

He will bring her up as his own, love her with all he has... that's all I want.

The smoke consumes me whole, and I wait for the flames to lick my skin and with one last exhale of breath, I whisper, "I love you."

CHAPTER THIRTY-NINE
TRIPP

My mom's screams haunt the hospital hallways.

Grief is a funny thing. It comes and goes in waves. Crashing over you and pulling you under, holding on to you till your very last breath before letting you resurface for one gasp of air before dragging you straight back down again. With each pull, the tighter your chest feels. But then there are moments when peace consumes you, knowing that they're in fact in a better place, but that's only momentary. A split second maybe, before you're back beneath the waves fighting for every breath.

We've lost far too much this year, I wasn't ready to lose him too.

My dad.

The fiercest of them all. Hard. Tough. Knew what was best for all of us. But over the years, the tough exterior slowly crumbled, and the final stroke was Lainey. She broke every wall down like a wrecking ball.

No one prepares you for what it feels like to lose a parent, and for those who have lost one, I understand them so much more now. I never understood the pain that comes with it, the immense grief that tears you inside out. But here I am. Living without the man who has always been my hero.

Always imagined he would die in his sleep peacefully, next to my mom.

But he died saving Dixie.

He died saving the only girl I have loved, saved her so her daughter didn't have to grow up without her mom just like she did.

Choking on my intake of breath as silent sobs rattle through my chest, I sit beside my dad, my head resting on his blanket covered body when I hear a sound of footsteps filling the room. Lazily looking up, I see my brothers.

All a little broken, all have tear-stained cheeks.

Riggs gives me a shallow nod as he walks towards me, Pacey next to him and their hands are on my back.

"I'll take it from here dad, I'll look after them all," Riggs' voice trembles, "no one will get our legacy dad, I hope we all make you proud... I hope we *have* made you proud," he stammers over choked sobs. "*Live by the ranch, die by the ranch,*" and with that, we bow our heads and grieve our father.

THE MINUTES SLIPPED INTO HOURS, and I am finally being wheeled towards Dixie's room and my heart thumps when I see her eyes on mine. A soft smile gracing her lips and I know I am about to wipe it away in an instant.

Riggs gives me a soft squeeze of my shoulder before he walks out of the room, leaving me and her alone.

"I am so glad you're okay," I whisper, pushing from my chair and kissing her on her lips.

"You have your dad to thank for that," her smile is still on her pretty face and my heart goes from racing to aching deep inside my chest. "How is he doing?" she asks, an oxygen tube in her nose.

"Dixie..." I whisper, clutching her hand.

"Tripp..." and I hate that she has that playful tone in her voice. It's my favorite and I am about to destroy it within seconds.

I shake my head from side to side, my lips turning down as I fight off the onslaught of tears that are about to rip through me.

"No," she whispers, her bottom lip trembling. "No," she repeats again, and I swallow down the lump that is burning my throat.

I nod, tears brimming in my eyes and with one soft blink, they roll down my cheeks.

And the wave of grief drags me straight back down as she cries into her hands, and this time I can't come up for air.

It has hold of me, pulling me deep into the crevices of the darkest ocean.

***

TWO MONTHS LATER

The warm water of the creek washes over me, slipping beneath the surface, peace radiates in my chest for just a second. It's been a hard two months.

Dad's funeral was held two weeks after he died. The whole town showed up as we buried him at the foot of the field. He had already picked his spot and wanted to be one with his ranch. My mom is growing stronger every day and having Lainey here has definitely helped. She is crawling around and causing all kinds of mischief but watching her grow is something else.

I have healed completely and my god, the first time I was back on a horse, I felt free. I felt like this is where I needed to be. I needed to be on the ranch, more than ever. I didn't want to go back to being sheriff. I loved it, but now, I had a new purpose.

To be the best I could be. To help Riggs keep Rivera Ranch going. I can feel dad wherever I am, but I mainly feel him in the soft breeze as I ride down towards the creek, and each time I pass, I feel a warmth in my chest that I can't explain. He dances with the leaves before he disappears over the mountains. I will never be over his death, it's changed me. Made me a better man and I never want to go back to who I was before.

Lucian and Wallen went down for fraud and it turns out that they were also responsible for Clay's death. When they dug further, they contacted the coroner who gave his notes and he had found a high level of drugs that were in his bloodstream and caused the heart attack. When the Attaway's home was searched, they found the substance they had slipped into his drink that night. Lucian was the one who gave them to Wallen. They are now serving many years in Wyoming, and I hope that Clay can rest peacefully.

He never deserved to die, especially at the hands of his friend and brother.

My chest aches and I find myself rubbing it out.

And lastly, Kelcie was found guilty of arson, bribery and fraudulent documents in a murder investigation. So now, there is a new sheriff overlooking Lovelock Bay.

Pacey Rivera.

In agreement with the Mayor, Marty and me, we knew

he was the right fit and I will only admit it now and here because no one else can hear me, he is a damn good sheriff... better than I ever was.

But that's okay, because I have a new lease of life.

A new dream.

Hands clasp my face as I am slowly pulled up to the surface and I suck in a deep breath.

"Hey," she smirks as water drips from my hair and off my nose. "Thought you were staying down there," I watch the crease in her brows, and I don't miss the worry that dances in her eyes.

"Hey beautiful," I rasp as her legs wrap around my waist and I smirk against her lips. "And never, I prefer it above the surface."

She kisses me, tongue just dipping past my lips before she pulls away and my eyes are still closed.

"We have a few hours before your mom and Aspen get back from dress shopping with Lainey... plus, I am dying to use the new toy that I got," she wiggles her brows and I groan, my dick already hard as I begin wadding my way through the water, slowly walking up the bank, she grips onto me a little tighter.

"We better get back home then," I trail my kisses down her jaw, and nip at her soft skin.

Placing her down gently, I spin her wet body and pull her back to my front, my hands rounding the small swell of her stomach and my heart thumps inside my chest knowing that she is pregnant with my baby.

She slips away and I miss her instantly as she reaches down for her towel and runs towards the house.

"Hey!" I call out, my cock throbbing as I grab my own towel and follow her into the distance.

I AM KNELT between her legs, my fingers buried deep inside of her as the tip of her vibrator rubs against her clit.

"Shit," her head falls back, her muscles tensing.

"You going to come for me baby?"

She whimpers as I lift one her legs over my shoulder, and slip my fingers from her soaked cunt, gliding the head of her toy just inside her pussy.

Her hips lift as I slowly push it inside of her and her legs tremble. Lowering my smiling lips over her clit, I flick my tongue against her before sucking and her moans fill the room as she comes. Slipping from her, I drop her toy on the bed as she pants, coming down from her high. Turning her over, I stand behind her, ass in the air as I slide deep into her pussy, my cock stretching her tight little cunt out as I pull my hips back and fill her again.

Thrust. Thrust. Thrust.

"You drive me crazy," I groan, fingers kneading the skin on her hips, her legs widen slightly sliding my cock deeper.

"Yes," she pants, and I begin to moan as I chase my own high, desperate to fill her with my cum.

Ten more strokes and I am coming as she moans, her fingers on her clit as she reaches her own orgasm. Pulling out of her, I lean down and kiss between her shoulder blades, trailing them down until I am placing soft kisses against her pussy.

"Let's go shower," I whisper against her skin, and she hums in agreement. She rolls over softly, and I take her hand in mine as I walk her upstairs, mindful that mom and Aspen could be home any minute.

Locking the door of the bathroom, I drag her towards the shower and turn it on. Hot water spurts out, the room filling with steam as I step under the shower and wait for her to follow.

"Always wanted to fuck you in here," I groan, my lips on her neck, hands kneading her full tits and her head rolls back. "And the stables."

"Then fuck me," she whispers and my skin breaks into goosebumps.

I smirk against the pulse point on her neck, twisting her around so she is looking out the window, small palms pressed against the steamed up glass as her legs widen slightly.

"I promise I won't be long, then I will spend the rest of the shower washing every single inch of you," I whisper just as I slip into her tight cunt again.

One hand curls around her hip, the other is in her hair dragging her head back as I pound into her, and with each stroke, her moans grow louder as one of her hands slips between her legs as she rubs her clit. I fuck her hard and fast and as promised, I spurt my hot cum deep inside her pussy as she clenches around me, her cunt pulsing as my cock throbs deep inside of her, snatching another orgasm.

WE LAY IN BED, her head on my chest as I dance my fingertips up and down her spine.

"You ready for your show tonight?" I ask, looking down at her as her head lifts, nerves bouncing in her pretty blue eyes. "Baby," I whisper, cupping her cheek, "don't be nervous... you were born to do this."

Her bottom lip trembles.

"You know you were darlin'," and I grip her chin, lifting her lips to mine as I kiss the nerves away.

"I love you Tripp."

"Do you know how good those words sound coming off your lips?" I rasp between our kisses.

"I love you," she repeats and my heart soars.

"And I love you my little dreamcatcher," I smile against her lips, "you're my wildest dreams," *kiss,* "my wildest love," *kiss,* "my wildest forever, Dixie."

She climbs onto my lap, hands clasping my face as our kiss deepens, my hands lazily stroking up and down her thighs.

"I love you," I choke, "it's always been you; it will *only* be you."

EPILOGUE

"Quiet," I whisper as I link my fingers through Dixie's and pull her out of the house.

"Tripp, where are we going," her voice is panicked as we walk down the stairs "the wedding starts in half an hour,"

"Then we better be quick," I throw her a flirtatious wink and her cheeks turn pink as we walk towards the stables.

"I promised I would fuck you here when I could, and well..." I trail off, spinning her into my arms and placing a kiss on her soft lips.

"Oh god," she whispers, arms locked around my neck as my lips trail down her jaw and dust over her collarbone, fuck I loved kissing her there.

"Wait," she pushes softly on my chest.

"What is it?"

"The horses... it's empty right,"

"Completely,"

"Good," she moans against my mouth as I lead her towards the back, pressing her against the cool wall.

"This has played out in my head so much," I admit, my fingers fumbling with the button of my suit pants.

"Well, now you get to show me just how it played out," she smirks as her hands wrap around my cock, slow and teasing pumps as she strokes me up and down.

"Dix," her name vibrates in my throat, dripping off my tongue.

"Tripp," her voice soft as she blinks at me all innocent.

"You're such a tease," and she kisses me, my greedy hands grabbing the skin on her thigh, hoisting her pretty dress around her waist and my fingers slip into the side of her panties.

"So wet," I nip at her jaw

My cock pulses in her small hands and I am desperate to be inside of her.

Lifting her leg up and over my hip, my fingers slide deeper as I rub against her g-spot.

"Yes, please," she begs, her pussy rubbing against the palm of my hand.

"Tell me how much you want me? How much you need my cock, little dream..."

"I need you," she whines, my fingers still fucking her, bringing her closer to her orgasm.

"How much" I taunt, a teasing grin on my lips.

"Like the air I breathe," she whimpers on a breath, and she makes me feral.

"Fuck," I groan as my eyes cast down and I slip my fingers from her cunt.

"I am going to fuck you hard and fast baby, then tonight, I will spend the evening loving every inch of you Dixie Walker," I pant as I edge the thick head of my cock in her soaked pussy.

"You know I love you right?" I whisper, my eyes lifting to hers and she nods.

"Well remember that, because I am about to fuck you like I hate every part of you," I grind my teeth as I roll my hips, my cock slipping into her cunt and fuck she feels like a dream.

"Oh my god," she moans, her fingers digging into my shoulders through my suit jacket as my cock slips out to the tip then pounding back into her.

"I want your orgasm baby, I want your pussy coming all over my cock," I rasp, and I feel the familiar build of my own orgasm growing as I fuck her hard.

Stroke after punishing stroke, she takes me deep, sucking me in further with each pound.

"Come baby, I can feel it, I can feel you tightening."

And that's all it takes to push her over the edge, coating my cock in her wetness as my own orgasm spills from me, filling her full.

We're panting and I lower her leg gently down, pulling her panties over and covering her cum filled pussy.

"I love you, Dixie," I plant a soft kiss on her lips as she smiles at me, eyes all hazy but twinkling with her post orgasm high.

"I love you more, Tripp."

I kiss her again.

"I want to spend every moment here, in this moment but..."

"But we have a wedding to attend," she pushes me away softly in the chest.

"We do," I nod, doing my pants back up and tucking my shirt into the waistband.

"Come on baby, let's go and watch them get married,"

I lead her back towards the house and where the

wedding party is waiting, she disappears into the bedroom upstairs and I walk into the kitchen where Riggs, Austin, Pacey and Buck wait with huge smiles on their faces.

"Where did you sneak off to?" Riggs chuckles as he swallows a mouthful of whiskey.

"Seeing through on a promise,"

"Oh yeah?" his brows raise,

"Yeah," and my mind takes me back to just moments ago.

I was besotted with her.

"Dada," Lainey coos as I sweep her up, holding her on my hip before I stand next to Dixie, fingers dusting across her delicate bump as I place a soft kiss on her lips.

"You look beautiful," I whisper.

She is wearing a sage green bridesmaid dress, brown hair thick and in loose curls, eyes all dreamy and full of glistening stars as she waits to walk down the aisle.

"What's that?" Sunny's brows furrow as she plucks a strand of straw from her hair and discards it to the floor.

Buck walks towards us and gives us a nod just as *wild love - james bay* begins to play and we watch as everyone stands.

Austin stands at the top of the aisle, Aspen and Riggs asked him to officiate the wedding. With Riggs and Pacey by his side, I give Dixie one last kiss.

"Fuck, I can't wait to marry you," my heart flutters in my chest.

She gets all teary and I tilt my head.

"This will be us soon," I whisper as I drag her hand to my lips and kiss her ring finger where a thin gold band sits with a heart diamond.

"I can't wait, just family as we marry under the blossom tree by the creek."

"I love you," I smile as she leans in and kisses Lainey on the top of her head.

Sunny sneaks up behind us and passes Dixie her wildflower bouquet. Moving quietly down the side of the seats, I manage to escape being watched as everyone waits with bated breath to see the bride. My mom steps up and takes Lainey from me and I give her a kiss on her cheek. She is all red eyed and I know she has been crying. My eyes glare to the two empty chairs that have feathered angel wings tied to the back.

One for Harlow. One for my Dad.

"You ready big man?" I ask Riggs as I take my place next to him, pulling on my black dickie bow.

"So fucking ready," he smiles, "I have been waiting ten years for this moment."

"Worth the wait then," I chuckle, my eyes landing on Dixie as she begins her slow walk down, and just in that moment, everything around me blurs.

"Yeah." Riggs rasps, pulling me back into the room as Dixie takes her place across from us all.

"Just need to find you a woman now, Pace," I give him a boyish grin as I look at him over his shoulder.

"I'm enjoying it just being me at the moment," he nods, as Sunny takes her spot next to Dixie and I catch Conrad's gaze, a wink passing between the both of us.

And then there was Aspen.

"Jesus Christ," Riggs rasps and I hear the crack in his voice.

"Damn she looks..." I trail off.

"Fucking beautiful," Pacey finishes my sentence.

"Yeah, she does," Austin chimes in and me and Pacey give him a soft smile.

She's wearing an ivory gown, flowy from the hips, little

laced sleeves and her golden blonde hair down in soft waves with a flowered braid and suddenly I see us all as teens again. When I look at the empty seats, I see Harlow smiling, tears rolling down her cheeks and my dad, who looks like the proudest man ever. I give a sad smile along with a knowing nod as a tear escapes and with one blink, they're gone, and I am back and about to witness one of my best friends and my brother *finally* get their happily ever after.

"Dearly beloved…" Austin speaks loudly and my eyes skate to where Dixie is, and that's when realization settles, she's always been my wildest dream, and I finally got her.

No more dreaming.

No more wishing.

She is mine.

PACEY

We incorporated the wedding with the cow branding. Call us crazy, but us Rivera's like to be different.

We branded the calves in the morning, lunched, danced and then just as the sun was about to set, we watched Aspen and Riggs get married.

The soft country voice of Dixie rolls over the field, her fingers working her guitar as she sings Riggs and Aspen's first dance song, *Invisible String - Taylor Swift.*

Tripp is dancing with my mom and Lainey, Conrad is dancing with Sunny and Austin is dancing with his mom, Blue.

Me? I am sitting alone on a bale of hay whilst nursing a whiskey.

I know I'll get my happily ever after, but for now, I have too much to do to save my ranch, to save all the ranches.

I haven't wanted to stress Riggs and Tripp out with the news that I have heard, but the sale of land is moving forward, along with the second biggest ranch, Cottonwheel Ranch, just outside of Lovelock Bay.

I have a meeting with Mr Wheeler at the beginning of next week and I am hoping we can work together to finally squash these suits once and for all, because it seems this runs much deeper than just Clay and his lot.

We have a much bigger problem.

Shaking my head from side to side, I drain the rest of my glass and push myself to my feet. Slightly missing my footing, a hand reaches mine.

"Careful there, sheriff," and my eyes connect with hers.

Dirty blonde hair hidden under a cowgirl hat. Beautiful green eyes. And a smile to drag you into her soul.

"I don't think we've met," she holds her hand out for me to shake. "I am Morgan Wheeler."

"Pacey Rivera..." and just as our hands clasp, the ground begins to tremor before a loud bang echoes around the ranch followed by screams.

"I don't think we caused that," her eyes widen.

I whistle, calling the cowboys and Marty. Rushing towards the stables, I grab my horse, Morgan hot on my tail as she grabs one of my boy's horses. I kick my horse on, following the still echoing bang and it doesn't take me long to find out what caused it.

"Shit," I groan as I look at the old back entrance of the gold mine that runs under the ranch blown, smoke coming through the ground.

"What's happened?" she whispers, just as Marty and

the boys catch us up. I look at them before my eyes find hers, and I honestly could lose myself in them.

"They've started a war," I tilt my head, before opening the rein to my horse and kicking him down the field towards Riggs and Tripp.

And I know this is going to be the biggest fight of our lives. The breeze dances around me as I gallop towards the party and I hear my dad's words echo around my head.

Live by the ranch, die by the ranch.

The End

Wildest Forever follows the story of Pacey and Morgan. Tripp, Dixie, Lainey, Baby Rivera, Riggs, Aspen and the rest of Lovelock Bay will all return for the final instalment of The Lovelock Bay Series.

ACKNOWLEDGMENTS

Firstly, my readers. Thank you for taking a chance on me, whether this is your first book by me or your twentieth, I am forever grateful for each and every single one of you.

This book broke me in places, but it felt like my own dreamcatcher whilst writing, taking all the dark and bad and absorbing it all, replacing them with so much light.

Leïla, thank you for being my sprinting buddy for Wildest Dreams. I would never have finished this book if it wasn't for your support.

Lyndsey, thank you for being my personal cheerleader, again, this book would never have crossed the finish line if it wasn't for you and your continued support.

Robyn, my amazing friend and my wonderful PA. Thank you. Thank you will never be enough for all you do. I am grateful for your friendship over the last six years and I could never imagine you not being in my life. You're a best friend. One I treasure greatly. Thank you for sticking with me through not only the sunshine, but through the heaviest rain as well.

Leanne, thank you for messaging me back six years ago when I slid into your DMs asking you to help me with my book baby. I was a brand-new author with no clue what I was doing. You were, and still are an important part of my author journey and a wonderful friend.

Lea, thank you for editing my work and being such a beautiful friend. We met when you were a reader, me a baby author, and look at us now.

Working together, a little dream team.

My BETA's, thank you for your feedback, notes and continued support. Forever grateful that I get to work with such beautiful people.

And finally, my husband.

My own personal dreamcatcher, I adore you with all I have. It's my turn to be your dreamcatcher now.

Thank you for pushing me to pursue my writing, thank you for keeping me going when I felt like I was drowning, and thank you for always standing by my side, shoulder to shoulder... Well, sort of, you're a lot taller than me.

But honestly, without you, there would have never been her, Ashlee Rose.

So, thank you, thank you.

If you're still here and stuck around to read all of the above, thank you! I hope you enjoyed Wildest Dreams.

If you're new here, hey, hi, welcome! I am so glad you're here.

You can find me on the following social platforms if you fancy giving me a follow:

Instagram: http://bit.ly/38NEN4B
Facebook: http://bit.ly/38QuJYI
Reader Group: https://bit.ly/3dKAXfA
Goodreads: http://bit.ly/2HMUXPZ
Amazon: Author.to/AshleeRose
Bookbub: http://bit.ly/2SSvISD
Tiktok: https://bit.ly/38FUEan
Discord: https://discord.gg/Rbmdbs8DGH

You can sign up to my newsletter here and receive a
FREE eBook:
https://dl.bookfunnel.com/ezg8i65hhj